BEST
EUROPEAN
FICTION
2019

BEST
EUROPEAN
FICTION
2019

EDITED BY
ALEX ANDRIESSE

DALKEY ARCHIVE PRESS

www.dalkeyarchive.com
McLean, IL / Dublin

Cover design by Gail Doobinin
Printed on permanent/durable acid-free paper.

Contents

PREFACE

The Marketplace at Toledo

I CAN'T HELP but consider all the innumerable ways I, American-born, am unqualified to write a preface to these thirty-two works of fiction that are united mainly, if not solely, by their having some connection to an entity called Europe. The language surrounding the publication of international literature today is, besides, so crowded with extravagant claims that I'm hesitant here to stake any of my own—except to venture that the work of Alberto Olmos, Sheila Armstrong, Ádám Bodor, Christopher Woodall, Lars Petter Sveen, Hélène Lenoir, and the other writers represented in these pages is incontrovertible evidence that there continues to be something like a Republic of Letters, whatever else may be unfolding in the world.

I do think, however, that I might be minimally qualified to say something about literature in general—which would of course include European literature—and the necessary gulf that separates literature from its so-called *national culture* and from the people who write it, the so-called *authors*, who, though they technically exist, are in fact nowhere to be found. Not at the dinner table, not at the lectern, and not, once the final paperwork has been filed, in the volumes of biography and correspondence attached to their names. Much as there may be to admire in, for example, the collected letters of Kafka, I don't believe even these can be said to derive, in toto, from the same substance as his novels, stories, or parables. The person who writes in one of his letters to Milena Jesenská, "If the occasion presents itself and you don't have anything against it, please say something nice to Werfel on my behalf," is not the same person who wrote *The Castle*. I am not sure it would be correct to say that "a person" wrote *The Castle* at all.

Writers have often made this point themselves, by crediting their work to the Muses or the deity, ascribing it to imaginary authors, or inventing manuscripts from which their own purport to be transcribed or compiled. Fiction writers in particular have favored the latter two practices: Daniel Defoe presented *Robinson Crusoe* as the work of Robinson Crusoe. Jonathan Swift attributed *Gulliver's Travels* to Lemuel Gulliver. Voltaire insisted that *Candide* had been compiled from the posthumous papers of Monsieur le docteur Ralph. And Nathaniel Hawthorne recounted at length how he was prompted to write *The Scarlet Letter* after discovering, on the second story of the Salem Custom-House, an affair of red cloth twisted around some dingy paper that contained many particulars regarding a woman named Hester Prynne.

All of these writers were, one way or another, following in the footsteps of Miguel de Cervantes, who claimed to have stumbled on the manuscript of *Don Quixote* one day while strolling through the marketplace at Toledo. Because this stumbled-on manuscript—signed by a historian named Cide Hamete Benengeli—was written in Arabic, Cervantes (not unlike the hapless editor penning this sentence) hired a translator, a Spanish-speaking Moor who happened to be hanging around the market, and who agreed to take the job for a fee of fifty pounds of raisins, three bushels of wheat, and a roof over his head until the work was through. "I took him to my home," Cervantes tells us, "and there in little more than six weeks he translated it all exactly as it is set down here." So it was that *El ingenioso hidalgo don Quijote de la Mancha* was born.

Of course, there's no question who really wrote *Don Quixote*, unless we decide to take Cervantes at his word. But why shouldn't we? In Paul Auster's *City of Glass*, the character called Paul Auster does just that. In the course of a conversation with Daniel Quinn, Auster outlines an essay he is writing about the authorship of *Don Quixote*—not the authorship of the book itself, he explains, but of "the book inside the books Cervantes wrote, the one he imagined he was writing." Seeing how Cervantes goes to such great lengths to assure the reader that the events described actually took place, it follows—says Auster—that the true author of the tale has to have been an eyewitness to those events. However, Cide Hamete Benengeli never makes an appearance in the book's pages, which would suggest that he cannot be, as Cervantes says he is, the true author of the tale.

What Auster proposes instead is that Cide Hamete Benengeli must be a conglomeration of four people: Sancho Panza, the illiterate eyewitness, who narrates the story aloud to Quixote's friends the barber and the priest, who in turn take down what Panza says in Spanish and hand over the results to Sansón Carrasco, another friend of Quixote's, who translates the Spanish into Arabic. This Arabic manuscript is the one that Cervantes discovers and has translated back into Spanish by the unnamed Moor he meets at the market. But there's one last twist to Auster's argument, and this is that Don Quixote himself orchestrated the whole "Benengeli quartet," probably posing as the Moor in the marketplace and, as it were, lying in wait for Cervantes:

> We shouldn't put it past him. For a man so skilled in the art of disguise, darkening his skin and donning the clothes of a Moor could not have been very difficult. I like to imagine that scene in the marketplace at Toledo. Cervantes hiring Don Quixote to decipher the story of Don Quixote himself. There's great beauty to it.

There's great beauty to Auster's exegesis as well. Fanciful though it may be, it perfectly enacts the lunatic logic of a madcap reader, tilting at the windmills of Cervantes's text. And what is a writer, anyway, if not a reader gone mad, a person—as the character called Paul Auster puts it—"who has been bewitched by book"?

"Bewitched," if you'll indulge me, is not an idle word. There is indeed something demonic about the writing of fiction, something that cannot be accounted for by common sense. The writer is, first, a reader possessed by literature, a reader who casts out the demons of literature by writing, journeying forth from his study to do battle with the phantasmagorical hum of language that his reading has put into his head. No writer perhaps sensed this demonic side of literature more acutely than Kafka: "I don't have literary interests," he famously wrote in a letter to Felice, "I'm made of literature, I'm nothing else and can be nothing else." And, less famously, in a letter to Robert Klopstock a few years later: "You need only keep in mind that you're writing to a poor little man who is possessed by every possible evil spirit, of every type." It's little wonder that in the third of Kafka's blue octavo notebooks, when he came to consider Quixote's creation, he did so in demoniacal terms:

Sancho Panza, who, incidentally, never boasted of it, in the course of the years, by means of providing a large number of romances of chivalry and banditry to while away the evening and night hours, succeeded in diverting the attention of his devil, to whom he later gave the name Don Quixote, from himself to such an extent that this devil then in unbridled fashion performed the craziest deeds, which however, for lack of a predetermined object, which should, of course, have been Sancho Panza, did nobody any harm. Sancho Panza, a free man, tranquilly, and perhaps out of a certain sense of responsibility, followed Don Quixote on his travels and had much and profitable entertainment from this to the end of his days.

Here, in Kafka's parable, the man bewitched by books is not Quixote but Panza, who's so successfully avoided being possessed by the devil he names Quixote that this Quixote becomes harmless—to everyone, but particularly to Panza, who is now free to follow his devil's exploits from a safe distance, without the necessity of taking part. So Sancho Panza reveals himself to be Quixote's author. Miguel de Cervantes is absent from the scheme.

Different as they are in tone and scope, Auster's outlined essay and Kafka's twelve-line parable point in the same direction. Whether Quixote conspired to bring *Quixote* into being or Panza drove Quixote out of his own soul onto the muddy roads of Spain, one thing is clear: Don Quixote and his adventures are not the patented invention of a single mind. They belong rather to the collective imagination—the mercifully individual collective imaginations—of their readers. This is what so fascinates both Auster and Kafka about Quixote's creation. It is also, we might speculate, what incited Cervantes to narrate his discovery of the "original" manuscript in the first place—a narrative that dramatizes the mysterious means by which narratives make their way into the world.

This is the way of it then. In the marketplace at Toledo, a Spaniard so ravenous for the written word he has "a taste for reading even scraps of paper lying in the streets" is invited to inspect a bundle of manuscripts, an invitation he cannot turn down. Indeed, this Spaniard is so ravenous that, even when he realizes these manuscripts are written in Arabic, a language that he cannot read, he immediately seeks out another man who *can* read them, buys the manuscripts, and hires the man to translate them—all so that he'll be able to read them himself. By the time he reads them, though, they will have been multiply transformed: first by the Moor's translation of them into Spanish, and then again by the Spaniard's unacknowledged additions, for after all, whoever Cide Hamete Benengeli was, he could not have foreseen the Spaniard's discovery in the marketplace at Toledo. Thus Cervantes's desire to read the story of Don Quixote in the end requires him to write the story of Don Quixote—a story that he insists, less whimsically than it may at first appear, is not his own. The manuscripts from the market have by now become a great work of fiction, and like all great works of fiction, they are the property of whoever goes to the trouble of opening them up.

ALEX ANDRIESSE

BEST
EUROPEAN
FICTION
2019

ALBERTO OLMOS

Every Last One, Place and Date

MY NAME IS Salvador Barahona and I always tell the same story.

I had come back to my country after twenty years in Mexico. I'd made some money there as an accountant for a multinational corporation. I married a woman from Guadalajara and, seven years later, I got divorced. A mestizo boy is currently maneuvering my surname through the Guadalajaran streets. It wasn't so bad, all told. I was nicely pensioned off.

The homecoming was bittersweet. A lungful of one's country refreshes you, it brings things back to your memory, for a few moments it brings back the speed of your life. But during my long absence, all my friends had fallen away, since I didn't do anything to keep in touch, and the same went for the few relatives I'd left behind, from whom I'd always kept my distance. In short, I was as alone as when I'd first set foot in Mexico. A bit more alone, perhaps.

I lived in a modest apartment in a newly built neighborhood. It had a boulevard with landscaped borders and tall lampposts, unassuming bars, and an asphalt path where kids rode their bikes. I would go out for a walk twice a day. When I got back home, I'd sit down in front of the television, which I usually left turned on. I also drank a lot of water, and in the end I took up playing the multi-million-jackpot lotteries.

It was a dull life, but for some reason I thought it was all I deserved.

This happened one evening in the summer of 2009. I was sitting next to an ATM, on one of those benches they have in the plaza by the major intersection. I was watching the passing cars and buses, police vehicles, a few brave cyclists. Across the street, on a bench like mine, I saw a man sit down who was more or less my age. For a second or two, the symmetry of our old age flustered me; it made me sad.

Then I felt like smoking. I took out my pack of cigarettes and patted myself down for a lighter. With the cigarette waiting between my
lips, I was forced to the conclusion that I had indeed not brought it
with me. I looked up to immediately petition some passerby, no matter if it was a man or woman, young or old, and ask for a light. I only
tried two people before I gave up. It's funny, the way we smokers think
we can recognize each other.

I looked back over at the man on the other side of the street and
thought I could make out that he was smoking. My eyesight isn't what
it used to be, and it's getting worse. The urge to light my cigarette grew
so pressing that I decided to go to the crosswalk and then up to the
bench on the other side of the street just to ask for the use of a lighter.
While the stoplight was still green, I stared with a degree of anxiety at
the man sitting there smoking—I had the sense that if he got up before
I reached him, a curse would fall on me. That didn't happen. I made it
over to him.

I asked for a light and he handed me a metal lighter that emitted an overwhelming stench of gasoline as soon as the top was flipped
open. While I was sparking my cigarette and taking the first few drags,
this man had unbuttoned the breast pocket of his short-sleeved shirt
and taken out a small white card with red lines. I assumed it was from
this same pocket that he had produced the fountain pen he was now
holding.

"Excuse me," he said. "Would you be so kind as to give me your
name?"

"Come again?"

"Your name. First and last. If you don't mind."

It didn't seem like a bad exchange to be able to smoke if all that was
asked of me in return was my personal details. These I let him have.

"Thank you very much."

The gentleman jotted down my first and last names on the card and
then put it in his shirt pocket, with the other cards he was carrying. He
buttoned the pocket, where he then nestled the fountain pen, whose
golden clip gleamed for a few moments. He had a completely white
head of hair, a tiny nose, and untrimmed eyebrows.

"Enjoy your evening."

I watched him walk away. His bearing was noble and light—

elegant—despite the short polyester sleeves. I wished he'd been wearing a hat. I wondered if he had perhaps been a policeman.

My next encounter with him brings us to the Christmas season of 2010. I walked into a grocery store to pick up a loaf of bread and found him noting something down on one of his ruled index cards. He left right away, unaware of my presence, or intentionally disregarding it. A young woman was waiting at the cash register for her change; but she was looking, as was I, at the store exit. Then we glanced at each other, and I noticed the remnants of a great bewilderment still lingering in her eyes.

The third time I saw the strange man with the cards, I decided to follow him. This was a couple of years ago. I stalked him with the utmost caution, always trying to keep at least one person between him and me and maintaining a distance of some eighty or ninety yards. I was using a cane by this time. I hooked it over my shoulder for the duration of my spy mission.

At first I assumed the man was going somewhere, since he was walking with the determination of someone who has an appointment to keep, or errands to run. But as we were leaving street after street behind us and rounding corners, I realized he was just out for a walk. He finally paused at a certain point, after fifteen or twenty minutes, and looked over at the other side of the street. I, too, directed my attention to the opposite sidewalk, where there was a large concentration of people, this being the area where the neighborhood bars were to be found, along with their outdoor seating. The man went on his way again, as far as the next crosswalk, which he crossed with what, once more, seemed to me like a clear purpose.

I decided there and then to throw in the towel on my pathetic escapade (one old fart tailing another old fart). I let him gain a few extra yards on me and brought my cane to rest on the ground. But the distance between us soon began to shrink as the man advanced along the other sidewalk—he was heading back to his starting point, perhaps intending to round off his walk. I watched him wend his way through the thronged patios, at a slower pace now, because of the obstacles that waylaid him, and at the last patio, he stopped. Somebody had spoken to him or ordered him to a halt—an acquaintance, perhaps. The next thing I knew, my quarry was writing something on one of his registration cards, and then he continued on his merry way.

A pleasant, youthful tingling shot down my spine.

I ran, after a fashion, to the same crosswalk the man had taken, and then hurried over to the last open-air patio on the sidewalk. The table he had stopped at was now rattling with the laughter of its occupants. For some inexplicable reason, their laughter grew even more hysterical when they caught sight of me.

Despite this, I stuck to my guns and spoke to them.

I asked if a man my age had stopped there and written something down on a card, and also, what it was he'd written.

A young man, probably in his twenties (apparently the same age as the other boy sitting there, and both the girls), volunteered to settle the matter.

"My name," he said. "First and last."

I lapsed into thought. The young woman who I assumed was his girlfriend went to whisper something in his ear, but she didn't want to leave the other two out, so I could hear it when she told my informant: "Give him your name, too."

They all laughed. The truth is, I didn't really care about the name.

"No need, miss," I said. And I decided to indulge in a small lie. "He's a friend of mine, he goes around all day pulling these weird stunts, and doing other things I probably shouldn't mention. I'm trying to help him." I weighed my words. "So, did he want your name for any particular reason?"

"No. Just straight out of the blue."

"What's wrong with your friend?" the other girl asked.

"Well," I said, "it's a long story."

"What's he want my name for?"

I smiled meaninglessly.

"Anyway, I'm going to see if I can catch up to him," I said.

"Stay on the scent of his lighter. He dropped it about twenty times just now."

The laughter started up again.

"Sure," I said to say something. "He's rather absentminded."

In accordance with my imaginary plans, I set out, rather unenthusiastically, to look for the name-collector in the neighboring streets; but I didn't turn him up. It's possible I didn't put enough effort into it. Admittedly, it was time to head back home and hear the lotto drawing.

As was to be expected, I bumped into him again around the neighborhood two or three months later. It was something I wasn't just counting on, but was dying for. There wasn't anything better to do in those days. But in any case, I'd already decided on approaching him.

"Good morning," I said. It was just past eleven a.m.

"Good morning, Salvador Barahona."

I was rattled for a moment, seeing he'd remembered my full name. I took the pack of cigarettes from my jacket and offered him one.

"I think it's about time I asked what *your* name was," I said.

The terms of the transaction hadn't changed much. Now it was one of my cigarettes for the other man's name.

The man took what I was offering him and immediately began to smoke. I followed suit. I had some kitchen matches in my pocket this time. Then I waited.

A couple of minutes went by; neither of us said a word.

"I'd be honored if you'd come visit my home," the man announced, at last.

"It would be my pleasure."

I accepted, prompted by the intuition that our chat needed this movement if it was going to continue. We walked a good ways, both silent; I could sense the impatience mounting with each step, as much his to give me his name and an explanation of his census work, as mine to be filled in on these things. Our canes knocked against each other at the door of his home.

It was readily apparent to me that he lived by himself. Neither the layout of the rooms, nor the style of the furniture, nor the decorative elements on the walls had anything to do with those of my place. Nevertheless, everything reminded me of home. Stillness filled the room; breathing inside the house of a solitary man verges, to an almost unacceptable degree, on indecency.

"So, Salvador, where do you live?"

I mentioned my street, in the new part of town; I gave some more directions so that he could find his way. Still, he insisted that I give him the full address, which he didn't write down on one of his cards, using instead a grid-lined notebook lying beside the phone.

"In case I get a chance to visit you someday," he said. "Come over here."

We went into a small, windowless room with a lamp that gave a serene and beatific light through its paper shade. The only other piece of furniture in the room was a large double filing cabinet; it was dark green, with six metal drawers, which each had a slip of paper on the front.

He opened one of the drawers and there appeared several rows of white cards, each threaded by a metal bar, like in the offices of yesteryear. He had obtained the names of a vast quantity of people, I suddenly thought, at the sight of that never-ending catalog. He extracted one of the cards and showed it to me. I read the first and last names of a woman, and below, a street and a date, with the day, month, and year.

"Is this why you wanted my full address?" I asked.

"No, not at all."

He rested his hand on one of the ranks of cards and began to explain. Every day, he would leave his house to take a walk, without any ulterior motive. He led a normal life, he made clear. Nonetheless, whenever he exchanged words with a new person, he would ask for their first name, their last name, and then make a note of where they'd met and the date. Back at home, he would file the new card with the others, in chronological order. Sometimes, he admitted, if he had gone for a certain number of days or weeks without adding material to his archives, he would be driven to despair, and only then would he force contact with a stranger, on the flimsiest pretext, like simply asking for the time.

I took everything he told me in stride. It would be safe to say that it even awoke a certain admiration in me. All the same, curiosity drove me to ask the fatal question.

Why?

"I'll help you understand it perfectly."

"I'd greatly appreciate it."

But I didn't really think I'd need much help to understand his explanation, whatever it turned out to be.

He took a card from his pocket and handed it to me. Then he lent me his fountain pen.

"Now you'll understand everything," he said. Adding, rather nervously, "Go ahead."

For a while, my head was in the clouds, but then I figured out that he wanted me to imitate him and play the notary. So I did. I asked for his first and last names, wrote down the address in which we found ourselves, and then the day, the month, and the year.

He invited me to put the index card in its corresponding place.

"Wonderful," he said.

Then, without much tact, he gave me to understand that the time had come for me to leave.

A couple of weeks went by, and quite a few ungenerous drawings. I decided to get rid of some furniture and buy myself clothes that wouldn't look so emblematic of the shadow of death. I fell in love with the host of a new morning television show. One day, there was a knock at the door.

"Salvador Barahona?"

From the threshold, a foreign boy measured me against the notes from his briefcase. I nodded.

"A delivery."

I didn't have a chance to ask for more details, since suddenly the boy rushed down the stairs, then climbed back up with a companion and the freight in question.

"Here you are."

The name-collector's filing cabinet was now standing in the entrance hall of my apartment.

Needless to say, that monstrosity wouldn't make my life any more pleasant or my home any less unwelcoming. Even so, knowing that the errand boys wouldn't be able to provide me with any clue about the matter, I signed the receipt and closed the door.

The next day, I headed for the home of my peculiar benefactor. I knocked and nobody answered. I returned in the evening and didn't find him in then either. I tried my luck in the following days, with equally scant results. The man must have moved.

His name was the last that had been registered in that immense hoard of thin identities. Obviously, I couldn't resist the temptation to browse through it. Many are the evenings I pass almost all of just looking out the window at the kids riding their bikes along the boulevard. There was a whole pack of blank cards in one of the drawers. But I had no mind to keep the inventory going. The task's uselessness made it ridiculous, and a bit pathetic.

Names, streets, dates. I fiddled with the index card that identified me. Then I pulled out several dozen of them in search of some current acquaintance or even somebody from my past who, by pure chance, had run into the name-taker. It was owing to this crazy notion that I ended up investigating the origins of the archives and seeing dates as far distant as 1978, 1960, and 1934, with their subsequent names; names, now in many cases, of people who'd passed on.

Intrigued, even enjoying myself, I decided to locate the first card of the archives. I opened one of the two drawers that grazed the ground and put my hand in all the way to the back, disturbing some cobwebs. I removed the card from its long, dusty confinement, and read it.

The pioneering name meant nothing to me; the date, however, filled me with shock. It was March 2, 1823.

I had already noticed, though without any particular interest, that the handwriting on the cards didn't always appear to be the work of the same hand. When I saw that nineteenth-century dateline, I had to swallow the fact that the archives were the work of successive scribes, and that the responsibility of continuing the record had fallen to me, almost two centuries after its inauguration. My question had finally come up against its answer. In short, there was no reason why.

At first it was easy to resist this duty that had burst in on me, since most of my days are spent in complete solitude, and few are the people who'll stop a retiree in the street to make conversation. But in the end a young man asked me some trivial thing about the bus route, and I did it, I asked for his first and last names, which I wrote down later at home. From then on, I was a goner, damned—busy.

After several months of faithfully performing my new obligation, I found myself living for it, and it alone. Yes, I, too, would drop some object (my cane) on the ground so I could then ask for the full name of the person who helped me to pick it up, normally a person I'd selected beforehand for incorporation into the archives. Women, those around my age above all, and kids were the most common victims of my ploys. Curiously, nobody refused to indulge a harmless old man.

I took note of several dozen names over the course of a couple years, until new health complaints began to prevent me from moving ahead with my records. It was less that my strength was failing and more that my faith was failing too. What was the point of all this? I wondered.

I needed a successor, and I knew the correct procedure for bringing about the transfer.

So, during the rare forays that followed this decision, I always waited a few seconds after writing down a name, in case the person registered should take it upon himself to ask for mine, a request that would set in motion the subtle wheels of inheritance. I don't know how many times my predecessor had tried it, or if the whole thing had perhaps been no sooner said than done, with me; the truth is, in my case the ruse just wasn't working.

I changed my tactics and surrendered myself to forthright honesty. I have offered the archives to other elderly people, in keeping with the inheritance model I know best, but also to slightly younger people, and even, one day, to some teenager, when despair had made me irresponsible. Only yesterday I harangued a man of forty-something who'd given me his seat on the bus. Taking advantage of his kindness, I asked him what his name was.

"Alberto," he said.

"Alberto what?" I asked.

I wrote down his first and last names, and then I told him everything.

TRANSLATED FROM THE SPANISH BY ERIC KURTZKE

SHEILA ARMSTRONG

Lemons

HIGH-FLUNG HANDFULS OF white polystyrene shapes, falling in gentle waves.

A package has come early for Christmas, and the two children have stolen away the S-shaped filling to make snow showers in their small, street-facing garden. Leaping into the air from balled toes, they catch pieces in their mouths, biting down so hard their teeth meet in the middle and slip to the side with a dry, squeaking noise. The taller girl spits a chunk of soft plastic out, and the other copies her in echoing delight. With it comes a smear of blood; a loose milk tooth has left a pinkish trail across the surface. She begins to cry, in fright, and panic fills up her eyes.

The older one laughs at the sight of the blood; she is eight years old and afraid of nothing, fierce as the sun. A thick headband scrapes her hair back against her skull, and she is barefoot through the cold grass, weaving around the thistles stippling the cramped front lawn of their terraced house. Her sister's brief terror subsides, and they resume their dance. They are whirling together in a snow globe, and they must catch each piece of polystyrene and launch it skywards again; if all the pieces fall to the earth at once, they will become figurines, frozen in place forever.

Across the road, a wet-lipped man leans against a gray cement windowsill and watches the handfuls of soft foam float down. His right hand is hidden in his trousers; the dark jeans full and bulging. He has cut a hole in the scooped lining of his pocket so he can grab himself through it, to pull and pull and pull.

The girls look up as one, sparrow-like, to see him staring. The older one becomes suddenly afraid, unsettled by the man's jerking motions;

a marionette moving without strings. They run inside, hand in hand, and the last of the polystyrene settles down on the lawn to wait for the wind to carry it off and up against the chain-link fence.

The girl is thirteen, and her teeth are chattering, like they do in cheerful adventure stories, but this is a painful, jumping thing and her jaw hurts from the strain. The sun had lashed whip-cracks of red across her back where her mother's suncream-coated hands had missed, but the ocean had been cold, so cold, so cold the shock of it had stunned her, and it had taken the scraping of a foot against a line of needled rocks to shock her back into breathing again. Lacey, a friend so new the thread between them remains spiderweb thin, had jumped in straight after her, almost on top of her head, and they had been pulled under together into a swirling, gray-green crypt.

Now they are shivering in the single shower cubicle together, clinging to each other in a giggling, salty mess. Lacey rubs her sanded hands up and down her own body, pulling her swimming togs away from her chest with an elastic snap. For a second, her soft, rounded breast is on display; a puppy-fat nipple the color of strawberry lollipops.

The shower is only warm compared to their chilled skin, and as they thaw they begin to shiver again, so they rub themselves dry with rough, over-washed towels before throwing on sweat-damp clothes. They walk from the beach to the shop to buy chocolate cigarettes, eating them in nibbles, paper and all. A shared dip-bag of orange sherbet grit-coats their lips.

Later, as the girl cycles her bike home alone, her salted togs wrapped in a towel and lodged in her armpit, she will think of the nipple, wet-sleek and smooth as a pencil-top eraser.

Just like a period, but heavier than usual, the instructions had said, in fractured English, but the cramps are coming faster and harder, so she is pressed against the side of the mildewed bath, the chill of the porcelain nibbling at the edges of pain. The room spins unfairly, shuddering up and down, and closing her eyes makes the feeling worse, so she stares at the wall, counting the tiles from the top to bottom, making sure the diamond pattern repeats cleanly.

The pills had sat in her mouth for too long, turning her spit thick and choking and bitter, and the memory of the oval outlines still remains under her tongue. They had come in an anonymous package from France, wrapped up with a silken scarf and some almond sweets that had been stale as soon as they had come out of the box. Her disapproving cousin, a pharmacist, hadn't added a postcard or note, and she had suspected the tablets were fake; a blast of B12, or a dose of iron to combat pregnancy-related anemia. But now she can finally, finally feel the movement inside her, and she raps her forehead against the rim of the bathtub in gratitude, once, twice, and again.

The whine of the Smashing Pumpkins seeps in; her housemate is listening to music as he works on his final thesis corrections. She is angry at the intrusion into what should be hers alone, in a sealed-off container of experience. But now reality has wiggled through the walls and is drawing lines from the pain in her abdomen to a cassette player in the next room, across the sea to an American singer with a razor in his throat, and all the way back to this flat, this bathroom, this tiled floor.

The pain crests again, in anger.

The clumping will be lemon-sized, she has heard, but this is too strange for her to understand. Lemons are tart and firm, waxy and unyielding; joyful exclamation points that are too bright, too yellow for this comparison. Her teeth clamp into the fleshy part between thumb and wrist, hard enough to dent, the outline of each tooth individually carved.

The singer hits a high note, a belly-song of hurt, and then there is a final wetness, a pulling from deep inside, and the pain comes stronger and truer than ever.

Her little sister is twenty-two, drunk, and sobbing; those wet, clunking things that come up from the diaphragm in retches to spill out over the lips. They are sitting on her couch, leather-backed and designed to fit the angled walls of her rented apartment. The room is small; cramped and low ceilinged, but the orange couch wraps around it like a hug.

A row of half-drunk cups of tea move from hot to warm to cool along the table, and she taps them gently with a teaspoon while she waits for a pause in the flood, each singing out a different note, weaving a song that is bright and pure. The cups are white china, a gift from an elderly aunt, and usually live on a shelf above the microwave, with chunkier supermarket mugs for everyday use. But the nighttime knock on the door, the sour, nostril-burning tang of vomit; this moment requires more help than those mugs can provide, so the china has come out, to fill up with heartache.

Her sister's head comes up from its hollow in her lap and falls backward against the arm of the couch, her neck a convex of misery. Her upper lip shines with mucus, and a silvery trail dances along the backs of her hands, up the black sleeves of her knitted jumper.

The telling is not easy—a party, a couch, a drink—the words that come out are put together wrong, the sentences fall apart, and tears overwhelm meaning again. So she smooths her sister's hair down again and again, but the red dye has made it rough and sticky, so it is an uneasy thing, like stroking a cat backwards.

It is so late it has become early, and she has work in the morning—a performance review—but the contract between sisters is old and stronger than sleep. A soothing, careful hum fills up the room with looping layers of softness, until calm descends like a parachute.

Clara is almost two, all soft edges and pudge, and she is sleeping, making wet, rumbling noises in her white pine crib. Her daughter is named after the sick girl in *Heidi*, and her first, halting steps last week had truly seemed those of an invalid escaping a wheelchair. The Victorian sicknesses of her childhood books had always seemed curable through laughter and fresh air and green things, but her daughter's lungs are weak, so she wraps her in two jumpers and a jacket for visits to the playground, and carries hand sanitizer in her bag at all times.

The bars in the crib have been raised higher, because Clara had scaled them the night before. She had bum-shuffled her way into the bedroom, pulling herself upright at the end of the bed, to see why Ma and Da were fighting, moaning, banging into each other with exhausted passion. An unclaimed leg had arced out to catch their daughter across the cheek, and the cry of pain and shock had caused her boyfriend to lose focus and ejaculate in fright. They had both leapt up, sticky and dripping, catching up their daughter in warm hands, shouting at each other in wordless, mindless guilt.

The baby sleeps well, now, and the high jail-bars of her crib do not bother her, but her eye socket is yellow-dark and bruised. A puddle of shame lies in the center of their double bed, and the surprised shrieks of their daughter will echo through the bedroom for months.

At night, they still hold hands, but turn their backs to sleep.

The fresh teethmarks are dark smudges on her daughter's neck, but she wears them with satisfaction, hair slick-stiff with last night's hairspray. Clara is fifteen and her breath is still sugar-sweet from alcopops and stolen cigarettes; eyes bright, she vibrates at a black-and-red frequency as she sits at the kitchen table, sipping from a pint of water.

Midmorning, and the spare key had shuddered in the lock just an hour before. She is making an omelet for Ben before his football practice, but the tension is rust-scaling the walls. Ben, oblivious, flicks brightly colored questions at his sister, and she bats them back across the room with morning-after wit. There will be screaming and accusations later, when her husband returns, but for now, a quiet fury splays itself out across the table like a dog in heat, throbbing and raw.

When Ben leaves to gather his football socks, she hands her daughter a silver dessert spoon and tells her to press the cold bowl against her neck until it begins to hurt, to soften the bruising. Close up, her daughter smells foreign, the way other people's houses smell wrong, and her spit-white eyes leak a giddy mixture of resentment and pride. So she cries softly after Clara stumbles to bed at lunchtime, cries as she plates the leftover omelet onto a separate dish, cries as she scrubs baked-on egg from the curved rims of the heavy-based frying pan.

The heat comes on her at night, mostly, but her sweat-soaked body begins to cool almost as soon as she gasps herself awake. She grips the duvet, easing it away from her sleeping husband, until the roaring in her ears subsides, and the sounds of the house slip back in.

Ben is awake and moving down in the kitchen, but she resists the urge to go to him. Her son spends the day in VR and ghosts around the house at night, and enough trust to leave him alone does not come easily to her. The medication drives him to eat, and she finds loaves of bread half spilled on the counter in the morning, butter-stained knives balanced on the edge of the sink. He has put on weight; his belly flops outwards over his jeans, but he refuses to leave the house long enough to buy a new pair. Clara doesn't understand his worries, his dark times, his scratchings at the wall; she calls her younger brother a waste of space when she visits home at weekends.

But mothers are burdened with second sight; she sees the terror behind his eyes and knows he would gnaw off his own leg to be free of it. She has terror, too: he will be learning to drive next year and her nightmares are of dark metal shapes twisted around roadside oaks. With the terror comes anger, when her womb pumps rage straight into her veins in a last, dying convulsion, and she is filled up with a muted, foggy fury that cannot find a target.

She will find her slippers, go downstairs to speak to Ben, hear his hurts; show her body that motherhood is not so easily thrown off. But instead she lies in bed until dawn glows on the horizon, and the flushes of warmth pulse through her body every few minutes, like a great, beating heart.

The smooth place beneath her collarbone where her left breast used to be takes up space in her mind, but it is negative space, like a scoop removed from an ice-cream tub. It doesn't bother her anymore, really, and her husband kisses her there when he remembers to, or when he sees her tracing a circle around her upper ribs in the mirror. But now the other breast is pulsing too, the poison is heavy and angry; her lymph nodes have jumped into the fray. She fingers it, testing the weight, trying to decide if healthy tissue feels heavier or lighter, and the fatigue drips down from her shoulders to spread like honey across the tiled kitchen floor.

She has seen an image online of a row of lemons, all lumpy and pockmarked, each darkened with a different malformation. Spot the signs of cancer, the caption had said, but sometimes signs are unnecessary, and knowing comes as easily and suddenly as the breaking of the day. Her husband also knows, or thinks he knows, because he sits up late most nights with his laptop and files, but the arrangement of paper never changes, because he stares at the wall instead of working and comes to bed benzo-drenched and snoring.

Clara is in Australia, too pregnant to fly; Ben sits in university in Dundee, racing through final accounting exams she wouldn't let him skip. But her sister is coming to visit soon, and they will drink tea out of their aunt's china cups and cry and talk about the future, or lack of.

She will not say things about unfairness, or stolen time; her sister is pragmatic and knows that things are how they are, and will be as they will be.

The smart lighting changes automatically as the sun goes down, and the room turns buttery-soft, like the gentlest of sunsets. She can see herself in the darkened windows; her reflection floats on the surface as if a sharp knife could peel it free.

A digital chime calls out as the sliding door pulls across, and a red-dyed head pokes through, bringing with it a whip-lick of December wind. She turns away from the sound and cocks her head to one side as her sister scrapes her boots against the doorframe.

Polystyrene snow, she says, as if resuming a long-interrupted conversation, do you remember the polystyrene snow?

PAWEŁ SOŁTYS

Jurek

IN THE AUTUMN of 2006 we drank beer as if our stomachs had been lined with peat, hot, smoldering peat that had to be drenched, but the foam and the beer only caused it to smoke, and we belched furtively, and the smoke came out of our mouths, our noses, even our eyes, it seemed, because we could see more and more, but less and less clearly, we could see all of Warsaw, all of Poland, nearly all of Europe, but only through billows of gray smoke. Jurek had the largest nose among us; it was not only long but also (for balance, perhaps) very wide, as if someone had glued together a fairy-tale crone's nose with that of Louis Armstrong to produce this singular Warsaw nose. And from below this monumental nose words rushed out, words that had to be washed down immediately because they were cruel and scorching and they might burn right through the tables of that bizarre pub where everything was made of wood except for the kegs and the taps.

We drank Żywe—this was before the craft revolution and the thousand breweries with a hundred thousand idiotically named beers—and it was a novelty, this Live brew, it foamed as you poured it into your mouth, bubbling up on the palate, it cleaned your teeth better than any German toothpaste, it flooded your taste buds so that you weren't sure what its taste actually was, and then it fell on the smoldering peat in our stomachs, without extinguishing it.

Jurek would tell us about Beata and about his divorce but most of all about his little girl, the three-year-old Helenka, taken away from him by a judge whose facial expression as she gave her verdict could haunt you in your dreams, and it did, it haunted Jurek every few nights, so that he'd get up and go straight to the boxing club in Grochów and start punching a bag with his stronger, left hand. And with his right and, when no one was looking, with his forehead and his monumental nose, and he'd rip his heart out and bash it against that hunk of leather, an ordinary brown punching bag without a logo, and in one glove he'd hold his liver and beat the shit out of it too, so that blood sprayed everywhere and the small workout room looked like a slaughterhouse, until at last Kociuk the coach, an old jailbird who after doing fifteen years had returned to life, to boxing, and to doing good works among the troubled youth, Kociuk the coach would grab his arm, shove his liver and his heart back inside him, heal his wounds, and say quietly, "Fuck, sonny, this ain't the way. It's not worth it. What you're doing is no good."

"But I've never hit anybody," Jurek would reply, and he'd let himself be held in that funny embrace, and Kociuk the coach would pat him on the back with one hand, and with the index finger of the other make little circles at his own temple—which looked the same as the rest of his head because he'd been bald for ages—to show the troubled youth that here was a madman, that this was no good, that they should all get back to their own speed bags, punching bags, and skipping ropes.

So we drank bottle after bottle of Żywe, a beer that behaved as if it were truly alive, burrowing through us, foaming up like crazy, flushing out eager words of comfort whose effectiveness was of course minimal. And we kept having to ask the barmaid for another round, to fizz up more soothing phrases, while Jurek drew things for us in his smooth notebook, things that he would have drawn for his daughter if that damned judge and that damned Beata hadn't taken her away from him except for every fourth weekend. He drew us houses, gardens, flowers, horses, cats, dogs, and other animals, and it was all terribly beautiful. He added shading, he made corrections, the horses would snort and drink Żywe with us, the cats and dogs would chase each other, while the other animals, taking no notice of their blue skin (because Jurek drew with a blue pen, a cheap ballpoint), would climb on top of the house, chew through the perfectly drawn roof tiles and fall inside, making a horrible mess, causing confusion and squeaking, squeaking like when you shift a wooden pub chair across a wooden pub floor. The smoke coming out of the chimney mingled with our cigarette smoke, and when Jurek busied himself with another detail we swayed a little in our squeaky chairs, to check whether we too hadn't turned into blue figures drawn in that smooth notebook.

In the autumn of 2006 we still weren't that old, so some of us, trying to emerge from Jurek's tale even for a moment, would glance over at the pretty student barmaid, but the barmaid looked right over our heads, probably because we had more beer and blue ink than red blood inside us, or maybe she had other things on her mind. But drunk men don't much believe in other things. I didn't, and as I swallowed another sip of that damned beer, I tried to catch her eye. I don't have a wife or kids, I'm not divorced, so if you'd be up for . . . But then someone would nudge me, and I had to speak words of comfort, even though I myself needed comforting, not as much of course, I hadn't been touched by such misfortune, but smaller misfortunes can also chew through the roof tiles and fall inside, making a mess, causing confusion and squeaking, squeaking like your lungs after you've smoked twenty cigarettes.

A few weeks earlier, I had been woken up by that sort of squeaking; sharp as the tip of a compass, it had pierced my sleep and kept repeating at regular intervals.

"What's wrong with you, kitty?" I asked Lopek, who was trying to vomit in the corner.

Barely awake, I didn't worry much at first. Cats puke. Obsessed with their hygiene, they lick themselves clean and in the process swallow their own hair, which they have to get rid of later. But this squeaking was worrisome; it was as if Lopek had swallowed a miniature referee's whistle and every spasm of his stomach was setting it off. I made myself breakfast and served him his morning meal as well, but he didn't even glance at it. He lay on his side as if everything were fine, but something didn't quite sit right with me; this was not ordinary cat laziness or disdain for people and the world but something more like resignation. His paws also seemed drawn up slightly differently than usual, if only by a few millimeters. I couldn't describe it exactly, but when you've lived with someone for seven years, you just know when the way they're lying is off, that they don't lie like that when everything is fine.

"What's wrong with you?" I repeated, stroking his head and then, more carefully, his belly.

This should have had a bloody outcome, with his front and rear claws coming out. Nothing happened. That's when I got scared. I took down the cat carrier from the high cupboard and slowly transferred

Lopek inside. The floor where he'd lain was stained with urine and feces. I felt as if someone had kicked me in the heart. I ran to the vet. There was a line: a small black female cat missing a paw and a lethargic spaniel. And various people. Finally we went inside. A blood test, IV, words of comfort.

"We have to get him warm, his temperature's very low, please leave him here overnight, we'll keep him warm in an incubator, we'll wait for the results, we'll be wiser in the morning."

I don't know if I was any wiser in the morning. I picked up the phone at nine, the vet spoke in a measured, calm, compassionate voice—practice, experience, tact.

I went to pick up the body.

According to his health records, he's a middle-aged male. A gray, long-haired male with awful test results. He can see himself reflected in the glass, but he's all blurry; his watery eyes have receded into his head. Beyond the reflection and the glass, there's nobody. Only equipment, wires and blue-and-white walls. Where are the hands that have brought him here? The hands that touched him tenderly over the past seven years, that were there to rub his head, his back, and, less often, his plump belly? The IV tube bothers him and he can feel a painful sting whenever he moves, but he doesn't move much, he doesn't have the strength. He lifts his head for a moment and after a few seconds lowers it again. The real pain is lower down, spreading from below his stomach, so bad that it's impossible to even complain. Where are those hands, he lifts his head again, he doesn't know if it's day or night, his instincts are silent, as if the pain had cut them off. It's warm, so warm one could fall sleep. He'd like to fall asleep, but he'd also like those hands to be there, so that he wouldn't be afraid, so that it would hurt less. But they're not there. The hands appear in the morning, when it's too late, when it's all cold. When there's nothing.

You remember some stories, and other stories remember you and reach out a hand to choke you when you least expect it. Teary-eyed, I kept glancing at the barmaid, who kept looking everywhere except at me and flicking her dark bangs off her forehead with a quick movement of her index finger, and with every passing moment I grew more and more convinced that this gesture was for me, to show me that I'm a madman, that what I'm doing is no good, and all my courage would sink into the burning peat. At last we'd go outside, trying to pick out lit-up yellow taxi signs with our unseeing eyes, and we'd ride home and dream our dreams, in which blue animals, objects, and buildings would mock us to our faces. I would also dream about the barmaid, who would pay me as much attention as in real life. Then we'd wake up and go about our daily business, only to sit down again each evening in that strange, entirely wooden pub and drink Żywe, which caused vicious hangovers but was a novelty, so we kept drinking it, and we sniffed the smoke and the blue flowers in Jurek's notebook, sniffed them in place of his daughter, on her behalf. That was the autumn of 2006.

In the winter we sobered up. Jurek came to an agreement with Beata without involving the court. Instead of going to Kociuk's, he'd take his daughter to the zoo. I started writing a book I would never finish. In this book, the sky was pink, the barmaid and I had a hundred different adventures, and wicked people always got punished. There is no punchline; what's past is past. The pub was demolished, one of us died, the rest have children or a therapist. Jurek has a new wife, the barmaid finished her studies and now teaches at a university. Sometimes I go and watch her come out of the gate in Oboźna Street. That gesture of hers hasn't changed; she still shows me that I'm a madman, that what I'm doing is no good, although she doesn't know I'm looking.

TRANSLATED FROM THE POLISH BY ELIZA MARCINIAK

[SWEDEN]

LINA WOLFF

From *The Polyglot Lovers*

IN TRYING TO find "the one," I'd never have thought the web would be my thing. There was something commercial about it, never mind I'd yet to write a personal ad, or anything else for that matter, and had no idea how to sell myself in writing. My boyfriends had always been regular guys from my village. The first one was called Johnny and there was nothing special about him at all, at least not on the surface, at least not until it became clear that he was in fact sick. We were in the same class at school and it started with him saying:

"Is there anything you've always dreamed a man would do for you?"

I guess he'd heard it in a movie and already back then, no joke, actually thought he was a man. And I suppose he wasn't expecting the answer I gave him, but something more like "Yes, I've always wished for a man who could make me lose my mind in bed." Or a concrete wish that would help him along the way. But I said:

"I've always wanted to be taught how to fight."

And when he didn't look as surprised as I'd thought he would, I added:

"Fight like a motherfucker."

Johnny nodded slowly, spit on the ground, and said:

"If that's what you want, doll, then I'll teach ya."

That very night he took me to what he called the "fighter's club." It was a bunch of people who'd seen and been inspired by *Fight Club*, but unlike the people in the movie, they actually practiced various martial arts and met up three times a week in a room to fight. Everyone went up against everyone else. You had to go under a school and farther down into a basement. It was tiled in tiles that shifted from brown to orange; a strange matte tile that didn't behave as tile usually does, but seemed to absorb every sound. From there, you went far into the culverts. Everyone was dead silent, barefoot, and had bags full of gym clothes slung over their shoulders. Only the fans made a noise. Then you entered the room and there they were, the people from our village who wanted to fight. A temporary captain was appointed, and we all warmed up together. Everyone was flexible, even the boys, and no one was ashamed of showing that they could do forward or side splits. People farted loudly stretched out like that, but not laughing was an unwritten rule. Then we fought. I was the only beginner and had one thing going for me: I was scared to death. Being scared to death gives you an edge, Johnny said. If you're really fucking afraid, you got a lot thrown in, the body was smarter than you think, and when you let it run on autopilot, it was capable of almost anything. But then you had to take control.

"Most people aren't angry because they get attacked, they're angry because they can't defend themselves," Johnny said.

Johnny could do more than fight; he could shoot, too, and we used to visit a firing range on the road between our village and the next one over. We walked around wearing orange earmuffs, watching the people shooting guns and then the ones shooting rifles. Johnny showed me how to take a wide stance, lift the rifle, and nail a clay pigeon. First in a simulator and then in real life. One day he said he could take me hunting now. He talked a lot about that hunt before we went, how you had to go out after dark, use your night vision, and keep real quiet the whole time.

They only pulled the trigger once when I was with them, at a wild boar. The shot cracked the silence, and you could hear the boar still running, not like before, but clumsily, branches breaking around it, and in the end limping and confused, as if it knew it were close to death and was pulling itself in a panic through the brushwood. As we advanced, Johnny suddenly pointed the beam of his flashlight upward. I saw the beech's bare branches reaching for the night sky like long dark bones. Johnny took my hand, clamped the flashlight between his legs, and started rubbing his buzz cut, back and forth, and I wanted to ask him why but kept quiet. He was just about to whisper in my ear—I think it was going to be something big, about us—but one of the hunters interrupted, saying he'd found the pig. He shined a light on it. A clean shot to the shoulder, blood pumping out over the black bristles. It was a large sow, and we all had to help carry her on a pole to the pickup. The next day, it was going to be cut up in Johnny's friend's yard. We headed over after breakfast, and by the time we arrived, blood and bristles were everywhere because no one actually knew anything about butchery. Everyone went at it as best they knew how, all the while saying it had to be fast. I never went poaching again.

One night I told Johnny that if he was ready, so was I. He smiled at me, and I was thinking that this was the first time I'd ever really seen his teeth, and they were big and white like sugar cubes, perfectly set in his mouth, an odd contrast to his face, which was irregular and acne-scarred. We did it on the bed of his pickup, and the jacket he'd spread underneath me got covered in blood.

"Girls today don't normally bleed their first time," the school nurse told us during sex ed. "Because they go riding and biking and bounce around, their hymens aren't normally intact."

I must have had an incredibly subdued childhood, because my hymen was absolutely still intact. The sight of all that blood didn't disgust Johnny at all, in fact he came within seconds. I didn't know what to say when he was done. But I could already tell that Johnny was a person to watch out for. Of course, like most of the guys in my village, he had violent tendencies, was uneducated and horny and would be for the rest of his life. But there was more to him.

"I didn't know you were a virgin," he said.

"What about you?" I asked.

"Yeah. I was too."

He looked at his stained jacket and said:

"I guess you gotta start somewhere."

The next time was much better. Not to mention the third, fourth, and fifth times. Johnny said he thought the two of us, we fucked like porn stars.

When we were sixteen years old, I broke Johnny's nose with the back of my hand. It wasn't on purpose in the sense that I wanted it to happen, my arm just flew out by reflex, it had nothing to do with martial arts. Anyway, it turned into a big thing, because we were in high school and everyone heard about it, the teachers and the nurse and Johnny's parents and mine. Johnny's mother said:

"I don't want you seeing that girl anymore."

We were in the schoolyard and his nose was bleeding. His mother had rushed over as soon as she found out and was standing there giving me dirty looks.

"Mom, Ellinor isn't some little girl," Johnny said. "She's a lady. And what a lady she is."

He smiled at me, hair falling over his eyes.

"And what a lady she is," he repeated, smiling even wider with those sugar cubes of his.

I wanted to say don't stand there grinning, remember how hot the blood got you, you're a sick fuck, Johnny, there's no hiding that kind of thing. That's what I wanted to say, but I suppose it was the bloody nose that made me feel differently, and so I went over and hugged him. The gesture was unusual for us. We did everything together. We helped each other with the repeating rifles and the other weapons, we fought and we fucked, but we never hugged. And yet here we were, and I could feel his hot blood dripping down my neck.

"Now you've learned everything I wanted to teach you," he said.

But he added that if I ever used what he'd taught me against him again, then he wouldn't think twice about killing me.

"Just you try," I replied.

"Don't piss me off," he said, and his eyes went black.

Soon we fell into a sort of sexual routine, even if you can't really talk about routines the way we were back then.

"Let's go to my place," he'd declare, sliding his hand between my legs while driving.

Going to his place meant the hunting cabin his dad had outside the village, where one could be left alone. It was a small cabin with gnarled bead-and-butt paneling and bright-yellow curtains with white stripes that his mother must have hung. The cabin had two small bedrooms plus a living room with a stove. We went into one of the bedrooms and he said:

"Take your clothes off and get on the bed."

While I did that he went to the kitchen and made coffee. He returned with his cup, dragged the chair over to the bed and, while he drank, he looked at me lying there on my back, legs spread. It felt like he could see right into me, up and through my interior, if you can say that, as if there were a dark channel inside me, and if you followed that channel, you would surface somewhere else entirely.

"Do you have to stare like that?" I asked.

"Think about the porn stars. They've got no problem showing themselves off."

"Think about when I broke your nose," I replied.

"You're like bread between my teeth," he said and raised his cup, as if in a toast.

Then he went on sitting there, drinking his coffee. When he'd finished it, he put the cup on a shelf and started taking off his trousers.

"When are you going to let me do you in the butt?" he groaned once, when we were getting it on.

I replied that if I were a truck driver and had access to a nice, comfortable garage, I'd never park my vehicle down in the drain. Johnny laughed, but never asked about it again.

A few years later I put on some weight. I never really got fat, but it was enough for Johnny to stop finding me attractive. We met up less and less, and eventually he stopped calling. Once I plucked up the courage and called him.

"Should we go shooting one of these days?" I asked. "Or fight?"

He told me he'd met someone. After that I saw him in the village with the other girl. She was thin and fit with long dark hair tied in a ponytail that hung all the way down her back. I wondered what it was like for them in bed, if he sat at its foot, drinking his coffee while taking her in, and if so, what she thought about it.

I kept up the fighting over the years. Like other people play bridge, sing in a choir, or dance a few nights a week and take comfort in it as they get older—a pursuit, so to speak, that provides a foundation for your old age or at least allays its effects—I stuck to that basement venue and spent time with the people there. Fighting was good; you got better with age. Being young and good-looking didn't buy you any cred, nothing came for free, and every last thing had to be fought for. Later, when I found friends who came from other places, they said they couldn't understand why a person would choose to spend their time like that when they could be spending it with a good book, good company, and a glass of wine instead.

"Not much in life compares to fighting," I'd replied.

I knew how it must have sounded to them, but I still think it's true. I've never been as close to anyone as I have in that basement room over the years. It has to do with concentration and how you read people's eyes. Sex doesn't work like that. There are people who close their eyes and jack off all their lives, into their own hands or between someone's legs, but nothing ever goes on in their brains. But when you face an opponent, there's a moment when you can see right into them and understand exactly who they are. Not to mention, and this is what I told my friends, you're not really old as long as you can kick a person who's taller than you in the head.

Sometimes I thought about Johnny and how he was a sick fuck. But sick or not, I'd come to understand that wasn't what's important. What's important is not being alone.

*

I ended up having a number of boyfriends over the years, pretty normal ones too, at least compared with what was to come. I never moved in with them. I was more the kind of person who lived, took each day as it came, and didn't get worked up for no reason. I wasn't really serious about any of the men in my life before the thing with Calisto and the manuscript happened. And that began with me creating a profile on a dating site with the following introduction:

I'm thirty-six years old and seeking a tender, but not too tender, man.

I left "interests" blank, I left "favorite authors" blank. Same with "favorite food" and "favorite places in the world." But in the space for your motto, I did write: *Meeting the aforementioned man.* Then it occurred to me that a motto is actually something else, a sentence or phrase that can act as words of wisdom in various situations. But I've never had that kind of motto so I left the sentence there, even if it would say something about me, suggesting a laconic side that might put some people off. But on the other hand I wasn't after a verbal person. I also included a picture of myself. It's a picture a friend of mine took, and I'm lying on my stomach on his bed. The signs of my age aren't visible because the only light source in that picture is a few candles, and like my friend says, most people look pretty decent in the glow of a few of those.

A week went by before I logged on to that site again. I'd received a ton of replies. Surprised, I worked my way through them, one by one. I've never been the kind of girl that gets appreciated. Once Johnny said I was like an onion, that you had to peel away the layers to get at me. Most girls would have been insulted if you said something like that to them, but I could tell Johnny meant it as a compliment. And now when I opened my e-mail in the mornings I had dozens of replies. An older man promised me "economic freedom" in exchange for "satisfying him" sexually three times a week. A twenty-year-old wondered if I could school him. I sat there, coffee in hand, laughing out loud. I felt touched, but not so much because these men were appreciating me (the photo, when all was said and done, was a con) but because I understood that the people writing to me actually believed in love, in the sense that I'd be able to give them what they were looking for.

Then some time passed before I next visited the site. Things came up, but when I finally went back I saw that several of the men who'd replied had kept writing to me. Some of them had written practically every day for several weeks. The twenty-year-old who thought I could teach him something seemed to almost have become a little obsessed with me, and wrote in a message that *I've always had girls who talk and talk, they never want to do anything but talk, but you seem wordless and genuine.* Wordless and genuine. I thought that was nicely put. I wrote to him:

> *I guess you're inviting them to conversation, plain and simple. Try inviting them to something else. Kind regards, E*

Some sounded threatening. Not that they themselves were threatening me, but because they were telling me about other men who were threatening other women on the site.

This world is no exception to the real world, wrote one. *Girls get threat-ened here, just like anywhere else, you have to watch out here, too.*

So I guess I'll block you now, you psycho, I wrote back and that was the end of that.

Sometimes I thought: Why did you leave, Johnny? Why couldn't you just take care of me? Now I'm afloat in this cold water and who the hell knows if I'll survive.

But I survived, otherwise I wouldn't be sitting here writing this.

My next boyfriend was called Klaus Bjerre and came from Copenhagen. He liked that I called him my "boyfriend," it made him feel young, he said. In Danish you say *käresta*: dearest. He lived in an apartment not far from one of the heroin rows. At that time there were still real her-oin rows in Copenhagen, and you could see people standing and sleep-ing on street corners in the December fog. Klaus Bjerre said they were harmless, and they were. I mostly stayed at home, since Bjerre used to say that "anything can happen in Copenhagen," and would gesture at the window. On the other side was a red brick façade. I've always liked Copenhagen, but I wondered why Bjerre was looking for a partner in Sweden. I thought there might be something about him that the Danes saw at once, but that he hoped Swedes wouldn't figure out. Danes think Swedes are dumb. Being from Skåne is no exception; same shit, they think. We're good for selling food, building a bridge, and keeping up our forests so that they can come over on the weekend and go for walks. Maybe we were even good enough to be wives or at least lovers, I guess that's what Bjerre was trying to find out.

"I only have one small defect," he said the first time we met, "and that's that I drink quite a lot."

It didn't worry me then, because I didn't know anything about drinking and thought it wouldn't have any effect at all, at least not to begin with. But then he touched me, and later I still stank of his hands. The bed we slept in also smelled of him, and sometimes when he got up I buried my nose in his pillow, thinking I might vomit. It smelled of liquor and dirt, a physical dirt, like the body didn't know what to do with all that poison and so had started to produce its own musty anti-dote. In the beginning he made me feel sick, but I got used to it. I liked the apartment he lived in. It was in Frederiksberg and was warm and had a heater just under the kitchen table that you could press your leg against while drinking your coffee.

Nothing special happened between us, nothing that doesn't happen between normal couples. The biggest thing that happened between us was when Bjerre talked about our future. He sketched it out before him like some sort of castle, and as he did so a look of happiness appeared in his eyes, and he'd even forget to drink while he was talking. He said I could come live with him, and he'd buy a bigger bed and other things I might want. We'd have friends that we could invite over, and he'd make sure there was money in the bank account and a year's salary of savings in case anything happened.

"I'm going to make sure of it," he said. "This is my responsibility, you should be able to relax with me and know that I'm behind you, taking care of everything."

I said that if he wanted to get his life in order the first thing he had to do was stop drinking. He nodded and took a drink from his glass.

"True," he said. "You're not telling me what I want to hear, you're telling me what I *need* to hear. And that's why you're a true friend, Ellinor."

He looked at me with those bloodshot eyes of his when he said it. His eyes had a shine to them, as though he were always on the verge of tears. He took my hand; his fingers were long and his nails chewed-off. He leaned in for a kiss, but the smell coming from him was so nauseating I turned my head away. He took another sip and blinked away the shine.

"When I think about the life I want," he said, "the calm, warm, cozy life I want to have with you, Ellinor, I feel like I can do anything. I'm prepared to do anything. Tomorrow we'll get out all the bottles I've hidden, and we'll pour them down the drain. It'll be like a fresh start."

He gave me another smile, and his hand gripped mine.

"Should we get a car?" he asked. "Then we can drive all around Skåne on the weekends. Walk in the forest and buy cheap food in Malmö."

I said that we didn't need a car; one of the nice things about Copenhagen was that you could borrow bicycles everywhere, and if you wanted to go to Skåne there was a train. Bjerre looked worried, as though the car were a prerequisite for all the rest.

"What about a dog?" he asked.

I shook my head.

"We have it good as it is," I said. "You just have to stop drinking."

The next day we were supposed to throw away all the bottles. Pour the liquor out, throw away all the bottles, and start that new, stable life. Klaus Bjerre got up early that morning, showered and perfumed himself and drank coffee, but without touching any of the bottles in the kitchen. When he looked at me, the whites of his eyes seemed less bloodshot.

"You'll see, everything will be fine," I said. "With enough determination, you can make anything work."

"Yes," said Klaus. "I'm going to the office now. Then I'll come home, and we'll eat dinner and drink water with the food. Then we'll deal with the bottles."

I lingered in the doorway as he made his way out. He turned around when he got to the banister, waved at me and smiled.

I went back into the apartment, sat in the kitchen and had breakfast. Maybe half an hour had passed after Klaus left when there came a knock at the door. It was a hard, firm knock. I hadn't heard any footsteps on the stairs, so I thought that the person knocking must have been standing outside the door for a while. Mustering the courage, then lifting their hand and pounding out three determined knocks. I stopped chewing and set my cup on the table. It must be a salesman or a Jehovah's Witness, I thought. But I knew that a salesman or a Jehovah's Witness would never knock like that. With their very first knock they'd make sure the person in the apartment perceived them as a friend, as someone who could improve your life. When I didn't respond, they knocked again. Hard and insistent, as though the person knew for sure that there was someone inside and wanted to let them know that they weren't about to give up. I got up and stood in the middle of the room. I stood there in my nightgown and stared at the door, unable to make myself open it. They knocked even harder, and I heard someone say:

"Open up, Mrs. Bjerre, please, Mrs. Bjerre, open up!"

I opened the door a crack. It was one of Klaus's neighbor ladies. I'd never spoken with her but knew she lived on the seventh floor together with her daughter. Klaus called her "that nutjob." She was just as poorly dressed as I was, or maybe even worse, because the bib of her night-gown was stained with coffee, or maybe it was marmalade.

"Yes?" I asked through the crack.

"You have to come with me," she said. "Regina's locked herself in the bathroom and is saying swear words."

"Regina?" I said.

"My daughter."

"I don't think I can be of any help," I said.

"But you have to," she insisted. "Regina might die in there."

I wanted to say that I had a lot to think about today in particular, and besides I don't usually go out this early in the morning. So I said that, while trying to shut the door. But then the woman began to panic.

"*No no,*" she shouted. "*You don't understand, Mrs. Bjerre, Regina might die in there, you have to come out and help me, otherwise she might die in there!*"

I don't know why, but I opened the door and joined her on the landing. All was silent. It was like we were completely cut off from Copenhagen's hustle and bustle, like the two of us, without knowing it and in separate apartments, had cultivated something all our own, something unpleasant and frightening. Our own vacuum, or our own sick universe. That's what I thought, and then I thought that I shouldn't have to know anything about vacuums or sick universes.

"What do you want me to do?" I asked.

"You have to help get her out of the bathroom," the woman replied.

"I'm sick," I said, not knowing why.

"What kind of sick?" she asked.

I tried to come up with a disease and said the most contagious one I could think of, that I'd caught some sort of pox.

"But I don't see any spots," she said. "What kind of pox is it? Impetigo?"

"No," I said. "Regular pox."

"Regular pox?" she wondered.

"What do you want me to do?" I repeated.

"Help us," she said. "We have to help each other."

"Isn't there anyone else you can ask?"

"You're the only one who's free around this time."

She was right. Of all the building's residents, I was the only one who wasn't busy. The rest of the doors were closed and locked and would be until six or seven o'clock when people started coming home from work. I was the only one free around this time.

"So I guess I'm coming," I said.

I went into the apartment, got my key, and followed her into theirs.

Their place was stuffy and messy. Almost no daylight came in and the apartment was lit up with lamps. There was a small shaft in the center of the apartment, probably an old garbage chute that now served to let light into the apartments in the building that didn't have windows on the courtyard or street. So, from certain rooms in the apartment, you could see into other rooms, and from the kitchen you could see into the bathroom. I stood there, looking in. And there, through the shaft, was a woman staring out the open window. She was sitting motionless, just a few meters away from me. A pair of thick eyeglasses distorted her eyes and her expression was hard to read. Her mouth was set in a thin line, and she too was wearing a baggy nightgown through which two oblong, sagging breasts could be seen.

"Can you show me the door?" I asked.

We walked through a narrow hall.

"Here it is," she said, showing me the bathroom door. "She's in there."

I grabbed the handle and rattled it. The door was in fact locked. I knocked.

"Hello?" I said.

"Is that Mrs. Bjerre?" Regina asked.

"Yes," I replied, even though I thought this Mrs. Bjerre business sounded silly.

"You'll have to kick down the door," the mother said.

"Yes," I said. "I'm going to kick down the door now."

I bunched my nightgown up around my waist, tucked it in the waistband of my underwear, and stood there for a few seconds. The neighbor lady's eyes wandered up and down my body slowly, with displeasure.

"I'm going to kick down the door now!" I shouted to Regina on the other side. "Stand as far away from it as you can! Got it? Watch out!"

I backed up. Then I kicked. It was the first time I'd ever kicked down a door, and I didn't hold back like you do with a sparring partner. I put my weight on my left leg, lifted the right, and kicked straight ahead so that the sole of my foot would meet the door. But right then, as I'm about to kick, I hear the mother say, quickly and weakly, like a peep:

"*Think of someone you hate.*"

And before I had a chance to think, before I could think about what she'd actually said, I saw Klaus Bjerre's face in front of me. I saw his face, his bloodshot eyes, and I caught a whiff of his sick breath. That face smiled crookedly at me as my foot hit the door with full force. My heel landed right in Klaus Bjerre's mug. The hinge exposed, the door swayed back and forth. Finally part of the frame fell onto the floor. And inside, on the toilet, sat Regina. Cross-eyed, heavy-breasted, and scared to death. The woman beside me let out a whoop of joy:

"Mrs. Bjerre opened the door!" she shouted. "There you have it, Regina, no need for a man!"

Regina got up from the toilet seat, came over to me, and draped herself around my neck, and soon the mother did the same thing. We stood there, lodged in the soft smell of their armpit sweat, and maybe mine, too, I don't think you smell your own sweat in the same way. They dragged me into the kitchen, offering me liqueur and cookies.

"Come now, Mrs. Bjerre, sit down and let us show you our appreciation."

Their bare feet shuffled beneath their nightgowns, back and forth across the linoleum. Their heels were dry and cracked, their toenails long, and their feet left prints on the floor, which seemed to be slicked with grease.

"I have to go back down to my place," I said. "Mr. Bjerre will be home soon."

They nodded in understanding. Then they waved goodbye to me in the stairwell as I walked down. I opened the door to the apartment, walked in, and was confronted with Klaus Bjerre's despairing odor. I stood there for a while, looking around. The breakfast table. The heater. The brick wall across the way. The bottles we were supposed to pour out that night. Our little life, the existence we'd managed to create.

Then I went into the bedroom, took out my bag, and packed my things. I walked out of the apartment, through the lanes towards Hovedbanegården. I spent a while watching the flurry of people under the glass roof and someone selling flowers nearby. A few minutes later I was on the train home to Skåne.

TRANSLATED FROM THE SWEDISH BY SASKIA VOGEL

HARO KRAAK

Dusk Blindness

I WAS GOING so fast I could feel my heart beating in my temples. Biking down Middenweg, I could feel the wind and sweat streaking down my lower back. The road was long and gun-barrel straight. I caught up to the tram, where a kid was looking at me, his eyes following my trajectory from behind the window, his head turning from left to right. For a moment I saw myself through his eyes. That's when the civil defense siren went off.

Because there were no further signs of a serious situation, I knew for sure it must be Monday. The sky was still empty; though I suppose fighter jets could fly above the clouds, none were visible to the naked eye. In any case I heard no sound. So I clung to that single certainty: Monday, twelve o'clock.

I used to be instinctively aware of the time all hours of the day. I'd get up five minutes before the alarm clock rang. But these past few weeks I've been swimming in time. And by that I don't mean that I've had oceans full of it.

The siren stopped as abruptly as it had begun. The tram was waiting at its stop and now I really had a decent lead. The farther ahead I looked, the better I could control the traffic. I focused on the cars, the cyclists, the pedestrians, and made them all move. They shaved past each other. These people seemed to shuttle each other forward like interlocking gears. In the distance a scooter came to a standstill. I kept pumping my pedals, harder and harder, but the scooter wouldn't move. My tires screeched on the asphalt, right under the guy's nose.

He said, "Those who go when the light is red, often end up mighty dead."

There was a white hair growing out of his nose.

I wanted to say, "Rhymes are for idiots and weirdos."
It would've been better to leave it at that.

They told me I needed a haircut. I didn't *need* to do anything. Other than sleep and eat. And then not as often as people say. I could, in any case, easily have gone another day without it.

"It's time you get a haircut."

Figures. My hair is long, and unruly (whatever that really means), but I don't see the point of anyone going to a hairdresser. I try to remember the last time I was on the receiving end of a shearing, but nothing comes to mind. For a while now, my memory and I have been less than simpatico. Sometimes I look at a childhood photo of myself and think, "That's not me at all."

I'm not overly fond of hairdressers. They're always looking at you. They ask you questions without caring what the answers are. It's not their lack of interest that bugs me—I myself have no need to know the banal details of other people's lives. But then again, I don't ask. What annoys me most about these questions is the way they compel me to lie. It's completely beyond my control. Not that it keeps me up at night—I believe my insomnia has other causes—but it always surprises me. The lies we tell.

Had I seen the movie, my sister recently asked. "The one with Jack Nicholson."

"Yes," I said. "Didn't like it. A crappy film."

"Oh," she said, and looked at her phone. "I thought you'd be into it."

The doctor said there were five things that might help:

- Taking my medication
- Going to talk therapy every day
- Getting regular sleep
- Facing my problems (by which he meant, no longer denying my problems)
- Giving order to my life, preferably by making lists

I found the last piece of advice especially appealing. I immediately made a note of his recommendations and stared at the other four tips, but I was distracted and decided to get it all down in an orderly fashion. I wrote, "There are things I do not understand."

- Why prices still end with 95 cents
- How an airplane takes off
- Why Wi-Fi doesn't cause cancer
- How the hell subway tunnels are dug
- Why white cars are cheaper
- How microwaves can heat up food
- Why we keep printing money
- How it is possible that toothpaste comes out of the tube layered into three neat colors

You might think, "Why does it matter?" But I don't. I simply know that it does matter. It's like I'm standing next to a radio tower—I feel it in my head.

Yesterday was the start of winter. No way to tell whether you've lost or gained time. The clock is set back one hour. When you wake up, you've slept one hour less. You've lost that hour. Then again, since the day begins earlier, it also lasts longer.

This didn't used to bother me. I'd escape the dilemma by watching the Teletext screen. It would happen at three in the morning. The clock would tick from 2:59:59 to 2:00:00. And that way you'd know you could stay awake for an extra hour. Now that I no longer have a television, I can't follow Teletext anymore. It's better this way, the doctors say.

The other problem I have with winter is the darkness. Or, to be precise, dusk. I can't go out at dusk because I can barely see anything. It could be that my eyes aren't able to adjust; I don't know. All I know is that I can only start looking around normally again once the sun has set completely.

Look around without everything humming.

Without seeing my heartbeat in the outlines of the buildings.

It's impossible for me to enjoy the week before I have to set back the clock. Nor is the week after much fun. I never liked change. Maybe that's why I'm right where I am. At least I know where I stand. The only thing I'd change is the food. Not because it tastes bad, though a change would be nice, but because it's pre-prepared. Every morning when I wake up and head down, and every evening when I take the elevator back up again, the tray waits behind the roller shutter. I pull on the cord to open it. I always think of this system as something magical: you pull the cord downward and the shutter moves upward. They put the trays there from outside, where there's a similar hatch. That way they don't have to disturb me when they bring the meals.

On the tray, each dish is individually covered in cling wrap. All I have to do is put it in the microwave. But that's where I have a problem. I couldn't eat something after it's been through that. The radiation can't be good for you. There's a lot in this world that I don't know, but I do know this: eating microwaved food will lead to a painful death.

Rightly so.

The self-help books say you should apologize to those you have hurt. But how could I know who it is I've hurt? Sometimes I feel so dulled by the pills I don't know whether I am myself capable of feeling hurt. I produced two columns.

Lies that I regret:

– Saying that I didn't kick him when he was down
– That my parents were dead
– That I hadn't climaxed

Lies that I don't regret:

– Saying that I'd climaxed
– That my twin brother died in the womb
– That I was baptized
– That it was only the one time
– That I used to get beaten
– That I was good at skateboarding

I did go make an appointment in the end. By which I mean, I walked into the hair salon and asked the hairdresser whether he had an opening. In an hour, he said. The salon was empty. Maybe he was startled by my hair and needed a moment to collect himself. Or he thought, "That hippie can wait. With his dirty hair."

People have been staring at me recently. When I sit down on the train, I can feel their eyes on my body. It's as if a small part of me disappears with each disapproving gaze. When they look away from me, they take something from me. I begin to crumble at the edges.

Someone said to me, "You have a wall around you."

I replied, "If only that were true."

In order to stay whole, I decided to take action. I looked at myself in the mirror and noted:

- Shoulder-length hair
- A long, dark-gray coat
- Black jeans
- Moccasins

My hair was actually the only thing that stood out. So it had to go. While I ambled through the city, killing the hour that the hairdresser insisted on, people had already stopped staring. It was as if I were one of them, just another inhabitant of the city.

The hairdresser said, "Well, it's really long, isn't it."

I nodded, not sure whether he was asking a question or stating a fact. And then I said, "It was for a role in a movie. I played a guitarist. Things didn't turn out well for him."

"Well well well," he said. "An actor in my salon. Now there's something that doesn't happen every day."

"Scissors in my hair, there's something else that doesn't happen every day."

He laughed. He was wearing a short-sleeved shirt and a belt wherein he could carry the tools of his trade.

He said, "That I believe. Do you also play guitar in real life?"

"Yes," I said. "By now I do. It has to look real, of course."

"Ah, I wouldn't know."

"No, I guess you wouldn't."

There was silence while he washed my hair. He massaged my scalp, digging deep with his knuckles into my temples. After which he asked, "How would you like it?"

"Short," I said. And after a moment, "Yes, take it all off."

Watching my locks fall to the ground, I thought about the people on the train. The clumps of hair on the ground were no longer mine, it's true. But nor did they belong to them. I looked in the mirror and tried to avoid making eye contact with the hairdresser, but to sit there staring at myself the whole time seemed equally inappropriate to me. I followed the hairdresser's motions. How he attached little clips to my hair and then later put them back on his belt. How he pushed a wet comb through my hair and how—when he was almost done and the shape of my skull was starting to become visible—he bit his tongue while he carefully shaved the back of my head with his clippers.

I used to think: People only ever do things for selfish reasons. Now I know: People only ever do things for other people. It's entirely about how others see you. That's why people listen to music, read books, go on holiday, brush their teeth, do their work, and dress their children. And that's why I went to the hairdresser.

This morning, during our session, we made a number of resolutions:

1. I am to listen to others carefully.
2. I am to lie only when it is entirely unavoidable.
3. I am not to hold anything in my hand while I talk, not even my other hand.
4. If I go to my session every day, I'm allowed to skip my pills once a week.

The shadows began to grow longer. I was cycling on Rijnstraat, at the part where there is a stretch of paving stones between the road and the bike lane. There was a woman standing right in that no-man's-land, throwing green bottles into the recycling. She was wearing a plastic raincoat, the kind to which raindrops like to cling. She checked in her bag for a moment. Then she turned around and took a step away from the road, into the bike path. I smashed my knee into her bag and heard something crack.

I clutched my knee and steered into the next bottle bank. My tire rolled over the jagged bottom of a broken bottle and immediately lost all its air. With a sigh—is that what people say? Either way, it's what it was; you could hear the tire emitting a miserable sigh. The woman gathered empty jars of peanut butter off the ground and put them back into her bag. She almost looked like a toffee, covered in her shiny plastic jacket. A toffee in its packaging—ready to roll out. I suspected that she must have said something, because I saw her mouth move.

"What?" I asked, taking out my ear buds.

"Are you in a hurry?" asked the toffee.

I think that I probably am. "What time is it?"

The toffee pulls up her sleeve. "Almost ten past five."

"If I'm not home in a few minutes, there will be more accidents."

The woman looked at me in consternation. My knee became warm. She said, "People shouldn't be in such a hurry."

And I, "People should look before they walk into a bicycle lane."

She gave no sign of having heard me.

"I have to be home on time," I said. "Before dusk sets in."

I saw her looking at my hair. She frowned.

"It's because it's wintertime," I said.

"Did you not take your pills today?" she asked.

"No," I said, "I don't have to today."

The frown again.

"It's wintertime," I said again. "I never know whether that means gaining time or losing time."

"Oh," she said. "There's a trick for that. The word says it all. Wintertime," she said again, slower. "Win–tah–time." She was looking at me, waiting for a reaction that didn't come. She said, "You win-the-time in win–tah–time. Get it?"

"Thanks," I said. And I meant it. "I will remember that, ma'am."

She laughed. For a moment we stood there in silence. I was tempted to tell her that I'd just had a haircut. That I don't always look like trash. But I didn't, because I knew that I usually did look like trash. I finally got off my bike and mounted the sidewalk. Then I said, "I've got to go."

She nodded and held up a shopping list. "Me too," she said.

On the way home I thought about the woman and her shopping list. I also thought about my own lists. What I could cross off. I thought about the hairdresser and even about the man with the white nose hair. I did not know who knew me best. No one seemed to be noticing me on the street. I could already smell the dark.

TRANSLATED FROM THE DUTCH BY JAN STEYN

TEOLINDA GERSÃO

Behind the Dreams

My wife liked to tell me her dreams every evening. Not in the morning, because when I left for work she was still sleeping and didn't wake up even if I made noise in the kitchen.

Sometimes, if I asked her about it when I came home at night, she'd say that early in the morning she'd heard the refrigerator door opening and closing, the banging of pots and pans, the scraping of a chair on the floor. Yes, she'd been vaguely aware of it but she didn't want to wake up and had gone on sleeping.

For her, sleeping or waking was a matter of will. And apparently she had no desire to wake up.

When I returned she'd tell me her dreams, as if during the day nothing noteworthy had happened. Things happened to her at night; they were almost always absurd and had no connection to reality, but they stirred up intense emotions.

She wrote everything down in a notebook, when she finally got up. She told me it was the first thing she did, before the dreams disappeared. If she waited she'd forget them, and that was the last thing she wanted.

I imagined her writing, in her nightgown, sitting on the edge of the bed. She wrote by the light of the lamp because she hadn't yet opened the windows. As she wrote down her dreams the night was prolonged and that act of detailed recording, in millimeter-sized handwriting that I could not decipher without great effort, would be the high point of her day.

She started a new page for every dream, with the date at the top of the page. It was a kind of alternative calendar in which only the nights counted. And reading me her dreams had in time become her way of sharing her life with me.

Truth be told, my attention wandered while listening to her, although I made an effort to concentrate. If those fleeting memories were so precious that she didn't want to lose them for anything in the world, they should also have meant something to me.

But for all my good intentions, I didn't find them interesting in the least, they were random things that you forget in the morning, or should forget, because nobody has time to think about them.

At least that's what I thought, and I was sure that was probably everyone else's opinion. But I tried to listen to her because that's what she wanted.

Nevertheless, as I listened, I'd look around, thinking she'd had all day to clean up the house, do the shopping, and make dinner. She could have had coffee with a friend after she'd done the shopping, before she went home. She could take a walk when the weather was good. She could knock on Maud's door, our next-door neighbor, and chat a bit, or arrange a dinner for the four of us, at their house or ours.

She could plan an evening of bridge with Daisy and her husband. She could read a newspaper that the mailman dropped off in the mailbox, or read a magazine or book. She could watch the soap operas on television, go to the hairdresser, to the gym, the spa or the mall. She could knit or take golf lessons. Or she might go to the movies in the afternoon with Louise.

She had more than enough time for the kinds of things that normally filled women's lives, or at least the lives of normal women. I suggested these activities to her repeatedly, as if she weren't capable of discovering them on her own.

She didn't lack for time or money, because I was well paid for facing an ocean of problems and stress, day in and day out. I was paid to deal with stress.

She had it better than I did, free time, light work, a tranquil life, which she could fill as she wished. But apparently all that mattered to her were those inconsequential dreams, as fragile as a breath of air, bubbles breaking the surface of a lake. Or soap bubbles.

I noticed that I only seemed to exist for her as someone to listen to her dreams, or as a character in them. In the dreams I was with her, we were in a sinking boat, she was about to drown, but I swam more quickly and saved her, keeping her head above water and pulling her to the beach. We were climbing an endless staircase, she was so tired she couldn't climb any more and I had to carry her on my shoulders and we continued to climb but the staircase never ended. We were sleeping in each other's arms, but a tornado was tearing off the roof and destroying the walls, all around us the houses were collapsing, one after the other, and she knew that when she woke up our house would no longer be there. Maybe that's why she didn't want to wake up and she nestled against me, seeking a safe, warm place as long as our bed didn't fly through the air and break apart. Or we were dancing at a party; maybe it was the prom where we first got together, because even though we'd known each other for a long time, apparently we still hadn't noticed each other. She didn't want the music to stop so we wouldn't stop dancing.

Sometimes I asked myself what time she'd wake up. Perhaps she stayed in bed whole mornings because she didn't want to wake up. Maybe the dreams were a way of hiding the fact that she was lazy; she seemed to be able to control when she woke up. Because it was true that she'd always been like that, somewhat indifferent and inactive.

She was too indifferent and inactive—the kind of woman who doesn't stand out in a group, a gathering, or a party, who doesn't try to be seductive, who doesn't laugh or gesture spontaneously. She was a quiet woman, simple and reserved, and that made me feel safe and it pleased me.

We hadn't had children, but that never seemed to bother her. I'd regretted it a little, but I carried on and didn't mention it. It comforted us both to affirm that after all life had many other things in it and that children are often just a source of problems and anguish.

In any case, I gave her a comfortable life, she had no reason to complain.

But in time the house began to suffer from neglect. Sometimes she did not even get up for lunch. I suggested she get psychological help so she could learn to see the world from another perspective. But she took offense and got angry, she assured me that she was perfectly fine and that I was the one with the problems. She didn't want to hear the word psychiatrist, all they did was diminish and belittle people, as if they were shrinking them, and it was appropriate they were called "shrinks."

And outside of the narrative of her dreams, she didn't show even a minimal interest in my day. Or in me, except as the person who listened to her dreams. I was even starting to disappear from them.

Again I mentioned casually, in passing, that she should see a psychiatrist, but she blew up again. It wasn't a psychiatrist she wanted to see, she wanted to see me.

She read me that night's dream, and reread the previous ones.

"I wanted to see you and I couldn't. I looked for you everywhere but you weren't there. You were at my side but I couldn't distinguish your features. Your face appeared blurry, as if in fog. And you were nothing more than a shadow. I stood by the window, watching you disappear. You left the house and your footprints were visible in the snow, but they kept receding. I knew you wouldn't come back and it wasn't worth making dinner. I was sleeping and you were shaking me and calling me, Meg, Meg, but I didn't wake up, as if I were a rag doll. And you were angry because I had turned into a rag doll and I was ignoring you and didn't like you, not wanting to know if you were happy or not, and you shouted at me for only being interested in dreams and giving up on life for my dreams. You shouted and shouted at me, but it was as if I couldn't hear you, because everything was happening far away, inside a dream. And you were slipping out of the dreams, from all of the dreams, and I remained alone, sleeping."

You had stopped having dreams for both of us, now they were just yours. I was on the outside; you had expelled me, even from the dreams.

The house was still, as though it were dead, when I arrived. And now I found you in a nightgown and robe, your hair uncombed, trying to make dinner. No matter how much I shouted at you and shook you and wanted to wake you, you went on sleeping with your eyes open. You weren't there. Even if you were standing you remained stuck in bed as if glued to it, or as if you'd fallen into sticky mud, or quicksand, that was swallowing you little by little.

This went on until I couldn't stand it anymore and I abandoned you, before you dragged me into that quicksand which would end up swallowing us both.

I didn't want to hurt you, Meg. But Helen was there every morning, at work, so close and available, and all I had to do was reach out my hand and touch her. I thought this was a passing phase and that everything would get back to normal between us.

But now I know I won't go back. You won't change and there's nothing else I can do for you.

Maybe I shouldn't have listened to you for so long, giving you the illusion that I put stock in what you were reading me, as if your dreams had some value, or I was interested in where you'd been and what had happened to you while you weren't there and you were running away. Because you hadn't been there for a long time.

I'm unable to imagine you waking in the morning and writing down your dreams, on the edge of the bed, before opening the windows, knowing you don't have anyone to read your dream journal to. Maybe now you only see a black square when you close your eyes. Maybe you can't sleep and you take pills, because you are going to continue wanting to escape into your dreams, because you can't live anywhere else.

But I gave up trying to follow you.

It occurs to me that one day you might swallow a whole container of pills at once. But I won't be able to stop you if that happens. I know it's terrible to say this, but now nothing that happens to you, whatever you dream or don't dream, has anything to do with me, or matters to me. I left the house, closed the door, and I won't come back.

TRANSLATED FROM THE
PORTUGUESE BY ELIZABETH LOWE

OLENA STIAZHKINA

From *In God's Language*

THEY DID SEE each other later, after his wife, Varda, had left—and not just in their dreams. Not often, but they saw each other. They would say hello, they would chat. "Here are mine," she'd say and show him photographs. First in her wallet, later on her phone. Revazov didn't show her any photos. Ten minutes. Five. Three. Too little time for anyone other than Inna to be "his" in that moment.

They didn't let themselves get carried away, or fool around. Old friends—family, you might even say. It felt comfortable. No reason for yelling, sobbing, kisses. What would be the use? But each time, after their meeting, Revazov regretted that he was leaving her without the yelling, without the embraces that would be impossible to break.

Once a year he'd send her his best wishes on some holiday or other—on whichever one was on the horizon when he felt the longing rise up in his chest. It was always different holidays. She understood. And about once a year, when the longing welled up in her, she wrote to him . . . In the beginning it was telegrams, later e-mails and text messages. "How are you?"

Of course, they never answered each other.

There was just one time. At an investment forum, where Revazov had brought along two partners and Inna had come with her translators. The moderators were disciplined, but there was chaos behind the scenes; the local bigwigs who were meant to open the thing were late and messed up the whole timetable, and got the speakers drunk at the beginning and not at the end. The whole forum turned into a party in the hotel lobby, and it was impossible to get anyone to go in to the conference rooms. Revazov's partners had dissolved themselves in vodka, and Inna's translators were practicing their Chinese, as the only ones who weren't drunk were the guests from China.

"Let's get out of here," Revazov suggested.

She nodded.

It was autumn then too. It was cold, but underfoot there were still leaves and not yet puddles. She was wearing high, and most likely uncomfortable, heels. She speared piles of leaves with the narrow toes of her shoes; the leaves flew awkwardly into the air, and she even managed to kick them as they descended, as though they were small, deflated footballs. His daughter, Miriam, walked through leaves in exactly the same way. First in her baby shoes, then in her trainers, and now, more and more often, in shoes with narrow toes.

By the house where Inna lived (both then and now) they stopped and turned to face each other.

"Shall I read your palm?" asked Inna. He shook his head.

"No. I know everything about myself already," he smiled. She took his hand and pulled it to her. This had all happened to them before. And so Revazov wasn't surprised when Inna kissed him on the wrist.

This year he couldn't find a pretext to write to Inna. There was nothing to celebrate. But when Varda's absence stopped being so painful, he wrote: "Where are you?"

The commonplace of the whole summer. An essential phrase. It was the beginning of every conversation. Or every "contact," as they'd begun to say. Beyond the frontline, in the rest of Ukraine, there was a different life. And there was a frontline of a different kind. His clients would report the shifting geography of the country. Friends too. Only Varda and the kids were in Mordor. And that was hard to take. And it was clear that everything was lost, precisely because they were in Mordor, and that the shadow would lie across that land for far longer than Revazov's miserable new life . . .

Not everybody was leaving. Not everybody. Those who remained would say, "I'm in the city." The city no longer had a name.

Inna wrote back, "Nowhere."

Revazov called her landline. Over the last twenty years, only the first numbers had changed. There had been two, now there were three . . . The number of landline users had clearly gone up.

"What's happened?"

"They've taken my husband. They want money. I think they've killed him already. I can just feel it somehow."

Her voice was dull, her tone resigned. Everyone had already learned to live in that resignation. And it was more or less clear that, if not now, then tomorrow, It, or they, would come. For us. For *them*. And you knew you should run away, but it was too late, there was nowhere to go, no strength left. No faith that, beyond the checkpoints, there was actually a horizon. And no more Tyulpan rocket launchers spewing their bloody mess all around.

"I'm on my way," said Revazov, "I have connections." He gave a bitter laugh at these words and left. The taxis, unlike the trolleybuses, which were reliant on electricity, were running efficiently . . .

Revazov recalled, against his will, his son's former history teacher, who was now working for *them*; the unwelcome, shapeless, toothless, giggling apparition, wearing its pince-nez, looking just like Beria; the image of his face kept crawling its slimy way into Revazov's head, and just as the mythical seafarer couldn't escape Aeolus, Zephyr, and his other companions, Revazov couldn't get rid of this picture . . .

Revazov arrived at the local administration building, now occupied by *them*, and spent a long time searching for the "historian," wondering how this drunk had managed to carve out his new career selling human beings for peanuts. In the office marked "SMERSH" they said that the historian was now a colonel in the Interior Ministry, but in the Interior Ministry they were pleased to inform Revazov that the historian had become a general, only now attached to the Public Prosecutor's Office. Revazov didn't know if he could handle a meeting with a marshal, but the Prosecutor's Office relieved this worry, informing him that, "Your friend has been transferred to agricultural work." Revazov wanted to ask: "Where to? Central Asia?" From what he could remember of Soviet life, any kind of agriculture was a demotion. And the warmer the locations to which the party dross was punted off, the more humiliating the demotion . . . Having to earn your daily bread felt like a bitter failure to those who'd made their names breaking fingers and knocking out teeth.

He eventually found the historian in the "Ministry of Transport." The office had no windows, and several other ministers of some description sat in the adjoining reception area. It stank of toilets and cabbage pies.

Everyone here looked despondent and out of sorts. And you could feel that their revolution was over, that it had taken to drink from grief. Now it was wandering around somewhere nearby, its face blue and swollen, but the historian and his colleagues no longer had the desire to try to decipher its garbled, dirty hints.

"They've ruined the transport system . . . It's a wreck . . . Can't even find a decent train car or a cattle truck to send all that filth off to Siberia," the historian grumbled. And muttered something about himself, about his bitter fate and the vicious battle against the private minibus drivers, about the time before the Gregorian calendar was introduced, about the outdated methods of collecting taxes from the fat-cat taxi drivers . . .

He muttered, yelled, and fell silent by turns, as though pausing sometimes to listen to someone answering him. Above his desk hung a portrait of "Givi"—one-time parking attendant at Donetsk's Covered Market, today Marshal of the United Armed Forces of the South of Russia.

"I have to find someone," said Revazov.

"The prices have gone up. I have to go through middlemen now, and that costs more," the historian said gloomily.

"First find out if he's alive. I won't pay for a dead man . . ."

"You will, no getting around it . . . Fucking intelligentsia—don't want to have to bury your friend in a ditch, eh? Well, just you wait!" The historian threatened Revazov with his index finger. Revazov thought the teacher looked like a cartoon dinosaur: big body, small head, and tiny little hands with little sausage fingers. Although dinosaurs didn't have sausages. Or fingers. And as Revazov looked at him it struck him that he'd be able to kill not only strangers, but also this guy—real, familiar, harmless, his son's old teacher . . .

His heart started racing again. And Revazov only now understood for the first time that the historian looked like Beria. But could Beria really be similar to a dinosaur?

*

He really was dead. Inna's husband. Vlad, it seems, was his name. Revazov found him at what used to be a training complex belonging to a football club. The complex had been built out in the suburbs, and sparkled, as people used to say, like something foreign, something imported, with its blinding green pitches like the green contact lenses in the eyes of Hollywood stars, with its gravel paths and subtropical bushes that flowered and gave off intoxicating, suffocating scents and in winter were wrapped tightly in white material so that they looked like unmelting snowmen, with the neon-lined contours of its buildings; all of this garishness brought to mind the American oilcloth they used to cover Dostoevsky's murdered heroine Nastasya Filippovna. It was too luxurious, too foreign, too inappropriate, and somehow resembled a synthetic shroud covering the grim suburb's corpse.

The complex had been taken in May. They started calling it "the barracks." They made a mess of it, trampled all over it, stole everything there was to steal, broke everything basically, they helped it blend in to the surrounding architectural landscape. In June, it started taking incoming fire. It was bombed with precision, professionally. And *they* couldn't quite believe at first that they could also be on the receiving end of something like this . . . They had thought that their ticket to the war, issued to them somewhere far away from here, guaranteed them immunity, a sure-fire investment, a sort of insurance policy; for them, the enemy was a fictitious object. And therefore it was possible to kill him, he who was fictitious, but not them, who were supposedly real.

The first stage of this surprise passed quickly. And when the complex became dangerous, they started calling it "the concentration camp." Without any shame. To end up in the concentration camp meant you were so close to death that you were good for neither digging trenches nor for trading with your relatives. They didn't even guard the prisoners here particularly closely, because they didn't have the strength to escape . . .

The historian said that Vlad was at the training complex . . .

He needed someone to go with him. Not Inna. Someone who could drive a car or dress wounds. Who could, if necessary, call . . . someone, some relative and say: you can stop looking for him now, or look in such and such place . . .

That was one of the simple desires people now had—to be identified. Nobody was too picky about being put into a mass grave, although ending up lying underneath a pile of *them* was something that neither *they* nor Revazov found appealing. To be identified is not to prolong another's suffering. Not to force them to wait for you.

Revazov went alone. Because anybody who came with him would end up a target, a traitor, an innocent victim, or maybe even a guilty victim—an aggressive victim who got into a fight deliberately and got mown down by a machine gun. Shot in the back, as usual . . .

Grandad Lazar used to say that Jesus was a human being adopted by God. Not born, but carried through the passionless body of Mary. And he had always had his eyes open wide. And Peter hadn't denied Jesus three times. It was He who had denied together with Peter. And together with Judas He betrayed. And together with them He was ashamed, and died. And rose again.

"And if you," said Grandad Lazar, "give to another more than he can bear, then you are a coward, and also a traitor . . . And you're the one who should die for this."

He could have called Igor, the neighbor with whom he'd killed the Russian mercenaries before. That would be some party—you, me, and my ex's husband . . .

Inna's husband had been dead for several days. He lay among the other bodies in a room at the complex that they'd fitted out with refrigerators. By the door, there were three lawnmowers, two metal buckets full of bullet holes, the frame of a Gazel truck, and some packs of yellowed leaflets that for some reason had never been distributed, but would come in useful soon as fuel for potbelly stoves, bonfires, fires in metal barrels . . . There was a shortage of paper now in the city, but not here. Paper is a great reason for hope.

"Take whichever one's yours," said the caretaker grimly.

"Can I call a hearse?" asked Revazov.

"A hearse?! I'll give you a hearse!" he spat, and snorted. Then he remembered he had a gun and shot lazily into the ground, almost without anger. He proudly adjusted his woolen *papakha* hat.

"Did you come here on foot or what?"

"On the bus . . . then on foot."

"Haha . . . on the bus with a stiff . . . Hehe . . . Now that's funny."

"Where are you from, bro?"

"We're from Nalchik . . ."

The name of the foreign town rang out joyfully. Revazov gave a short, quiet sigh. He looked at the face under the *papakha* and caught himself trying to commit it to memory, so as to be able to recognize it later. It turned out that it was perfectly possible to call a hearse. The funeral business was booming. Wooden crosses, paper flowers, inscriptions on graves. If people had money to pay for all this, Revazov thought, it could be a decent business opportunity. But judging by the texts on the grave markers they weren't paying much. They just copied, mixing stuff plagiarized from other graves with the drunken pathos of cinematic nonsense about "officer's honor."

During the siege of Leningrad they'd moved bodies on sleds. In winter. And in spring, when the snow had melted but there was still no food? How did they move them? Did they sling them over their backs? Drag them by the legs? They just abandoned them, because the winter had drained them of the ability to grieve, to feel . . .

"Ivan," said Revazov to the body, "I'm Ivan. And I never laid a finger on her after your wedding. Just know that."

He hauled the body onto his shoulders. He carried it to the bus stop. There was a smell. And the softness of a lifeless person. And yes, he began to feel sick. But it would have been even worse, impossible, to drag him by the legs.

The undertakers sent a car to the bus stop. They didn't ask any questions. Nothing surprised them anymore. They gave him a price that was tolerable. He had saved some money on the historian by telling him that he'd pay for Vlad upon receipt, at the training complex. And the whole time—on the bus on the way there, while he'd been talking to them, while he'd been identifying the body—by the jacket, by the most recent photograph, by the trousers with the white paint stain on the pocket—and while he'd been carrying him, the whole time he'd been thinking how he'd love to be a fly on the wall when the guy in the pince-nez tried to demand the money from the guy from Nalchik.

These thoughts made him smile.

But the other thoughts—about calling Inna and telling her to come and get the body from the morgue, about the emergency meeting place they'd agreed on, which was now already obsolete. He called her, and when he started talking he couldn't stop . . .

Two strangers can become communicating vessels filled with grief. It works well: a stranger's grief doesn't take up too much volume. It evaporates easily, like dew in the sun. When people know each other, their grief multiplies, and both vessels become full, and the glass is put under great pressure. The grief can't escape, has nowhere to go. The vessels break.

For Revazov, anyone who came to him carrying Varda's dead body over his shoulders would immediately become Charon.

And Charon doesn't get telegrams or text messages asking "How are you?"

We don't care how Charon is. And that's it.

These other thoughts made Revazov cry.

TRANSLATED FROM THE
RUSSIAN BY UILLEAM BLACKER

OLIVERA ḰORVEZIROSKA

Events Agency

1.

SHE HAD MADE a reservation for seventeen people in the pub at the Kapan An Inn. She was a little anxious about how things would go and so, half an hour before the booking time, she set off resolutely toward the Old Bazaar. She hurried, almost running across the Stone Bridge. A tight feeling wrapped itself around her throat like a scarf on an unexpectedly warm winter's day. She shot down the right-hand side of the street, past the Ibni Pajko Mosque toward the Daut Paša Hammam, and when she reached the stairs in front of the old department store called Most, she leaped up them in one bound. Her steps and the beads of sweat running down her neck subsided only after she found herself standing on the cobblestones. She slowed her pace, but she still reached the pub quite quickly, barely realizing she had crossed through the Old Bazaar. Suddenly she found herself descending the stairs to Kapan An.

"Good afternoon, good afternoon!" she said loudly. No one paid any attention to her . . . A harassed-looking waiter—about her own age, his face flushed, as though he was angry, as though he was annoyed, as though he was giving vent to pent-up rage—was wiping the counter furiously, like the balance of the universe depended on it.

"Good afternoon," she said to him once again, this time even louder, speaking directly into his face, the two words ramming into his flushed cheeks, while he, almost grunting, and suddenly recognizing her, muttered:

"You're a bit early, aren't you, Miss?"

"Yes, yes, I'm a teensy bit early, but still, I wanted to come a bit beforehand, you know, I've got Japanese guests coming . . . I want everything to be absolutely perfect . . ."

"It will be, everything's under control, now just sit down, take a seat . . ." Thoroughly agitated, he waved her toward a chair, and the rather short girl with the big eyes thought that if she didn't plonk her bottom down right then and there, he might clip her over the ear.

"I'm not in the mood to sit down," she said when she was almost seated on the chair. "I want you to tell me how the order's coming along, we agreed on locally produced meat, *tavče gravče* . . ."

'Yes, all right, yes . . . everything's ready. They'll be served as soon as they arrive."

"But there's still time, you know, before they get here, for the food to go cold . . ."

"It won't," he replied tersely as if closing the door to further conversation with a heavy, foreboding padlock, before dashing off into the kitchen like a man possessed. The girl was left entirely alone. A moment later, the sound of an argument the likes of which she'd never heard before came from the kitchen . . . A torrent of profanities escaped from there, possibly even to stave off a beating! The waiter, yes, that was definitely his voice, probably even redder in the face than when she'd first seen him on entering the pub, was swearing and hollering. This was followed by the sound of something falling and smashing. "Calm down, calm down, calm down . . . ," a female voice screamed at regular intervals, while she, all ears and a little bit afraid, just stayed in her chair . . . She gave a start only at the thought that her Japanese guests might arrive at any moment and witness it all, that is to say, hear everything that was going on. So, she stood up . . .

"Please, I beg you," she cried at the top of her voice, "please, sir!" The waiter shot out of the kitchen as though catapulted, glancing back over his shoulder, and repeating for as long as his voice would hold out:

"Fucking whore! Slut! You want to fucking push me around! Well, I'm not your fucking husband. Go to fucking hell, you damned bitch!"

"Sir, please, the Japanese guests will be here at any moment, please . . . What's going on here?"

"Oh, enough with you already! Let 'em come, as if the Japanese have never seen any depravity before! I've had it up to here with every fucking thing . . ."

Just as the Japanese guests entered the pub, a stout young woman wearing a white cook's outfit appeared behind the counter. She was in tears. The waiter flew at her and began strangling her right in front of everyone! At first, the Japanese guests made out as if they hadn't noticed anything, but then all sixteen of them turned to stare at the girl—their host—at the same time. She, in turn, didn't know whether to explain to them what was happening or whether to go and rescue the poor woman... No, no . . . She made out as if everything was perfectly normal, and politely began pouring mineral water into their glasses. Shouts resounded all around them, the woman screamed, the man had his hands wrapped around her throat . . .

Embarrassed and tired of acting as if this was a normal everyday sight in our cafés and drinking establishments, first she called the police, and immediately after that her cousin, who only yesterday had offered to help in any way he could to warmly welcome the Japanese guests to their city. He talked to her late into the evening, telling her that she should organize some kind of memorable event for them, that she had to make an effort for Skopje to be carved on their bones, etched in their minds and eyes somehow . . . At the time she'd said to him, "Don't go overboard, Cousin Milan," while now she muttered into the telephone receiver:

"Cousin Milan, come at once!"

As expected, her cousin rushed over from Taftalije, the neighborhood he lived in, followed by two policemen from the nearby police station in the Bit Pazar. The strangling had stopped, but fists were flying, food was being thrown around, cutlery was being hurled, glasses were being smashed, the Japanese were eating *tavče gravče*, locally produced meat, and cheese . . . "Well this happened, then that happened," she said to the policemen, while Cousin Milan tugged at her sleeve, whispering to her: "You shouldn't have called the police, you shouldn't have called the police . . . I would've told you, I would've explained to you . . ." But she wasn't listening to him. She put a great deal of effort into explaining the situation to the policemen:

"You know, I'm Alexandra Krstić, I'm doing postgraduate studies in Japan, and now I've come home together with my colleagues from the university in Kyoto. They're my guests, as well as the guests of my parents, Pavlina and Savo, and they've come to Skopje for the first time. I made a reservation here a long time ago, and now look what's happening . . . I don't know what to say to them. What is this—a brawl? . . . A family quarrel? . . ."

Without saying a word, the policemen went to the back section of the restaurant, followed immediately by her cousin Milan. They said something to the waiter and the cook, some sort of document was handed over to them, they nodded several times, and the policemen made to leave.

Her cousin was relieved, but she was still not appeased.

"What's happening? Where're you going?"

"Excuse me, young woman," said one of them, "we have no authority to intervene in family disputes."

"But they're not husband and wife, and even if they were, he was strangling her right in front of us, in full view of everyone else!"

"I'm sorry, young woman, you can come with us to the police station in Bit Pazar, make a statement, and we'll see . . ."

"And my Japanese guests?" she asked, as if all the anxiety of the world was pouring out from her big eyes.

"What about your Japanese guests?"

"Well, what should I do with them?"

"We don't really know what you should do with them. Let them eat, and then they can hit the road again . . ."

They ate and then left. She thought that her cousin had been very helpful to her, without really knowing what he had in fact done for her. For them. For carving images of our fair city on their bones, etching it in their minds and eyes. She was especially grateful to him after they came out of Kapan An. Once again, he'd proved extremely useful to her. He made the very polite and cheerful suggestion that they walk downtown, one foot in front of the other along the bank of the Vardar River.

2.

I've been in charge of the potted flowers and plants at the Events Agency for a long time. Actually, just the small ones because Florascope took care of the large ones. Once or twice a week, they'd send over one of their staff members to water the large plants, giant ficuses, Benjamin figs, fiddle-leaf figs . . . My duties each day were to tend to the potted cyclamens and violets on the windowsills. And to make cups of coffee, thyme tea, and cocoa. From time to time, I'd be told only ten minutes beforehand that I had to go up the long hallway and slowly pour some water into the bucket by the window. And not just with any old thing, but using the sleek white watering can with a long, thin, black spout. I had to empty out all the water from it into the bucket as though I were watering a delicate flower, an invisible orchid. The first few times I was accompanied by another employee who watched me carefully from a distance and told me to straighten up or bend down, to hold the sleek watering can higher or lower. Then, after I perfected my posture and the pace at which I watered the invisible orchid—actually, decanted water from the sleek watering can into an ordinary plastic bucket—they would just tell me to go to the hallway at such and such a time, giving me a knowing wink to take the sleek watering can that always stood on the cabinet like an objet d'art. I never used it to water the violets and the cyclamens on the windowsills. Nor, for that matter, for any other purpose either. Even though from the start I didn't understand the meaning of this duty, I made an effort not to think too much about it, not to try and understand things that couldn't be understood anyway. No, I never got used to watering an invisible orchid, as I referred to the decanting of water from one thing into another, from a watering can into a bucket by the large window in the hallway between the agency offices and the elevators.

Sometimes, on days when I felt like tidying things up, even though the agency had a cleaner, I'd also wipe a few windows and some of the numerous framed photographs . . . I always started with the biggest one, hanging on the southern wall. And no, not because I liked it; rather, there was something strange about it . . . A dozen foreigners with completely different physical features and clothing from ours are sitting in some restaurant, eating Macedonian food, while in the background, behind the counter, the waiter is strangling some woman wearing white clothes, maybe the cook . . . It made no sense to me how in the same room people were strangling each other, while others calmly sat by eating . . . In the far right corner, where the glass is scratched and the cleaning cloth somehow always catches under her fingers, barely visible were two policemen having an animated conversation with a rather short pretty girl with big eyes . . .

After I'd thoroughly wiped this photograph, rubbing it with glass cleaner a few times, then drying it off with a clean microfiber cloth, my hand would move across to the slightly smaller photograph next to it, in which some foreigners are standing in a street, pressed up against one another, all looking up at a window on the upper floor of a building opposite them. In the window two women are holding hands, dancing an *oro*! One of them—the taller one—is even holding a white hand-kerchief in her right hand, waving it in the air like the lead dancer in a folk dance group. Last time I was wiping this smaller photograph and my hand spontaneously came to the women in the window, it seemed to me as though the lead dancer was in fact the cook from the bigger photograph next to it . . . It seemed really strange to me, and I felt like sharing my thoughts with someone, but everyone was doing their own thing at their desks, staring at their screens, so I gave up on the idea right away. Since then, not only before wiping the framed photographs, but also before watering the small potted flowers, I've always stared hard at the photographs in the Events Agency searching for and find-ing the same people in all of them. The cook, I firmly decided, was also the lead dancer; the Gypsy, who in one of the fuzzy photographs is rob-bing one of the many foreign female tourists on the Stone Bridge, was "the strangler" from the biggest photograph . . . The foreigners, on the other hand, always seemed to be multiplying, which is something I'd noticed a while back, but they never reappeared from one photograph to another. At times they were narrow-eyed Chinese or Japanese, at others fat, pale Germans, and at others again Americans in gaudy pat-terned shirts. None of the foreigners from one photograph appeared in another . . . Gradually, over time, wiping windows and framed photo-graphs, especially photographs on the walls of the Agency, became my duty. I made it my duty simply because I found it interesting.

3.

A large cloud of foreigners floated down the gentle descent from the Central Bus Station toward the Olympic Swimming Pool. It was high noon on one of those hellishly hot days in Skopje, a time when noth-ing could compel the residents of the capital to leave their cool homes. The cloud was irregular in shape: a sharp point at the tip made up of the two least exhausted guides and an ungainly mass of tourists with cameras around their necks, small backpacks slung over their shoulders or fanny packs fastened around their waists. Straggling at the tail end of the cloud were three or four of the slowest tourists, absorbed in conversation, who seemed neither aware of the city, nor that the temperature had risen to above 100 degrees Fahrenheit. The sun bored through their brightly colored caps, injecting fiery thoughts into their minds. A middle-aged man with thinning hair, but with a taut, athletic physique, was trying to pick his way through the throng of tourists who formed the bulk of the cloud and to make his way up to the guides at the pointy tip. Encountering a thick tangle of bodies, an almost immovable resistance, at first he tried forcing his way past them all, then he tried almost leapfrogging over his frazzled traveling companions, but in the end he just gave up and stood stock-still as though in defeat. He poked around in his backpack, and had he just pulled out a white handkerchief to surrender to the sun, everything would have seemed quite unremarkable. Instead, he took out a half-filled water bottle with a label advertising the name of the statewide low-cost ISP, carefully opened it, and tipped the whole thing over his head. Just like that. The cloud of foreigners huddled together as though caught in a sudden downpour, umpteen pairs of eyes stared at him, then thunderous laughter erupted across the hot asphalt . . . Carrying their sodden laughter with them, they continued along Boulevard Kočo Racin, but the way they were moving around no longer resembled a cloud. They walked slowly in twos or threes. Approaching the Red Cross building, their attention once again wasn't captured by the city to which they'd all come for the first time, but by the same man with the athletic physique who was now hurriedly trying to remove his camera from its case. It was proving difficult for him because his eyes were glued to a different spot as his hands groped blindly to unfasten the clasp. One by one the tourists from the group began to follow his gaze, until the last pair of eyes locked on the spectacle framed in a wide-open window on the upper floor of the building across the street. Two women—one short, the other tall—holding hands, were dancing an *oro* in their room! The taller woman was even waving a white handkerchief in her right hand! The tourists stared wide-eyed at this unusual sight as though it were some sort of media screen stuck in the window of the building. They cocked their ears, trying to catch any stray sounds of music, but unfortunately the cars that were accelerating down the boulevard like crazy lunatics drowned out what they longed to hear. Still, they were able to keep on watching, because it wasn't just some sort of momentary rejoicing, but many minutes of wonderful circle-dancing. The short woman was twisting her body in pleasing, harmonious movements, bobbing her head joyously to a precisely defined rhythm and putting her left hand on her wide, fleshy hip from time to time. The other woman, the taller one—the lead dancer—was holding her head up proudly, waving and waving the white handkerchief! She kicked her feet up higher, especially her right foot, as if marking time to the inaudible tune. She had large breasts that uniformly followed the circling of her hand waving the handkerchief. Up, down, *opa-pa*, up-down with her head, her right foot, that's it, with her left leg merely following, her knee bent, her pose now on a level with that of her shorter partner. She straightens up, she's taller again, forward, forward, she turns her gaze back, while the handkerchief twirls around and around in the air. When her wrist isn't spinning circles the handkerchief doesn't twirl, when her hips are quiet her breasts don't bob up and down, when her hips begin to swing, one by one, her breasts slowly begin to bounce inside her T-shirt with the plunging neckline . . . The middle-aged man continued groping for his camera, only more and more slowly now . . . All of the skills he possessed, including the dexterity of his fingers, were rendered useless by the unusual dance framed in the window. The women had been so carried away by their own dancing, the swaying of their hips, the joyous bowing and throwing back of their heads, that it gave the impression they were merely getting on with their everyday lives in the best possible way. "Snap-snap-snap" sounded a few times; a random passerby photographed the spectacle, nonchalantly slipped the camera back into his pocket, and then continued on his way in the opposite direction from where the tourists had come. They, in turn, stayed as long as the sun would allow. The dance went on and on and on, lasting even until the middle-aged man finally freed his forgotten camera and snapped about a dozen shots. One by one, the tourists headed toward the crossroads with their eyes glued to the window. They walked slowly and distractedly, their feet of their own volition carrying them back, as though their agreement to return as quickly as possible to the Stone Bridge was lodged in some kind of a case.

4.

During the coffee break, the director came into the storeroom where I was normally to be found and asked me to take a photograph to a picture framer.

"Tell him to frame it like all the others, he'll know," he said.

I immediately put down my pen, with which I'd been doing the crossword in the newspaper and he gently tapped my arm, adding with a wide grin:

"You don't have to do it right away, finish your crossword, you can go later . . ." The photograph, which he leaned against the wall, was quite big and carefully wrapped in a large piece of white paper placed between two sheets of cardboard to protect it. I stared off and on at the six empty squares in the crossword meant for "a delicate tropical flower," and at the photograph that I couldn't see, let alone wipe. Somehow, at the exact same moment, the thought struck me that a six-letter word for a delicate tropical flower might be "orchid," and that I could carefully remove the photograph and just as meticulously unwrap it from the white protective paper in which it had been wrapped. I quickly jotted the word *orchid* with my right hand and my gaze flew to the sleek watering can on the cabinet, while my left hand was already taking out the photograph . . . I was dumbfounded! In it were the waiter and the cook, who were also the Gypsy and the lead dancer. I recognized their faces as though we had all grown up together as children! *He* was dressed up as a homeless violinist—sitting cross-legged in the round floral bed in the square facing the Ristikjeva Mansion—fiddling with all his might . . . while *she*—comfortably sprawled on a threadbare two-seater "Nanna Ditzel" wicker sofa, surrounded by pots of fake purple flowers, with a colorful drink with a straw in her hand—lovingly and through half-closed eyes is gazing at him . . . Roaming all around them are foreigners—tall and blond . . . Perhaps Russians.

After putting two and two together, I was left stunned as to the true nature of the activities of the Agency where I worked, and I was having no luck pushing open the heavy, metal door of the picture framer's shop. It would open a crack, hiss slightly, and then close again. After a few clumsy attempts, a cheerful stocky guy with an unkempt mustache opened the door wide for me from inside.

"Good afternoon, miss, please come in."

"Good afternoon. The door . . ."

"Forget the door, how can I be of help? . . . Oh! But you're . . ."

"Who am I?"

"Well, you're the woman from . . ."

"From where, sir?" I shouted in a too-loud and overly excited voice so that the framer's interrupted recognition might resume spontaneously.

"Forget it, it's not important . . ."

"I'm from the Events Agency. I was asked to bring this photograph to be framed. The director said that you would know . . ."

"Yes, yes . . . When is it needed by?" he said in a very different tone of voice.

"I wasn't told anything. I don't know."

"Fine, I'm sure I'll hear from them . . . And the previous photograph that they brought over has been ready for some time . . . I was just about to call them to send someone to pick it up, in case it might be needed . . ."

While he was expertly unwrapping the photograph that I brought, I glanced at a huge vertical photograph leaning against the wall opposite him . . . and in it . . . at the top, at the very top just below the silver frame, I recognized myself with the white watering can in my hands!

The photograph was bigger than all the other ones hanging on the walls at the Agency. It was narrow and quite tall . . . Most of it showed a giant flower drawn on the side of a tall building, like those huge sheets of canvas strung on the red buildings along the central station that read "Renovate me." On those you could also read the name of the bank advertising its new loan packages in this manner, while here—nothing, just a giant flower in beautiful colors and . . . at the top, where the only window is along the entire length of the object—there I am with the white watering can. Its thin black spout appeared as though it was watering the flower on the wall! The bucket in which the water was really being poured couldn't be seen in the photograph because it was by the window itself, but from inside, from the other side . . . "From the other side of reality," I thought to myself. Everything had been well thought out! What should and should not be seen from outside. That's why from the start they had instructed me exactly where and how to stand near the window, how high to hold the watering can . . .

From outside it had to look as though the flower on the side of the building was being watered! At the bottom of the photograph, standing on the street was a group of tourists with cameras held high.

5.

I hurried toward the Events Agency. I didn't return along the same road I'd come down, but along an entirely different one that would take me to the back of the building that housed the Agency, not to the front entrance. I wanted to see the flower, because I'd never seen it before. For months every morning I went to work in the offices of the Agency above the painted flower, which I'd never seen . . . Yet so many times I'd watered it as though it was an invisible orchid! I hadn't watered an invisible orchid at all, but a giant garden with the most unusual flower! From afar I caught sight of the back of the building where I worked. It was impossible to miss! There was the flower, at least fifty feet high, because from the ground floor up to the fifth floor there were no windows on that side. The first window above the flower was the one from the hallway at the Events Agency . . . I stopped and looked up high . . . There was no one at the window! It was closed . . . All of a sudden a commotion erupted around me. Some rowdy people wearing backpacks were pushing and shoving me . . . They were speaking English. "Tourists," I figured, and at the same moment I heard my cell phone ringing. I took it out of my pocket, and before answering it, saw that I had seven missed calls from work!

"Hello . . ."

"Where've you been all this time? We've been looking all over for you, you were meant to pour the water in the bucket! Oh God, the tourists are already down there . . ."

"Yes, here they are, right next to me . . . I'm down here as well," I said calmly, because everything became perfectly clear to me. "I'm on my way."

"No, no, there's no time, I'll find someone else at once!" said the director, and he hung up.

I knew what I had to do. I crossed the street, and from there I saw everything clearly and at a glance: at the window with the white watering can in her hands the secretary from the Agency appeared.

At the same time, the tourist leader gave the tourists a sign for them to look up. They crooked their heads and erupted into loud laughter. Some even began to applaud, because it was clear to see that a woman was watering the giant flower on the façade! It wasn't me, and in that moment I still didn't know whether I was happy about this or not.

"This is so cool! This is so cool!" the contented tourists muttered to one another, snapping photo after photo . . .

"This life is bullshit!" I said to myself with a resigned smile, and hurried back to work . . . My crossword was left unfinished.

TRANSLATED FROM THE MACEDONIAN BY PAUL FILEV

DEYAN ENEV

The Underpass

THERE'S A KIOSK with a sunshade by the underpass. In the morning, on my way to work, I drink my coffee there. Cars fly past along the boulevard, people run toward the bus stops, the sun crashes its cymbals on the windows of the big building on the other side of the street. When you take a step outside of everyday life, your thoughts get a little bit clearer. And you start noticing the details.

Take, for example, this red chemical toilet that some genius has plopped down right here on the sidewalk by the boulevard. It sticks out grandly, like a monument to progress, like a symbol of civilization, like a treble clef in front of the oratorio of our time. We no longer piss in the bushes but in the red toilet. Let's develop the plot. A jeep suddenly pulls up and parks by the toilet. A big hulking guy with a twisted face and a shiny head like a brass ball rushes out. He dashes into the toilet. He's so big, he lifts it up with his shoulders in his desperation. He can hardly believe his luck. And at this moment—I seize on the next bright idea—at this very moment his cell phone rings. It's not the end of the world, it could happen to anyone. A little composure is required in situations of this sort. But our protagonist doesn't think his movements through. Meaning he fumbles. And as he goes to take out his phone, he drops it in the toilet.

This would make a great commercial, I think. An in-your-face message of genuine quality from the heart of Bulgarian reality. From deep in its bowels.

But where's the catch? Where's the stroke of genius? Where? That from deep in those bowels the phone keeps ringing.

I have another idea for a commercial. For gum. Here it is: Summertime. A brunette's driving a convertible. The brunette's shoulders look

71

like they're made of chocolate. The wind blows through her hair. The brunette's driving her convertible and chewing gum. At some point she gets tired of chewing. She takes the gum out from between her pearly whites and drops it on the road. A dude in a tank top in the Ferrari behind her drives over the gum. The tires of the Ferrari drive through the gum, I'm telling you. But you can imagine. The dude hits the gas, but the car doesn't move. Not forward, not backward. Shit. Thank God the brunette looks in the mirror and sees what she's done. She stops the convertible and walks over the asphalt, she even kicks off her flip-flops and keeps walking, barefoot; she reaches the Ferrari with the dude and the dude gets out of the Ferrari. Startled, moved, enchanted. There is no need for pointless words. Maybe something short, if it comes down to it. Really short. *For life*. No need for pointless words. The message is clear—this gum will help you find love.

That's enough. I have no more ideas. I have to get to work.

There he is, the old man who plays a wooden pipe has shown up, so it really is time. You can set your watch by him. He takes his place on the tiles, he wipes his pipe. He always plays the same melody, a simple melody, like a bird's song. The day before yesterday he bummed a cigarette off me and told me his daughter worked in the building across the street. In the huge building, blazing in the sun. She's the secretary for the biggest boss. The one whose office is on the last floor and looks like a spaceship. The old man had wanted to call her, to at least see her for a moment, but he didn't feel comfortable—not in these clothes and in this state. And she was so busy with work she had no time for him. So he made up his mind to write her a letter. But I am supposed to give it to her, if I can. Just give it to her.

"You write it," I said. "The rest is a piece of cake."

Now, the moment he saw me, he stopped playing and came over to me.

"I wrote the letter," he said.

"Let's see it."

The old man pulled out a crumpled sheet of graph paper. His forehead was sweaty. There were all kinds of doodles. It began, "My girl, the only thing I have is my love for you . . ." After that it was illegible.

"What is this?" I asked.

"Well . . . it's the letter."

"This won't do. It's unreadable. We have to write it over again. Come earlier tomorrow. I'll come earlier, too. And we'll write it over again."

"Good." The old man rejoiced, pleased that we would get it done tomorrow. "Give me a cigarette."

I gave him a cigarette. He put the sheet of paper in his pocket and walked over to his pipe.

Now I glance up at the spaceship. The boss has just walked into the office. He's taken off his coat. He asks his secretary for a cup of coffee and waits for it, standing by the window, looking down at the intersection from the nineteenth floor. The world is his. And the secretary is his. We look at each other for a while. The secretary brings the coffee. He's a big boss and knows how to keep his distance. But the thought of this secretary lingers in his throat. His shaved Adam's apple stretches the collar of his shirt. He swallows and sits down behind his desk.

I have to go. A boy is approaching from the exit of the underpass. He's dressed in a baggy tracksuit, his face wide and calm like a golden mask. I know him. This is the son of the woman who sells tickets in the underpass. It's obvious the boy has a screw loose. The mother and son spend every day sitting in their plexiglass box. His job is to arrange the tickets—in twos, threes, fours, fives. In twos, threes, fours, fives. But sometimes he manages to break free, like now. The boy heads under the sunshade and starts going around to the tables. He asks for money. Now he has reached me.

"Give me a buck," he says.

"I gave you one yesterday."

"Give me a buck," he repeats, as if he's been wound up.

So I give him a buck. He goes to the glass stall at the bus stop where they sell pizza, buys a piece of pizza, and starts eating it right there.

I have to go now. But something is missing. Something important. I look at the grass, the shrubs. Something is missing. I see a first-grader hurrying along to school with his mother. He's late. His school bag is bigger than him. He hops along beside his mother with his heavy bag. Hippity hop. Hippity hop. I watch them until they reach the underpass. The school is on the other side. Now half of its yard is a pit. A tower crane sticks up over the pit. They picked up King Kong's body from the set with a tower crane like that, I'm sure of it.

I put out my cigarette. I go into the underpass. I buy a ticket from the boy's mother. I walk up the stairs to the tram stop. The old man has started playing his melody on the pipe. The tram is coming.

On the tram, I'm distracted by the newspaper of the man in front of me. He snorts a couple of times, but I keep reading.

Sparrows are becoming extinct, I read in the headline. And then: the population of sparrows in Europe is dwindling rapidly. This is a worrying phenomenon, and scientists can't explain it, agencies are alarmed.

According to the National Museum of Natural History in Paris, sparrows are now on the list of endangered birds. The decrease in sparrows, which greatly rely on people, is especially drastic in the United Kingdom. The sparrow population there has decreased by over ninety percent in the last ten to fifteen years. They've become almost extinct on the island, says Frédéric Barotto of the French Center for Biological Studies of Bird Populations. This alarming statement has been confirmed by studies in other countries. The population of sparrows in Hamburg has decreased by fifty percent in the last thirty years. In the Czech Republic—in Prague alone—the population of sparrows has decreased by sixty percent. The same tendency has been witnesssed in France, although at a slower rate: between 1989 and 2003, sparrows have decreased by eleven percent. The sparrow is one of the species that depend most on people for food and shelter. The reasons for the decrease in the sparrow population, especially in the cities, can't be clearly determined. It's possible it might be due to pollution of all kinds, and also to the effect of electromagnetic waves.

Then it was my stop. I got off the tram. The old man's melody was still ringing in my ears.

That's good. As long as I can set this melody going in my head, everything's fine. The melody is very simple. You can learn it, too.

TRANSLATED FROM THE
BULGARIAN BY KALINA MOMCHEVA

JOSEFINE KLOUGART

From *New Forest*

Light

BARE EARTH HERE. Here on the lawn where the wind has swept the snow aside. Up over the slope. The winter reaches deep into all things. Pebble-gray clouds in the sky. Three boys hanging over the handlebars of bikes, smoking in the underpass. The foliage is crisp with frost. The summer seemed almost without end. The light shone through the thin skin of the leaves in the crowns above us. We jumped from the bridge and swam out to the buoy in the harbor entrance. Sometimes I wonder if it was us. But then I remember again. The way we clung to the buoy when that big freighter sailed too close for comfort. In the water, I turned toward you. I looked at you and said: The waves will carry us like children. You shouted something back that I didn't catch. For a moment you seemed happy. We hardly believed it when winter came, but suddenly there it was and we stood in the window and watched the people cross the bridge. Through the gray-brown haze we watched them. Some in little clusters, others alone. In the big rooms facing the harbor, we stood and watched. Like two plants on gossamer green stalks striving toward the first light. The final darkness of morning. I placed a log in the stove and opened the air intake so the fire could catch. When I opened the front, the ash whirled up, then settled like paper-thin slices of birds. I put my finger to my lips and sucked as hard as I could to draw out a splinter. I can still see the splinter if I hold my finger to the light. The one who loves the least is in charge. The people crossing the bridge reminded you that you had to leave. You put your clothes back on, and your coat, and went back into the living room and stood in front of me as if you were going to say something and had forgotten what. Yesterday I walked northwards in the forest. The forest too still reminds me of you. The frozen leaves rustled as the wind drew its broken cart among them. The wind was strong yesterday. It gripped my wrists and twisted my hands behind my back and dragged me backwards the rest of the way, and my grandmother whispered: Here comes the wind with the cold of Russia in its coattails. Wrap up well if you're going out, and before you know it you're ordering veal in the shop on Holmbladsgade and carrying the cold steaks through the marrow of gray afternoon. And indeed the wind came as she said it would, battering the land like a great tumbling wall, whipping over the sea over the shores over the lawns over the road over the gardens over the houses. If you relax, the cold ceases to be unbearable. So no other may find you and put their cheek to yours as one might put a tuft of lichen to damaged skin. The wind came through the trees like that herd of horses that strayed into the abandoned church. They run through the gardens out there. I had already been walking for some time. Occasionally I sat down on the ground and untied the laces of my boots. I cleansed the sores with spit. The pus tasted like pine resin. I put my boots back on. As evening approached I came to the lake where I once played with my sisters. Its surface was a lid of thin ice apart from two holes where a pair of patient swans sailed stubbornly about like dogs that remain at their beds. I remember picking a blue stone up out of the sand and whispering to my sister: Look, it's shining. She probably couldn't see it then, but trusted me because I was older or because she didn't want to lose face. We could hear the light in the wind. The cold made us huddle together and we twisted our faces at every gust, eyes narrowed to slender slits. The clouds drifted apart and revealed a blue belt of sky above us. I think about you all the time. The clouds cast restless shadows on every face. I am a long time leaving you. The shadows sweep over the faces and roofs and cities and woods and seas and like your hand when you swept it through the grain in the field and later through my hair. I am an illness from which you will slowly recover. The sun rests on the tiled rooftops, warming up the attic rooms. I unfolded the piece of paper; it had been in my pocket all that time. It said: I will stay here the rest of the winter. Down in the harbor of Islands Brygge is a kind of raft, fastened to the wooden construction of the harbor baths. The swans nested on it all through the summer. Now it is overgrown with red-stalked flowers. How beautiful, you said, pointing. I agreed without hesitation, having noticed it too and thought the same thing. Nature works to make everything its own. Light-colored hairs hung like tiny jets of water from your fingers after you swept your hand through my hair. Remember that the sun is always on its way back, that ghastly April will soon be here again. The pale yellows and grays are in charge now. I feel as if I am carrying something that is not mine, something stolen, something I am hiding from you. A knowledge I can find no place to deposit, something I have seen and cannot forget. I paused on the old train tracks and listened to the sound of a bell ringing somewhere beyond the forest. There was something human about it. It spoke to me in a whisper as if from a place behind the dense hazel hedge at the bottom of my parents' garden. I know you will turn against me in anger one day. The most important is perhaps what we forget. The placid submission of evening to night. The stones in the grass were cold when testingly I touched them this morning, it was as if they remembered the night. A face that remembers having wept. Ants have no place in snow. There is memory in everything. The children ran over the hill on Christmas morning pulling their sleds behind them on ropes like little phantom horses. The dawn is a thin line in constant flux like the line drawn by the tide in the sand of the shore. I know you will return to me again and again like a nightmare or a story that keeps getting told. You must lie with your foot elevated, you said. You fetched some pillows so I could sit up. Death opened his face. Rest, ice. For the first time in ages it was like there was room for me. The hand that swept the strap of my dress from my shoulder had strangled a jay that crashed against the windowpane earlier that same day. RICE. The girl sweeps her hand through the bracken. Her passage through the forest is like the passage of a season through a landscape. She knows a fox has been past. Its smell lingers in the grass. She thinks to herself that such traces are nature's memory. The sun slants a shaft of light down through an open flank in the clouds, down into the trees. The girl wanders into its ray and tips her head back to look up. A red kite flies through the light. Its long flight feathers part it like a comb drawn through a landscape. Her eyes are wide and disturbing. Shadows fall on her face. A tiara placed on the bedside table of our homecoming queen casts its shadow against the wall before the light once more is extinguished. The shadows on my sister's face as we sat on the warm rock at the boundary between the fields. We were just children. We still are in a way. In the thin slivers of sunlight a deep voice speaks to us. *Please don't talk like that when the girls are listening.* I think I still look for my sisters in all my female friends. I miss them. The wings sheared the light, sprinkling its shreds from their feathers. Parting remains our most important task. I called you mine. I said I had you. All other undertakings turn out simply to be preparation for this: the nitty-gritty. Shreds of light litter the branches of the larch. Everything I remember is already myth. The iron sizzles in the bucket; we have ridden horses through the forest. A sickly smell of burnt hoof. Age has descended on my face like light. Sometimes my face becomes a child's again, though fleetingly, in a glimpse. Then perhaps it is autumn again, and again I stand and stare at nature that has spread a carpet of withered bracken beneath us. Your hand under my foot. The sun gleams like a bone exposed when the skin is peeled back. Chanterelles glow at the foot of the ancient oaks. I've started remembering things from my childhood, small details that had not escaped the body's memory after all. The fallen trees make the plantation look like a derelict cathedral. A ruin in marble and mortar. Nature is far too human. Humans will make everything their own. We are nature ourselves. In the storm, the trees were nature's chattering teeth. The larch lost their needles to the earth. I think to myself that just before, the forest was a heart that over some short distances was ours. We stopped in the clearing and listened. You thought maybe the forests were dependent on me, that without me they would vanish. Everyone has owned a forest in childhood. In the trees is light. We have all of us belonged to someone. A dream is perhaps transilluminated by a memory as the forest is transilluminated by a dream. The sunlight shone through the leaves. Something rising up from the forest floor, mingling into dreams like a mist wrapping around a tree, crawling up her leg like ivy and wild honeysuckle. The bindweed grew in the low stone wall at the bottom of the garden, putting out its pale-green shoots to entangle anything we left outside. Nature owns everything in the final end. Memory puts out its long shoots into dreams. Ceaseless sun among the trees. I remember retrieving a bike and discovering how the bindweed held it to the ground like a mother holding onto a child in grief. In the spring we planted rose bushes in the garden, American Pillar and Rose Awakening, and we fertilized them with little blue pellets that lay on the black soil until disappearing after only a few days. And winter came and the bramble stood like white arches of crystal on the slope. The girl kicks a football ahead of her into the plantation. Garish red and black pentagons sewn together. Select. In the weekend cabin farther toward the sea the family unpacks. Her sisters pick wood sorrel behind the cabin. It is autumn now. A tight posy of wood sorrel in the hand of a child. Her cheeks are heavy, her fair hair very fine and somewhat electric. Some strands fall into her eyes and she tries to blow them away, then sweep them from her face with the back of her hand. She has proceeded in a straight line from the cabin so as to be able to find her way back again. Maybe they think she is still in the car or in one of the back rooms. The trees in the plantation stand motionless in the ranks in which they were planted. Between the rows lie the fallen trees, their trunks and broken branches, and the needles that have already left the larch. She crouches down by one of the fallen ones. The bark is reddish brown with trenches of dappled gray. She is the child. The tree feels hollow now it no longer is nourished through its roots. The child peels off a piece of bark, watches as insects and crustaceans scuttle across the bare wood, woodlice, and wood-boring beetles, their sheeny shells, dispersing outwards like raindrops on the windscreen of a speeding car, outwards and away. She brushes the dirt from her hands. She walks into the wood through an opening between the trees. She halts. Inside the wood, inside the heart of the trunks, is silence. The wind rustles the tops of the trees, but still the wood is silent to her, as the world is silent if you listen for it from the marrow of your bones. Or the way I was silent that time in the cathedral in Málaga. Did you whisper something to me there, something I have forgotten? She turns around and looks back in the direction of the cabin. She has already wandered too far, she thinks: I am not afraid. As she walks on she cannot hear her own footsteps. The earth succumbs without sound. Occasionally, a twig snaps beneath her sandals. Mostly, everything is still. The sun shines down through the trees, drifts of glittering dust in empty columns of light. She walks among the rays as she might pass through the fine jets of the garden sprinkler, or the way the dead pass through walls. The wood is a house with walls of light that shift with the sun during the course of the day. The girl turns around. She lifts her foot to walk on, but hesitates. A beetle rambles, glistening like oil. She steps over it and crouches down. Observes. The way it moves across the needles and moss, blindly feeling its way, antennas sweeping. The little armored head, and behind it the half-moon of the thorax, whose shell is fluted with microscopic grooves visible only when the light falls in a certain way, as if some other insect, dragging its sting behind it like a plow, had walked over the beetle one day when its shell lay melted and blank as wax. The girl kneels and puts her hand down in the moss in front of the insect. She presses the back of her hand into the damp lichen so the beetle can crawl onto her skin. Only then it stops. Right in front of her hand. It is as if the beetle realizes that she might wish it harm, that her hand is a kind of trap. The girl's mouth hangs open, strands of hair once more fallen before her eye, swaying irritatingly in her face in time to her breathing. The insect moves on. Clouds gather slowly above the wood. The beetle's shell loses its shimmering luster as it crawls into the girl's palm. Calmly she closes her hand around it like a forest fire might close around a house. She gets to her feet, glances over her shoulder in the direction of the cabin where her family is unpacking. She walks farther along the shining path, past the ball that lies so still. She feels the beetle moving in her hand. She imagines it trying to find a way out and clenches her fist tighter. The path between the trees becomes narrower and narrower, she thinks. She carries on. The sky darkens over the path, blue-black as a boletus mushroom squeezed between identifying fingers. She walks on, the ball behind her becoming an increasingly smaller gleaming eye, a spot of light at the periphery of her vision as she squints at the sun. The clouds draw together, petroleum blue, descending on the treetops like soft flesh pressing between the slats of a couch. As evening comes the wind picks up and the clouds drift in tongues toward the south. The days of June were separated by nights that grew shorter and more transparent. The tops of the tallest trees are lances poking into the belly of the sky. The needles beneath her feet are darker now. She found them to be orange before, now they are grayish black. Most of the trees keep their needles all through winter, but the larch drops them every year. These are the needles over which she now walks.

There are no glowing coals. She thinks for a moment that she hears someone behind her, someone speaking her name, but when she turns to answer there is no one there. Don't you know your name when you hear it? The floor of the wood, scored where someone once tore up a length of moss to heal their skin. A bit farther on a screen of light behind the trees like a changeable backdrop she might insert behind the stage of a toy theater. She goes to the clearing, stands swaying at the edge. A low bank above the meadow, half a meter of bare, sandy earth. Only pale grasses, the odd birch, self-sown and poorly nourished, poking up among the yarrow and chamomile whose spindly arms strive toward the sky, not so much to reach the light as to be found. The clearing is a wound in the dark-green flesh of the wood. In the clearing is a house, a foreign object, like a rusty harrow or a corpse thrown into the bog a long time ago. She feels the beetle moving in her hand. She clenches her fist as tight as she can. She hears its shell be crushed. Its legs are still moving. The house is a sorry sight, its roof overgrown by various plants: Our-Lady's-bedstraw, wispy, dun-brown grasses of the same kind as those sprouting up from between the planks of the decking. A gutter of dented, lime-scaled zinc has fallen down at one end and is now a diagonal chute leading down into the ground like a shaft of light slanting from a high window in a church or stable, or angled through the branches of the trees. The dun-brown grass stands humble and hungry in the sandy soil. The landscape is open fields stretching away from the black-painted house. The house looks like a crater left behind by something that no longer exists. It is not a place in which anything will ever happen. Nature's takeover is already advanced, the place looks like an abandoned industrial area or some forgotten corner of a language. The black paint of the woodwork is flaked, little black wings exposing the raw wood underneath. The beetle no longer moves in her hand. For a moment she can hardly feel it at all. And yet it must be there. In the hand she closed around it. She uncurls her fist, one finger at a time: thumb, index finger, the last three like a fan or the sweep of a sprinkler in the rain. She straightens her fingers, and her palm is like an open space left in the woods by the fire. The insect is crushed, stuck to a line of her hand. One of its six skeletal legs has snapped off at the uppermost joint and lies now on its own, detached from the rest of the body. Bodies spread over a large area by an explosion. The shell has split open lengthwise. The girl turns her hand over and the beetle falls into the sand at her feet. She stares at the house, a black pupil in the midst of the open zone. She has goose pimples on her forearms. Her skin is tanned after a summer that continued without pause until one day perishing imperceptibly at the hand of autumn. Now it will soon be evening. The child hears the wind draw its trails through the pines and the near-naked larch, like a trawl dragging along the seabed. The sand sinks beneath her feet and she must step forward into the clearing to keep her balance. Promptly, she jumps back between the trees again. She looks around, but cannot see the path. Suddenly there seem to be a hundred paths. Her heart pounds in her chest, she pushes her hair away from her face and feels something sticky and sharp on her brow. She removes it with her arm, then wipes the shard of the beetle's shell off on her skirt. She starts to walk, faster now, tilting gradually forward until she begins to run, choosing a path she thinks leads in the right direction. She is unsure. She runs past the trees and everything looks the same. When she comes to the place where she left the ball she stops and looks around, peering through the trees at the adjoining near-luminous paths. The ball is nowhere to be seen. The sky grows darker and darker like a stable where the animals jostle to get to the fodder, the bodies of the heifers closing in on her like the thought she can no longer escape: that she is alone and lost. But at this very moment of capitulation she sees the ball only a few meters away among the trees. It shines like a planet, or a face into which one might stare without realizing it to be one's own until too late. She turns and stands in front of the ball, considering it for a second before going forward cautiously, as cautiously as she one day put her hand to her face to brush the strands from her eyes and shield her face from the sun whose rays now intensify as we step out into the clearing among the trees.

TRANSLATED FROM THE DANISH BY MARTIN AITKEN

PATRIK OUŘEDNÍK

From *The End of the World Would Not Have Taken Place*

ENCOUNTER

JEAN-PIERRE DURANCE emerged from the train station and was heading toward the bus stop on the other side of Boulevard Montparnasse when he saw, on the terrace of a café, a back that looked familiar. The man with the back was Gaspard, and he will be the main character of this tale. Jean-Pierre Durance's part, on the other hand, will quickly peter out. You don't need to remember his name.

Durance walked around the table to assure himself that it was indeed Gaspard, Gaspard Boisvert, a little over six feet tall, broad shouldered, salt-and-pepper hair, early sixties. He then said, "Hello, Gaspard." They only knew each other vaguely. They'd met two or three times, and back in the day, fifteen or twenty years ago, he certainly would have said, "Hello, Mr. Boisvert." But this was an age of first names, it was more personal, friendly, direct, more international, too: the whole world had become a conglomerate of first names.

Gaspard raised his head. He seemed to recognize his interlocutor.

"Hello, what are you doing here?"

"Oh," Durance responded, "just in town for some biz."

It was also an age of abbreviations.

"I'm heading back to Orléans tonight. But what about you? What are you up to? I heard you were back for good? I mean back in France? Nothing else tempting you across the pond, in the US of A, as they say?"

In the United States Gaspard had served as an advisor to the stupidest American president in history. It had now been over ten years, but every time he ran into someone he knew they felt authorized to ask the same questions. His American interlude had bestowed upon him, once and for all, his social identity.

This was, moreover, another reason for Durance to call Gaspard "Gaspard" rather than Mr. Boisvert: advising the stupidest American president in history was nothing to sneeze at. Maybe I could invite myself to sit down, Durance said to himself, I've got forty-five minutes.

"That's correct."

"May I sit down? I've got forty-five minutes."

With his hand Gaspard gestured toward the chair across from him.

"What have you been up to since your return? I imagine you've had some interesting offers. Advising the American president is nothing to sneeze at. Especially for a Frenchman."

"That's true."

"You should write a book. A kind of behind-the-scenes account. It'd sell like hotcakes."

"Yes, that's true."

Durance sensed a slight uneasiness. Gaspard's answers were not falling within the conversational norms of good-natured individuals.

"Do you come here often?"

"Every day."

"Do you live around here? Sorry if I'm intruding."

"In a hotel nearby, yes."

"Oh, in a hotel."

"Nearby, yes."

"My wife will be thrilled to know I ran into you. It must be at least fifteen years, right? Even more?"

"No doubt."

In order to spare the reader from tedious dialogue, let's summarize: the two men stayed on the terrace for a good half hour. Unsettled by Gaspard's nonchalant attitude, Durance had become even more insistent, as happens in such situations. Why, please excuse my curiosity, in a hotel, why not enter the diplomatic corps, such an astonishing career, by the way, he and his wife, they were immediately impressed. Did he remember their friend, what was his name again? And so on.

After his business conference, Durance returned to the train station. Passing the café again he noted that Gaspard's back was still there. This time, however, he did not approach him.

Here Jean-Pierre Durance's role comes to an end.

THE FUTURE OF THE WORLD

The future isn't what it used to be. You must have noticed this yourself: the future isn't what it used to be.

In the past, the future mainly unfolded according to one of the following modalities:

(1) The world would end, and everything would start again from zero, creating an identical world—the pessimistic version of most belief systems.

(2) The world would end in a horrifying and final bloodbath, from which would arise a world of bliss—the optimistic version of some religions.

(3) The world would never end, and bliss, which acted as the leavening agent, would continue to increase until the end of days, which were themselves infinitely extendable—the foolhardy version of the ends of History.

But at the beginning of the twenty-first century these theories had run their course. Forecasts had changed. All people endowed with a certain understanding of the facts on the ground agreed on one point: no matter how you imagine it, it's going to end badly. Either in a horrible bloodbath followed by nothing at all—the optimistic hypothesis. Or by bloodbaths here and there, followed by more bloodbaths here and there, without end, until the universe expands to the point that it becomes infinitely dense, which would in turn precipitate the destruction of the galaxies and the poor miserable wretches who live there. Some observers added a supplementary aspect: a concomitant and heretofore inconceivable dulling of the mental activity of humanity.

GASPARD, OR OPTIMISM

Gaspard was no stupider than anyone else. He imagined the future much as you and I would. But his education impelled him to act as if nothing were wrong. He had the gift, or the weakness, of occasionally disregarding what he knew for certain, such that for several hours, for a whole day, a cautious optimism would come over him. And what if you could influence the way of the world? So that man could realize his varied abilities, engendering within him an irrevocable desire for peace, making him love his brother, making it so that this love triumphed over his greediness, his egotism, his natural meanness? Inaugurating a peaceful coexistence, with people living in harmony, but which, at the same time, would not prevent creativity or imagination from blossoming? Protecting mankind from pure necessity, making work pleasant, granting a peaceful death to all, preventing the universe from expanding?

GASPARD AND THE BOMBING

Gaspard was born on February 13, 1955, on the tenth anniversary of the bombing of the German city of Dresden by the Allied forces. The Germans and the Allies were at war then. Later, when Gaspard was born, the Allies and most Germans had also become allies. He was born in a small village in the flat, gloomy countryside of northern France. I don't recall the village's name. His older sister died in an accident at the age of five, when he was three. Now the only child in a relatively well-to-do family, he felt the vague desire to please, as best he could, his parents, who were traumatized by what the neighbors called their family tragedy. Up to the age of fourteen or fifteen he would speak to his dead sister and ask her advice. Then he stopped speaking to her. High school in Lille, then university studies in Anglo-American Literature and Culture at the Sorbonne in Paris. His thesis, which he never completed, examined three of four novels by an American writer from the 1930s, Nathanael West: *Miss Lonelyhearts*, *A Cool Million*, and *The Day of the Locust*. The thesis shows an evolution in West's writing: in the first novel America is heading steadily toward its ruin, in the second it's plunging into a nightmare, the third ends at the edge of the Apocalypse. The end of the world already. After quitting school he spent nearly three years in the United States, where he became involved with the underground. It was the fashionable thing to do back then. It was during this time that he met the niece of the future president of the United States, an encounter that would later change his life for several months. They met at a rock concert, just like anybody else.

In those amiable days, America fought against communism and Soviet imperialism in the name of democracy and the free market, and communism fought against American imperialism and capitalism in the name of the proletariat and the end of History. The rest of the world had but limited importance.

Back in France, Gaspard began working as a translator. Besides the immeasurable amount of dross that his editors had him translate, he had been successful in imposing on them several authors who were dear to his heart: Donald Barthelme, Joan Didion, Richard Brautigan, and Kurt Vonnegut. Vonnegut was the author of a book on the bombing of Dresden, *Slaughterhouse-Five*. The bombing of Dresden had killed more people than the atomic bomb dropped six months later on the Japanese city of Hiroshima, but it was less well known. These deaths were the result of an ordinary weapon. The atomic bomb, on the other hand, was sublimely spectacular, and it's in the nature of spectacular things to be more enthralling than a simple death toll. For every death during the twentieth century, on average 2.55 human lives appeared on Earth, whereas the spectacles that left a lasting impression on the imagination were, when all was said and done, few and far between.

That night approximately 100,000 people were killed in the Dresden bombings.

For the first time 255,000 newborns cried out in fear.

But Gaspard had not yet been born.

BIG BERTHA AND ME

Now as for me, I was born on the twelfth day of August on the forty-fifth anniversary of the day that Big Bertha, a cannon with a 12.5-kilometer range, was put into service. This happened in 1914. At the time the Germans and the Allies were at war. An eminently modern war—people had noticed that the more cannons there were, the fewer the casualties. Over the course of several months the number of cannons increased while the casualties decreased. This perturbed several conservative generals but pleased the troops. Except the equipment that brought about this reduction in losses contributed, by its very essence, in prolonging the war and therefore in increasing losses. All things considered, a good old brawl with sabers or machetes is definitely much more charitable.

I was born in Prague, a city dear to those whose souls, in order to flourish, require decadence. It was the capital of a country whose name is impossible to remember, Czechoslovakia. Too long—once it has more than three syllables, unless you've won or lost an important war, a country doesn't exist.

THE BOMBING OF DRESDEN

Perhaps the bombing of Dresden didn't result in 100,000 dead. Other sources indicate different numbers. Accordingly, if we trust the humanitarian organization the Red Cross, there were 305,000. If we believe the German officer in charge of cleanup, 221,500. If we take the conclusions of the German newspaper *Die Welt* into account, between 60 and 65,000. If we prefer another German daily, *Süddeutsche Zeitung*, around 300,000. If we consult the Dresden police report compiled after the bombings, 135,000. If we refer to the one written by the government of the German Democratic Republic, 35,000. If we turn to the work of a commission of experts from the Soviet army, 250,000. If we give credit to the German Minister of Public Enlightenment and Propaganda, 200,000. If we place confidence in a commission of German historians, between 18 and 25,000, but another German historian posits the number at 40,000.

In short, between 18,000 and 305,000. Thus, the possibility that there were 100,000, plus or minus a few, is in accordance with all known data points.

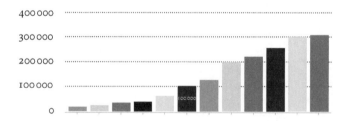

WHAT I KNOW ABOUT GASPARD

Notwithstanding the warm regard we felt for one another, we had spent rather little time together. Say somewhere around thirty meetings, which would make for somewhere between 150 and 200 hours of conversation—more friendly than intimate, tending more toward general than private matters. Most of what I know about Gaspard I gleaned from what one might call his diary if it weren't for the fact that these were just loose pieces of paper, some dated others not, randomly collected in two plywood suitcases, the kind of suitcase that, long ago, you'd see people carrying who were leaving the country to move to Paris, or who were drafted and going to join their regiments. All kinds of papers in all kinds of shapes and sizes covered with memories, reflections, aphorisms, minor observations—"*Today, Monday March 2, I noticed that my ophthalmologist has the head of a toad*"—now obsolete notes—"*Euro / Franc: divide by 3 + multiply by 20*"—newspaper clippings, excerpts from books, or short poems:

> *Splitting its shell hole a crack*
> *the dream pierces the black.*
> *The pale mien*
> *of being boiled in a blood-filled tureen.*

There were also some report cards, old photos, postcards, and even several of his parents' love letters from before they were married. In short, a kind of *disjecta membra*, but which nonetheless allowed me to piece together several scenes of the Gaspardian life.

MY PROJECTS

Writing a book about the end of the world was a long-standing project. I'd already written a play on the same subject. It was called *Yesterday
and the Day After Tomorrow*. But you're obsessed, my wife said when I
mentioned the idea of taking another crack at it.

I don't think so. But I might be wrong. According to psychologists,
the idea of the end of the world allows people to accept their own mor-
tality. What's more, the world doesn't even have to end. They say the
death of others in and of itself is soothing. To be on your deathbed and
to be able to say, *In any case, this is going to happen to all those stupid bas-
tards*, would bring peace to the soul.

Just as long as you don't believe in the afterlife. Imagine! Just imagine! To run into all of them again!

MY EDITOR

As for my editor, he sniggered. The end of the world? His tone betrayed his thoughts: a rather hackneyed subject. Since the last end of the world no one believes in it anymore.

"But this time it's for real."

"Ah, you've got some inside information?"

Increasingly ironic.

"You could say that. I've read some reports about it. Everything reputable."

"It doesn't sell anymore. You're going to need to spice it up with something less mundane."

"The end of the world is never mundane."

"More appealing, then. I don't know . . . a family secret, for example."

"That's the plan."

"Something about religion."

"Also the plan."

"With one or two wars as a backdrop."

"There are tons of them."

"A dictator. People like that."

"It's human nature."

"The bloodier it is, the more they'll like it."

"Even more human."

"Take Hitler for example. An age-old subject, but it still sells."

"I'm aware of that."

"But don't forget current affairs, of course."

"Of course."

"Something along the lines of the past resurfacing under the troubling auspices of today."

"Nicely said."

"Not too much sex . . . it slows down the pace."

"Not too much."

"A few biblical references."

"That goes without saying."

My editor would have made a pitiful writer.

Just as bad as the rest of them.

THE FOLLOWING CHAPTERS

The following chapters treat of family secrets, wars, divine action, and bloodthirsty dictators.

GASPARD AND THE FAMILY SECRET

Gaspard's grandfather may have been of Austrian origin. At least that's what his father maintained. This in spite of official documents that clearly indicated a French line of descent: Boisvert, Jean-Baptiste, born 8 June 1876 in Cassel, Maritime Flanders province, brown hair and eyebrows, brown eyes, normal forehead, average nose, average mouth, round chin, oval face. But Gaspard's father had a secret.

COMPUTER PROGRAMS

In the old days the French had an expression: "to be one war behind."
It meant to not be up to date on the latest events—the last presidential election, the evolution of sexual mores, developments in the areas of fashion and technology. During the twentieth and twenty-first centuries, however, the expression had lost its relevance: there were too many wars and they followed one another too closely. Live media coverage only added to the confusion. Except for a few military strategists, no one was up to date.

Then some computer programs were released with modules that could announce the start of a new war by emitting a specific sound. The default was BOOM! but it was possible to choose another among the following options:

CRASH!
WHACK!
WHAM!
BANG!
THUMP!
BADABOOM!
OUCH!

Or:

Some jokers had then hacked into the module to add: HA, HA, HA!

GOD AND GODLESS CITIES

The first bombing recorded in human history was God's strike on four cities in the Jordan River plain, the most famous of which was Sodom. The event is related in the holy book of the Jews. The inhabitants of Sodom lived in great sin. The men found pleasure in penetrating one another. God sent two angels to inspect. They confirmed the charges: after inquiring as to their genders, the inhabitants wanted to defile the angels. The Eternal consequently made fire and brimstone rain down upon Sodom. There were three survivors: the prophet Lot, known for his fondness for cheap wine, and his two daughters. His wife could have escaped the disaster as well, but, hearing cries, she turned around while fleeing. She was transformed into a pillar of salt. God wanted no witnesses.

There were no survivors in the three other cities of Gomorrah, Admah, or Zeboim.

GASPARD'S GRANDFATHER

"It's not one-hundred percent certain," said Boisvert, Pierre-Maurice, to his son Boisvert, Gaspard. "I'm not saying that. But there's a possibility."

Gaspard's father was more or less convinced that he was the fruit of a night of love between his mother and a certain German army lance corporal by the name of Adolf Hitler. His was one of the most famous names in world history: in the space of a few years Adolf had managed to kill by proxy some sixty million individuals. He was considered the greatest and most skilled murderer of all time. With an average of 22,810 dead per day, he was well ahead of his main rivals: the Soviet Stalin (10,163), the Chinese Mao Zedong (9,904), the Japanese Hirohito (5,562), the Turk Enver (2,857), and the Cambodian Pol Pot (1,574). All on their own, those six were casually able to wipe out 8.5% of the world population.

	RANK	PER DAY	PER HOUR	%
	1	22810	950.5	43
	2	10163	423.5	19
	3	9904	412.75	19
	4	5562	231.75	11
	5	2857	119	5
	6	1574	65.5	3

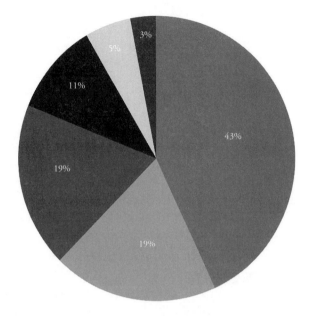

The night of love in question supposedly took place in August 1918, in what would later become the suburbs of Lille.

Pierre-Maurice obtained this information from his mother. "One day I was down at the river doing the laundry. On the other side a German soldier was drawing on a piece of thick cardstock he had on his lap. I was curious what he was drawing."

"I'd like to be wrong about this," said Pierre-Maurice. "If I'm talking to you about it, it's because you need to watch out if you start to get ideas. Heredity exists, whatever they may say."

TRANSLATED FROM THE FRENCH
BY ALEXANDER HERTICH

HÉLÈNE LENOIR

The Foreign Girls

THE GIRLS WERE always foreign, from good families. They paid for the bedroom and full board. In cash. Nelly would put this money in a box each month and would spend it twice a year, over the course of ten days. She would go away by herself with an organization renowned for the quality of the services it offered, combining cultural and athletic activities. For Nelly, it was walking tours. Every February and September, she took off, allowing herself this luxury with the money from the foreign girls whom she took care of as if she were their mother during their four-month stays.

In Madame Volterra's time, Nelly didn't need to know anything about these girls, didn't even need to recognize their faces before they appeared at the train station. She was sure they would get along immediately and, after a quick adjustment period, they would delight in each other's company and complain only rarely. Madame Volterra—head of recruitment and placement of interns, among other things, at Technitel—had a remarkable gift for choosing future interns, based on their applications alone, and housing them in the right place.

The foreign girls whom she had been sending to Nelly for the last four years all seemed to come from the same family. It was as if each new girl was the previous one's sister or cousin and borders were non-existent—their nationalities and languages were simply distinguishing marks. Lawyers, industrialists, and bankers apparently led the same lives and raised their children the same way—whether in Hamburg, Milan, or elsewhere, the variations were minimal: they were always well-mannered, wholesome, and conscientious girls. Transparent, without whims or vanity for the most part, they seemed to come from a different era, with their rigid ideas about love and marriage (of which their

100

parents were the ideal incarnation). They couldn't imagine living at all differently from their parents; the girls worked hard not to disappoint them, to excel and to behave, maintaining that boys were uninteresting, that they would wait for the boys to mature and get a good job before they would think about anything other than having a drink after class, or going to a tennis game or a movie, always in a group. Almost all the girls were like that, very sure of themselves yet blushing when the subject came up, when asked if they had a fiancé or a boyfriend, at twenty, twenty-two, it would be normal . . . Nelly watched them, emotional, remembering her own adolescence, seeing them get flustered as soon as a man showed interest in them in a simple, kind, friendly way—for example her sons, especially Gilles . . .

Gilles worked nearby and would often drop in while the foreign girls were there; she had noticed this and had worried a few times but she had no reason to shut him out or to object when he asked the girls, from time to time, to come over to babysit. His once-again pregnant wife needed rest, and if the young girl wanted to come over and help on a Saturday afternoon, then for the weekend, she could take their little boy out for a walk, play with him, and watch him in the evening if Béatrice weren't too tired: it had been an eternity since they'd gone out. The girls would accept, delighted, and they would come back happy, charmed by the cute kid and by the young family's life, exactly as they'd dreamed it, the husband so present and attentive to his wife, whose recent miscarriage or difficult pregnancy excused her nervousness and mood swings in the girls' eyes . . . "but she's really nice, look, she let me borrow this dress, this book . . ."

Nelly listened to each of the girls and watched them in secret, aware as the weeks went by of each one's elusive air, her desire to shorten their conversations at dinner and to take refuge in the bedroom. At first the girls would come home happy from a pleasant adolescent outing, but little by little it would become a torment whose cause not one of them confided in Nelly. Each girl had so quickly gotten into the habit of telling Nelly her every feeling in minute detail, but she would soon become distant, closed off, politely mentioning some migraine, stomach ache, or worry after a sad phone call with her mother . . . These changes would take place toward the end of her stay and she'd use this pretext to isolate herself in the evenings and on weekends: she was starting to write up her internship report, to get ready for classes to start again . . . "Sorry," she'd say, when Béatrice called her, she wouldn't be able to help her out next Saturday, and she'd stay in the bedroom when Gilles came by and asked about her in passing.

"She's working," Nelly would say. "You know, at the end of their internships they're all the same, they panic, they're overworked, but it's a good way after all to get over their homesickness, after three months it's rather intensified . . ."

"OK. I guess we'll have to ask the neighbors' daughter to watch the little one again . . . It's too bad . . . Béa liked her . . ."

So he would come by less often, and then would show up unannounced the day before she left with a little gift from Béatrice, who had usually already said goodbye over the telephone an hour before. The girls were always emotional, understandably, given the series of goodbyes they'd endured over the last few days. Most of them burst immediately into tears and looked at Gilles with an almost shameful embarrassment, justified in the eyes of the others present (Nelly; her husband, who'd made the effort to be on time for dinner that night; and two or three of the girl's friends, whom they'd invited at her request) by the surprise of the gift. Gilles never stayed; his wife was waiting for him. He kissed his mother and the foreign girl in the same affectionate manner and wished her "bon voyage and good luck," making her promise to keep in touch. At that moment, Nelly, overwhelmed by the girl's unease, hated her son, who beamed with the same candor and cheerfulness the girl had shown during the first weeks, and which she seemed to be stripped of now, as though he had taken it from her . . .

It had taken her time to understand, and still, she continued to doubt, having no tangible evidence to suspect her son over the last four years of having had with the girls . . . Because before, as a young newlywed, he had no need for their services or his mother's support and he went straight home from work . . . But now, with Livia, the last one, she wasn't an idiot, she had seen that . . . Even if the girls might have been of age and free to act as they saw fit, the thought that her thirty-year-old son, a father, fooled around with them, so naive, so stupid . . . And what could *she* do to stop these games? The first part of the game was so innocent that she only elicited surprised remarks from the girls when she tried vaguely to warn them, "You should do something with kids your own age instead . . ." "But why? I love babysitting . . ." And Gilles, when she suggested he call their neighbors' daughter, "But Béa prefers these girls, they have good heads on their shoulders—"

"Come on, Gilles, they're as immature as can be, it's obvious!"

"They're mature enough to look after the little one in any case, and for Béa it's the same as it is for you, they give her a break and take her mind off things—"

"What do you mean it's the same as it is for me?!"

"They're a breath of fresh air, you've said it yourself, you get to travel thanks to them . . ."

Stupidly, she told him it wasn't the same thing, getting worked up, hurt, changing the subject immediately as though he'd reproached her for going on vacation with the foreign girls' money. She had just signed up for a trip to Croatia in early September, making the arrangements very late, without pleasure.

Gilles had come over after work to complain as usual: the birth of the baby a month ago hadn't brought Béatrice and him together at all, as his mother had told him it would. On the contrary, "she's constantly over-tired, overwhelmed, oversensitive, I can't even touch her . . . it's hell." He wanted to know when the new girl would arrive and her nationality, her age, her hobbies, "I guess she's probably like the others . . ."

"I don't know anything about her. I don't know. For the first time, I don't feel up to it . . . This time I had to decide practically on my own. Madame Volterra retired at the end of May and the young woman who took over isn't . . . well, with Madame Volterra I was sure, she only showed me the file to be polite, I had complete confidence in her and I was never disappointed. But now, I had to look at the files myself and saw immediately this woman wasn't up to the same standards."

"Why?"

"I couldn't tell you, it's just an intuition. Obviously when all you have is a photo, a résumé, and a cover letter that they surely didn't write themselves . . ."

She'd skillfully put off Gilles's curiosity by suggesting he hurry home to his wife. After he left, she felt overwhelmed. She felt like canceling everything: Croatia *and* the foreign girl. Morocco in February would have been the last trip, and Livia the last of Madame Volterra's girls whom her son . . . It was him, the long weekend in May, he took her with them to visit his in-laws in the countryside. As soon as she came back, Livia started crying over nothing, no longer ate, barely slept. She wanted to go home, she left three weeks early, breaking off her internship and paying top dollar for her plane ticket . . . Nelly felt obligated to get her a doctor's note and to insist to Madame Volterra that she get credit for her three months at the company. She had called Livia's mother to set her mind at ease, both frustrated and relieved by the language barrier. Ten days later, she called Livia to see how she was and the young girl's voice reassured her: she was so happy to be home, apologizing for not staying till the end, the separation from her family, from her homeland, it was too difficult, but she missed Nelly, she had been so good to her, all those hours they had spent together, she would remember them for the rest of her life . . .

She had cried after that phone call (she cried so rarely) and was submerged by a heavy wave of dark guilt, by which she felt cleansed at the same time, repeating between sobs that everything was fine, "my God, I was so afraid . . ." without daring to clarify what she was afraid of, remembering the times when her sons were still there, when she sensed things . . . that's what she would say: "I sense things . . ." and they would laugh at her.

The same tears returned after Gilles's visit, heavy with a brown dust that, because of him (though she was never able to determine its exact origin), had showered down all over this "perfect arrangement," as her friends so precisely called it, and her whole life. Everything had been luminous since she began hosting these girls, to fill the void her children had opened up when they moved out, condemning her to live out the rest of her days alone with a silent, usually absent, man who when he was there was somewhere else—their relationship was nothing more than a lukewarm friction between two solitudes and she was suffocating in it. The foreign girls brought her an invigorating breath of air and a free-and-easy freshness that took shape in her and amassed like the money in the box. As little by little she emptied the box to put down a deposit and then pay for her trip, for some clothes and guidebooks about her destination, she felt this energy buoy her up and carry her along during the preparation for her travels. She was ready to spend lavishly.

But this time she had no energy left for it. Her distress about Livia, Madame Volterra's resignation, the birth of the baby, and fragile Béatrice, whom she had been helping a great deal, all exhausted her. First of all her savings were smaller, since the girl had cut her stay short and Nelly had refused to accept the rent for the month of May, even though Livia had stayed until the twentieth.

"No, no, it will be my contribution to your plane ticket or whatever you need, I'm so sorry you're unhappy and that I can't do anything for you. I don't want the money, keep it," she said, hoping the girl would confide in her in return.

She was so eager for their words, especially at the end, even if she didn't want them to say the name "Gilles," it was better that way, what could she, his mother, have said if they had suddenly told her . . . but what? What could he have done to them? Maybe he had just whispered a compliment, taking their hands, touching their shoulders or knees in the car, and the girls who had never tolerated even the timid advances of boys their own age (Nelly was sure of it) were unsettled in their naiveté. It was not likely that a man like Gilles would want to seduce them, there was nothing especially attractive about them; Madame Volterra chose plain girls, not really *un*attractive, no, but intelligent and happy with nice features that were always spoiled by some flaw: bad teeth, bad skin, bad eyes, they all had some rather spectacular imperfection. Livia was fat . . .

She'd never thought about it before receiving the files for the four interns that Madame Volterra's young replacement had sent her in early June so she could contact the chosen one before summer vacation. The résumés looked just like the previous ones, the same social origins, the same upbringings probably, but she didn't find the usual family resemblance in the photos. Disconcerted, she asked two of her friends to come over for tea and help her choose. They finally opted for an Irish girl without really knowing why.

"I have the impression," one of them said laughing, "that she's the least dangerous of the four."

"Dangerous?" Nelly was taken aback. "Stop joking around and tell me seriously."

"Well, you can see for yourself that they're nothing like Madame Volterra's pinheads! They were really nice, of course, but in my opinion, these new girls are going to be something different at the Technitel office and at your house too, of course . . . Don't make that face, it's good! Change is always good!"

"Yes . . . but for me Madame Volterra was still . . . And I don't know if I should follow in her footsteps and stop—"

"And your travels?"

"Oh, I wouldn't necessarily have to give them up. André doesn't mind if I go and he doesn't care what it costs. I came up with the idea myself to earn that money so it would be entirely mine, the girls and the travels, to breathe the fresh air they bring, it's mostly that . . . it's only that."

"But he breathes that air too!"

"Him? Oh, he sees very little of them . . . Honestly he doesn't give a damn as long as he doesn't have to contribute."

"But he does! He shares a certain responsibility with you."

"Responsibility? That's a strong word. They're adults."

The next day, she went to the Technitel office to return the files in person and tell them which girl she had chosen. She wanted to see the young woman, hoping she could begin to build the trust that was completely lacking in their relationship.

"The Irish girl?" she asked. "Too late, she's just been taken, I approved it just a half an hour ago, by a family who, like you . . . And among the other three, who was your second choice?"

"No one."

"Ah. You mean you don't want to—?"

"No, I'm just a little surprised. With Madame Volterra . . . I depended entirely on her, we usually . . ."

"But it's exactly the same with me. You know the girls have been preselected and it's a guarantee for you. We received over forty applications for eleven positions."

"You only gave me four files."

"There are boys too. According to my records, you only want girls. And among the girls, there are some who prefer to be housed elsewhere."

"Can I see the others? The boys, after all . . ."

She left the office empty-handed, without having made any decisions, asking for two days to think about it, "I have to talk to my husband."

"Certainly," the young woman had replied. "On the other hand, I don't really see why you're hesitating about the three other girls. They're more or less interchangeable . . . Unless their nationality bothers you?"

"Of course not, nothing bothers me."

She barely slept that night, feeling agitated and discouraged by the arrogance of this new Technitel employee who couldn't hold a candle to Madame Volterra and who'd given Nelly the impression that this was some kind of shady business where she would get swindled. She went around in circles, determined to take herself off the list of host families, "I'll do something else, volunteer work, sports, I'll keep busy some other way, but the empty house . . . and what about a boy, why not . . . but boys live their lives outside, I know, they don't talk much. For me, girls . . . even if their stories aren't spectacular, their little sorrows, their big ideas, their affection, their company in the evenings. We would often play cards, I made cakes with Livia, we watched television together and I gave her explanations when she didn't understand the language. She wrote new words in her vocabulary notebook, I corrected her mistakes, her pronunciation, I taught her so many things . . . To give it up forever . . . All because these four new girls have something else in their eyes, I saw it, a different sort of intelligence . . . Yes, a different intelligence that made them beautiful, they're beautiful, that's it . . . that's what Madame Volterra did: she eliminated the beautiful ones immediately. I don't see why I should close my door to them and deny myself at the same time . . . I'm going to call tomorrow and tell them to send me any one of them, I don't even remember anymore . . . but a girl, another one, one last time . . ."

She made an effort to be attentive and write down the important information, knowing it was rather careless of her to choose over the phone without looking at the photos again, helpless against the young woman at Technitel, who, trying to help her as she hesitated, hammered her with questions.

"Athletic or a homebody? Catholic or Protestant? Spanish? Lithuanian?"

And when she came to a conclusion, summarizing Nelly's mostly neutral responses, she became friendly, certain that Nelly had made the right choice, insinuating she knew it immediately when she saw Nelly the day before: Isabel was the right choice for her. Madame Volterra had often said that, but coming from this woman it had a totally different effect on Nelly . . . Disagreeable, all of this was disagreeable after all, even if it wasn't the girl's fault . . .

When Nelly turned on her computer to reread her first contact letter, she wondered if she shouldn't change more than just the girl's name and the dates; perhaps she should update it according to its addressee, who might find some of her turns of phrase ridiculous or fear she was too maternal, and who definitely didn't want to be "considered during her stay as a member of their large family." Written four years earlier for Madame Volterra's girls, these lines in simple French drew a picture of her that wasn't false but today seemed unflattering, like a photo of her in the kitchen with two or three grandchildren hanging on her apron. While a photo of her backpacking in the Atlas Mountains . . .

She tried some edits, found them clumsy, and erased them. She quickly printed her letter, signed it, and went out to mail it immediately. On the way back, she dawdled in town and made some useless purchases. She was unable to rid herself of her apprehension, but it faded a little when she read Isabel's rather quick reply.

"I'm relieved. She seems charming, active, motivated, smart, like the other girls after all," she said to André that evening.

"Good," he said.

"But this time, I won't let Gilles . . ."

He looked at her, startled.

"Those little shady games . . . with Livia . . . oh, you know what I'm talking about," though she was sure he didn't. She hadn't ever talked about it, to anyone.

He shrugged, finished his drink, and folded his napkin.

She looked outside, surprised that she was so determined to protect this new girl, who seemed completely able to protect herself, while she had abandoned the others, so much more fragile and exposed . . . "but I didn't know then, or I wasn't sure, I . . ." Without consenting to admit her guilt, she promised herself she would redeem herself for Madame Volterra's last interns through the next intern, Isabel, by redoubling her vigilance, even if it meant sacrificing the good relationship she had with her son: "I will not allow him near her."

"Those little shady games . . ." André said, cleaning his pipe, with a vague smile that appeared disdainful to Nelly.

"What?" she said, watching him, flustered, pleading.

He took his time, concentrated on his utensils. She knew she had to be quiet, to wait. She closed her eyes, squeezing her fists under the table, as though she had just heard a verdict and understood to what sentence she had been condemned.

"Tell me . . ." she whispered, her head lowered.

It turned slowly. A carnival wheel, where the foreign girls' faces alternated with the faces of the men who had courted Nelly during her travels, some of whom, even if they were rather old or closely watched by an attentive wife, had started her daydreaming. She liked to listen to them, to enjoy their thoughtfulness and sometimes outdated chivalry, to let their brilliant, spellbound gaze fall on her—all while watching to avoid delicate situations. Whenever one of them became more insistent, she immediately changed her attitude, growing distant, severe, inaccessible; and the rejected man's aggrieved air inspired troubled feelings in her, whose nature she refused to contemplate.

André didn't look at her.

She placed her elbows on the table and her face in her hands, looking at the pack of tobacco that he'd left open in front of him.

"You think it's me . . ." she said.

He calmly lit his pipe.

"The girls and my travels . . . if I canceled everything . . . if in the future . . . the future . . . in the silence . . . and you."

She spoke slowly, trying to catch one of those thoughts stuck onto the carnival wheel. He was making it spin faster and faster just by being there, emotionless, immense, in the center, at the beginning and at the end of what he'd just uncovered, content to repeat her own words that she had said without thinking ("those shady little games"). He had been the leader, the master, the dealer, the winner who takes all. She felt that, but too confusedly to put it into words, that is, to give a body to something between them that was destructive for her . . . He would be fine, like always, like Gilles, his life would be barely changed, structured from the start by an unchanging routine and a job outside that provided him enough distraction that he never felt the need to share anything at all with her, some meals, yes, if that . . . the rest, she didn't want to know how or with whom . . . Those torments belonged to the past; a sort of agreement had been tacitly established, each of them got their fair share of the deal. He didn't stop her from giving in to her electrifying desire to travel, to go on the most extravagant vacations; it was in her: formless, dark, elusive.

The fragrant smoke of his pipe spread out between them.

She whispered softly, below it, "What do you think I should do?"

He looked at her without understanding.

"Once, just once . . . if you could make an effort and not be a coward by repeating that it's my life, that these decisions don't have anything to do with you—"

"If it's become a problem—"

"Yes."

"Then you have the answer."

She laughed. "OK. So, I'll fix my problem by calling that woman tomorrow morning, and telling her about some crisis . . . yes, I'll have to invent some crisis, some catastrophe . . . I'll remain evasive, 'very serious personal reasons,' and she'll imagine . . . I don't care what she'll imagine, she's a horrible girl, I don't understand how they could have given her Madame Volterra's job . . . the way she treated me . . . but they'll see at Technitel, they'll see very quickly with these new interns—"

"What?"

"I don't know what, I just sense something, ever since I looked at the applications, the photos . . . and when Gilles asked me so many questions the other day, curious, impatient, it was disgusting, casting me in that role like it was nothing . . . and you, tonight you . . . you're rubbing salt in the wound . . . you—"

"Of course not."

"Instead of telling me it disgusts you, after four years, to see me play with these girls, just because I don't know, I don't see how or with what, after having spent my whole life in this house without you, where nothing, nothing . . . That's it. Nothing."

She stood up and walked toward the window, looked at the evening sky where some birds were flitting about.

"The boys left," she said calmly, "all four of them, one after the other. You barely noticed. I hosted the foreign girls . . . There are some who spoil their grandchildren, others who get a dog . . . Do you think a dog . . . ?"

She heard him clear his throat and pour himself another drink.

"But who would take care of it when I'm traveling? And how would my trips be if, waiting for me when I get back . . . ? Because knowing when I come back, I'm going to get the bedroom ready and orient my thoughts, my whole being, toward an unknown new girl whose very presence will prolong what I only experience on my travels . . . If there's nothing but you, you and me, all winter . . . if there's nothing but that . . . I can't," she said, returning to sit across from him.

"Honestly, I don't see what the problem is. No one's asking you to give up your travels or to—"

"No one. Not even you."

"I don't have any reason to."

"You don't give a damn."

He sighed.

"Except when I bug you like this and I try to see a little clearer . . . when actually, it's worse. I feel . . . It's horrible what I feel . . . If you'd really listened to me you'd know . . . but you didn't listen to me. You let me talk, hoping I wouldn't go on too long. You think I like complicating the situation, that I'm inventing the problem, that I'm making it up just to hear you say that you think it's great: the foreign girls and my travels, you like them, you benefit . . . that fresh air is thanks to me . . . and Gilles . . ."

"I don't understand what Gilles—"

She interrupted him: "Gilles is a little bastard."

"Ah."

"Yes."

She started to clear the table in order to resist the temptation to say more; it looked like that was what he wanted as he watched her, stunned. She went into the kitchen, her heart beating in a mix of triumph and rage.

She put the plates in the sink and rested her hands on its edge, her arms tensed, her head tilted backward, her mouth open, examining the ceiling in the dim light. She knew now. Everything was clear, brutally clear. She knew how her life would be, no matter what she decided.

The foreign girls and her travels would continue to give it a rhythm, on the surface, without evading the real question of her own future in this empty house with an absent man whom she should have had the strength to leave four years ago, or even earlier . . . even earlier . . .

She let her head fall on her chest, her eyes closed, her back hunched. Those thirty-five years of marriage were speeding by, abruptly stopping for a second or two at moments when she felt as clear-sighted and captive as she did now, in that childhood terror when they left her behind, alone, and she ran as fast as she could to catch up to them, to be with them, close to them, even if they would punish her, humiliate her, ignore her, it wasn't as bad . . . As if there were nothing other than "not as bad" . . . and her joys and pleasures floated like fresh herbs sprinkled generously into this bitter broth that must be swallowed completely and without complaint. There were so many people who would have paid dearly to have this pittance, so many women who would envy her for being so free, for never having to worry about money, for never knowing the pain of loss, of abandonment . . . Her life had been so calm, ordinary, and without mystery, except for her, in each of these moments of distress, when she foresaw that one evening she'd be here: finally forced to see what was beyond her, already very close, at the end of this dance between her travels and her foreign girls.

Slowly, she stood up straight, tightening her crossed arms against her stomach, staring at the handle of the cabinet. "I should, yes, but calling that woman . . ."

André had just turned on the light.

TRANSLATED FROM THE FRENCH BY ELLY THOMPSON

CHRISTOPHER WOODALL

Lying to Be Cruel

I WITNESSED A psychodrama yesterday. I think that's what it was. In fact, I played a part in it.

I was in Copenhagen to run my monthly seminar on social dynamics. The university gives me a room for the night and a canteen dinner, both adequate.

For once, however, on retreating to my room, I felt I needed company or at least conversation. I glanced at the screen in the corner then, knowing my wife would be too busy to talk to me, phoned my son in Hamburg but he was busy too. On an impulse, I decided to look up Jeanette, a woman I had a relationship with many, many years ago. If she were alive—and why wouldn't she be?—it wouldn't take long to track her down: she was the kind of person you could never imagine existing anywhere outside Copenhagen.

After some expressions of surprise and other preliminaries, when I said I happened to be in the city for the night she said I should come and have dinner.

You'll meet Per, she said.

Per? I said. *That* Per?

Sure, she replied, with a little laugh. Then she said where they lived and told me they ate at seven-thirty.

*

Per turned out to be a shambling, bohemian type, an amateur jazz musician, and either much older than me and Jeanette, or markedly less well preserved. Jeanette seemed the same as before: nervy, bright, angular, but reserved too. I was reminded why I'd fallen for her and

how upset I'd been when she'd jilted me. I recalled her frank explanation: "You're fun and I do love you. But Per needs me. You don't."

She had been right, I suppose, but it had taken me several years to
get over it, perhaps because her "I do love you" kept ringing in my ears,
an engine of equally unfounded hope and regret. The first New Year
after we separated, I received a card. Per had moved in with her and
they were "trying for a baby." I hadn't wanted to know that and I never
replied. After a few years when I fell in love again, I hurried into a marriage that has always been good enough but rarely joyful.

I was now sitting in their dining room, hearing Per's anecdotes,
while Jeanette bustled about the kitchen, preparing a tagine. Against
one wall, under some historic concert posters, stood an upright
piano flanked by matching rickety music stands, each carrying ill-se-
cured sheet music; a trumpet lay in a dilapidated leather armchair.
The wall shelving was stacked not only with books but with every
sort of knickknack, card, and photo of grinning or pouting children, none of whom, Per divulged, were theirs. Mostly nephews and
nieces, he said.

Ordinarily, when people ask me if I have children, I'm unembar-
rassed, matter-of-fact. On this occasion, I dreaded the question and
when it came—with all the leaden inevitability of conversational eti-
quette—I was momentarily tempted to "delete" one or two of them.
Four, I said, finally. Then, as if in mitigation: Though two of them
are twins.

Jeanette brought in the tagine and side dishes, placing them all on
the oval mat that occupied the center of the table. Per uncorked the
wine I had brought; Jeanette served.

Did you know Wolf has four kids? Per asked.

Jeanette's eyes squeezed half-shut for an instant. Four? That must
be nice, she said.

During the meal, we talked of anything but children: Per's perfor-
mances, compositions and teaching; Jeanette's work for the city council and her political commitments; my books and conferences and
consultancy. Repeatedly, I heard myself sounding either complacent
about my achievements or apologetic. There were several moments
when none of us spoke at all.

I was still picking at a damson and cinnamon tart that Jeanette had "thrown together" for the occasion when Per pushed back his chair and said: It's great to meet you at last, Wolf. I've heard about you over the years. If Jeanette and I seem a little muted, well . . . (here he turned to his wife) . . . shall I tell him about Tina?

Why ever not? Jeanette said, getting up to open a window and fetching a box of Toscanellos from the kitchen. Per lit his with a lighter and held out the flame for his wife.

We've had a bit of a shock, Per said, resuming his seat. Jeanette nodded in corroboration.

I'll tell it my way, Per said, looking at his wife. You can always interrupt, darling, if I misremember some detail.

Sure, Jeanette said, funneling smoke from both nostrils.

A couple of weeks ago, he began, we were seated here at this table, just the two of us, after lunch. It was a Sunday. Jeanette was sitting where you are now, flicking through a newspaper. I was about to do the dishes. Sunday domesticity, you know? Per appeared to ponder this for a moment.

The phone rang and you got up to answer it, Jeanette prompted.

That's right. We get a lot of nuisance calls, even Sundays, even sometimes—as on this occasion—in English. So when I heard a voice say, "Hi, I'm Tina," I gave my standard nuisance-call response: "I don't know who you are or what you want but please cross me off your list and do have a nice day," and put the phone down. But she phoned straight back. Before I could get a word out, she said, "Listen. I'm your daughter and my mother always told me you were at least a polite person and you're not being polite." "My daughter?" I said. "Like hell, you are. I don't have a daughter." At this point, I noticed Jeanie had pushed her paper aside and was removing her glasses.

Per paused and Jeanette took up the story.

The next thing I heard Per say was: "You're British, aren't you? English, I'd guess. Yorkshire?"

That's exactly what I said, Per confirmed. And Tina replied: "Uh-huh. South Yorkshire. Like my mother. Which is why you recognize the accent. Remember now? Sheffield? 1993?"

I didn't hear that part, Jeanette said. But I could see Per was drawing up a chair—the chair you're sitting on right now, in point of fact. Then he said, staring at me, his eyes wide open, "So—*Tina*, did you say?—you think you're my daughter?" At this point I got up and went and stood beside him and he put the phone on speaker.

"Look," Tina was saying, "If you don't believe me, give me some DNA and I'll prove it. My mother did sleep around a bit in those days. You were by no means the only one. But she's sure it was you. The condom split . . ."

Per coughed, as if the cigar or the memory—or, perhaps, the persistent lack of memory—disagreed with him. Then he took back the story from his wife.

"So how old are you?" I asked Tina.

"All grown up. Work it out," she replied.

"Where are you phoning from?"

"Paris."

"So are we going to meet?"

Christ, that was quick! I said, looking from Per to Jeanette and back again. Jeanette threw a cursory smile my way but I could see the conversation was all between Per and Jeanette now. I could have got up and left. Jeanette spoke again.

You glanced at me to check I was OK with Tina visiting. Maybe you wanted me to decide. Was that it?

Not really. Anyway, all you did was nod every time I looked to you for help or some kind of suggestion.

I felt she was your daughter and it was your call. Besides, I couldn't see any harm in her coming.

Per snorted at that and, with a quick glance at me, resumed his account.

So Tina replied, "Sure. I'd like to meet you." And I said, "Well, clearly you know where we live . . . Why don't you come and stay for a few days? We don't have anything planned." Jeanette just beamed, as if she found the whole thing hilarious.

No, not hilarious, Jeanette said. But Tina sounded so brash, so fresh: I was curious to meet her. And there was something else . . . I think maybe I liked the idea of someone we basically didn't know coming to stay. Life can get a bit stale as you get older. The spontaneity of our invitation and her acceptance recalled my youth, those shared houses where people—strangers—were always turning up, staying, then vanishing as inexplicably as they appeared.

Per nodded.

So I said to Tina, "Just let us know when you're coming. We'll pick you up." And Tina said, "Great. I'll come by train."

"When?"

"Tomorrow evening?"

At this point, Per stalled and Jeanette prompted him again: "How will I recognize you?" you said.

That's right. And Tina replied, quick as an eel: "Just look for my mother, the way she looked when you met her, and you'll find me. The only thing I ever got from you, Mum always says, is your skill at improvisation."

"Really? You're musical?"

"Not in the slightest. I just improvise."

And that was it, Per said, looking at me, as if he'd just remembered I was there, then back at his wife as if to confirm I might as well not be. Jeanette puffed on her cigar.

Wow, I muttered, reaching for a cliché: Quite a bombshell!

Absolutely, Per said, getting up and making for the toilet.

Jeanette's mouth was contorted in a gesture of evident demurral.

As the toilet door clicked shut on Per, I caught Jeanette's eye: What? You weren't that surprised? I asked.

Not really, no. After all, I'm the infertile one. And Per was always a frisky little rabbit. So it was on the cards, wasn't it? I'm sure you can remember the way things were in those days: men took no responsibility. If a woman wasn't on the pill, it was her look-out.

How could I not remember? Jeanette had had an abortion early in our relationship. It had been as much my fault as hers. Neither of us had felt ready to have a child. There was nothing to say about it. I figured there never had been. If that abortion had resulted in infertility, I hadn't known it. I returned to the subject at hand.

So you never knew about his affair in Sheffield—if that's what it was?

Hell, no, Jeanette replied. He was away for months on end. I had an affair too while he was away. Several, actually.

So did Tina come?

Oh! Sure, Jeanette said, looking up as Per returned to the dining table: Wolf was just asking whether Tina ever turned up.

Grunting as he sat down, Per turned to his wife: Why don't *you* tell Wolf what happened when Tina arrived?

OK, Jeanette said. But I'll tell it my way, all right?

Sure, Per said.

*

Jeanette went to the kitchen, returning with a bottle of whiskey, a jug of water, and three glasses. She poured the whiskey, lit another Toscanello, held it away from her to examine the lit end, then took a deep breath.

Tina had my attention—Jeanette began—from the first moment I heard her on the telephone. Let me explain. My English isn't so good. I never passed any time in Sheffield or anywhere else abroad. But I heard the young woman's mood, I heard her anger. Do you know what I'm saying?

I'm not sure, I said.

A woman can often feel empathy for another woman's anger, right? Especially if the anger is directed at a man. But in Tina's case, I couldn't tell where the anger came from. So I was intrigued. I figured it really had nothing to do with Per. So I felt protective. What had he actually done to anyone that was so bad? Tina's mother had got pregnant and chosen to have a child? Good for her. Tina had got to have a life. Great. Also, I could see how excited Per was to be meeting his daughter. Elated. Euphoric. He had a child at last! And for free! He hadn't needed to change nappies, lose sleep, worry about school results, deal with adolescent sulks and inappropriate boyfriends, or become an unpaid taxi driver for an ungrateful teenager . . . He was dreaming of having a fully formed child, the fruit of his younger loins, come home to embrace him. Am I exaggerating?

Per stared at his shoes. Well, a bit, he said.

OK, a bit. Anyway, Tina showed up and was charming—especially to me . . .

Per snorted again and said: To me she was polite—at least to start with—but unswervingly distant. Do you remember? Before I'd even told her your name, she'd kissed *you* on both cheeks—the English never used to kiss strangers—but, when it came to greeting me, English reserve kicked right back in with a vengeance: she shook my hand, keeping me at arm's length, and clenched her teeth.

Yuh, Jeanette said again . . . For about thirty-six hours, it was like having a paying guest—except we were the ones doing the paying. We showed her the city, treated her to meals in restaurants, got an extra ticket so she could come to the opera with us. I have to say I found her great company. She told me about the books she was reading, including a lot of the second-wave feminist classics I'd read at college myself. In fact, she reminded me a lot of myself at that age. All this time not a word about the reason she'd come. But little by little she seemed to be thawing out with Per. They seemed almost relaxed together.

Then, on the third day, over breakfast, we stumbled somehow into the conversation we had all been waiting for and also postponing.

We didn't stumble, Per said. I asked her point-blank if she had a photo of her mum. I was expecting her to show me something recent on her smartphone but, no, she ran upstairs and came back with an old-fashioned hardback diary, which she opened and shook till some photos fluttered out.

This is my mum, she said, showing me one of a woman with a baby at her breast. Everything in that photo was utterly beautiful: the woman, the baby, the breast. I was taken aback. "I don't recall her at all," I said, transfixed.

"Well, you wouldn't, would you?" Tina snapped, snatching the photo from under our gaze: "You were drunk. It was after a jazz gig. In Barnsley."

Per didn't reply so I turned to Tina and said: "Men get drunk sometimes. So do women. That happens. It isn't a crime."

"Anyway," Tina went on, addressing Per now. "Mum took you back to her place in Sheffield and you had . . . sex. You weren't very interested and far too drunk to be any good. Don't look offended. She refused to tell me anything about the night I was conceived till I was seventeen and then she told me the whole damn thing, blow by blow. No finesse, she said. No warmth." At that, both Tina and Per looked at me—as if for some kind of casting vote. I looked as blank as I could. I wasn't going to take sides.

"Why are you so angry with me?" Per then said. "Because your mother thought I was a lousy lay when drunk? Or because I was never around when you were growing up? How could I have been? I didn't know I had a daughter. Maybe if your mother had thought to contact me . . ." At that, Tina erupted, jumped up and paced the floor. "I didn't need a father. I had—and have—a perfectly good father. His name is Malcolm and he's been living with my mother since I was four. They're even married." Tina picked another of the photos that had cascaded out of her diary and shoved it under our noses. "See?" The new photo showed a man my age, my height, my girth, with a full beard just like mine.

Yuh, it was creepy, Jeanette said, lifting the whiskey and gesturing toward my empty glass. I shook my head and covered the glass with my left palm.

So, Per said, I asked Tina again: "Listen . . . Why are you so angry? From what you're saying, your mother and I had consensual sex. You were conceived. She never told me. What did I do wrong?" Tina replied: "My mother went to a lot of trouble to put herself in your way. She'd been hanging around you for weeks, really fancied you, and you never noticed her. Even when she got you into bed, you were barely interested and you never tried to see her again. You don't even remember her, do you?"

"Are you telling me that your mother felt or feels hurt or insulted by me?"

"No," Tina said, "I'm telling you that I do."

I could have laughed at that—it seemed so absurd—but the young woman had tears in her eyes.

Jeanette and Per stared at each another, unsmiling. Each seemed to be waiting for the other to continue. Then, with a glance, they seemed to agree it was Jeanette's turn.

After breakfast, Tina offered to leave, if we could just drive her to the station. We hesitated, then said she didn't have to go and that we were happy to spend the day at the coast as planned. To our surprise, she decided to stay. The rest of the day was filled with false smiles and inconsequential niceties, as if we'd signed a pact of non-aggression. We had a long, long walk. It was entirely relaxed and hypocritical. Which was fine. Just what we needed.

That seemed to be the end of the story. Per and Jeanette were both looking at me. I racked my brains for an appropriate comment.

Well, it's almost a happy ending, I said: father and daughter reunited, not exactly reconciled, but still.

I figured it was time for me to leave. I started to get up, but then Per pulled a face, waving at me to sit back down. Oh God, there's more, I thought.

That evening, Per said, we went to bed straight after dinner, exhausted no doubt by the sea air. The following morning we drove Tina to the station. On the platform, as the train drew in, she turned to me and, as if delivering a prepared speech, yet twitching with nerves, said, "I've had a great stay and it's been really interesting to meet someone my mother once slept with." I wasn't paying attention to her choice of expression and even if I had been I might have let it go, but Jeanette protested at once. "'Someone your mother once slept with?' Is that it? Look, Tina. Per has done nothing wrong and he is, after all, your biological father." "Well, actually, no, he isn't," Tina retorted, her eyes darting to left and right. "I've been fibbing from the start. Mum got pregnant all right but decided to abort. She didn't think his genes were worth preserving. I was born about two years later. Malcolm is my biological father." "Then why the anger?" Jeanette asked. "Because he broke my mother's heart," Tina said.

Per and I were so dumbfounded all we could do was wave her goodbye.

What else were we going to do? Per said.

I now lifted my glass and held it out for Jeanette to fill.

So, tell me, Per, I said: How does it feel to discover you're a father, meet your supposed child, be insulted and humiliated, and then find she's not "yours" after all? It must have been bewildering.

I was relieved, Per said. Sad, then relieved. How could I not be? She clearly didn't like me. I didn't much like her. Too mixed up, too bitter. Frankly, it was good to know she wasn't my flesh and blood and that her blue eyes and fair hair—common enough features, after all, in these latitudes—had nothing to do with me. Right from the start, I had no fatherly feelings toward her and I still can't recall a thing about her mother. No, I was glad to discover there was nothing between us.

Well, all's well . . . I said, glancing at my watch.

Neither of them took my cue.

Per settled back, seeming to sink into a dream.

Then Jeanette turned to Per.

I wouldn't be so certain there's nothing between you and Tina, she said, speaking so softly it was as though she weren't quite sure she wanted to be heard.

At first Per said nothing. It took a while for Jeanette's words to sink in. Then, sitting up a little straighter, he said: What do you mean?

Jeanette put down her glass.

We know Tina lied, don't we? That much is obvious. But do we know *when*?

Per's face enacted the dawning of a poisonous notion. Well, he flannelled, people sometimes lie out of sheer laziness. That's why I lie, when I lie. But then she's not like me, is she?

Jeanette spelled it out: If Tina was born two years later than she originally told us, she'd be little over eighteen now. Does she look eighteen? She said she was about to start her third year at college. That's a bit precocious even for a twenty-year-old. But for an eighteen-year-old? And she told me so much about her course work, the essays she's written, the dissertation she's working on. Could she make all that up? Anyhow, what about her touring Scotland in a camper van the summer before last? Since when can you drive in Britain at sixteen?

I see, Per said, putting down his whiskey. His right arm was trembling. I glanced at his eyes. Then I saw that Jeanette was beaming in what looked like triumph. I suddenly felt I was intruding on some obscure and ugly power play. This had nothing to do with me, did it? I had no business being there.

I drained my whiskey and got up. Per coughed and said I should come again next time I was in Copenhagen. Sure, I said. Jeanette showed me to the door.

*

Outside, in the breeze, Jeanette said it had been good to see me.

I stared up and down the street for a reply. If I hadn't had the whiskey, maybe I would have censored my thoughts better, or at least my words.

Do you ever wonder, I blurted, how things might have been if we'd stayed together?

Never, Jeanette replied. Do you?

No, I said—a finger tugging at the lower eyelid of my left eye—neither do I.

I didn't love you, she said impatiently. I'm sure I must have told you that.

Actually, you told me the precise opposite. I've never forgotten your words: "I do love you but Per needs me. You don't."

I was probably lying to be kind.

To be kind? I repeated.

Unlike Tina, Jeanette added.

Unlike Tina? I don't follow.

Tina could have said she was born *one* year later. That would have been a bit of a stretch but plausible. But she had to say two, didn't she? She wanted us to figure it out. That was cruel.

But Per hadn't figured it out.

No. That's true.

So why did you have to force it on him? Was *that* kind?

It's important we live in truth.

Ha! But only when it suits you . . .

I waited and waited but Jeanette only smiled. I walked away. Neither of us said "good night."

*

I went back to my room at the university. I felt angry with just about everyone: with Tina for being a new-model puritan, with Per for being a softy, with Jeanette for being cruel, with myself for . . . what? For ever having loved Jeanette? The worst of it was that there had been some kind of psychodrama and I'd allowed myself to be sucked in.

My mobile rang. As I entered the building, I had switched it back on.

Hi, darling, my wife said. Your phone has been off all evening.

Yuh, I er . . . switched it off.

So where have you been?

I looked up an old flame.

Ah-ha.

And her husband.

So . . .

I probably told you about her years ago. Jeanette.

The one who lived in Copenhagen? The frigid one?

Jesus! I never said that, did I?

Whatever. Actually you did. Was it fun seeing her again?

Not exactly, no. In fact not at all.

Tell me about it. What happened? You sound so strange . . .

There's nothing to tell. I'm fine. Really.

There must be something. After all these years.

No, darling. There's nothing to tell. Really nothing at all.

Honestly?

I laughed at that, laughed harder than I'd expected.

Sure, I said. Honestly.

XABIER LÓPEZ LÓPEZ

Discourse on Method

GOOD AFTERNOON. IT is truly an honor to be able to address you all from this podium after so many years of absence. Absence, yes, but not forgetfulness. Luck had it that there were some who disregarded the recommendations of the "curia" (no, I will not call it the Sanhedrin, do not tempt me), and I can assure you that I never lacked for news about this Academy and its prolific intellectual life, at my modest Californian retreat. I see Professor Mantiñán, who forwarded me Pérez Soto's introductory lecture and Vargas Méixome's valiant rebuttal. And Torres Pena, still quite youthful at eighty-eight, who overcame his proverbial enmity toward modern technology with patient dedication and used Messenger to keep me up to date on the raucous debate among those who felt I'd been duly anathematized, those who believed quite enough time had passed to consider a reconciliation, and, finally, that group of young researchers who had the outlandish idea of reclaiming me as little more than their spiritual father, sending me a sizable portion of their postdoctoral funds in a monthly deposit, and even setting in motion a sort of democratic initiative, if you will, so that each and every one of the research projects I carried out abroad would be validated. It is to them—and I know that if they are not here today it is due to immovable and inescapable obligations—that I dedicate these words with all my heart. All of them, dear colleagues, share some part in the incubatory idea with which I began my research career: what is important for humanity is not what we write but the why and the how of it, that is, why and how we write.

What is it that brings a human being, shackled to the satisfaction of their physiological cycles (sleep, food, urination, defecation, respiration, fornication, masturbation), to pick up a pen, to sit themselves in front of a typewriter or digital word processor? What is it that forces them to momentarily set aside their communal enslavements (family, neighborhood, work, consumer transactions) and throw themselves into the ether of creative thought? How are they able to break free of those chains, and, most importantly, why the hell do they do it? What are the most propitious conditions for bringing about this phenomenon?

You must all agree, cherished comrades, that despite the extreme effort it would require, we could all ultimately imagine a world without the *Quixote*, *Tristram Shandy*, or even *In Search of Lost Time*. You must also agree that that world would be nearly identical to the one we know. And if it is such with regard to true masterpieces of literature, nothing much would change if we accounted for the hundreds of thousands of minor titles we believe deserving of a space in our individual and collective consciousnesses. Just you try it, killing literature. If you are able to break the taboo once and for all and proclaim literature's fundamental contingence, you will arrive at the point to which I wish to take you. The only thing relevant is the literary act itself. There could be a world without books, or at the least a world without the books we know; what would be unthinkable, friends, would be a world without literary creators. Literature is an action, not an outcome. And from that point of view, believe me, the world offered to us is lush and stimulating indeed. Almost to the same degree, colleagues, as that surprising assertion of Thomas Mann's: "A writer is someone for whom writing is more difficult than it is for other people." If you will permit me, I shall give some examples that illustrate my modest words, which, in a moment of childlike inspiration—preoccupied as I was with not disappointing you all by my return—I have had the audacity to title: "Discourse on Method."

Antoine Raimond Frimer, the author of *The Next Chapter*, and I'll say it in French, *Le chapitre suivant*, for it is high time to reclaim my old abilities, was apparently only capable of writing outdoors. At first on café terraces, or on the balcony of his house; later on, in the Breton hamlet where he went to live in his old age, in a garden that surely had its grapevines and blackberry brambles, and on top of those last two details, which I confess to be the fruits of my bucolic imagination, a good bit of shade provided by some oak trees originating from the legendary Paimpont forest. As you might intuit, *Quercus robur* being a deciduous species, his writing sessions were intense and quite spread out in time.

There are some who only experience literary pleasure by availing themselves of uninitiated lovers, intimacies and obstacles, damp dreams where the world becomes a narrow gutter up which one has to claw and claw and claw in order to set free, finally, one's distressed and melodramatic brain. Yes, esteemed colleagues, there are some who give themselves over to writing in order to purge an unattractive appearance, the perpetual unease that has nibbled away at their insides ever since the first twilight they can remember . . . And only one person managed to confess it openly: "I've written, since I was very young, believing that writers fucked a lot; I continue to write now, old and decrepit, thinking, believing, complaining about . . ." Arthur F. Lie, gentlemen, or, if you prefer, "the Australian who wanted to be a writer when he read Hemingway in the military cantinas of Darwin and Port Moresby, New Guinea, with the Japanese attacking from Truk, Kusai, Jaluit, and the Caroline Islands." Arthur F. Lie, ladies and gentlemen, or that soldier who, completely safe, watched the Japanese Zeros, the trail of their engines, their silvery apparition in the Pacific sky, and immediately began to fantasize about the blueberry breasts of the geishas, with feet so childlike they could fit them entirely into their mouths.

The laundry list of maniacs—for writing remains an extreme mania—is certainly an extensive one. Signing contracts with the same pen, old and gnawed away by the damp. Marrying in red underwear. Stepping up onto the sidewalk with one's right foot. Eating the potatoes before the chop. Saving the best for last. Reading the paper backwards, that is, from back to front. Pretending one is not listening while in reality enthusiastically taking part in all these strangers' conversations: cataloging, taking sides, declassifying, condemning, absolving. Or, perhaps, *nouveau roman*: leaving a tape recorder at a café on a winter afternoon and stitching together stories from the recorded voices. But for that, distinguished audience, you have to be François Mensonge, not just anybody. Writing in *Les Temps Modernes*, marrying his cousin despite all pleas to the contrary, and having the stones to make confessions of this tenor: "Boubal is a peasant who's always looked at Paris with a hick's eyes; Vian, a clown; Prévert, a philanderer; Genet, a pederast; La Gréco, a portside whore; Sartre, cross-eyed; Duncan, a pathetic old man; and Bryen—then I'm finished—an unbearable child whose buffooneries can cause all kinds of quarrels." And that with some of them physically present. With the painter, E. Binnet, and his *Patrix, Saint-Germain-des-Prés* family portrait, his last paintbrush still damp.

Cheating at cards. Raging and foaming at the mouth when someone else holds the three. Believing in fate. Believing that love, or lack thereof, has anything to do with poker, tute, bezique, or subastado. Reading history books and always taking sides with the partisans, with the communists. Cheating at dice. Hating the yankees and loving the Russians. Hating the Russians. Enjoying intestinal troubles. Believing in fate, in tarot. Being excited by stories that come from far away.

Italo Calvino—as you all know, *ex-partigiano* and ex-communist, brought low by intestinal troubles per the intentions of a left-leaning socialist woman, ex-partisan and ex-communist—enthusiastically assimilated the Russian studies of the symbology of the short story, and there must have been something fashionable about it, as his compatriot Rodari, a teacher in the Reggio Emilia schools, also confessed—still a communist—an identical devotion. Pre-war and postwar Italy. Moravia denouncing the indifferent. Einaudi . . . Einaudi editore.

Rodari's father, esteemed colleagues, was a baker. Calvino's father, a professor of tropical agriculture at the University of Turin, and due to the glaring rhyme I will not call it Torino.

Italo Calvino, gentlemen, he and his *viaggiatore*, he and his castle where all destinies intersect, should have taken note of Vladimir Propp, like Rodari. Vladimir Propp and his thirty-one playing cards symbolizing every single one of a short story's functions. Vladimir Propp and the Russian school; and Calvino, married to a Russian-Argentine translator, stitching together a game from his discoveries and his tarot cards: each and every character to suffer the fate of this world.

Valéry getting out of bed at four in the morning, always at four, in order to write until daybreak. Breton and the surrealists defending automatic writing. The *Dada*—which means nothing—jotting down words on a piece of paper that they tear up and immediately toss into the air.

Huxley wearing Baudelaire's old jacket, or Thomas De Quincey's, or that of countless others, in order to poke his nose through the doors of perception after finishing up his stupefacient mush—etymologically anything that produces numbness or stupefaction, according Eduardo Belendi's ineffable dictionary, that which makes us stupendous.

There are trends, you might argue, and as always you are not wrong. Only a fool would dare deny the role trends have played in history, the extraordinary strength they possess in configuring codes of conduct. An example? As you all know, few mothers gave teat to their little ones before Rousseau wrote Émile. For that there were wet nurses, who quickly weaned (demeaned) their offspring in order to take their swollen black breasts and introduce them into the mouths of the Madam's children. But it would appear that character comes from the mother's milk, and Enlightenment education encouraged the bourgeois new mothers to free their swollen, virgin breasts, full of strawberries and cream, from their little bodies' cages. What had in times past been a vulgar admission of the most abject bestiality became a marker of progressivism and distinction.

Trends . . . Any time I've trusted a line of reasoning based on precedent, if you will permit me a small ludic parenthesis, I have enjoyed imagining Balzac's reaction. But, you may be wondering, why Balzac? Well, simply enough, because I am certain he was the most ill-humored and hot-tempered writer in all of history. Do you disagree? There he is, furrowed brow, jutting and puffed-out lip, hammering the table with his fist: "No and a thousand times no! I wholly refuse to give teat and lose my imagination all for the effect of an elixir!"

Balzac, when it came to trends, already had an antidote: his character. When it came to literature, a quotation by Lavater, the great physiognomist: "God protects those he loves from worthless reading."

In any case, esteemed audience, a dissertation which seeks to concentrate on the creative act and its circumstances, or in more academic terms, the ethics of aesthetics, must shed its abstract-theoretical chains (much as it may adorn itself with elements of an anecdotal nature) and seek experiences which are not purely referential. None of the authors I have cited, not even the most recent ones, have I ever met in person. For last, I have saved a figure of transcendental importance in my life, and by consequence in my firmest convictions about these matters which currently occupy us, in large part, and I do not believe I am mistaken here, against our mothers' wishes. Undoubtedly. Last comes Theodor Lüge, the prolific Polish novelist, because to a certain degree it was primarily he who brought me to intuit the truth of that which I am telling you.

If you have the opportunity, gentlemen, to obtain a good history of literature, if you have a moment to pause on the chapter dedicated to early twentieth-century Polish literature, if curiosity takes you so far as to go out beyond the generic guidepost for the Młoda Polska, or Young Poland, you will surely encounter a large number of authors who, without writing in either Russian or German—for in that case they would have been included in the Russian and German literature sections—took part in forging a proud nation within the Universal Republic of Letters. You would necessarily be informed about Zenon Przesmycki, founder of the magazine *Life*, as well as Stanisław Wyspiański, the bountiful playwright who alternated between prose and verse. You would necessarily come upon Karol Irzykowski and Władysław Reymont, authors of the lengthy novels *The Witch* and *The Promised Land*, respectively. You would necessarily run your finger, in a rapid and bewildered internal pronunciation, over the names of Brzozowski and Staff and Żeleński. But none of them, esteemed colleagues, cast even a shred of shadow over Theodor Lüge, architect by profession, a writer who went up against the one and only Rabindranath Tagore for the 1913 Nobel Prize in Literature, and if in the end he did not get the cat into the bath, it must be said, it may have been due to the dearth of translations that had been done of his work and surely due to the jury's fear of the reactions of the Prussian and Russian governments, because a prize like that would necessarily entail a formal recognition of the Polish nation.

Not Musil, nor Proust, nor Zola. None of them, despite their reputation as prolific monsters of the pen, accumulated as many pages as those written by Lüge during the course of his life. Just his novel *I Am an Invented Man*—which many posit as a precursor to Musil's *Man Without Qualities*—numbered nearly three thousand pages. His verse-novel, *Occurrences in the Life of a Peasant with Holes in his Pockets*, numbered one thousand. To put a figure on Theodor Lüge's work, gentlemen, is an almost impossible task, because to the hundreds of novels he published in his life we must add the two or three dozen posthumous ones, and a large number of stories, articles, and collaborations scattered among journals and magazines of every description. The professor Emil Bausseric, the only madman who swore to counting them, gives a terrifying number: the titan Theodor Lüge wrote five hundred and thirteen complete novels. You heard that right, five hundred and thirteen!

One afternoon, in the twilight of his life—Lüge turned one hundred in Cyrankiewicz's communist Warsaw—he was interviewed at his house by a young researcher, later a journalist, who was notified by his colleagues at the cultural supplement he had been assigned to for his scholarship of the writer's absolute reclusiveness when it came to speaking about the intricacies of his creative rhythm and process. This researcher, bold like all young people, decided to prepare in great depth for the interview, such that he tirelessly visited bookstores, archives, and libraries, out of a desire to familiarize himself with that long-winded theory which breaks down the methods, channels, and motivations employed in literary production dating back to the earliest times. You are familiar, dear friends: fresh firewood and young people . . . "Do you not sleep?" Lüge's wife, a thin little old woman, though she was perhaps twenty or twenty-five years younger than the novelist, could not help but smile upon hearing such a thing. She placed the small tray with *schnaps* on the table and glanced at her husband with that strange and playful look that seemed to say: "What's this boy talking about, Theodor? He's asking the dormouse if it sleeps." The writer, seated in a rocking chair, patted the folded blanket covering his legs. "In fact, young man, you just plucked me from a delightful nap." Indeed, he struck the first blow. Nevertheless, the researcher was unperturbed. It had taken him so much work to arrange the interview that under no circumstances was he going to walk out of there empty-handed. "You told me to come just before three," he said in his own defense. His voice, distinguished colleagues, sounded small. He, in his entire being, felt small due to the enormous number of books crowded into that room which smelled of liquor and old age. And, believe me, Theodor Lüge also appeared small, on his perch, like a little bird that's just fallen from the tallest part of a tree.

Without really knowing why, and despite the hostile reception he had just received, the investigator-acting-as-journalist felt pity for that

little, defenseless-looking old man. He tried again. "You gave up your
profession as an architect in order to devote yourself entirely to literature. When did you realize architecture wasn't for you?" The prolific
writer, gentlemen, narrowed his eyes: "Journalism doesn't do well when
it relies on sources as unreliable as those implied by your claims. I never
gave up my profession, sir. I designed this villa. And all the other villas
in this neighborhood. And all the expansions to Warsaw and Kraków
and Katowice . . ." Imagine, if you will, the expression of the young
man, who was beardless back then, naive, insolent, and perhaps inti-
mately wounded by the insecure realization of his youthfulness. All
his lines of reasoning from the days prior went down the drain in that
moment, as well as the documenting he'd toiled over, and which ultimately meant he would have to toss out the interview's central frame:
the recourse to the handy model of "parallel lives," that framework
that meets with such success among any public which loves or hates
or is simply unaware of Plutarch. Let me be more specific: the hermit,
Marcel Proust, evaporated like a wisp of smoke and, with him, all pros-
pects of uncovering, in a little villa on the outskirts of Warsaw, a man
who had so happened to come to the same conclusions toward recon-
ciling life and literature.

From that moment on, ladies and gentlemen, the blunders followed
in succession. Have you ever taken a moment to ponder what would
happen to a tree if you removed its trunk and branches? "So you live
a normal life?" the young man asked after a little while. The old man's
face trembled with indignation: "Do you mean to insult me, good sir?
What in God's name do you mean by that? Do I leave the house to visit
friends? Do I stroll around on Sundays, go to the cinema or theater,
and then dine at a restaurant in the city center? Of course I do. What
did you come to this house looking for, a damned monster?"

We will honor the truth, dearest colleagues: despite his rapid and
forceful statement to the contrary, despite his varied and clumsy apologies, that was exactly what our young man had come looking for in
this clean and tidy house. A monster. He tried his luck with automatic
writing, mentioning the surrealists, but all he achieved was an irritated tap-tap-tap from the old writer, who quickly furrowed his brow
in a show of disdain for Breton and those of his ilk, who continued
to click his tongue at each and every one of those questions fruitlessly

inquiring into alcohol, psychotropic substances, even—such awful desperation!—habitual submission to hypnosis. At this stage of the game, you'll no doubt understand that the researcher no longer felt any sureness of foot within his mind. He even went so far as to think that his time in that living room was actually part of a joke, a prank played on him by his coworkers in the editorial department. However, he did not give up. In case you weren't aware, this young man of whom I speak never, ever, ever gave up: "Do you look at the world through any specific lens? Is observation, as it is for many other writers, your principal method of study? Does the key to the miracle of literature lie within the de-automatization of one's perception of reality?" In a kind of resigned pragmatism, the novelist resolved to place a timid, forced smile on his lips. "Come now . . . I have eyes in my head."

By the way, esteemed public, Mrs. Lüge had now re-entered the room. She was carrying a tray with some large pieces of *makowiec*; for anyone unfortunate enough not to know what I am referring to, it is a delicious poppy-seed Christmas-time treat quite common during the era I am recounting—a simply delightful winter pastry. She must have sensed their mood in the air, for she gazed maternally at the distressed journalist, and at the same time, hardening her expression, at her husband. She left the tray of sweets on a small table, directed the steely gaze at her husband once more, and slammed the door on her way out. I choose to believe that silent warning had its desired effect. "What were you asking me, my dear friend?" Our amateur researcher no longer had the slightest idea what to ask. He felt shame burning his ears and all the blood in his body was rushing up to his face. Pushing the over-accelerated gears of his brain just a bit further, he remembered the harsh words of a high-school teacher, truly indignant over the quality of his verses. "You'll all get stuck if you're waiting for the muses. Read, dammit, read; not a single person has ever become a writer without reading." This prompted him to ask the question, gentlemen, and truthfully, you can be sure, with the sole purpose of picking up and ending the torture as soon as possible. It was certainly not what the supplement's subscribers would be expecting, but at that point it mattered little to him that his report on Theodor Lüge would become, plainly enough, a concise list of his favorite readings. Nevertheless, my friends, even this easy alternative was unable to wrap things up in simple fashion. His unsociable host quickly opened his mouth in a gesture you could all easily imitate by biting down: "Well in truth I don't read very much. I don't know, maybe three, four novels when I was young, that's all . . ." You will understand, esteemed colleagues, that his question could not be held back for even a tenth of a second: "YOU'VE ONLY READ THREE OR FOUR NOVELS IN YOUR WHOLE LIFE?"

I will say it once more: "YOU'VE ONLY READ THREE OR FOUR NOVELS IN YOUR WHOLE LIFE?" The young man rose from his chair a bit impulsively and approached the shelves where the enormous number of books that had made such an impression on him—as well as giving him a sense of extreme diminution—lay collected. Essentially, it was as expected: T. Lüge, T. Lüge, T. Lüge . . . There was not a single book in the room not authored by the man of the house. He simply could not take it anymore, gentlemen. Patience, especially in those young men who think they hold the world in the palm of their hand, has its limits. He left his just barely bitten portion of *makowiec* on the edge of his plate, grabbed his wrinkled knee-length coat, and after bidding farewell to the old man like someone running to catch a train that will not wait, he dashed out of the house. For a few seconds he was incapable of forming a coherent thought. He snaked through the deep-black streets of the city's humble suburbs, and only when the threat of snow reminded him of his jacket did he feel the unusual lightness of the garment covering his shoulders. He searched around in his pockets with growing anxiety until he told himself that no, unfortunately he was not mistaken. Not just his gloves, my dear colleagues, but his gloves, his wallet, his keys . . .

The idea of having to face the writer once more turned his stomach. A few minutes with that tiny, temperamental old man, and not a single one of the sturdy intellectual constructs it had taken him so much time and effort to erect remained standing. But he had no other options. He could either return to Lüge's cave and retrieve his keys or he could prepare to spend the night outdoors, a prospect which could not but send a sharp chill down the spine of anyone familiar with the draconian temperatures of Warsaw in December. He retraced his steps, recalling the outline of a back door shaded by a small curtain, and confirmed the truth of his intuition when approaching the villa from behind. Fortunately for him, the latch was not thrown, so that he dropped all pretense and decided to enter without further delay. There was no one in the room. He saw Lüge's blanket folded on top of the rocking chair, and further along the tray with *schnaps* and squares of poppy-seed cake. At the feet of the chair he had occupied, impossibly balanced on the rug, his starched gloves and the coin purse with his keys. He rushed to gather up his things and leave the place once more. However, that is not what he did. He held his breath and pricked up his ears. From the hallway—from some place beyond it—came the metallic slicing of scissors that round the ear in the course of a haircut. *Chik, chik, chik . . .* In reality—we will get on with it—the precise and disjointed clicks of a typewriter. His curiosity, distinguished colleagues, was more powerful than his fear. The noise was coming from a room set up in the space beneath the stairs, a small, dark cubicle from which trickled a faltering, caramel-colored tongue of light. He gave it no more thought. He brought his hand to the doorknob, wrapped his fingers around it as if he feared it would escape him, and opened the door, his heart in his throat. The mystery was revealed at last. A bare bulb hanging from the ceiling. A table. In front of the table, Lüge's narrow back, Lüge perched atop the typewriter, and, at that moment, an explanation that eliminates the fleeting sensation that the old man has eyes in the back of his head, because Lüge looks at him, surprised, without even turning his head. Mirrors, gentleman. The walls of the room were completely covered in mirrors.

TRANSLATED FROM THE GALICIAN BY JACOB ROGERS

COLM Ó CEALLACHÁIN

Orphans

June 2013. Fermanagh.

G8. G8? G8? Oh yeah, the G8. It meant nothing to Aideen, nothing at all apart, perhaps, from the opportunity of a week's holiday. The whole county, as her boss had been warning her, would be in lockdown as soon as the summit began.

"Isn't it always?" she had replied.

She took his advice nevertheless, and booked the week off.

"Where will you go?" he asked her.

"Belfast first, and then the sun."

"A wise decision. Yes indeed, George Best Airport, the best thing about that town."

More often than not, his droll humor was lost on her.

She could also stop in with Charlie for the week, of course. Would his two sons be with him now, she wondered? Charlie shared custody of the boys with their mother, a fact that Aideen tended to forget. She would be fifty soon, and with no children of her own she had very little comprehension of what living with two teenagers entailed. Charlie didn't mind this and seemed willing, indeed, to put up with any amount of her idiosyncrasies. Or put another way, her selfishness, something she herself was only too willing to own up to. She called him now, and no sooner had she told him of her plans than he was offering to come and collect her.

"Traveling light?"

She ignored the question. Her travel bag, a glorified wallet, was thrown in the back before she jumped into the passenger seat. She started flicking through the stations but the summit was the only show on the airwaves.

"How was the road down?" she asked Charlie. "Did you bump into the rulers of the world? Any demos?"

"Nothing. Not a secret service fella to be seen, nor even a crustie."

The roadway snaked its way through drumlin country, blue skies above them and the occasional glint of lakeside silver to their left. The placards which were nailed to a tree every now and then were objecting, not to world domination by an elite, but to the hydraulic fracturing of the very earth beneath these farmers' fields. "Fermanagh says no to fracking," they proclaimed or, more imaginatively, "Tamboran Resources Frack Off!" Other roadside signs appeared then, for the Marble Arch Caves this time, prompting Aideen to ask Charlie to pull in.

"Can't we keep on for Enniskillen?" he said. "We don't know when they're going to start blocking off the roads. It's too hot today, anyway, to be crawling around under the ground."

"What's the matter? Afraid of the dark?"

He grunted noncommittally, but turned off all the same.

She bought the tickets. It was the least she could do, considering how reluctant he was to come here. As soon as the little boat dropped them off in the heart of the cave, however, his mood lightened. The limestone formations, sculpted over millennia by the slow trickle of water, started to capture his imagination. He saw angel wings rising from dark pools, grotesque carnival masks leering at him from natural alcoves in the rock. Aideen simply saw formless lumps of stone. Dinosaur snot at best, elephant scrotum.

Squinting in the sunlight, the tour group gathered around the cave entrance. The tour over, their guide started leading them back toward the visitor center, but Aideen lingered behind. Below them, the subterranean river they had been following emerged from a deep cleft in the ground. Picking her way carefully down she headed toward it with Charlie, more than a little reluctantly, following behind. When they reached the bottom she found a flagstone by the river's edge, and stripping off briskly she started laying her clothes down on it.

"What are you doing?" he asked her.

"Isn't it obvious? Might as well take a quick dip as we've come this far."

Stripped to her underwear, she stared at her reflection in the bog-dark water. Her ribcage so clearly defined, her slight frame shivering. A jolt of cold pain as she jumped in then before swimming hard, with rapid strokes against the current, toward the mouth of the cave.

"You're out of your mind," she heard Charlie say.

Long hair the color of copper merged with the water as she rose and dipped. Half turning, she winked at him, and swam on.

June 1977. Nottinghamshire.
"D-A-V-I-D. David. S-O-U-L . . . Sally?"

"Soul. David Soul."

She was coming home from school, her little sister Rosie lagging behind her as usual. Still only six, Rosie would have always struggled to keep up with her but in this case she was staying back intentionally to read Aideen's latest schoolbag graffiti.

"A-D-B-A. Adba."

"Abba. A-*B*-B-A. Abba. Hurry up, Rosie. It's too hot today to be hanging around."

"Is that Daddy?"

It was Rosie who noticed him first, the solitary figure on the ridge that stood between them and their pit-village home. Aideen shielded her eyes and looked up, and even in the sun's glare it was apparent that he was waiting for them.

"No, it's not our dad," she said at last. "He's not tall enough."

Continuing on up the pathway to the summit she would, from time to time, peer suspiciously at the unmoving form.

"Can you still see him?" Rosie asked, breathless now as they neared the top.

"I can. It's Steve."

For as far back as Aideen could recall, Steve and his wife Grace had been a presence in her life. He lectured in the local Poly, but before that he had been an engineer in her father Mike's pit. When Mike lost a couple of fingers in an accident below ground, Steve had helped him file a claim against the mine company. When his award finally came through, a pittance that worked out at roughly a thousand per finger, Steve advised him to go back to school. Those were lean years, with Mike studying for his degree as their mother, Nancy, fed and clothed the girls. They had come through them, however, and Mike himself was teaching now, grateful, as always, for Steve's advice and support. But what was he doing here today, Aideen wondered, as they crested the hill?

"Hello, girls. Want me to take your things?"

"Yes, please! Can we have ice cream?"

"You sure can."

Bought off by that bribe Rosie skipped ahead, but Aideen, still skeptical, refused to give up her own schoolbag.

"Where's Dad?" she snapped. "What have you done with him?"

In the middle of an English lesson, Mike had suffered a heart attack. Sudden, massive, and fatal. Still only thirteen, Aideen now had the misfortune to lose a father for the second time. About her natural father she knew, admittedly, very little. A miner from the west of Ireland, so her mother had told her, a man who had fled back down the mine before Nancy even realized that she was pregnant. A one-night stand, literally, against the back wall of the sports and social club. At this stage she hadn't yet slept with Mike, her regular beau, but after she explained the circumstances of her pregnancy to him he had stuck by her. Ever the gentleman, he married Nancy before her bump was even showing. He loved her of course, as he loved Aideen and Rosie when they came along. His two daughters, without distinction. What bond did Aideen share with her biological father, after all, apart from her name? It sounded like Aidan, which was his name, or so Nancy claimed, although knowing her she might just have liked the sound of it. She argued, in any case, that her daughter was owed at least that from her otherwise anonymous father. When she was old enough to understand, Mike would tease Aideen about her origins.

"You've got coal dust in your veins, girl. Mind you don't end up like poor Persephone, fated to spend half your days underground."

She could only laugh at him. As if she would live her life in the shade, a troglodyte, destined never to shine.

———

In the years following Mike's death, Nancy self-pitied and self-medi-
cated in equal measure. Having no children of their own, Steve and
Grace kept a close watch on their neighbors' daughters, giving them
the guidance and stability that their mother sometimes lacked. In due
course Rosie became a teacher just like Mike, while Aideen, in spite of
her earlier misgivings, followed the career path of *both* her fathers. She
studied geology, hoping, at the same time, to avoid the carnage she
saw all around her now. As the eighties progressed her little village had
become a battleground between strikers and scabs. Whatever else happened, she assured Steve that she would not cross a picket line.

"You won't need to," he told her. "The mines will all be shut before
you even get your degree."

Why, then, she asked him, had she spent the last four years training
for an industry that seemed to have no future?

"Don't worry, love. There'll always be some sore on this earth that
needs scratching. That's the beauty of this work. This is your opportunity to see the world, even if it'll be mostly from below surface level."

Where had this cynicism come from? Aideen didn't question him
further. A few more years of postgraduate studies and she would be out
of here, with Steve only too willing to help her get away.

"I've got contacts in this business," he told her, as the miners' strike
entered its death throes. "Old friends, working far away from this cold
and muck, far, far away from all this bloody strife."

June 1987. Transvaal.
Within days of her landing at Jan Smuts International, a state of emergency was declared throughout the country. Aideen, so principled when
it came to her hometown dispute, had been ignoring the news reports
in her rush to get away. She imagined herself, naively, as a positive role
model, an example of someone who would take people on their merits
alone. What she did not realize was that the goldfields of the Rand, her
future place of employment, were just another front in the battle for
the soul of the nation. Everything, meanwhile, was new to her, and she
welcomed it all. It was a chaotic affair, admittedly, this relentless grind-
ing of the wheels of industry, greased, as always, by human sweat and

toil. Every morning at six she would be awoken, as if a switch had been flicked, by the hum of traffic. Still shivering in the Highveld chill, she would leave the little apartment the mine company was renting her and jump into a battered old Renault. In ten minutes she would be clocking in at the twisted, bountiful heart of the Rand, the lode-bearing, land-locked reef that sustained this city of millions. Beneath its vermilion clay, vivid as a fresh wound, lay sand that matched the color of her own blond hair. As the winter storms blew up from the Cape this sand was swept from the mine dumps that dotted the city, coating everything and everyone in a fine white powder.

Years afterwards, it was the scents of that first winter that remained with her above all else. The smoke of sweet-smelling brush fires wafting her way, the tinder-dry vegetation which had not tasted water in months combusting almost at will. Paraffin too, pungent but not unpleasant, burning constantly in the shacks on the far side of the railway line. From here also came the acrid scent of burning tires that accompanied the frequent clashes between police and populace. It was in the wake of these demonstrations that she first came to know the women traveling in from homelands and townships in search of a missing husband, son, or father. She helped them, in as much as it was possible, to retrieve the wages that were due to their men. Were they not alike now, she and them? Orphans, all of them, of the mines.

"You're not going to drink that baboon's piss, are you?"

It was at a braai, a company barbecue, that she first got to know Meyer. Fresh out of medical school, he was cutting his teeth in the mine's clinic. Taking her aside now, he introduced her to dagga, the local weed. After a few tokes Aideen pushed away the cider she had been sipping. This was to be the start, if not of a romance exactly, then of something more than just the mutual pursuit of pleasure. Aideen was happy, for now, to put her trust in the deep-brown eyes of this man she had barely said hello to before this. She wanted to be entertained, and Meyer knew how to do that. Through the canyons of his hometown they would drive, past endless blocks of deserted offices and apartments, in search of clubs and shebeens that were a world away from the horrors of the news reports. He was obviously smitten with her and, as spring approached, she found that she, almost in spite of herself, was reciprocating. Summer came, and the hoar frost that had lain on her heart since her father's death began to melt. A new year was dawning, and with it would come a new challenge.

On New Year's Day they lay in bed to escape the noonday heat. Too hot to do anything, or so she thought until she noticed Meyer watching a trickle of sweat cut through the gully of her breasts. The wet season, finally, had arrived.

"Eish, why don't we just stay in bed all day?" he asked, damming the stream with his little finger.

"We're meeting your parents later, or have you forgotten? Take a cold shower, and call them then. Tell them we'll see them in the restaurant around four."

"Will I book a cab too?"

"No, I'll drive. I won't be drinking."

"An early New Year's resolution?"

"Not exactly. But you're the doctor, you figure it out."

When he *did* figure it out he put his ear to her stomach, as if listening for signs of life.

"How long now?"

"Two months. You're not worried?"

"Why should I be?" he asked, kissing her belly.

"Because I'm scared shitless. But as you're down there, you might as well make yourself useful."

She pushed him further down on herself, but almost immediately he turned to face her again, grinning.

"Happy New Year to you both," he said, before lowering his head once more.

Some weeks into that new year, in the middle of the night, Aideen lost her child. She knew immediately, before Meyer had even driven her to the hospital. From that point on he hardly left her side until, as June came around again, he sensed a change in her. Then, as regular as the winds that blew up from the Cape, as permanent even as the re-imposition of emergency powers, she started to feel that familiar graveyard chill grip her heart once more. A chill that had been suspended, temporarily, by his love for her. Although she felt that she too might love him, she would not remain with him now. She would return again, barren, to the bleak places within herself, just as Persephone had bidden farewell to the land of the living.

June 2012. Nottinghamshire.
She was awoken by an otherworldly keening coming from the back of the house. Opening her eyes Aideen gazed down at her bedclothes, and at the orange mesh which shone on them. Her childhood bedroom, illuminated through the gaps in the window blind by the light of a streetlamp. Beside her on a chair lay her clothes. The bedroom was otherwise devoid of furniture, as the whole house was now, just a year after Nancy's death. After the funeral Rosie had asked her if she wanted to keep anything.

"Take it all," she had replied, knowing that Rosie could do with any help she could get.

Her little sister had a young family of her own now, with a mortgage in tow. What would Aideen have done, in any case, with the furniture? After twenty years working in what was euphemistically termed the extraction industry, following the money around the world? Tired of it all now, admittedly, but a girl has to make a living somehow. This was just a short trip home for her, a chance for Rosie and herself to tie up the loose ends before their parents' house went on the market. After that her next stop, incidentally, would be to the homeland of her birth father. Beneath the fourth green field of the borderlands lay methane galore, provided you didn't mind fracturing the bedrock to get at it. Which a lot of people *did* mind, as it happened. Aideen was hoping to have her wells dug and to be long gone before any fracking got underway.

"Dig a hole, and then fuck off. That's my motto," she explained to her sister. "Just like my Irish dad did, all those years ago."

Aideen threw on a T-shirt and headed down the stairs. Looking out on the back garden she saw that Nancy's flowerbeds, her pride and joy, were fast becoming a wilderness. Beyond them two foxes, the source of the wailing, were humping furiously. A bulging vixen eye, glistening in the moonlight, stared nervously back at her mate as his mangy tail decapitated the few remaining flowers. She stood watching them for a moment and then returned to bed.

In a far corner of the cemetery, away from Mike and Nancy's grave, their neighbor lay buried. Steve had remained strong up to the day that cancer was diagnosed, but declined rapidly thereafter and was dead within months. Grace had told Aideen all this on the morning of her mother's funeral, but she had decided against visiting Steve's grave.

"I thought you'd have wanted to pay your respects," Rosie had said to her afterwards. "He was your mentor, after all."

While Rosie played outside with her friends, he had prepared Aideen for her upcoming A-levels. As her mother was usually passed out on the sofa, they would go upstairs to her room. She was sixteen, in full bloom and proud of the attention her father's old friend was paying to her. As soon as she told him that she had missed her period he started making arrangements. He told Nancy that he was taking her daughter to see some universities down south.

"Your life is just beginning," he said to Aideen. "Don't throw it all away now."

She knew that he was thinking of his own future, but what choice did she have? He had been the bearer of bad news before, on the day that her father had died. She knew that sooner or later he would lead her to a darkness as deep as she had experienced that day. If not to the underworld exactly, then at least as far as London.

On the way home, they stopped off at a pub in King's Cross. A clear-blue London evening, restful and still in the early summer's light. Aideen had been discharged with a clean bill of health. Her judgment clouded, perhaps, and still in an anesthetic haze, she had disagreed. She knew now that she would never give birth. In the pub, the drinkers' chatter and the game on television merged for her into one dull background noise. Steve sat beside her, pint in hand, watching the game.

"What will we do now?" she asked him.

"What's that?"

As the doors opened and another punter entered the bar, the city outside briefly intruded on their conversation. Harsh noises, man-made, were borne in on the evening rays.

"What will we do now?" she repeated, more impatiently this time.

"Let's go," he said. "The game's over. Forest have won."

Finishing his drink, he rose to his feet. Smiling contentedly, he spoke softly to her.

"We're champions of Europe, Aideen. Again."

June 2013. Fermanagh.

Searching for the cave's wall Aideen swam, in complete darkness, toward the sound of water lapping against stone. Finally her hand brushed against a flat slimy surface, too smooth to gain a foothold on. She thought about swimming on, but the swift current and a creeping chill convinced her to turn back. She stripped quickly, shivering in the sunlight as dark water ran off her goosepimpled flesh. Drying herself with Charlie's fleece, she laughed quietly to herself.

"What?" he asked her, a little apprehensively.

"Nothing. Nothing at all. That was good, though."

Before they got into the car, Charlie spoke again.

"On to Belfast then?"

"I've got another suggestion."

"Oh God. What now?"

"I want to make some inquiries about my birth father."

"What do you know about him?"

"Only his name, and that he came from County Mayo or Roscommon. Were you ever in that part of the country?"

"I was, unfortunately. It's quiet there. Very quiet."

"Good. It'll make a change from all this G8 bollocks."

"Why don't you come back to Belfast with me? You could spend weeks searching for news of him, months even, with nothing to show for it."

"That's all right. I've got the time."

"What about your job?"

"Frack it, as they say around here. Will you come with me?"

"For a day or two, maybe. I still have a job, remember, and two kids to look after."

"Oops," she said, smiling faintly. "I'd completely forgotten about that."

"One more thing," Charlie said, as they got into the car. "Have you considered the possibility that he might be dead by now?"

"I have. And if he's not, I'll kill him myself, the bastard."

TRANSLATED FROM THE IRISH BY THE AUTHOR

[SWITZERLAND: FRENCH]

CÉLINE ZUFFEREY

Contortions

I WAS LATE. I'd run in vain through the long hallways alongside the crowded moving sidewalks: the metro had left, and on this line they ran fifteen minutes apart. During the summer, the air in the metro stations is stifling. To stay dry, you have to walk slowly and keep a bottle of water close at hand. It was late August, and I'd been running and had forgotten to buy water. Sweat was pouring down my back, plastering my T-shirt to my skin, which made me look thinner than usual.

The platform was deserted and silent. I was the only one there, sweaty and out of breath. "You must never forget that you're a dancer. Dance is what you are and what you must never stop being." That's what the Maestro used to say, it's one of the many sayings of his that you can see written on the walls of my school, in the hallways and classrooms. This one was printed in red. Seeing them, we were meant to internalize their message. We were supposed to discover the hidden meaning, we were expected to think about it later, when we were outside, at home, or waiting for the metro. That's what I was doing now, after a year in that school: the constant repetition and discipline were bearing fruit. Which was why, almost without noticing it, I was practicing my pointe technique there on the platform, wiping away the sweat that covered my forehead. It was becoming second nature: at the crosswalk waiting for the light to change, in a checkout line at the store, in front of the mirror brushing my teeth, it was imperative to practice, practice, and practice still more. "Talent alone is not enough; hard work is indispensable. Go beyond talent with work." That message was printed in blue.

"Your heel turns out too much, you have to hold it straighter."

147

At first I didn't react. I thought I was hearing a murmur in my head, one of the numerous remarks made by my professors. I often repeated them to myself. Sometimes I'd even imagine them uttered in the voice of the great Maestro in person. Supposing that he would take the time to correct me. But a cough followed the remark, and I understood that the murmur was coming from behind me. Looking around, I saw a man I hadn't noticed when I arrived, or rather a pile of rags sunk into the long, concave bench and propped against the wall at the far end. I dropped down on my heels and took a few steps toward him, but I stopped abruptly when I saw that he was a derelict, a panhandler. A beard, tangled hair that was dark and filthy, sunken eyes: that was about all I could make out through the heap of drab fabric covering him. I wondered why he wasn't suffocating from the heat. In front of him, the inevitable plastic cup, containing a few spare coins. I told myself he must be either drunk or high, that the best thing to do was to give him a bit of change and keep my distance. But when I leaned over his cup, I saw a foot emerge, wrapped in several layers of socks, and set itself on the tile floor perfectly *en pointe*.

"Like that, you see?"

I saw it well, even very well, but I was so stunned I was wholly incapable of telling him so.

"You do it like this."

He shifted his heel slightly to the right.

"You see how the line of the foot is broken? But, if you align your heel correctly, you'll be able to execute the other steps more easily."

Still seated, one foot on the floor, he was executing a series of basic steps *en pointe* with all the precision of my ballet teacher. Still silent, standing in front of him, I tried to replicate his movements, to arch my foot more.

"Yes, like that, that's better already." He coughed. "You just have to practice more, go beyond talent with work."

"Hey! That's what the Maestro says."

He started and, letting out a long and sonorous *shhh*, he drew his foot back under his body and cowered under the coverings; I no longer saw anything but the top of his head. A tramp who knows how to execute his pointe technique, but a tramp nonetheless, with all the madness and nonsense that go along with it. But even so, he was doing the steps perfectly and quoting the Maestro. Instead of moving away, I couldn't help asking:

"Are you a dancer?"

The question echoed in the empty space, underlining the absurdity of asking a beggar if he could be anything other than a beggar. He shook his head wildly, gasping for breath between chesty coughs and clutching the covers with his grimy hands.

"But then how could you do that? And those movements? You must have been in a dance academy."

"No, noo, *shhh.*"

I should have left then, cast him a parting glance, shrugged, and walked away. Several minutes later the metro would have arrived, my boss's reproaches would have quickly put this encounter out of my mind, and it would have come back to me only now and then, over a drink among friends: "One day I met a derelict whose pointe technique was superb, yes, I swear to you!" But instead, for some unknown reason, I persisted.

"You're a dancer, there's no doubt about it. And a good one. Ah, I know! You're working on some choreography, is that it? About street people. With which choreographer? Are you part of a troupe?"

"Noo noo noo noo." His droning was like a song, like an undertone.

"Can you help me? I'm having difficulties with this step, do you see? When I do this, I . . ."

Suddenly, he threw off his coverings, scattering them around us, and revealed a stump where his right leg should have been.

"You think I can be a dancer with this?!"

His shout made me recoil in surprise, a little frightened and more incredulous than before. He started mumbling things I couldn't understand, visibly enraged. Still seated, with his good leg folded under him, the other dangling barely below the bench, he was trying to gather up the rags strewn on the ground. Speechless, I leaned over and offered him one of them, which he tore violently from my hands, before stopping mid-gesture, his eyes downcast, his gaze suddenly filled with immense despair. He sighed, pinched his lips together, and shook his head.

"I *was* a dancer!"

———

I made no reply, and he surely wasn't expecting one anyway. He covered his stump with the pile of tattered fabric.

"I had talent, so much talent. It was a gift, I was made for it. Made for it and everyone saw it, yes, everyone saw it."

I felt stupid standing in front of him, too tall beside a man who was holding his head in his hands, so I sat down next to him. He didn't seem to notice, his palms were over his eyes, and he was rubbing them and pressing on them as if to shove them back into their sockets.

"There were some jealous ones, you bet there were. Fernando with his ferret's eyes, his goddamn ferret's eyes. He'd have been happy if I'd croaked—haha! Incapable of executing a spin. Pathetic. Meanwhile, I was working, I never stopped working. It was never enough. I had installed a ballet bar in my studio, an old bar. The school used to close at eleven p.m., but I needed more practice. I had splinters in my palms. The varnish, the varnish was peeling so much, they were going to throw the bar away. I found it in the street, behind the school, where it was waiting to be picked up by the trash collectors. I should have sanded it. They didn't understand what I was trying to do, I had to go beyond, beyond, but no one understood, no one knew, and there . . . No one knew, except . . ."

He suddenly sat up straight and looked around frantically, to the right, to the left. He was a skinny man, skinnier even than I was, skeletal, unhealthy. His head shook with tremors, and I was sure he wasn't even aware of them. He began to gnaw at a fingernail that was already cut very short, his hand masking half his face.

"I miss the splinters. He had only smooth and harmless bars, a waxed, gleaming floor, a practice room set aside for me, just me. There were students who would have given anything for that, to be in my place. As for me, I was ready to lose everything. That's what it was—that, it was that. He recognized it, I'm sure of it now, he had seen it, that was the reason: more than talent . . . something else was called for . . ."

Now that he'd begun to talk, the flow of words was unstoppable, always somewhere between muttering and shouting, as if he were going to burst, as if the yelling were caught just at the surface, without ever being able to emerge freely. I wondered if he wasn't delirious, I was almost sure he'd lost his mind, but the metro wasn't there, I had no excuse for leaving. I didn't dare budge, and though flustered by the people who'd arrived on the platform, I kept listening.

"It was a winter day, a day in February. It was cold, I felt chilled, everyone was keyed up. We'd been looking forward to this day ever since it had been announced: he was coming to visit our school, he was coming to observe some classes. We would see him, and above all he would see us, he would perhaps observe several of us, a few rare privileged ones would receive some comment from him, they would repeat it to everyone, distort it, embellish it, and in all the bars of the city, they'd boast of having received a few words of advice from the great Maestro. I didn't go to bars, not at all. Who has time to spend in bars when dance practice is all-consuming? It takes effort, you have to go farther, nothing will ever be enough—beyond, you must go beyond. At night I had to practice, late, late into the night, with the splinters and the different tempos, leaping higher, stretching farther, farther . . . farther from him. I have to . . . leave."

But he didn't stir, he didn't budge, he went on staring into his plastic cup, which held, at the bottom, a few yellowish coins.

"He came into the class, I knew he'd be coming, that was what had to happen. I wasn't surprised, I didn't lose my nerve like all the other idiots. His blue eyes seemed to pierce everything but never stayed fixed on anything. I danced. I looked him right in the eyes, and he saw me. He saw me and he knew. From the beginning, the beginning. He applauded. Three times. Three sharp claps of his too-delicate hands with their too-slender fingers. He applauded me, looking at me. He applauded me. And the ensuing murmurs, and the envious, hateful glances, everywhere, the reflections in the mirrors and him, and his eyes, and I, silently pleading, hoping so fervently, finally, that someone would understand, and if he didn't understand, if he didn't see, then no one . . . no one. But he did see. And somewhere he was expecting, he was expecting me, my aspirations and my devotion, me and my hands full of splinters.

"And then everything went very fast. It was what I'd anticipated, it was the logical unfolding of events, like a gliding step, like a predestined future, like . . .

"He moved me into his house, opened his practice room to me, observed me at length, corrected me very often, over and over, and I was always eager for more. I had to go farther, there was something to go after, something that didn't exist yet because no one had even dreamed of it. I sensed it, and he did too, he knew it. I couldn't make out its dimensions, but I knew there was a veil, and there was some-thing behind the veil, and I had to struggle, to go beyond everything and earn the right to lift the veil, to pass through it. Very soon, he barred me from going out, I was already going out very little. He put me on a diet, I was already thin. He made me work more, already I was hardly sleeping at all. I was so afraid of disappointing him, so fear-ful that he'd no longer see anything when he looked at me, he'd let me go, he'd abandon me, that I would fail. Aside from correcting me, he was barely speaking. We weren't there to talk, we weren't there to get acquainted. We knew each other already."

His hand brushed the bench where his right calf should have been. Little by little his fingers climbed toward his truncated thigh.

"And then one evening when we were beginning to realize we were approaching a dead end, when I reached the last extremity, the limit of despair, my feet bloody, my muscles spent, my skin on fire, the Maestro presented the solution. That was what I was expecting from him, I knew he would. Not the practice room, not the advice, not the train-ing. He had to bring me something more. It was he who had to lead me beyond. He asked me if I was truly ready for anything, but he hadn't expected me to speak, he knew the answer, he had seen it. Long before, in that classroom, he had seen it. So he said to me, 'We're going to cut off your leg.' That's what had been missing, the decisive answer, the way out. The step, moreover, toward the veil, behind the veil, at long last, dance brought to the next level. Yes, obviously yes. Which leg? The right, that was clear, that was the one that had to go, that was the loss that would let me reach, let us reach, let everyone reach the revelation, the stage behind the veil."

Filled with terror, I gazed wide-eyed at him, his hand resting on his stump, his head nodding, his head endlessly nodding.

"So, we did it. A privately engaged surgeon, no questions asked, a quick operation, a thin scar. And then months of rehab, a specialized center, sequestered, isolated, and then he, present as always, and then his eyes, which were looking at me differently, looking at me more approvingly, looking at me, I was sure, like they'd never looked at anyone before. I was the very incarnation of the evolution of art. The metamorphosis, the mutation. Was the world ready for that? Was the world advanced enough to understand it? I was barely sleeping, I had become muscles, rhythm, and dance. I was getting there, it was simple now, I was almost there, so close. And I touched the goal at last, a moment of grace, a white veil, and then nothing more, nothing but movement, pure movement, different, perfect, unique. So I danced, over and over, just for him, the two of us alone in the practice room, my leg and him, the music had become superfluous, everything was there, perfection needed nothing else."

The man was becoming more animated, talking faster and faster, trying to get up, yet still seated, agitated by a movement that was shaking his entire body.

"And he was filming everything. Cameras everywhere. To capture every angle, and above all, not to miss anything. 'People will spend years watching you,' he'd tell me. 'They'll spend years breaking down your movements and trying to understand, to understand the quintessence of dance.' The video recordings were piling up, accumulating more and more, I never had enough, I didn't imagine that one day it could stop, that I could simply stop and never dance again. Why do that? Why do that now that I finally know how to move?"

He looked at his half leg, panicked.

"One day he turned off the cameras and told me to take a break. A break. That was the first time I heard those words from his desiccated lips. I protested, he left the room. I continued to dance, he did not return. I finished by collapsing in the middle of the floor, no longer sustained by his two blue eyes."

He stopped talking. For a very long time, he said nothing more. People were walking by us. Plenty of other people must have passed without my noticing them, so hypnotized was I by his story; plenty of other metros must have escaped my attention while I was slipping with him into the reality and horror of his story. Eventually, he resumed in a dull, lifeless voice:

"It was the sound of his footsteps that awakened me, resonating in the empty hall. Only one neon light was still on, but I could see the large knife shining in his hand. He approached me, murmuring to me that we were almost there, murmuring to me that this was the last stage, I had to understand, he was sure I understood. His eyes were shining, shining even more brightly than when he used to watch me dancing on my one leg, than when he was filming my first time *en pointe* as an amputee. He told me I must die, that perfection is not something living, art is only an abstraction, an absent Beauty, and he could not let me live. He told me I must have suspected as much, I had always known it deep down, and that it was up to him to say it out loud, up to him to carry it out. Coming very close, he said in a low voice that I shouldn't worry, everything had been filmed, everything would be preserved, he had made multiple copies. He told me I would exist forever, but for that to happen, it was essential for me to die. He told me I was born for this."

His eyes closed, he was breathing deeply, steadily.

"But I couldn't go through with it. I was afraid. I was afraid, and I wanted to continue, to continue dancing, no one could take that away from me, and I wasn't sure of being able to dance any more after the blade had opened my throat. So while he stood behind me, one arm holding up my head, I thrust myself backward and toppled him over. He was old and feverish, he didn't react fast enough, his breathing had been impaired by the shock of falling, and I snatched the knife from him. Looming over him, I held the knife close to his eyes, extremely close. I was afraid, I didn't know what to do. I had to leave, he had to let me go, but I knew he'd never let me go, I was his creation, I was the means by which he would inscribe his name in the annals of art, I was his glory and his ultimate contribution to the world. But I couldn't, I had his knife, I had his fate in my hands. I scratched his eyelid, a little blood flowed. I dropped the knife and fled, I took my crutches and I scuttled off. Far, far from the practice room, far from my school, still farther, as far as possible. Night came very quickly, and very quickly I was hungry, very quickly I realized I had no money, that I could no longer have any. There was no longer anything but the street, with its corners never obscure enough to hide me from him. Because I knew he was looking for me, I knew he would never stop looking for me, ever. I was the last stage. The last stage before the Sublime."

For the first time, he turned his face toward me, a face deformed by strain, and he looked at me with eyes transformed by horror and dread.

"He'll find me, I know he'll find me. Even if it takes years, he won't stop looking for me. And I know, I know that very soon I won't have the strength to hide myself, that very soon I'll no longer have the will to flee."

His eyes no longer looked at me, they were somewhere beyond, they were imagining something or remembering something else. I didn't know what to do anymore. I looked at him, him and his nearly empty cup, him and his coverings, him and his lopped-off leg, and I heard the metro pulling in, and I saw it stop. I got up and stepped on board.

TRANSLATED FROM THE FRENCH BY PAUL CURTIS DAW

GEORGES HAUSEMER

The Fox in the Elevator

ON A FOGGY March morning, the fox made his way across the parking lot. It was bitterly cold. Crouched low to the ground, he slipped through the rows of parked cars. The windshields were covered with a gray layer of fine, Styrofoam-like snow. A sharp wind was blowing. The top of the old water tower, encased in wooden planks, had disappeared into the clouds. There were no reflections in the dull, frozen puddles. For a short stretch, the fox used the footpath meant for employees, patients, and visitors. Patches of asphalt lined with leftover snow. What had once been innocent, pristine white was now dirtied by the passage of time, peppered with tiny, dark flecks.

The fox barely left a trail.

Up above, at a window on the fifth floor, stood the man with the bandage behind his right ear. Squinting, he peered out into the snow. Behind him, the patient with the incessant cough was already passing by, strapped tightly into his transport chair. The attendant pushing him down the hall had a ring in his nose and tattoos winding around his neck. Next to the lapel of the attendant's hospital coat hung a nametag with the name Pawel on it.

The man with the bandage watched as the fox approached the stairs at the front of the main building. He wondered how it could be that not a soul was in sight. There was nobody who could put a stop to this, who could trap the wild animal before it got any farther. Instead, the pierced, tattooed attendant passed by again, now free of the transport chair and the patient who'd been in it. He was heading for the room across from the elevators, the room with the ISOLATION sign out front. A set of instructions below the sign directed visitors to notify hospital personnel before entering.

Occasionally, cries for assistance emanated from behind the door: "Nurse! Nurse!" Someone had likely forgotten to help him put on his socks before leaving for the night.

The man at the window wondered whether he should have spoken to Pawel. And what the actual difference was between a transport chair and a wheelchair anyway.

Before him, like an unexpected gift, lay the town square. The local bank, an Italian restaurant, a newspaper kiosk, and a flower shop. An ambulance pulled up in front of the building next door. Its lights were flashing, but the whine of the siren was absent. Total silence. Even the town square seemed momentarily frozen. The only perceptible movement was coming from the lift ramp at the back of the ambulance. The speed of its automated rising and falling made for a ridiculous spectacle—like something you'd find in hidden-camera footage. The cries for help were still coming from behind the door. On some evenings, a muffled beeping could be heard flitting down the long hall. An alarm clock, perhaps, that nobody felt responsible for.

Eventually, the ambulance lights went out and the man briefly turned his gaze away from the window. When he looked back out, the fox had vanished. At first, the man was startled. He scanned the snowy landscape below with a furrowed brow. There was a hedge of bushes near the water tower. Flour, milk, or powdered sugar? No movement. Until a box truck appeared, driving toward the hospital from the square. It had bright lettering on its side. In an effort to make out what it said, the man bent forward until his forehead was resting against the windowpane. When he straightened up again, there was a greasy patch where his forehead had been. He tried to wipe it away with the sleeve of his jacket, but that just made it bigger, and uglier. And it certainly didn't help him see any better—quite the opposite in fact. By now, the fox, provided he hadn't gotten scared and run off, could easily have made it to the door unseen. As for the door itself, the new motion-sensor system meant that it opened even without the touch of a human hand, its glass panel sliding back and forth as if operated by a ghost. All it needed was for someone to be approaching. As long as someone was approaching.

The man turned around and went back to his room. He regretted that he hadn't thought to bring his radio along. Or fresh underwear, for that matter, or his toothpicks, or the wax earplugs he almost never left the house without. For a while, he forgot about the fox.

It was a long wait for breakfast. But finally it came, and after he had made his way through two rolls topped with sliced cheese, a croissant with currant jam (and far too many seeds), pineapple yogurt, a glass of orange juice, and two cups of coffee, he spent a while rummaging through the old newspapers the attendant had brought him. The same attendant who took his temperature and blood pressure every morning and who served him his meals. Impatiently, he searched for articles he hadn't read yet, finally coming upon a story about the diseases afflicting bordello patrons and members of swinger clubs. His feeling upon finishing it was, honestly, that he'd expected better. He took an absent-minded sip from the water glass that had been sitting, neglected, on his nightstand. The nightstand had plenty of room for that old radio he kept on the kitchen shelf at home.

Suddenly, the man with the bandage remembered the fox. Ever since the day he'd arrived, he'd been surprised by the lack of activity in this hospital, especially compared to the other hospitals he'd been forced to visit in the past. Unwanted intruders would have no problem avoiding detection here. Often, several minutes would elapse before somebody passed by his half-open door—and this wasn't just at night-time, but during the day as well. Sometimes he would get up and stand insistently at the entrance to his room, just to see what happened. But nothing happened. At most there was the ringing of a telephone in the distance. One time, he watched a heavyset man in pajamas shuffling across the linoleum floor, his beer gut wobbling back and forth with every step. An oxygen tube had been inserted into his nose, and the man was dragging the tank, strapped to a carrier with wheels, behind him, like a stubborn dog. The man whose socks they always forgot to put on started screaming for the nurse again, rattling the rails on his bed. But Pawel was nowhere to be found.

When the man with the wound behind his ear had come to, on the night before he was admitted, he had been lying on his kitchen floor, his left shoulder propped up against the refrigerator. The other man had been standing over him, holding the bottle they'd finished earlier that evening.

It had to be more than just curiosity. Soon, the man with the bandage was standing in the hallway again. But instead of a wild animal, he saw one of the nurses approaching. The one with the big brown birthmark on her left cheek. She gave him a wordless smile. The man with the bandage reciprocated, matching the sparseness of her greeting with a subtle smile of his own.

To his left was the metal staircase that led to the lobby, four floors below. The hollow booming of shoes in the stairwell reminded the man—after he had eaten his fill of beef goulash, cabbage, and corkscrew pasta for lunch—of a stomach rumbling with hunger.

There was also an elevator—one so big that an entire bed could fit inside. And even then, there would still be room for multiple Pawels, plus a few assistants, a cleaning cart, and some IV poles. Anyone who stepped off the elevator on this floor was immediately confronted by the ISOLATION sign on the door directly opposite. The unlucky ones were also accosted by the cries of the patient within—"Help! Nurse! Help!"

Why doesn't anyone ever do anything about him? the man who'd left his radio at home thought to himself. But can somebody who makes so much noise really be that sick?

But he'd never read or heard anything about a fox being able to use an elevator.

The bleeding and the bruise behind his right ear were now almost healed. But in the meantime, they'd noticed something else and ordered X-rays of his head and upper body. Abnormalities lateral to the trachea. They had to get to the bottom of it, and while they were at it, check to make sure that the skull and the brain were still fully intact. Which meant he had to stay. Further analysis required. Which also meant more spiced cucumbers and tandoori chicken, more soft cheese and Oberländer Hell.

He had even forgotten his phone at home. And now he could have really used it. Now or a bit later, when the fox actually made it up to the fifth floor. He'd taken up his post in the doorway and was now just waiting. He'd had a lot of experience with waiting. He was good at it. He was good at being alone, too. And for the most part he enjoyed it. He even enjoyed waiting. But without a phone? But who ever thinks to bring a camera along to the hospital?

Thankfully, he hadn't had to wait long for a single room to open up.

Around noon, the fog began to lift. He took his time with his meal—*Zigeunerschnitzel*, mixed salad, roasted potatoes, and ambrosia for dessert. The only beverages available were water, tea, and coffee. "In that case, nothing," he replied to the nurse with the brown patch on her cheek. She nodded. She was wearing a blue-and-white striped T-shirt under her white hospital coat. Like sailors used to wear, the man thought to himself. Which was probably not true. Hadn't he recently seen photographs of sailors wearing little more than tattered rags? And why didn't she have a nametag?

After he had finished eating, he made his way back to the window at the end of the long hallway, where there was also a lounge, which both patients and visitors were encouraged to use. A small, wobbly table and three armchairs that nobody would miss if they ended up in the garbage heap one day. So far he had yet to see anyone take the room up on its offer of peace and restorative comfort.

The grease stain from his forehead was still there. A fat retired couple was walking across the town square below, laden down with shopping bags. A car turned into the parking lot in front of the bank. As the driver got out, a lone, harsh ray of sunlight fell at her feet. A split second later, it had disappeared. The woman, holding a child in her arm, probably hadn't even noticed it. The child was certainly big enough to walk on its own, the man thought to himself from behind the window. It was then that he realized his vision had become much clearer over the past few days, even without his glasses, which had fallen victim to the wine bottle the night before he was admitted. They'd simply shattered, without a sound. He'd almost laughed about it. But then the pain had come, and everything had begun to flicker and tremble before his eyes. And then things had gone dark.

Which made it all the more amazing how much his sight had sharpened since he'd been here. The parking lot, the water tower—even the fog-shrouded top—the passersby, the fox, who had looked a bit shy: was it a miracle? The man made a mental note to ask one of the doctors the next chance he had. Or at least the nurse with the mariner's shirt. To make sure he wouldn't miss her, he went back to his room—the one with the numbers 3 and 2 on the door—and lay down on his bed. By force of habit, he reached for the remote and pressed the big, red button at the top. This remote was tiny, and unusually thin. Even more unusual was the fact that it didn't have any numbered buttons on it. All it had was a +/− button for the volume and another similar one to change the channel. Flipping through the paltry selection of programs available to him, he came upon a story about a group of gold hunters who had managed to extract three million dollars worth of precious metal from the Alaskan permafrost. ". . . but Parker was so fixated on his goal that even the most experienced members of his team quickly became exhausted," a sonorous male voice reported.

Wasn't the young attendant named Pawel? At any rate, he got on well with the maritime nurse. When the small cuts on the back of his neck and on his throat hadn't stopped oozing after three days, she changed his bandage for one with a thick layer of marigold ointment on its underside. "This should noticeably speed up the healing process," she assured him. She could not help but smirk at the dry formality of her words.

"Especially during the night," she added quickly.

"Even if I can't sleep?" the man asked.

He suspected that the nurse had her fun with other patients as well. When she'd left, he resumed his post in the hallway. All quiet, even the crybaby in his isolation bed. He squatted on his heels and blinked serenely. The pressure next to his trachea was becoming more and more noticeable. But he ignored it, just like he ignored the phlegm that had started coming up his throat and onto his tongue when he coughed. It was just a matter of time, anyway, until the tip of that bushy tail would slip into the elevator, just fast enough to avoid being caught in the door. Oh yes, that sly devil would manage it eventually. If not up the stairs, then certainly in the elevator. And without a sound, thanks to his soft paws, supple pads, and underdeveloped claws, which resembled those of a dog. The ravenous beast wouldn't make so much as a peep— he'd simply wait until the number 5 lit up on the panel. And he'd certainly know what to do with all the food.

TRANSLATED FROM THE GERMAN BY JEFFREY D. CASTLE

ANDREJ HOČEVAR

Another Happy New Year

WHEN THE GLASSES were once again clinking over the table, the drink was splashing out of them, and the hands were like rays shining from them, Maja and I grabbed our things and fled, wordlessly. We put our coats on and pushed our way through the throng. We were in a hurry to get out, to the surface. Once outside, we quickened our pace and didn't stop until we made it to the square about a hundred meters away, near the town center, where the taxis usually waited. I spun toward her. "What was that?" I said. "What?" she said. "I don't know," I said. We stood motionless for a few moments, staring into each other's eyes, then fell into an embrace. "Everything all right?" I said. "Yes," said Maja. "But, really, what was that?" she said, and we broke into embarrassed hiccups of laughter.

"What was actually going on in that other room? Did something happen?" I asked once we were on the move again. "It was just another room, a smaller dance floor. I'm not exactly sure," said Maja. "It started off fine, we talked a bit with those Serbs, even danced, then some woman appeared, a total buzzkill. Right in front of everybody she started going on about her tragedy, with some violent husband who kept on abusing her. She and her daughter had to make a run for it. They came here and eventually she found a new husband. Look at this one, she said, he's only violent toward others. A total softy with her. If the new guy ever ran into her ex—she hasn't seen him for years, doesn't even know where he is now—he'd kill him on the spot. Whatever. Anyway, she was drunk and rubbing up against every guy there. But she wasn't from our group, she was some Macedonian, Vasilija or something. Doesn't matter . . ." said Maja.

"Vasa!" I whispered to myself. "Oh, yeah, by the way, I forgot to tell you something. I've had enough of this. Next year we're celebrating in Germany. I got an artist-in-residency," I said, as we got in the cab.

We had a few agonizing weeks behind us, especially this last one. December had, as usual, dragged on and on as I tried to ready myself for family gatherings and heed Maja's demands that I behave more festively. She was running around the apartment, bitching to herself about the mess, and planning away—where best to put the tree, when to have the parents over for a meal, the menu—and I, meanwhile, was doing my best to ignore her. I was acting like someone who doesn't want to divulge it's his birthday because it's the middle of the week and his co-workers either don't know or have all forgotten about it. In such cases it's better if they simply don't know. Two years ago Maja and I had told each other in no uncertain terms what we were thinking: the more she insisted on the importance of holidays and rituals, the more I closed myself off into a sad, amoral place and tried, passively, to push her as far away as possible.

And so our Christmases had the air of an unexpected compromise: the first chance she could (over the first glass of wine), Maja would admit that this whole Christmastime circus really was a bit too much and that she was willing to make do with less of the clutter if only we might fight a bit less and if only I showed at least a little understanding, while I, in the end, was always at least somewhat softened up by her efforts—something that was hard for me to confess even over the second glass of wine. This year had been particularly tense. Adapting to life with a baby meant we were always exhausted and the apartment was even messier than usual. The slightest of slights and we'd explode. It would be hard to identify the low point: the paltry Christmas tree looked more like a plaything than a real tree, never again would we invite both families over at the same time, we both fell asleep before ten on New Year's Eve. "Why are we even together?" said Maja at some point. "Call it stubbornness," I said, with a forced smile, even as it occurred to me that I'd, again, gone too far. "Stubbornness," I said, "is mightier than any random day on the calendar or couple of weeks off."

By the first few days of January, we were both in a somewhat better mood, glad to have survived December. In fact we were both relieved. And that's why I suggested we have the neighbor over to watch the kid so we could go out for a drink. "Like we used to, remember? When we were two young people," I said. Once the kid was asleep and the babysitter was comfortably ensconced on the couch, we, to underline our effort and ambition, dressed up almost like it was New Year's and left in a hurry. "We won't be long," said Maja, closing the door on the way out.

Everything was looking pretty dead in and around our bar of choice, so we strolled through the town a while, to ward off the bad mood that sitting, by ourselves, in an empty bar would immediately put us in. When we returned an hour later, people in parkas were hanging around in the street and there was music spilling out of the bar. Through the ground-floor window we could see the DJ dancing around as he mixed. Maja wanted to turn back, but I, out of obstinacy, swung open the door in a highly determined manner and went in. The place was packed. We walked alongside the bar and in between the tables. There were beautiful young people dressed in carefully selected but not necessarily festive attire, probably straight from work—no families—sipping their craft beers. I gestured toward the two squished-together tables in the corner where a woman in a tight dress was sitting. The benches around her were empty. "Mind if we sit down?" I said. Without waiting for an answer, I yanked Maja behind me onto the bench. The woman mumbled something incomprehensible or inconclusive and a few moments later explained that she was waiting for some people, but for the moment it wasn't a problem. She devoted herself to her phone; I went to the bar for some drinks. By the time I got back, the bench was also occupied by a few men who paid us no attention. Still, Maja had nudged herself along to the edge and was staring stiffly ahead. I sat down and set myself to pretending I was having fun.

We drank slowly, without any real pleasure, while our table grew more and more crowded. By the time we'd finished our first drink, we were crammed in tightly and the tables were crowded with drinks. We couldn't hear each other for the noise. Somebody noticed that our glasses were empty and asked loudly if we wanted another round. He yanked a bottle from somewhere and nodded at us, a huge smile on his face. "Want some Serbian *rakia*?" While Maja and I were gawking at each other, the guy was already calling out for two more glasses, and the next instant there they were, filled to the brim, in front of us. I shrugged my shoulders and toasted the strangers.

"You two are probably friends of Zvezdan's, no?" a woman asked us under the raised masculine arms, and smiled. "Zvezdan? Who's that? Actually, we're here just by chance. There was no room anywhere else," I said, and returned the smile. While I was explaining, the guy who'd been pouring the drinks listened in, cheerfully bellowing, "No harm done, today we're all friends and there's drink enough for all." Maja gently inquired whether it happened to be the drink-guy's birthday. "Mića? No, no. Today we're celebrating New Year's. Orthodox New Year's!" said the smiling woman. Then she got up, hollered something into the air and, along with the others, raised her glass high. I looked at Maja, eyebrows raised. She gave me a wide smile. "We've been given a second chance! Happy New Year!" she said. I kissed her on the lips, then we hugged and raised our glasses. Our hoots blended with the screaming that surrounded us.

Soon we were chatting away with at least half the table. We drank fast and paid no attention to what we were ordering or where the drinks were coming from. Eventually a few of us went out to get some air. A few more disappeared into a second room that was half hidden behind a narrow entrance where, as I found out later, there was also a little dance floor. That's where Maja disappeared to. Out of the corner of my eye I caught a glimpse of an accidentally exposed thigh, belonging to one of the women in the too-tight dresses Maja had been talking to. A moment later, the women were gone. I stretched out my arms and laid them on the backrest of the bench. With closed eyes, I tried to imagine the point at which the difference between silence and noise vanishes.

"You and your wife are a beautiful couple," someone said, quietly. I opened my eyes, slowly. Staring at me was a dark-haired guy I hadn't noticed before. He was sitting opposite me, down at the other end of the table. "You're married, right?" he said.

It took me a moment to come around. I studied him a little more carefully. He had a thick beard and a soft but penetrating gaze that somehow made me feel strangely and suddenly sober. He was looking right at me and evidently waiting for an answer.

"Yes," I said, "married. Three years. You?"

"Divorced," he said and kept right on staring at me.

"Um . . ." I mumbled and began looking round the room.

"I hope you know how to appreciate what you have. The years I spent with my wife were the best years of my life," he said. It was like he wasn't staring at me but through me, into the wall, into another place, another time.

"It's true, I do have a great wife. But I know I'm not always the best of husbands. Ever since the kid came along, our relationship has been put to the test," I said, theatrically reaching for my glass and emptying it in one go. I found another more or less full glass and drained it too.

The guy just sat there for a while, calm. Then he said I was right, and knocked back a shot of his own. We filled our glasses.

"What do you have? A son or a daughter?" he eventually asked.

"A son," I said.

"Congratulations!" he said.

I raised my glass to interrupt him, but this time he didn't follow my lead.

"Today it's almost nothing but Serbs, but I don't know most of them either. Now I live here, outside of Ljubljana. I'm building a house in the Karst region," he said.

I was starting to think of how I might interrupt him and when the others would get back.

"My wife, Vasa," he continued, "was Macedonian. I loved her immensely. My parents were against us, but, you know, love is stubborn."

Surprised at his choice of words, I looked up. He talked on. There was no stopping the guy. "In spite of everything we got married and a year later we had a kid. I wanted a son, but, still, it was the most beautiful moment of my life. I just adored that daughter. You know what I mean, you have a wife and kid, you know what it means. Young people today don't get married anymore."

I was starting to miss the crowd, wanted to be part of a group again, to be able to talk to everyone and no one. There's no room for anxiety when you're crammed in tight. The bunch of us were mere strangers using a shared pretext to celebrate. Nothing of substance.

"But those were tough times. There was no work, you know," continued the guy, who wouldn't be stopped. "A lot of guys I knew went abroad. A few years later I decided to go too. But when you have no papers it's tough to find work . . . You know why the Germans are so successful? Because of us southerners. In Germany I did all sorts of work, under the table, mostly construction, helping out in warehouses, stuff like that. For months I lived in a container next to the construction site. Every night me and the other illegal workers heated up tins of goulash like we were truckers, on the road. And when you come down to it, we really were living like truckers. Like refugees. Homeless people. Maybe you can't imagine it, but even homeless people have their territory, an area they guard with their lives. Well, that's how illegal workers guard their jobs. If two guys start fighting, everyone else turns away, I know how it is, I know it all too well! There's some sort of unspoken agreement. Let those illegals kill each other, who cares. If you have no papers, you're a dog. And when they have to, dogs will gnaw each other to death. It's a tense situation, sooner or later someone's going to pull a knife and . . .

"In spite of everything, I sent my wife an envelope each and every month. I slaved, you get it? I earned more money up in Germany than two families make down there, almost nothing left over for me. But no harm done. You know what gave me strength? My daughter. Thinking of my daughter. That was the only thing that kept me alive. Alive, you get it? Up there nobody cares if you have a family depending on you down south. That you're walking around in overalls so your wife can buy herself a new dress. That sometimes you have nothing but a cigarette for dinner so your daughter can have a watermelon.

"But, OK, the past is the past. No? We all have some sort of stain on our conscience, under the skin we're all blood. Back then, in the containers . . . It wasn't easy, it really wasn't. Everyone has to deal with his own problems and let strangers be. No point mixing yourself up in things that don't concern you . . . Family's sacred . . . Well, like I'm saying, the past is the past, you can't change anything, even if you'd like to. That's why I'm here in Slovenia, building a house, no permit of course. Where are you going to get a permit? There's no work here anyway. The difference, though, is that I'm no longer mailing my money away, you get it? Whenever I can, I put a little to the side. I don't know, maybe for my pension or something, since I have nobody, nobody. Let me tell you something: I'm never ever again going to send my wife and daughter money.

"Long story short, when I came back after two years she told me she couldn't anymore. I asked her what it was she 'couldn't anymore.' Was there someone else? She didn't answer. I asked her what she was doing with the money I sent her. She started to cry. She went on about how hard it was, alone with the child. I asked her what more did she need. She lived in a house, had a full fridge, and a daughter with clean clothes. What more did she need, dammit? She was standing in the middle of the kitchen, in a long black dress, with arms crossed, tears running down her cheeks. I could have hit her. I wanted to kill her, you get it? But I held back and just sat myself down, calm. I've taught myself that you have to keep your cool. Be cold-blooded. I told her to just disappear, that I didn't want to see her ever again. That same day she really did disappear. And she took my daughter with her.

"The next day I decided that I'd disappear too. Nothing was holding me there, I didn't have anything. At first I wanted to burn down the house, but I changed my mind. Let her have it, if she wants it. By now she's probably long since moved away and left the country. There you have it. And I've stayed here. Alone. Thinking of my daughter used to be my salvation, now it's torture. But I can't stop thinking of her. I don't know her, I don't know what she's become. That's what I blame my wife for most of all, you know? So she's got some other guy? That's bad, but it doesn't matter. But she took away my daughter. She took away everything I had. That's why I could kill her. Kill. That's also why I had to flee, because I knew that if I ever ran into her again I really would kill her. Love is stubborn. It's capable of anything. If love can overcome the sorts of obstacles it did when we were first together, then love can kill, too."

When he stopped talking, he raised his head, almost imperceptibly, and kept staring at me with those eyes whose softness now frightened me, as much as his seeming calm. All this time, he hadn't moved in the slightest.

I understood that this time he wasn't expecting any response from me.

I could imagine the guy back in that kitchen, sitting in the same position as now, cold-blooded, besieging his wife with that voice that was all the more dangerous because it seemed so controlled. By the time you realize you're having trouble breathing, that his voice has wrapped around you like a snake, it's already too late. I saw him suddenly jumping up from the table and, wordlessly, strangling his unfaithful wife, his eyes all the while radiating immaculate love.

Then the other members of the group began to return to our tables.

Right away we were all crammed in again and the glasses were once again in the air, once again full. The guy looked me in the eye, motionlessly, for a few more moments, as if there were no noise and nobody around him. I was paralyzed. The only thing I felt was something trembling inside me. Then he smiled and turned away. Somebody gave him a glass and the very next moment it was already in the air, united with the others.

TRANSLATED FROM THE SLOVENIAN BY JASON BLAKE

CHRISTOS IKONOMOU

Salto Mortale

THE ITALIANS ARE always the first to arrive. It's a mystery, how they always manage to snag the best seats, under the mulberry tree whose green leaves are as big as elephant ears. Iasonas thinks they're a couple, but to me they seem more like father and daughter—the woman has to be at least thirty years younger. Though there's no family resemblance, in fact they're like night and day: the old guy is short and stout like an owl, while she's got legs that go on for miles. Her legs are as long as he is tall, and her body tight and sun-browned, with merciless curves, shiny black hair, cat eyes, and a smile like a dagger.

Her name is Laura, but that's not what we call her. Whenever we see her coming, we stand at attention, glue a fist to our chests, and say, "Hail, Hottie, we who are awaiting execution salute you." She doesn't speak a lick of Greek, of course. She must think we're hitting on her, but who cares, she's earned it.

Then there's the Chief, who's had her in his sights since day one. And now, catching sight of her coming over all crackling and crisp, arm in arm with the little owl, smiling like ten Cheshire cats all in a row, he goes and stands at the very edge of the roof in front of the crumbling parapet and struts his stuff, hair blowing in the wind like a salt-and-pepper flag as he pretends to stare off toward the horizon, beyond the ruins of the tower, beyond the vineyards and the olive and orange groves, far off, at the sea—unsmiling, unmoving, like a warrior gazing out to sea waiting for enemy ships to appear, or like a seafarer ready to set sail for unknown seas, over dark and wild waters. He stands just like that, unsmiling, unmoving, until the Italian woman down below raises her hands high and shouts, "Yoohoo, Pietro, allo!" and the Chief turns and looks down at her, feigning surprise, and she snaps a photo of him with her iPhone—the first photo of tonight's performance.

"I don't know, I've got a bad feeling," says Iasonas, looking at his father, who's starting his warm-up—stretches, toe touches, jogging the perimeter of the roof.

"Me too," I say. "I told you, Barba Pietro's going to beat us to the punch."

He throws me a sideways glance, starts to say something, then thinks better of it. He lights a cigarette, stands up, and starts to unfold the chairs and set them out in the courtyard.

"That's how it goes, though," I say. "Gods belong with goddesses. Or virgins."

*

Iasonas's father's name is Petros, but we call him the Chief because he looks just like that Indian guy in *One Flew Over the Cuckoo's Nest*—a huge hulk of a man, two meters tall, big and solid, with gray hair down his back. He and Iasonas don't get along too well, but I think he's a god. It's been two years since they came to the island from Athens, and since the day they arrived I've been following him around like a groupie. I want to be close to him, to smell his scent, track his footsteps, his gaze, how he talks, how he smokes, how he drinks his whiskey or *tsikoudia*. To me he's a god. Even after what happened this winter, when Iasonas's mother ran off with some Dutch guy who used to paint landscapes down at the port, and the Chief took it hard and started drinking *tsikoudia* by the bucket and his hair went white in a single night—even after all that, I still think he's a god.

Now more than ever before. Because for the past month, since the beginning of summer, the Chief has been doing this show up at the castle every night, driving the crowds wild. It's an incredible sight, you'd have to see it to believe it. He's like Samson, wrapping himself around the few columns still standing at the entrance to the tower, shaking them as if they're made of Styrofoam, lifting huge cornerstones into the air, clambering up the wall without a rope, all the way to the parapet. The best part of all, though, is him wrestling with the Crisis. The Chief comes out into the courtyard with this short white chiton on, like an

ancient hero, slathered all over in oil, shouting some kind of gibber-
ish, and then all of a sudden Elvis, an Albanian from Katergo, appears
under the archway carrying a scythe on a short handle and dressed
as the Crisis: in rags, with a witch's hat that says *IMF* on it, dragging
empty pots and pans on a string tied to his ankle, and with an EU
flag and another from Germany hanging from his belt. Growling like
the Minotaur, waving his scythe in the air, Elvis pounces on the Chief
and they start to wrestle, and one of them falls, then the other one,
and they're rolling around on the ground, the tourists staring at them
with their mouths hanging open, and when the Chief finally grabs the
scythe and pretends to slice off the Crisis's head and Elvis falls writhing
into the dust—then everyone jumps to their feet and claps and shouts
"Yeah" and "Wow" and "*Vive les Grecs*" and "*Viva Grecia.*" The Chief
raises his fist, bows, then takes the witch's hat off of Elvis's supposedly
severed head and gives it to Iasonas, to collect money from the tourists.

That's the Chief's finest act, but tonight he's going to do something even better. Tonight, for the first time, he's going to do the salto
mortale: he'll jump from one of the castle's rooftops to another, a sev-
en-meter jump. Seven whole meters, without a helmet or knee pads
or anything. Iasonas is scared, because it's really dangerous, a trick for
those lithe little martial arts guys, not for the Chief, who's 120 kilos and
can down a barrel of *tsikoudia* at a sitting. Last night they almost came
to blows, because Iasonas has been nursing a grudge for a while—he's
ashamed, he says, to see his father making a fool of himself like that,
acting like an idiot with all those masks and scythes, and embarrassing them both every night in front of the tourists. But the Chief won't
listen to reason. Tonight he's doing his jump. It's over, it's finished—
tonight he's going for the salto mortale.

What can you say? He's a god, he does what he likes.

*

Bit by bit the others gather and take their seats for the performance.
Germans, Russians, Scandinavians, a group of Chinese with camera
lenses like telescopes. Some are regulars, for others it's their first time
there. Iasonas plays the tour guide, tells them the castle was built by
a Venetian family called Da Molin, points between the ruins at the

enormous chiseled rock with the phrase *Omnia mundi fumus et umbra* carved on it, which means "Everything in the world is smoke and shadows."

As soon as everyone's seated, the Chief makes his appearance and walks to the middle of the terrace. He stands there motionless, eyes closed, taking deep breaths. Then he opens his eyes, spits on his palms, shouts, "ei-o, ei-o," picks up speed and jumps over the narrow gap between the two towers and lands with his knees bent on the rooftop across the way. Then he picks up speed again, jumps, and lands again with his knees bent. It all happens so quickly, so simply and calmly, that everyone is struck dumb, incapable of believing what they just saw happen before their eyes.

"What happened?" Iasonas asks, standing beside me, bathed in sweat, his eyes closed and a finger plugging each ear. "What happened, is he alive?"

"Of course, he's a god," I say. "Have you ever heard of a god dying?"

The Chief comes back to the edge of the roof and makes his bow, one hand on his chest, the other behind his back—and only then does everyone start clapping, shouting "bravo," snapping photographs again.

Iasonas takes the hat and goes to collect the money. He weaves his way through the crowd, and when he gets to the mulberry tree, the Italian woman takes out a fifty-euro bill, holds it high in the air for the Chief to see, then blows him a kiss with her fingers and tosses it into the hat.

*

Night is falling. The red sun is disappearing behind the mountains, the sky to the west is bloody. When the very last of the foreigners leave, Iasonas tells me to follow him. We climb the stairs to the rooftop. A cold wind has picked up, carrying the scents of jasmine and orange blossom from a distance.

The Chief is sitting with a bottle of *tsikoudia* between his knees, looking at the darkening sky. Beside him are two more bottles, both empty. Iasonas goes over and asks him to do the salto mortale again. The Chief raises his head and gives him a blurry look.

"What'd you say?"

"I want you to jump again."

"Get lost," the Chief says, then turns to me.

"What do you think this is, you bums? Cirque Medrano?"

But Iasonas insists.

"If you can do it for money, you can do it for me," he tells Chief. "If you can do it for money, you can do it for love."

Father and son look one another in the eye for a minute, then the Chief lowers his head and takes a swig from the bottle. He gets to his feet, faltering, and stands in the middle of the terrace. He looks at the sky, at Iasonas, at me, and now there's a sadness dripping from his eyes—a bitter sadness like you wouldn't believe. Then he gathers speed, runs, but when he gets to the edge of the terrace, he stops short, waves his arms in the air like a drowning sailor, and falls headfirst over the edge. By the time I've reached the top of the stairs, Iasonas is already down below in the street.

The Chief is curled in a heap on the cobblestones, Iasonas cradling him in his arms and murmuring to him. The Chief is trembling all over, his hair spread like a gray octopus over Iasonas's arm.

"What happened?" I shout. "Quick, we need to call an ambulance."

Iasonas holds up a hand.

"We're fine," he says. "It's fine, go home, I'll bring him in the car."

But I don't go anywhere. I stand there staring at father and son who are now just one tangle of yarn.

Iasonas is stroking the Chief's cheek and saying something to him.

"Oh, Chief," he says. "Chief, you fell fighting for Iasonas and love."

TRANSLATED FROM THE GREEK BY KAREN EMMERICH

ULF ERDMANN ZIEGLER

Detroit

I GOT INTO rowing because I was tired of scouting and Rotary Club didn't do it for me anymore. But that had more to do with Falk Blohm's disappearance. He was a natural scout leader, the kind who sang "La Paloma" by the campfire. Head tilted, he'd gaze slightly upward and his limbs would make these very broad gestures, more or less what passes for charisma among boys. He carefully chose the younger boys whose bunkhouse he was responsible for. He'd get us into bed on time and then get us back up by candlelight. No leader would ever have managed what Falk achieved effortlessly: two minutes later, everyone had their pants down. Falk touched everyone, just briefly, as if it were a blessing, and later cleaned the floor in the dark after we were already back in bed. He called this servicing the team. Not a word the next morning, but the fire of curiosity still smoldered in our heads, the pulse of excitement magnified by seven pairs of eyes.

He couldn't do this kind of thing at the Rotary Club. Those kids were from the Elbe suburbs. They'd spill the beans in a heartbeat, sitting at their walnut tables with crocheted tablecloths. Still, he had recommended me for the club, and he knew what he was doing. He had the keys to his father's yacht. We would disappear into it once a week. He showed me the techniques for touching another man so it was fun and wasn't over too quickly. Afterward we'd drink Balle brand rum from the bottle. I'd get quiet, and he'd tell me stories from *The Lord of the Rings*. Then came his conspiracy phase: Trotsky, Mata Hari, Kennedy. In the end he took up with some scientists, a team of psychologists, I thought at first, or a church group, rather, based in the Rocky Mountains. I wasn't listening as closely then. Which was a mistake of course.

We wore the label "exchange student" like a badge, something which spared us uncomfortable questions. We knew the word shouldn't be taken literally. The whole program had been invented to show democracy to Nazi Germany's young people, up close and personal. It was the twenty-fifth or thirtieth year of the program, which had grown into a philanthropic society. We wanted everything that was spelled out in the application forms and that was repeated during the weekend seminar after we were accepted: to understand other cultures and all that—or so I would say. When you're so young, sixteen, without a hair on your face, platitudes spill out easily. You even come to believe them yourself, as long as they're useful.

The seminar took place before Easter, south of the Elbe, where it flows down to Cuxhaven, in a villa that reigned over the thoroughfare. We were all from Hamburg, the boroughs of Wandsbek and Barmbek and Eppendorf. Where exactly didn't really matter, or paled at least in comparison to the destinations of our journeys: Portland, Oregon; Allentown, Pennsylvania; Greene, Iowa. Response letters had already arrived from families readily offering information about themselves, about the number and names of their children, the parents' professions, their religion, and the make of their cars. I had just learned about "my family," as we said, the week before I got there, and assured everyone I'd already written back to them in Ardmore, Oklahoma. I had started the letter; it lay on my desk between my monstrous Latin and math assignments.

The educators worked hard to loosen our preconceptions about the United States until it became unrecognizable, as if we were setting out into an uncharted land, a blank space on the map. They were experts in clichés and prejudice of all sorts. They wanted to make us believe that no two individuals' experiences would be identical. But they seemed nervous. No one mentioned Falk Blohm's name. Only on the way back, on the suburban line, did it come up. I remember the helpless laughter, but there we were on our own, a loose collection of adventurers evanescing one by one between Neugraben and the Hauptbahnhof station. We wouldn't see each other again until the airport.

I spent the months until then exclusively with Willie. Either we were at rowing club or at the movies or at his mom's house. She was a fantastic cook and didn't have anything against me sleeping "next to" Willie. It couldn't have escaped her notice how sad and lost Willie had been before he met me, and how cheerful and full of verve he was since we had been together. I helped him with his English, which was kind of funny, seeing as Willie was half-American after all, visibly, cocoa brown with black frizz. His father only appeared in a black-and-white photo: very serious in a white collar, a narrow, ethereal face, like an athlete's. Willie was round and soft in comparison but with hydraulic shoulders and calves of steel. He was the motor of our four-man shell.

Before those months with Willie, at Rotary Club one Thursday, it would have been time to sneak off again, but Falk told me he had lost the keys to the yacht. I read the expression on his face, and I was relieved. The following fall, Nixon was gone, but Falk Blohm had downright disappeared, and they weren't advertising much for the year abroad in America. They took pretty much anyone. Me, for example, and Wilfred McGregor, Willie, that is, whom I saw for the first time when he sat with me during the selection announcement. The groups were always random, to see whether we had any class-based attitude: "we" being the children from west of the Alster lakes. Willie and I got along at once, and took a long walk together after the meeting. It was October, and it felt as though the Elbe River was not so much running through the city as raining down onto it. That same evening, down in the Portuguese quarter, I met his mom. You could see how hard it would be for her to be without Willie for a whole year, and before it was even Christmas, Willie withdrew his application.

As for rowing, I showed up at the right time. Willie's four-man had just lost its cox, an ambitious boy named Joachim who did well goading the team on but who lacked the right timing for the sprint. The rowers felt no one would ever be able to do it like Blomsky. Blomsky was like an iridescent soap bubble, here today and gone tomorrow. When Joachim gave up, Mecki, a strong, silent type, jumped ship too, and I took his place in the now-coxless shell, which soon launched back into competitions.

There came a day when I told my mother I didn't want to go to America. There came a night at Willie's when I suddenly understood who Blomsky was. There came a day when I brought Willie to our place near Klosterstern, and afterward my mother said he "was really quite a handsome boy." And I was dumb enough to say "Yes." Anyway, she replied, either before or after Willie's visit, I don't remember now, that I had made up my mind to go to America and it wasn't possible to call off plans like that. When she said that, it was as if a light switched on in my head. Then I knew I wanted to retrieve Blomsky, that is, I wanted to track down Falk Blohm in Utah. I'd talk him out of this sect or whatever it was of his and bring him back to Hamburg. Not for *Bild*, the newspaper that had trumpeted his disappearance for days, just for us, for Willie and for me. And for our four-man.

We flew out of Fuhlsbüttel at midday to Detroit where we landed in early evening. There were a hundred and fifty North German students on board, and I spoke with none of them. From my window seat I marveled at the many lakes and ponds until I realized that they were swimming pools in the suburbs, one for every house. I stayed seated until I was the last one on the airplane and watched a man unload my faux-leather, pine-green suitcase. My mother had bought it for me a week before, in the arcades. I kept my carry-on close like a little brother. It was a shame about the suitcase, really. I wouldn't be able to use it on my journey.

Those with direct connections continued on that evening to Seattle, Houston, Los Angeles, or in the other direction toward Atlanta or Boston. A dozen of us stayed behind at the airport. We were each assigned a room and given a voucher for the restaurant.

I dumped out my suitcase and my carry-on on the giant bed and packed everything I might need into the smaller bag—a second pair of shoes, a yellow rain slicker, a camera, and a book. What I was missing was a sleeping bag. With a little luck, the drivers here might take hitchhikers home with them like they did in Sweden.

The wood, brass, and leather of the airport hotel's lobby gleamed elegantly. Outside, in front of the automatic glass doors, was a starkly lit half-circle driveway. Liveried black men opened the doors of limousines with tinted windows. Wives dropped off their husbands, who plunged into the hotel with heavy, boxy briefcases. The cars were as massive as expected, with powerful, blubbering engines. Some emitted a complex purring, drowned out when they stopped by the howling of the air conditioning. The station wagons were long enough that you could comfortably sleep two or even three in them. A certain type of station wagon was lined with wood or some material that resembled woodgrain. One small round car consisted solely of curved windows, as if its body were surrounding a glass balloon. When the passenger doors opened, you could see automatic seatbelts passing through a grommet or—when the front seat of a coupe was pushed forward—fluttering like a loose hem. Trunk lids, like gaping maws, opened automatically. No one would turn off the engine while the cars were stopped and then they'd drive away as if drawn by distant magnets.

At the farther end of the half circle was a black bench, lit only indirectly, where I shoved my carry-on. From there, I watched every vehicle that pressed its way through the half circle. Some didn't have any license plate in front, so I could only read where they came from once they passed me. Some came from Ohio or Indiana, but most were from Michigan, a few from Ontario across the border. I couldn't see the fumes coming from the cars' exhaust, but the drive was sometimes more, sometimes less, obscured by bluish fog. I sniffed at the cars like hope. One driver with long hair called to me, "*Eh wehrer yug oh-ing,*" and my legs tensed to stand. Then he called again, but I felt the liveried men staring at me and hesitated. And it was only when he got back in with a shrug and drove away with a clattering front axle that I understood he'd called, "Where are you going?" The most important question of my life, if not the only one I had that night in August.

I sat there for a few hours and contemplated how one might go about finding Blomsky in Utah, or in Los Angeles, rather. Scientologists aren't Mormons after all. I had read up on these things in the Hamburg State Library the week before my departure. I wondered what would take longer, hunting down Falk Blohm or spending a year in Ardmore where my host father worked buying groceries for the state penitentiary, which must mean the prison. He had a well-upholstered wife with curls like an Airedale and two blond daughters living beneath a steely blue sky. I knew that much from the colored photos.

Whatever the case, I had left Willie behind, and the longer I breathed in "the ole Detroit perfume," the less I could remember what had brought me there. I felt exposed in the middle of America, an order whose delivery had become absurd. When the blush of dawn became visible, I took my pine-green suitcase and, without clearing away the rest of my luggage, lay down on the massive bed and sank into a dreamless sleep. When the telephone rang, I didn't answer, just stumbled into the bathroom where I threw up.

TRANSLATED FROM THE GERMAN BY DUSTIN LOVETT

GARY KAUFMANN

Coffee and Cappuccino

A SURGING HUM signaled the arrival of the ICE train in the Munich Hauptbahnhof. Not long after, Ulrich was fighting his way through the throngs entering and exiting the cars. He was wearing an expensive black suit over a plain, white shirt. A thin red necktie adorned his chest. The only other items he had with him were his suitcase and briefcase. There was not even a hint of beard growth on his cheeks. Had he been dressed differently, he might have been mistaken for a teenager.

The situation was dire enough that Ulrich didn't have time to be picky—he raced into the nearest establishment. Apparently, being part of a world-famous fast-food chain didn't guarantee any certain standard of hygiene—but at least half the toilet stalls were empty. As was customary, he fished some change from his pocket to give to the woman at the window before going in.

But relieving himself did nothing to quiet Ulrich's frantic manner. When he looked in the mirror while washing his hands, he couldn't help but notice the cleaning lady standing at a nearby sink. Her white gloves had stained patches on them from the chemicals she used, as did the rest of her clothes. Her hair was long, red brown, and unkempt. It smelled like fryer fat. For some reason this woman looked familiar. Ulrich often had trouble with names, which was not exactly helpful in the political profession. He was very good at recognizing faces, however, and he was sure he knew her.

But from where?

He thanked her as she handed him a paper towel. He took his time drying his hands.

"Excuse me, but do I know you from somewhere?"

No answer. Instead, she cast her eyes downward, got on her hands and knees, and began mopping the floor with a cloth. Maybe she hadn't heard him. It was also quite possible that she didn't speak German, or that she only spoke a little. Ulrich tried again. Still no reaction. He watched her work for a while, still struggling to answer his own question. Just as he turned his back to leave, he heard a quiet snicker behind him.

As he turned back around, it hit him: "Now I remember! You're little Julia! We went to elementary school together."

"I'm sorry, but I think you've gotten me confused with someone else," she replied, continuing to mop the floor.

Anyone else would have just left it at that. But Ulrich was not the type who gave up easily. Memory after memory was springing back to life, strengthening his conviction that she was exactly who he thought she was. He walked closer and pointed his finger admonishingly. "I know your games, Miss Hardner! Didn't you ever grow up?"

She threw her cleaning cloth to the floor, but before her foot could hook around his leg, Ulrich had stepped lightly to the side. "Did you really think I'd forget that move?"

The old friends embraced. Julia was smiling. "You're just too smart, aren't you, Ulrich?"

An uncomfortable silence set in. The last time they'd seen each other had been years ago, and since then their contact had dwindled. Neither really knew how it had happened.

"My break's in a half hour. Do you want to grab a coffee?" she asked.

The taut corners of his mouth widened. "Now there's an offer I can't refuse."

To pass the time, Ulrich took a stroll through the train-station shops. He spent the longest at an international-magazine kiosk. A good opportunity to catch up on some reading. With the latest edition of *kicker* under his arm, he returned to the restaurant.

He ended up having to wait another fifteen minutes, but he didn't mind. Rid of her uniform and with now significantly neater hair, Julia was far easier to recognize. The latent beauty he had always seen in her when they were kids was now in full blossom—she was unmistakable.

She waved, beckoning him to follow as she made her way toward an empty café.

They had hardly sat down before the waiter descended on them. "Julia! How's it going? What can I bring you two lovebirds?"

Ulrich gave the waiter a puzzled look. Julia, however, broke into full-throated laughter—which only made things more uncomfortable. Ulrich was beginning to regret his decision. He could have spent the evening in his hotel room, with a nice glass of wine. What was he thinking, getting into a situation like this?

Julia gathered herself and answered first. "The usual for me. And how about you, my love?"

"I'll have a black coffee, please." As far as he was concerned, the waiter could not leave soon enough. How somebody could possibly think that was appropriate baffled him. At least Julia seemed to have found some humor in it. The whole place had a sort of feel-good atmosphere, but still. While Julia stared up at the ceiling, he continued to read the menu.

What was there to say after all this time? And how could he even be sure that she was still the same?

Finally, he broke the silence: "I see you haven't lost your sweet smile."

"Oh, please. Stop it!" she whispered, waving her hand in an effort to repel his words. "You know you can't just compliment me like that."

Her cheeks had flushed slightly—another relic of their earlier years. The boys had always had an eye for her. Even at the age when girls were still gross. Many of them had envied Ulrich for his good relationship with her. One had resorted to bullying to try and stop him from walking Julia home every day after school. But Ulrich never backed down.

Ulrich put the menu aside, using Julia's wandering gaze as an opportunity to study her. Why wasn't she saying anything? Back then, she had been the biggest chatterbox he knew. No matter how banal the thought, everybody who crossed her path had to hear about it.

He wanted to wait—to see how long it would take her to start the conversation back up. Surely then she would show more interest. And after a couple of false starts, the words finally came: "I'm sorry I ignored you earlier," she said cautiously. "Of course I recognized you."

Ulrich nodded. "It's fine."

Her reaction was understandable. She was ashamed of her job. How had she ended up like this? It was probably hard for her to get excited about anything these days. Julia had never known what she wanted to do, and had always preferred to postpone rather than decide. The only thing she'd known for certain was that she wanted to live in a big city—her hometown was too dull.

"Do you remember when we did swim team together?" Ulrich asked.

This, it seemed, provided the necessary catalyst—all of a sudden, Julia felt the memories welling up inside of her too. For the first time since they had been sitting there, she looked him in the eye. "I used to call you my everyday hero because you always made sure I got home from practice safely, even when we'd stayed too long talking."

They had both joined the swimming team because it was what you did. As a kid, playing some kind of sport was for all intents and purposes required. But when the balance between school, friends, and athletic ambition became harder to manage, Julia slowly lost interest. And from then on, the two had started to grow further and further apart, each becoming more firmly rooted in a new circle of friends. Soon, they only saw each other at public events. It was around this same time that the formerly timid Julia began to recognize the power she wielded over the opposite sex, and not long after, her metamorphosis into a bona fide party animal was complete. It seemed like she was always in a relationship, casting her line for the next boy as soon as the current one started to wear. And with each smitten suitor, her vanity deepened.

The waiter brought their drinks, and Ulrich wasted no time in taking a sip of the black brew. He let out a satisfied groan and set the cup back down. "So you live in Munich?"

"Yes."

She hadn't touched her cappuccino yet. Instead, she leaned over the table and began to straighten Ulrich's necktie. "And what has brought my hero so far away from Liechtenstein?"

"I have a meeting with the finance minister tomorrow morning," Ulrich answered. He'd been hoping to avoid this topic—the conversation was already uncomfortable enough. But there was no way around it. "I wish I could stay here a few more days, but unfortunately I have to go to Berlin right after, to see the chancellor."

Her eyes widened, and his smile faded. Now she would never look at him the same. Not like she used to. But he didn't look at her the same either. Finally, she lifted her cup. He continued: "As minister of economic affairs, I have a lot of these meetings."

"Minister of economic affairs?!" She almost spat cappuccino in his face. Even the waiter, who had made his way to the other end of the café, jumped a little. Taking care not to spill, Julia placed her cup back down on the table and sank a little lower into her chair, as if following an unspoken command.

"I would never have thought that shy little Ulrich would turn out to be such an important man. Back then, we could barely get you to say a word."

Ulrich wasn't sure how to respond. True, he didn't have a leader's disposition, but he managed to slip effortlessly into these roles. People valued his trustworthiness, and his reserved manner meant that few disliked him. He'd gotten into politics on the recommendation of a former coworker.

Ulrich and Julia sipped timidly at their coffees, avoiding further conversation. Occasionally, Ulrich would look her in the eyes and open his mouth as if to say something, but he couldn't bring himself to speak. He kept thinking about all those hours they'd spent laughing together. Things were different now. The person sitting across from him might as well have been a complete stranger. Any remnant of the former Julia was an illusion. He stared at the bottom of his empty cup.

"You never called me."

"I . . . I couldn't . . ." she stuttered, visibly struggling to continue speaking. "I'm sorry."

Ulrich looked at his watch—it was getting on time for him to go back to the hotel. Julia nodded and finished her now-cold cappuccino with a single gulp. Within seconds, the waiter was at the table with their check. But before she could dig her wallet out of her purse, Ulrich handed the man a twenty-euro bill: "Keep the change."

Whispering a frantic "Thank you," the waiter disappeared behind the register, depriving Ulrich of the opportunity to reconsider his generous tip. Ulrich stood up and reached for his luggage.

"I'm sorry. The next time I'm in the city I'll call you. I'll certainly have more time then."

"I'd like that very much," Julia whispered quietly. She took out a pen, wrote her number on the receipt, and handed it back to Ulrich, holding the door open as he walked out of the café. Before the door had shut behind him, she was making her way through the crowd, and just like that, Ulrich was spared the task of deciding how to say good-bye. He watched her walking away for a while, and then crumpled up the receipt and threw it in the nearest trash can before hailing a taxi.

TRANSLATED FROM THE GERMAN BY JEFFREY D. CASTLE

CARYL LEWIS

Against the Current

PIOTR WAS ON his way to work in the slaughterhouse when he saw the old man walk into the water. His shift started at five, and he thought at first that the tweed jacket and the cap he could see through river mist must belong to one of the fishermen he'd come across, tickling trout out of their element. Piotr held off a while. But when he realized the man was up to his chest in water and that his cap had been captured by the current, he threw down the butt of his cigarette. The river was in full spate following nonstop rain, and the man was holding his own against the flow that threatened to topple him any minute. A heartbeat, then Piotr watched as the white face and the dark clothes went under without a word.

"*Kurwa*!" he swore.

He ran along the path, shrugging off his rucksack. He knew that pressure would hold the man under, forcing him fast through white water. Pulling his sweater over his head, only stopping to hop out of shoes, into the river he went. The cold was a body blow. He took a deep breath and upended himself. All night the rain had hammered the roof of his caravan behind the pub. Flat on his back and wide awake, the storm had kept him company. By this morning, with soil washed from its banks and its depths stirred to a frenzy, he could see nothing in the river. He was blind. Surfacing, he rubbed the wet from his eyes.

"Old man?"

The current beat against his body and took him also in its grasp. Along its banks and down toward the old bridge, the river's waters folded and were enfolded in creamy clouds of foam.

"*Dziadek*! Old man!"

There was no noise except the water's terrible roar. He had been stunned but now he felt the cold. He couldn't resist the pressure as the river took his legs from under him. He felt the skin on his shoulder rip. He breathed bubbles as the air was gone. The sheer weight of water was on his chest, with no chance of a breather before being taken under all over again. Then he was spat out of the main channel. Under the bridge he came up, took a deep breath and coughed.

"Son of a bitch!"

He groped for the limb of an old tree lying limp across the water but then saw a white hand in the black. He fished for the hand and pulled the old man toward him, turning his face toward the light. Supporting him under his chin, he kept hold of the branch with his other hand.

"You're trying to kill me too, eh?"

Taking him in his arms, he could feel the slightest movement in the old man's back. Piotr looked up at the old bridge's underside. Decades of damp had coated its stones in black slime. If he let go, back they would both go, underwater. Nor could he drag himself out with one arm only. Waiting was the only game. Waiting for someone passing by.

Passing by, walking the dog, maybe. His workmates didn't take this route. They'd rather meet at the wall of the pub where most of them lived in single rooms, call at the *polski sklep* for cigarettes and porn mags, then head on en masse, taking the mick all the way along the main road. Piotr was the only one who went the river way.

He didn't even like rivers. Back home, the only time he went to one was with his dad, catching carp for Christmas. It was their job to go fishing, bearing home their live prize in a bucketful of water in the trunk. Carp feed off the river floor, so they'd have to clean its system by starving it for a day or two in the bath. Every year he'd sit in the tiny bathroom watching that fish swimming back and forth, its dead, blind eyes staring at the white tub.

When his dad left, it fell to him to kill the carp on Christmas Eve. All he'd feel was numb when he'd pull it from its element, watching it gasp then drown. He'd hit it with a stick, slit it with a knife. His dad would keep back a fish scale for luck, pressing it between the *zloties* in his wallet. But Piotr didn't bother. By the time he was thirteen, luck and magic were only empty promises.

He was always first to arrive at the slaughterhouse. Radio on, rubber boots and rubber apron. Once the others had wound their way from the village, the killing would start. Making the lambs their own willing victims. A wooly head made to face ahead and the others would follow. One two three. Instinctively. Trustful not one of them would be the unlucky one. A mechanical system. Kill them, open them up. Each stage effected with industry and indifference. Bleat becoming meat. The blood piped into tankers, transformed into liters of fertilizer for faraway fields.

But sometimes a lamb knows its own mind: farmers admit it. It has a sixth sense, a flash of something other in the eye. It tries to jump out of the pens. Struggles. Pushes itself, panting, farther back in line. Gets kicked into place by the other lads, back into the system. Them laughing and texting girlfriends back home. Piotr would stand, midflow, watching them without a word.

His arm hurt. He shouted for help but the mist muffled his voice. His clasp was strong around the fragile body. He was mumbling.

"It's OK, old man."

He'd been one of those who go with the herd. Home the town that time forgot. School-leaver. Work whatever and wherever. Girlfriend, baby, promises, out of there. His little girl was in his mind as the cold took hold of his body. The old man's eyes began to close. He whispered into his ear, as though telling her a bedtime story, his breath warming his old cheek. He could sense him letting go. How thin his hair was, how slack his flesh about its bones. His skin gave off an oily sheen and a whiff of tobacco. Piotr felt him coughing.

"*Ma nhw'n mynd â'r ffarm*," he said, his voice faint as memory.

"Shhhh."

"*Y banc, wi 'di ffaelu talu*," he said.

"It's OK, old man."

"*Ddeith pawb i wbod.*"

"I don't understand."

"*Ddeith pawb i wbod.*"

"I don't know who's crazier, you or me, old man."

Now even Piotr's lips were trembling. He'd never felt as cold. His arm muscles were straining. All feeling had gone from his lower body.

He thought again about his daughter. Her smooth skin. Who would catch her Christmas carp this year? It was years since he'd spoken to her mother. Of course he'd send her part of his wages, but that was a face-less business, done through the bank. He didn't know if she had a new boyfriend nor whose job it was to put their little girl to bed. That carp, he thought, swimming back and forth in the whiteout.

He felt the man catch hold of him. Those old fingers clawing at his shoulders. Piotr turned to look him full in the face, staring at him. His shallow breath on his face. Eyeball to eyeball. He said not a word, so Piotr searched for that look. The flicker that meant a lamb wanted out of there. But there was nothing. No struggle. No scramble for dry land. And then a message passed between them. Piotr pulled him closer and for a second the old man leaned his head on the young shoulder. They listened to each other breathing. And Piotr loosened his grip, little by little, and let him go with the current. He watched him become one with the water; listened to the river swallow him up. Then, his whole body shuddering, he pulled himself up out of the river. He stood a moment on the bank watching the morning mist dissipate. It was a new day. He picked up his stuff and walked home, against the current.

TRANSLATED FROM THE WELSH BY GWEN DAVIES

GÁBOR VIDA

From *History of a Stutter*

The Other Side

IF THE FAMILY were only the Székely relations, convinced that they are living their quiet, unassuming, God-fearing lives in peace and love while hating each other half to death, and to each question or half-swallowed utterance, some silenced or repressed figment of reality unravels, and the one who insists on asking questions is threatened with a paternal slap in the face or a maternal disavowal on account of the intention, assumption, or utterance alone: if all I had to account for were everything that passed in Barót, Szárazajta, in the Székely land at large between the entrance of Horthy's army and the Soviet occupation, or what Maniu's raving legionaries and the comrades administering the collectivization wreaked, what Socialism arranged up to the fall of Ceaușescu, and what heritage it left behind, there would be material galore for the Great Transylvanian Novel. For sometimes it seems I have always aspired to write something of the kind, that's what I'm ceaselessly preparing for, the reason why I keep researching my narrower and broader homelands, going through the woods, villages, towns, and archives, although I know perfectly well that I'm just trying to hide from myself. If the family were only the Székely relations, that alone would be more than enough material, and excellent material, because the image we have of ourselves and the reality are so far apart that a novelist could wallow in this fairyland neurosis to the end of his writing days. Here's the *roman fleuve*, one only has to transcribe it nicely, ably, skillfully, to structure the whole thing with a fair bit of verbiage: stern father, abandoned child, religious frenzy, Trianon, Northern Transylvania, Ceaușescu, Hungarians, Székelys, Romanians, and lies everywhere, behind which linger not truth, not even several forking truths, but lives, men and women, a lot of suffering, little sex, a lot of alcohol, or let there be a lot of sex with a lot of alcohol, incest is no longer in vogue or no longer a problem, so let's stick in a bit of pedophilia, nowadays it's in high demand and you can pass it off with just the thinnest justification, throw in a helping of pseudodialect and a few musts: Transylvanian gastronomy, virgin nature, spritz water, and bearshit. What if my tractor-driving uncle went to hell because he was a homosexual, or perhaps he'd been raped as a child, and of course there's also the somewhat more heroic version, that he was involved in some Székely resistance movement: rough riders in the Hargita mountains who wanted to reconquer Saint Anne's lake from the Securitate, or put up the Hungarian flag on the Csala tower. In the end the Securitate screws got the upper hand, we can't exclude the hypothesis that they administered a massive dose of opium to Tom, because he resisted to the very end, even if one doesn't quite know what or whom. There's room for variation.

God will punish you if you write things like that, Mother says when she reads the first draft of this manuscript. She doesn't say I'm lying, that it didn't happen like that, but from her point of view one doesn't tell such things, not even to oneself, let alone to others. At this stage she is not yet aware that she, too, is a character in the story. She only senses that I'm being denigrating, ironical, she doesn't see that almost everything I tell is gleaned from her recollections, that it's from her I know all these things. About which we don't speak, which we only utter, throwing them at one another when for a moment we forget about the prohibition and our temper hurls us over the jumps of speech. There's a whole world hidden, suppressed in her, which erupts every now and then with primal fury, until she realizes what she's saying, and that I'm listening. Then she puts an end to the flow with some practical message. I learn only very late that she'd burned a good part of the carefully preserved letters and records, that she'd culled the family pictures and gotten rid of all the negatives: for a long time she used to be the family photographer. Like an inflexible censor. She's not alone in this: her little and elder sisters are the same, as is their ideology, but of course sometimes the details they remember differ, which is only natural, and later they'd lecture and shout each other down because that's not the way it happened at all.

If there were only this, it would be more than enough to keep me busy, but there's more. Because Father, who's convinced that "but" is something with which one ought not to begin a sentence, in fact looks down on them, a common attitude on the Pannonian Plains, and for him this goes so much without saying that no discomfiting second thoughts occur to him, that this might be wrong after all, partly because Mother is a Székely and so I'm half one too, and partly because, since he himself has a connection with them, it means either that he himself can be looked down on, or that the people with whom he mingled of his own free will, at first not fully grasping what it all might lead to, are not to be looked down on either. But afterward, because with us it's always afterward, he begs to differ: he's not like them, after all he's Hungarian, which can only be made clear to other Hungarians, in part because the linguistic nuances are only worth employing in Hungarian; a German or a Frenchman or even a Romanian can't possibly understand what it's all about, even if such differences and divergences exist within every nation. Behind every egalitarianism there lurks a strict hierarchy unconnected to rational argument, and it doesn't take much imagination to see that everything's best the way it's done in one's own village, town, or street. At any rate, those were the days when he used to have his own village, town, or street, which is all the more striking since there's no longer any village, town, or street he can call his own. You can think this ironically or in all seriousness: that there must be terrible queer creatures at the latter end of the world, where they don't put any paprika in the sausage!

In the aftermath of the Romanian army's 1916 incursion, a flood of Székely refugees appears first in inner Transylvania, many of whom eventually reach the Plains. A mass of a hundred thousand, with carts, animals, and bundles, poor, distraught, and bewildered, along the highways from which, every now and then, the army derails them, onto side alleys, though in no way protecting them from looters and thieves. This is far from the first wave of refugees in modern Hungarian history that catches the country unprepared and at a loss, but unlike the Galician Jews, Székelys are Hungarian after all—at least that's the official line. Today, this is hardly ever mentioned, but it left indelible marks on the collective memory, and every subsequent wave of refugees will support this: the authorities are helpless, the people suspicious and hostile, fearing for their own possessions, they have enough trouble on their hands already. Months pass for the wandering Székelys, to whose relocation to their domicile the government allocates huge sums of money. The Székelys are in no hurry to get back home and, as it happens—although it didn't used to happen this way, only afterward did this become the pattern—those funds don't even exist, or if they do they invariably land in the pockets of ruthless government officials and speculators; not a penny reaches those in need, but everybody blames them, it's because of them that they're left in the lurch. Trianon comes next, World War II, and the wave of refugees after the severe 1946 Transylvanian and Moldavian droughts inescapably impresses it into the collective consciousness of the Hungarians of the Plains—who ended up this side of the Romanian border—that something is definitely wrong with the Székelys. They may be Hungarian, but Hungarians with a different speech, a different frame of mind and behavior; abject poverty follows wherever they come, whenever they are allowed to come, whenever they are sent to us. In any case, Hungarians cannot possibly be different, for who are we then, because in the eyes of Hungarians, especially those of the Plains, all diversity is intolerable and suspicious. A Székely may eventually count as Hungarian, but hardly as a human being, just as Gypsies and Romanians are not human either, and at any rate not Hungarian, and can never be assimilated, nor want to be of course. There are villages where no Hungarian has sold a house to Székelys ever since then. At least that's what they say.

So my father's family, close and extended, officially looks down on Mother on the grounds of Hungarianness, because she's just a Székely cutie. Somebody says so with a shrug when their plan to marry, or their intention at any rate, is revealed, and it's not long before Mother finds out. They never say it to her face, but she knows precisely what they mean. They could just as well say she's Romanian, it would be just a mistake she could immediately and indignantly correct and take issue with, but in this case she can't, there's nothing to feel offended about. Father doesn't take issue, I don't know if then and there he picked up this condescension to her, or if it's something only a Székely can hear, but they do hear it, all the time, everywhere, ever since. Trianon is brought home here, although this Székely sense of inferiority dates much further back, intensifying over time until it reaches well-nigh pathological dimensions. The gesture with which somebody's Hungarianness is withdrawn or at least questioned at the sign of the first regionalism of speech, the first quaint intonation, is like a verbal lynching. No one should take it seriously, but in the course of the twentieth century Pannonia has amply proved what a grievously serious matter this is, for anyone's Hungarianness can be withdrawn at a moment's notice.

Quite apart from this, Mother has an all-round sense of inferiority. She comes from a poor family and my grandfather's Baptist faith was considered rather extravagant, even in the Transylvania of alleged religious freedom and tolerance. Although in the Romania of the 1950s the prime public enemy is not the Baptist community but the so-called "historical churches," openly belonging to any strict sect is a dangerous thing. Mother will soon get kicked out of the Communist Youth Organization for going to a church event rather than a school event, to service rather than the comrades' gathering. Being booted out here is like pillorying, a public humiliation enacted because the family and the father are the way they are, and in those days it's not wise to stand up to the authorities, people go to prison for much less. And Mother's at a loss, as if everything were happening over her head: what's more, she'd been baptized a Catholic, according to Grandmother's faith. Yet another source of confusion in the family, which for a long time I don't understand and nobody bothers to explain. My grandfather Unclegyurika makes everyone go to the Baptist congregation hall whether they like it or not, he's not one to have heard of religious tolerance and the 1542 Edict of Torda, regarding the freedom of religion—that's not in Scripture. The matter is further complicated by the fact that according to the old Romanian law it's the father who decides in what religion the children born to mixed marriages should be baptized, but my grandparents agree that the girls should follow the mother's religion and the sons that of the father, as was the custom in Transylvania. Formally, the Baptist Church makes no demands on anyone until immersion, let them decide for themselves, after all it's supposed to be a liberal church, and American at that. No use questioning what a fourteen-year-old girl could decide there and then, or what it must have cost her, psychologically speaking. Mother is an eminent pupil, a striver, she is diligent and obedient and of course goes to the Baptist meeting hall, but for some reason she refuses immersion, she's the only child to resist point-blank, she herself doesn't understand why, not even in retrospect. Without a second thought. But she's humiliated because of the Baptists. No one can serve two masters, this we know—but three?

And then Mother finds out in 1963 that for the Ágya Hungarians she's just a Székely cutie. Six children in the family, Grandmother Zsüli says in horror. My God, like Gypsies, not even they have that many. In those days in Father's village there were at most two children in a family. With my generation, an only child becomes the general rule.

My grandfather Joszip Vida is a hardened alcoholic, as was his father, another Joszip. Everything crystal clear, strictly no euphemisms, we don't try to cover it up, nobody believes that it can't possibly occur in a simple, hard-working, God-fearing family. God is not feared, nobody likes hard work, there's always poverty, fucking poverty, in vain does my great-grandfather try his luck twice in America, but then he drinks it away. According to the family legend, the only reason why he didn't perish on the *Titanic* was that all the tickets were sold out, but it's not true because he sailed off in 1911 from Fiume, that's what I found in the Ellis Island digital archives where his name is preserved among the many millions of immigrants, together with the ship's name from which he disembarked on the ninth of May: the *Ivernia*.

In keeping with their simplicity, I wouldn't dedicate too much space to my paternal grandparents if I hadn't spent the first five years of my life with them, and if I hadn't felt for a long time, in fact for as long as I can remember, that Grandmother Zsüli is in fact my mother and Grandfather Joszip Vida my father. I have parents, too, of course, mostly on the weekends, but they're always tired, always rushing off to work, they are building that nice, big, uniform square house in Kisjenő where one day I'll be entirely theirs, when the most nondescript nine years of my life begin. In Ágya we don't even live in the kitchen but in the outkitchen that's built against the stalls. During the night we can hear the sheep ruminating through the plaster walls, a soothing buzz in the dark, and if we go in with a storm lantern their eyes glow green. There's no electricity, it won't be installed in the house until 1980, because Grandfather's transistor radio, on which he can listen to twenty-six different Hungarian-language radio stations, breaks down, and you can't find any battery-run radios in the shops, only plug-in

ones. If you die I'll buy a TV, Grandmother threatens him, and she
will indeed. We listen to the radio a lot, Free Europe, Voice of America,
Radio Subotica, in those days even Istanbul and the Beijing radio used
to broadcast news bulletins in Hungarian.

Our favorite program is "The Ten-Minute Musical Quiz."
Grandfather can't stop wondering how anybody can distinguish
between those musics that all sound the same to him. In fact he quite
likes music; during the program I have to keep silent. He usually lies on
the bed with the green bedspread, I perch on a small stool in the half-
light, he smokes, the fire in the stove flares up now and then, we listen to the radio, sometimes he gets up, drinks a bit of pálinka or wine,
lies back. Once we listen to *Ábel in the Wilderness* from start to finish
and he doesn't understand every word or turn of phrase, but I do, and
when the installment is over I try to explain what the mountains and
the woods are like, I'm a Székely after all. At that age I'm sorry there are
no bears mentioned in *Ábel*, I'm a bit disappointed, because we've visited parts of Csicsó and seen bears. Only much later do I find out that
in fact in those times there weren't many bears in the Hargita mountains, and just a few scattered across the whole of Romania: only starting in the sixties would there be bears in any number, for the sport of
Communist comrades, to the chagrin of shepherds and farmers, to our
joyful surprise.

With Grandfather we also listen to *Peter and the Wolf*. This is the
first such cultural experience in my life, and it will forever remind me
of my obscure, boundless terror, of being alone, of anxiety. It's summer, or at least warm, because the door is left open, he is sitting at the
table cutting tobacco leaves, he does this when he has no money to buy
cigarettes, he's smoothing out and wetting the leaves he gathered, then
he cuts them up with the sharpest knife. He's telling one of his wartime stories, he served in the Romanian army, was a military gendarme
in Temesvár and the Banat. I remember a warehouse in flames where
the Russian soldiers tried to get tobacco at the risk of their lives, some
burned to death, and there's a bit of tanned leather in the larder, of the
kind the officers had coats made of when the Temesvár leather factory
was bombed to smithereens and looted. I can hardly make out what
Grandfather is talking about, the way the wartime yarns spin together.
The village is full of men like him, when they gather to drink and

play cards they talk about little else but the war, and when are the Americans or the Brits finally coming? Never, Grandmother Zsüli says curtly, and with her all the other old women in the village. They are a bit like the women in Tiszazug who conspired to poison their husbands, their point of view and the realm of experiences identical, it's only their headscarves pulled down almost over their eyes and their dark hatred that they can pit against the battalion of drunken old men. There's been little, if anything, pleasant or good in their whole lives, and even if there had been they wouldn't remember.

With my Rhédey grandmother, it never occurs to me that we might be related to aristocrats of the same name. There's no way. She's an embittered woman filled with hatred, who takes her mother to court over a little plot of land and afterward refuses to speak to her for thirty years, although they live in the same courtyard. When Grandfather falls off the attic ladder and can't get to his feet, she says, "Go in alone, Vida," and goes out into the village. Grandfather crawls inside, from the mud into the bed, he happens to be sober, but his broken heel bone will never mend. It's from Grandmother Zsüli that I find out that Uncle Will isn't Mother's real brother but only her stepbrother. But Grandmother seems to be a born mother-in-law, or old witch; she sees and understands everything, she's outspoken, merciless, and will not behave, she loves no one—not even me.

I can't get away from Prokofiev. Grandfather somehow vanishes behind the music together with his war, his bay horse on which he gallops past a building in flames, they shoot at him with a machine gun but can't hit him. In the meantime the wolf has devoured the duckling and I know that the wicker fence around our garden is frail and tumbledown. It would be no hindrance to a wolf. I can't climb up the walnut tree, its lower boughs are too high up, and I'm not good at climbing trees anyway, I'm thin and weak-chested. Everywhere we live we live at the edge of the village. In Ágya there are immense orchards the size of football fields, the street is fifty meters wide, allegedly it was Empress Maria Theresa who decreed this, so that, in case of a fire, the flames couldn't leap from one row of thatched roofs to the other. Besides, there's plenty of room, this is the Romanian side of the Pannonian Plains. In back of our garden the fields begin, a barely tended orchard, the Kenderes Gardens, and beyond that the pastures, the wasteland,

marshland, reeds, boggy clumps, mirages, the whole arsenal. For a long
time Petőfi is my favorite poet and I spend entire days leafing through the
1878 volume, looking at Mihály Zichy's engravings. My favorite poem
is "From the Inn to the Dog's Grave," later I'll swap it for "National
Song," the first poem I'll learn by heart, in an upflare of patriotism,
but for some odd reason I keep mixing up stanzas four and five. On
our roof there's a crane's nest, we have to watch over the newly hatched
chicks because, however tenderly the nursery rhyme's Hungarian boy
cures its wounded leg, the bird is not picky, it descends in a flash and
snatches away a chick, it's not afraid of the hen or me, darts its long
beak at my hand when I try to grab it by the neck. A flap and it's gone,
up on the chimney where it clatters triumphantly. No chance to get
my revenge on him with a slingshot or arrow. Grandmother vows that
one of these days she'll call the hunter to shoot him, but I wouldn't like
that, so it's indefinitely postponed. Cranes are useful, they eat snakes,
and there are plenty of snakes in the neighborhood, I'm afraid of them.
There are also many toads and all the rest, but those I'm not afraid of.

My third defining radio memory revolves around the events of
1956—some horrid radio play about the war in which the bloodbath rained down by the counterrevolutionaries is described in graphic
detail. I can recall exactly how a wicked counterrevolutionary tears
out the heart of a man who's been hanged upside down, but how that
heroic heart goes on beating for a while before it's tossed on the ground,
and by the time it lands in the mud, the liberating Soviet soldiers have
already turned the corner. In retrospect I'd say, the Corvin Lane group,
but at that time I don't understand anything. Grandfather, too, is listening, then suddenly switches off the radio and bursts out in fury:
Motherfucking Communist cunts! An elaborate oath, like when he's
cursing the stove that gives off smoke, the grainy coals, everybody's
whore of a mother, toward the end the Lord God Himself makes an
appearance. What happened in 1956, I ask, frightened, and Grandfather
explains that the keykeys called in the Russians, who blew Budapest to
pieces, yet again. And ever since then the Russians and the keykeys
have been ruling, because the motherfucking Americans didn't lift a
finger, they didn't bugger Moscow with their atomic bomb. I must have
been eight or nine, for all I know the socialism in which we live and
which we're building is the world's best-ever social system. I can even

enumerate the reasons, this is what we learned in school, and Mother too says that in the old regime people never had enough to eat, well, she never lived in the old regime, Grandfather says; but she's learned all about it, I say. I would defend Mother now and then.

Then Grandfather tells me that in 1956 he sold two heifers and wanted to buy a horse, but his younger brother Alexander persuaded him to buy a tractor instead, and they took it away, together with the land, what little land they had, and some people were beaten to death because they wouldn't give everything over, and others just went home, lay down and died, died of grief that the land and the horses were no longer theirs. Grandmother just nods, then snaps at him, what land are you blathering about, you never had any land, Vida, the land was mine, and they took it all away, yes they did. It rarely happens that they agree on something, in fact they've hated each other their entire lives, for the fifty years they've lived together. This first political lesson of mine made the world look threatening, because it's clear to me that nothing's the way Mother and the school teacher have been telling me. How can we possibly have everything when they took away Grandfather's tractor that ought to have been a horse? And the radio play goes on, obviously a serial, a long string of horrors, but now I know that it's not the way it happened, the very opposite is true.

TRANSLATED FROM THE
HUNGARIAN BY ERIKA MIHÁLYCSA

HELENA JANECZEK

From *The Girl with the Leica*

Buffalo, NY, 1960

DOCTOR CHARDACK WOKE early. He washed and dressed, made a cup of instant coffee, carried it into his study along with the Sunday *New York Times*, flipped through the pages devoted to American politics, which he intended to follow more closely now that the race for the presidency was getting tighter. Then he put the paper down, took out paper and pen, and began to work.

It was quiet outside, apart from the sporadic chirp and caw of martins and crows and the distant hum of the odd car in search of a gas station. Later, the neighbors would get into their own cars and go to church, or visit family or the restaurant serving the Sunday breakfast special, but fortunately none of these were things Dr. Chardack had to do.

He had just written the beginning of an article when the telephone rang. It came as no surprise to him. "That'll be for me!" he shouted toward the rest of the house, as much out of habit as to keep his wife from staggering sleepily toward the phone.

"Dr. Chardack," he answered, leaving off the "hello" as always.

"Hold the line, please; call from Italy for you."

"Willy," said a voice muffled by the intercontinental line, "I didn't wake you, did I?"

"*Nein, absolut nicht!*"

He knew right off who was calling. The old friends were still there, the marks they left as deep as those impressed by a bad fall from one of the stately big trees in Rosental Park. The ones who were still alive sometimes got in touch.

"Georg, has something happened? Is everything all right?"

In the days when he'd been Willy, he was the friend people went to for practical assistance: money, that is, for he had always had more than the others. At this, his caller laughed loudly and told him he didn't need anything, but that yes, something had happened all right, something Willy had done over there in America, so big that Georg couldn't resist calling him rather than writing a letter.

"Congratulations! It's great what you've accomplished, you could even say it's historic."

"Thanks," Chardack replied, somewhat automatically. He wasn't good at taking compliments, and although he did have a witty streak, no wit came to mind.

They had been champion wits once upon a time. Well, maybe that was an exaggeration, but they had been good at livening up a deadly dull debate with stabs of irony, and Willy Chardack had always been as good as the others. Now his American colleagues appreciated his dry sense of humor, intensified by the German accent (the mad scientist!), and he was happy not to seem cantankerous by American standards, to be a character.

Chardack, hearing the distant voice of Georg Kuritzkes, imagined him *en plein air* with the whole crew, not necessarily out of doors but in the luminous, light-hearted atmosphere of a French film, although Paris hadn't been part of the story back then. But Rosental could hold its own with the Bois de Boulogne, and Leipzig was famous for its narrow, hidden alleyways. Leipzig had industry and trade, centuries-old traditions of music and book publishing, and that bourgeois solidity was a magnet that drew people from the country and from the East, making the city ever more a real metropolis, even in its conflicts. That is, until the protests and strikes turned bitter and the world economic crisis pushed Germany toward catastrophe. At home, Willy's parents were tense, his father nervous about the lines of people seeking jobs, any jobs, when he was already struggling to keep his shop boys and warehousemen on the payroll, because even the market in furs—a source of Leipzig's prosperity since the Middle Ages—was faltering.

Willy and his friends didn't have to deal with bankrupt clients, but they were ready to do battle against whatever they must, even if they did come from prosperous families. And they were also free to do so, free to take off and sleep under the stars, free to laugh and joke, free to court girls (and there were some pretty and even sensational ones: Ruth Cerf, who'd shot up from a skinny beanpole into a majestic blonde, and Gerda, the most enchanting, lively, and amusing person he'd ever met in the entire female universe). The desire to have a good time survived even when Hitler was about to take power and they were getting ready to pack their bags. It was inalienable, that quality that made them equals, comrades, a challenge to the Nazis simply because of the way they lived and laughed. They weren't really equals, though, and Georg was the best example of that. Georg was brilliant, but to excess, like something squandered, like those shirts (of fine Egyptian cotton) that had languished in a Chardack wardrobe ever since Willy began to dress like his friends on the Left. Georg Kuritzkes was intelligent, handsome, and athletic. Honest and reliable. Excellent at uniting, instructing, organizing. Confident on the dance floor. Passionate, knowledgeable about the latest music from abroad. Courageous. Resolute. And even witty. How could someone like Willy Chardack ever be a girl's first choice? He'd been nicknamed "Dachsie"—for those legs of his with the Dachshund proportions—long before the name turned sour, when he heard it pronounced in Gerda Pohorylle's light Stuttgart accent. He'd never be first. However, the fact that Georg was amusing meant he was liked even beyond the limits of the young and their pecking orders, and the affection was persistent, Willy had understood, feeling it just now.

Georg had gotten the news from his brother, who had married and moved out west to a place with a view of the Rockies. The newspaper clipping took eons to arrive, but somehow, through the dead branch lines of the Italian mail service it did, a complete, wonderful surprise.

"Sounds like you're going to get the Nobel."

"Oh, come off it. We're just one engineer who does his experiments in a barn next to a house full of kids and two doctors in a Veteran's Hospital. In Buffalo, not at Harvard. The medical industry scouted us out and delivered big pats on the back and promises. But up to now, we've had no funding or requests to license the patent."

"OK. But a machine that boosts the heart so a person can swim, play soccer, or run for the bus is a revolution, dammit. They'll get it, sooner or later."

"Let's hope. When you called I expected it to be the hospital or some patient we've sent home. *Any problems*—by now I speak like the telephone ladies—*Let me put the call through.* But sure, I'm pleased."

"Well I'll bet. In the end, you'll be the only one of us who has changed anything. The only one who did anything revolutionary."

Chardack had an answer to that. He was thinking about the students who had waged revolution in America by sitting at lunch counters where blacks were not allowed, until Woolworths and then other five-and-dimes and drugstores in the racist South opened those counters to persons of color. Their certain, pacific belief, guided by a reverend named after Martin Luther, reminded him of the English carpenter's son, his partner, who'd become an electronic engineer thanks to the GI bill. "Providence puts me on the right path, dear Chardack," the IT man Greatbatch would say when the doctor rushed out to his barn with an urgent new problem, "and you'll see, it will all work out." It was he, Willy, the nonbeliever, who was reborn with every electric impulse guiding the heart of a cardio patient, his prayers heard by the only deity he answers to, Aesculapius.

"My work's enough for me," he said.

The other laughed, a deep, mellow laugh, in sympathy, but Chardack heard a crack in his voice and he let Georg go on.

"Sadly, miraculous inventions are pretty rare in my field. If only we could hook up something like your machine after a stroke."

Chardack sensed unhappiness once again. Maybe some levity would help. "The heart's mine, the brain's yours! We'll divvy up the vital organs the way the superpowers divide the world—even the cosmos."

"What matters is having something to divide up, no? Now that you'll be invited all around the world, make sure you look me up if you're passing through."

Chardack was relieved, they'd made it to the courtesies. In the end, it was no mean feat that of their shared aims and ambitions—medicine, Gerda, the triumph of anti-fascism—both could still lay claim to the first.

The two exchanged addresses as the conversation wound down. Kuritzkes told Chardack he was thinking of retiring from the FAO and the UN altogether. "So, Willy, I await you over here, whenever worn-out old Europe decides it too needs a machine to keep it going."

Standing by the phone after he put it down, Chardack heard again his friend's laugh, so warm despite the sarcastic undertone. But then it struck him what lay beneath the laugh, the hints Georg had dropped, and he stiffened.

Why had Georg gone to Rome, to the FAO? Had he really believed that the UN food and agriculture organization could defeat hunger, no less? He'd never been naive, or a true believer, quite the contrary. Who knows if he'd even have gone to Spain if that crazy girl hadn't come along to persuade him. To say no to Gerda, impossible! She was truly crazy, even crazier than Capa, who in turn had been horrified to learn that not only had she gone on a long holiday in Italy with the famous Georg, but the foolish woman had taken photos of the Republican militias into Italy, the cradle of fascism! Gerda, unflustered, shot back that his objection was petty, just a pretext to stage a row—and those listening, above the cozy din of a Paris café, could only stifle an admiring smile.

In any event Georg Kuritzkes joined the International Brigades, the Communists, and stayed in Marseille, and when Willy Chardack sailed for the US, Georg remained in France and joined the Resistance. But before going to the *maquis*, he got his degree and after the Liberation wrote a thesis that earned him a research post at UNESCO.

Chardack stayed away from politics, although politics didn't stay away from him. It was tough to accept that the US didn't want scientists as qualified as Georg because of their holy terror of anything Red. But maybe Georg had no regrets. Or maybe he'd returned to Italy because the UN sent him there, but was fine with that.

This conclusion cheered Chardack, and when he returned to his article the clouds that had swept in from the Atlantic had been brushed away.

Pleased to have finished a first draft of his article, hearing the doors on the ground floor bang as everyone went out, thank heavens, it wasn't immediately that he felt his distance from this world he'd landed in. It was after lunch, when he decided he would make the rounds of his patients and then head down to the east side of town, to Polonia, Kaisertown and Little Italy, where you could find some decent pastry shops. It was something that maybe he ought to do more often, not that anyone in the family expected it. Chardack had never been one

to aim beyond his capacities. Fine to bring home a cake; not fine the
abstract effort to become a *real American* when what he'd done and
was doing was already plenty. He let himself be called William, pronounced his surname American style, served two years in Korea, and
got two medals for the pump made out of a grenade that he devised to
deliver transfusions. He was proud, sure, proud of the boys he was able
to save, just as he was proud of all those American lives he was saving
with his subcutaneous pacemaker. Therefore, do not ask more of him:
America, in his view, was a country to belong to, not a religion to be
reborn in. Sometimes he missed the good things of Europe. Anything
wrong with that?

Now that he had ascertained that all his patients were stable, he
decided to leave his car at the hospital and walk over to Hertel Avenue
where there were various cafés and restaurants both Italian and Jewish.
Weather permitting, Dr. Chardack liked to walk, a habit not entirely
American. He was, as it happened, just about the only pedestrian on
his route, and the only one in jacket and tie (a light jacket over a short-
sleeved cotton/polyester shirt) on that late summer Sunday afternoon,
and of course these were the streets of North Buffalo: straight as an
arrow, punctuated with young trees to justify the term *Avenue*, lined
with freshly painted—a few were slightly peeling—clapboard houses
in pink, yellow, greenish, blue, cream, and snow white, some with
American flags, small and not so small, and each with a nice carpet of
grass out front (no picket fences!) that was surprisingly able to survive
the snow and keep the heat (the cool, not so well), as he had discovered over the years.

The only nuisance to guard against was someone wanting to give
him a lift. "Thanks, no!" he'd say, lacking any convincing reasons why
not, until he had the clever idea he might justify his eccentric pedestri-
anism as heart disease prevention. "Is that so, Doctor?" his neighbors
would reply, clutching their car keys in nervous hands. But today the
sidewalks were empty except for a pair of young girls trading secrets
and a squirrel or two so brazen you could see it came from different
stock than its poor, frightened cousins back in Europe.

Walking in a place that knows nothing of you while you know it
rather well either sets your thoughts spinning or drives them out with

every pace. It hadn't been in Leipzig that Chardack had developed the habit of taking long walks in the city, but in Paris, along the boulevards of the 6th, the 7th, and the 15th arrondissements, sometimes going as far as the elegant and even the popular quartiers of the Rive Droite. The metro cost little but it was the first expense cut by Ruth and Gerda, who didn't have an allowance from their families. It was a waste of money and anyway walking kept them slim, they maintained. Dachsie had grinned, saying that was the least of their problems. The girls would let him buy them a coffee, but only very rarely a metro ticket. What was the fun of traveling underground, squeezed into a cage, when they were in Paris? At the word "cage" Willy decided not to point out that it was about to rain. Gerda had been in prison; it was a miracle she'd gotten out, and good luck had been with her when she made her escape from Germany, too.

"Where are you headed?" he'd asked. "Do you know how to get there?"

"Thanks, Dachsie, I can manage, but if you've got nothing better to do you could come along with me part of the way."

Maybe he did have things to do (hide out in the library and stay there until it closed) but he lugged those heavy medical tomes of his well past the Pont Saint-Michel and came back with the marks of his briefcase handle carved on his fingers.

She was tireless and, after a month, seemed to have been born in Paris. Maybe that day she was going to pick up the money she'd earned for odd jobs, but they'd have to march all the way to Opéra and, on the way back, stop for a croissant and strawberries for Ruth, who was probably back in the room by now.

"That girl—not yet eighteen and already so tall—is going to faint on me if I don't bring her something sweet!"

Or else she needed to go to the post office in Montparnasse to send a letter to Georg, well, actually a mailbox and a tabac to buy the stamp would do—and while he was at it, maybe he could get her some cigarettes? There were times, when she was already sticking on the stamps for Italy and he was still waiting for his change, when Gerda would claim that dachshunds, well, if they didn't exist, you'd have to invent them.

Then she decided to study privately for her *baccalauréat*. Georg was full of encouragement and urged Willy to help her with the scientific subjects which she'd never studied. On a park bench in the Jardin du Luxembourg, she'd take the Periodic Table and Basic Physics Formulas from her handbag and the two of them would hold up the sheet, now dangerously worn along the fold lines. They sat there, hunched together in that papery intimacy of chemistry and physics until Gerda lost patience or felt the cold. How many minutes of contact with Dachsie's flannellled thigh, how long could he study the silk stockings that poked out from beneath the formulas, the small feet keeping time with the equations as she repeated them?

In the morning, opening the shutters, Willy observed the clouds above the hotel courtyard. When they were heavy enough to suggest they'd have to skip the outdoor study session, his mood, too, grew heavy. For him, cloudy skies and moderate cold were fine, but he could never guess when Gerda would want to come indoors. She would suddenly rise and begin to walk along the green wall of trees bordering the path. Her step was light but slightly nervous, or maybe it was just the gravel being ground under her heels as she advanced one stride after another. Dachsie stayed behind, sheet in hand, ready to correct her. Gerda would stop and look back, hoping to find the formula or recall the sequence of elements before he caught up with her.

Should he slow down, Willy wondered? Whether to give her more time or simply to hold that gaze of hers, he wasn't sure. Gerda almost always succeeded in tossing him an answer, pleasing him with a quick smile of triumph. Sometimes, though, watching the students come out of the Lycée Montaigne, Gerda kept walking, as if the nice coats and shining hair worn by those young things, so animated now that classes were out, made her own lessons look silly. Enough, let's quit, her feet seemed to say, picking up the pace toward the gate on rue Auguste Comte, where the kids from that venerable Parisian school were exiting the park. Willy lengthened his stride, ready to tell her firmly that those young people were no excuse to get irritated and walk off and leave him. Strangely enough, Gerda would slow down, as if she'd suddenly understood, and then Willy would hear her clear soprano voice—"Lutetium, Hafnium, Tantalum, Tungsten, Rhenium, Osmium, Iridium, Platinum, Gol . . ."—as if this were some Surrealist poem. The lycée students squeezed back to let her pass, and here and there he saw a smirk. But the eyes of a few boys sparkled with a light that Willy Chardack was quite familiar with.

Chardack would never forget block D of the Periodic Table recited in those dramatic tones, a group of elements that curiously included mercury, used in his pacemaker battery. In truth the mercury battery was no good and that was a problem he and Greatbatch had to deal with, one he couldn't wait to tackle. Chardack wasn't afraid of a challenge, as it happened. Greatbatch had never asked where the good doctor got his *sang froid* and that unshakeable confidence in the power of inventions. Maybe it was because he thought only Providence could have found him a cardiac surgeon so skilled and yet willing to spend nights in his barn. During those nights Chardack had talked a bit about his life in the Old World. He'd had enough of cafeteria lunches and dinner parties where colleagues and even perfect strangers asked the same questions over and over.

"So you went to college here or back in Germany?"

"In Europe, but not in Germany. Paris."

"Uh . . . Paris?"

"You know, even in Paris, the morgue doesn't smell of Chanel No. 5," he said once, casting a chill over an entire dinner table. Finally their host began to laugh at that med-school joke, *not bad*—but not appreciated by the wives for whom Paris was elegant and *romantic*. When the ladies went out to the kitchen to clean up, though, the fellow brought up the question again. "We've seen some pretty awful stuff, what do you say, Bill? There's nothing, except maybe death, as democratic as what a doctor does, and I see they teach that in the same unpleasant way everywhere. Hey, can I pour you another couple fingers?"

"Cheers," said Chardack, who lifted his glass and swallowed what he was about to say.

The problem, in truth, had been the living. It was certain professors who flunked a student at the exam for stumbling—not over a concept understood wrongly—but a word mispronounced or wrongly declined. "We've been invaded!" declared the posters on the streets, and the classrooms filled up with knots of students arriving in Paris from everywhere fascism and chauvinism were rampant. There were Italians here, Hungarians and Poles there, Romanians and Portuguese in smaller numbers. The Kraut Jews were here, there, and everywhere, the straw that broke the camel's back because there were so many of them, and they were feared on account of that, and also because they were often the brightest and best prepared.

Commit everything to memory, spit it out like a recording, word for word, texts five-hundred pages long. Study your eyes out long past midnight to the penny-pinching glare of two bedside lamps shorn of their flowery pastel shades (those had actually seemed rather romantic once upon a time), trembling from fatigue and the damp chill, not to mention the acid in your stomach after too many cafés crèmes to keep you from collapsing on the hotel room mattress.

"Soon a Frenchman won't be able to find a French doctor to look after him," pronounced the students who hung around Catholic youth organizations, keener on defending French ethnic purity than on glorifying Jesus Christ. In those loudspeaker voices, arrogantly tossed at a classmate.

You had to be the best to pass the exams. You could never miss a deadline. You had to hurry. And hope that the *Ligues d'Extrême Droite* didn't stage another, more successful February 6, 1934. "They're good at making champagne, but they don't know how to make a putsch yet" was the contemptuous, exorcising comment on that bloody demonstration by a fellow student from Berlin. You had to hope that the government didn't give in to the most reactionary pressures, and that the Left would win the next elections. Otherwise there were likely to be enrollment quotas, to give the French universities back to the French, and who knew what else they would come up with to make life impossible for immigrants.

Two years of uncertainty. Then, after the Front Populaire won (and there were celebrations until dawn that fourth of May, 1936), the nationalists and just plain anti-Semites among the professors grew even more vile, convinced that France's only defense now lay in them, and that they must stop the invaders by blocking them from their studies, pushing them out one by one, exam after exam.

But the privileges conferred at birth or by mother tongue vanished at the door of the morgue, where the air was stagnant, clammy, cold as death. In the morgue everyone's skin took on a cadaverous hue, whether you were the fortunate scion destined to assume the practice of your distinguished father, or the lower-middle-class son borne up by family savings and the ambitions of his kin. Those macabre-scientific rites applied to corpses didn't reveal anything about a doctor's eventual capacities, Willy used to reassure his fellow students.

Still, the morgue was a moment of testing, of vindication. A moment when no professor could deny the evidence laid out on the autopsy slab. Objective know-how. For Willy and his Leipzig friends this was all they could rely on, otherwise they could only hope that the fate they refused to acknowledge would elude them. Otherwise they would be handing control to the thugs who'd expelled them, they would validate the hateful "destiny of the race," the phony legends of people who claimed to be descended from divinities extinct for millennia. Destiny was a false myth, a cheat, a reactionary ploy. Still, they had to take their fates in their hands here in Paris, using every means at their disposal. Willy didn't hesitate to pick up the scalpel. Gerda, the only one of them in that group who'd come to Paris with a skill, kept to her typewriter until her lightly calloused fingertips first embraced the neat body of a Leica.

"Gerda plays the Remington like Horowitz the Steinway": that was the word that went around the cafés that their crowd, who slept in cramped hotel quarters or narrow dormitory beds, used as their living rooms. Those cafés were also the exchange floor for the volatile black market in jobs. Gerda's French, acquired in a boarding school on Lake Geneva, was excellent, but it also made her appear a privileged young lady who'd never lifted a finger. Her first jobs thus arrived not because people thought she might be a good typist, but just because they liked her. Imagine their surprise when she came back, very quickly, with impeccably typed documents. Her renown grew as rapidly as she typed. It might have been anyone who coined the phrase about "our Gerda" and the Steinway, anyone who needed something typed *vite vite*. But no, thought Chardack—almost colliding with a bike in his path—it had to have been Fred and Lilo Stein, who put up Gerda and the Remington in their apartment and saw her at work back then.

Willy hadn't been convinced the Steins' place was best for "our Gerda." "How's it going up there in your Montmartre exile?" he'd ask, once in a while. "Fine, very well," she'd say, and sing the praises of her room, shared with the perfect roommate, Lotte, a journalist who was also chasing odd jobs. Nor did she fail to praise her wonderful land-lords to the skies. Her landlords the Steins were not, officially; the pro-ceeds of the young women's informal sublet compensated for the rent the Steins had lost when the French photographer who'd signed the lease disappeared on them. The other tenants paid the rent more punc-tually than Gerda and Lotte could dream of, but unless the apartment was silent starting at a certain hour, they had threatened to withhold the entire sum. The two young women, if they were to meet their dead-lines, had little choice: once Lotte finished her cacophonic hammering, Gerda began beating out a fast march with drum rolls and squealing trumpets at every paragraph, the noise thundering well beyond the closed door.

And so the Steins, having offered the tenants a nightcap ("un petit cognac . . .") and many apologies (Fred wanted to give them a discount but Lilo was adamantly opposed) moved the Remington to the point farthest from the bedrooms, the dining room table where only they, the landlords reclining on their sofas, had to endure the full impact of the ratatap background music. They claimed they were used to it, they claimed Gerda's tempo reminded them of the crazy percussion beat of Gene Krupa in Benny Goodman's swing combo, not to mention the vigorous revolutionary artistry of Shostakovich and Khachaturian. "Our Gerda plays the Remington like a Steinway," they'd say, and she'd laugh, happily in tune with their praise for her solo act.

Willy had lost touch with her somewhat during that period, although she was always delighted when he showed up in Montmartre, a decent bottle in hand. The Steins were pleasant and relaxed, and often invited him, but the occasion never presented itself to get to know them better.

Years later, though, he'd met up again with Fred and Lilo on a fate-ful day, May 6, 1941, the date stamped on his ticket for the Marseilles–US passage. Willy had come down to the dock as tense as the ropes holding the ship to the pier. He watched the moorings coming off, saw the coastline disappearing in the distance. He recognized Fred as they were both heading inside from the deck. "Wonderful to see you," they'd said, with all the incredulity, the relief, the lump in one's throat those formulaic words could contain. They'd gotten to know one another during the crossing, the Steins talking and Willy happy to listen. They were already thinking ahead to their new life in America, but they spoke at length of Gerda, of the good times with Gerda, as you would expect. She was the connection that made their friendship, and ultimately, a topic of conversation not subject to those anxieties they must leave behind at least for this month on the high sea. And knowing that she was dead and buried in Paris at least meant they didn't have to wonder where she might be and what else might happen to her . . .

Chardack looked around and realized how monstrous this thought seemed in the context of a lush green, peaceful suburb where the biggest concern people had were the raccoons that ransacked their garbage cans at night. It seemed one woman had come face to face with an intruder in the bin, and the animal had stared at her in amazement, before bolting just in time. Tales that someone born in Europe had trouble taking seriously, but which nonetheless earned a column or two in the *Buffalo News*. Gerda would have gone crazy about such tales, although she'd also have wondered how anyone could live in a place where the most thrilling thing you could meet was a, what was it called, a *Waschbär*. A raccoon.

In any event, Gerda had been essential in making the Atlantic crossing bearable. From Fred and Lilo's stories he'd learned various things he hadn't known. For example, the fact that Fred had been so enchanted by her typing skills that he'd photographed her at the Remington, her light hands on the keyboard, her face lit up with a smile, a grimace, determination, concentration, defiance, wisps of allusive smoke between typewriter and camera.

During her Montmartre exile, Willy had been convinced that Gerda's interest in photography was only a passing fever. True, she needed entertainment like she needed air, and André Friedmann, who'd been buzzing around her for quite some time, did make her laugh, no question. What other reason could she have for hanging out with him? What ambitions or possibilities did that charming windbag from Budapest have, with his messy hair and silly French, a guy hoping to sell a couple of photos to the papers, like hundreds of others? He tried to make himself interesting, pretending that his miserable appearance was a look he'd chosen, but Gerda didn't fall for that, and the fellow, who wasn't stupid, had eventually stopped courting her and accepted the role of friend, mostly clownish, that she'd assigned him. Photography and the photographer were just a hobby, and a way to meet people (people like Cartier-Bresson, who had those elegant manners that betrayed his wealthy upbringing) before Gerda moved in with the Steins.

It still seemed inconceivable to Chardack that Friedmann—Capa— had become such a well-known name that even an Italian-American girl from New Jersey knew of him. "Robert Capa? You never told me!" his wife had burst out that day, seeing him blanch at the wheel of the car when the radio news announced the photographer's death in Indochina. He would have bet a lot more on Fred Stein, who'd been respected in Paris and hadn't done badly in New York, but Capa's huge success was something else, sensational.

Stein came from Dresden and had gotten his law degree in Leipzig, and he was known in Paris as an anti-fascist and a photographer. He'd taught himself photography, had earned the respect of his colleagues, and had even been able to set up a studio in Montmartre. Gerda admired this, she admired the way a professional who'd been deprived of his right to work, first by Hitler and then in France, had become the craftsman and even artist that the acrid smell of chemicals from his bathroom-darkroom betrayed. Furthermore, had noble France not been a country where even a so-so building had apartments with their own bathrooms, the inhabitants and the studio would have shared the same space with difficulty. The bathtub, however, was perpetually occupied by a clothes rack festooned with drying prints, which probably didn't please Gerda, thought Willy.

One day, when she was still sharing a hotel room with Ruth Cerf, she'd asked for help, urgently. It was a ridiculous problem, also slightly, well, embarrassing, involving bedbugs. The two young women had discovered the real cause of their rashes, misdiagnosed as allergies, and set to work to rid the room of the pests, beginning with the parasite stronghold, an ignoble mattress. They thought they had resolved the problem. But now, dammit, they were in need of a hot bath, from which to emerge with rosy faces and the wrinkled fingertips of newborns, rid of that coat of grime that always seemed to stick to the skin no matter how thoroughly they washed twice a day in the rusty sink. They didn't have the money for a bath, however, and anyway the hotel bathroom was almost more revolting than the place itself. Before Willy could do much more than send Gerda a dazed look, she launched into her request.

"You just think of something to distract your concierge, and we'll go up. From there on, it's simple; we'll take care, and leave one at a time. You don't have to do anything, just bring the key to the bathroom. Don't forget it, now."

Willy's first thought was to send them to the municipal baths, but the only one nearby, the Bains d'Odessa, had a terrible reputation. And so he resigned himself to the risk the concierge or the maid would discover he brought girls to the room (two at a time!). But everything went according to Gerda's plan. That night, however, he was still sweating, his heart pounding, and finally had to resort to a humiliating mechanical remedy to calm his state of agitation. It was knowing they had undressed there, just a few steps away down the hall. And then, a turn of events he hadn't anticipated, when Gerda came back to get her bag, took out a tin of Nivea, and said to him, "If you like, you can turn around." He quickly placed himself in front of the wardrobe, while she took off her clothes and applied the cream to her skin.

"Sorry, you'll have to wait until it's dry."

"No problem, I can wait."

"Fine, but I hate making you stand there in detention."

And in fact, when she told him she was finished, Gerda hadn't yet applied the cream to her legs. When she did, there was another wait of a few minutes before she rolled up her stockings and pulled down her skirt. What a joke, turning around when he did. He could only hope he hadn't blushed too hard when she gave him a peck on the cheek, whispered, "*Danke*, Dachsie," and hurried off, the door closing behind her.

TRANSLATED FROM THE
ITALIAN BY FREDERIKA RANDALL

VESNA PERIĆ

What Has She Done Wrong
She Hasn't Done Anything Wrong

ONCE THERE WAS a little children's song that had lyrics I didn't understand, and nobody explained them to me. No one at school sang this song to anyone, and it was apparently only my family that loved it. I don't know who started it, Mom or Dad. The little song was awfully brutal, but it had, like, a happy ending . . . They always sang it to me as a lullaby.

Mama was Kukunka, Kukunka, and Daddy was Taranta, Taranta. They had a son called Yuyu. Once they were walking, walking, out beside the Nile so deep, the Nile so deep where lived the great crocodile . . .

I walk up to Harun, who's leaning on a low wall in the park behind our school. Harun raises one eyebrow above his geeky glasses, scrunches himself up like a little pussy, and continues drawing. He mumbles softly:

"*Salam.*"

"*Salami* up your ass."

I sat down next to him.

"D'you know what's the only good thing about you people being here? The fact that the old farts won't let us go to school, as a protest. If only this would last till summer break. And then you have to get the hell out of this town. Got it? Hear what I said?"

Harun moved away. But goddammit, I'm not giving up. No, I'll never change my mind. I give that jungle bunny a mean look.

"You guys are dirty, and my dad says you Turks all smell like hogs, even though you don't eat pork. Oink, oink, oink, little piggy. What're you shitting bricks for, you little pussy? C'mon, look sharp. Come on . . .

Sit down. Look what I've got for you! Are you hungry? You have to be
hungry. Take a bite. Let's do this . . . Why're you clenching your teeth?
Take it. It's not nice to say no to things. It's not polite to turn something down when somebody's offering it to you nicely."

Harun shakes his head no. But I don't let up. I won't ever relent.

"Hey, you have to eat when I say so!"

I spread his jaws apart and push a sandwich into his mouth. Harun
growls and struggles to get away, but in the end he gives in, because he's
a pussy, a two-meter-tall pussy, and he accepts the sandwich and swallows bite after bite.

"That's it! All the way to the end. Cucumber, imported from
Macedonia. Mayonnaise, Serbian. Bun, white flour additives. Serbia.
Ham, pork. Hormones, antibiotics. Serbia. Did you eat it up? Well,
fuck me, you did eat it all. You see, there's nothing horrible about eating pork. You see—you didn't die! You didn't die, right? You're breathing. And stinking. Stinking up my city. Now beat it!"

Harun scoops up his little notebook and goes to the camp. I
mooch a cigarette and puff away contentedly. Slowly the demonstra-
tors arrive. For twenty days now they've been gathering in the park,
demanding that the fucking refugee camp be relocated outside the
city. The refugees just keep coming and coming. It's an occupation.
This isn't my country anymore! Then again, things aren't so boring
anymore. The old folks won't let us go to school, for safety's sake. We
shoot the shit all day long. Fun. In the afternoons I usually go over
to the King Spa Hotel to spy on my sister. Jelica's the prettiest girl in
Banja Koviljača, not because she's my sister but because the heavens
smiled on her. From time to time the guy who fucks her comes by.
She thinks, she believes, that he's her boyfriend and will marry her
someday, but I know that's never going to happen. Maybe this happens to some people, but not Jelica. It's karma. Mladen is an IT manager from Belgrade. He comes across as a goody two-shoes, but what
a good-looking goody two-shoes! A hipster. At some point he developed aches and pains and came to the spa for treatment. That's when
Jelica's obsession began. She follows him online, to see when he's
on Viber, when he's read her message; isn't he supposed to respond,
what's he posting on Facebook, what's he posting on Instagram, is his
wife beautiful like in the photos or only from a certain angle? He's

here again after an absence of three months. And he lies, saying those three months were the longest of his life. Then Jelica changes the tone of her voice and turns into, like, his doctor, or physical therapist, wrapping herself around him like a pampered pet. Mladen hands her a little package. She opens it as if it contained that ring from *Lord of the Rings*. Mladen tells her he thought of her every day, while she caresses the powder-pink silk nightgown. She melts from happiness seeing that he remembered the color that she loves. Jerk that he is, he apologizes for not coming to visit.

"But you did come . . ."

And I can see that she's never been happier in her twenty-two-year-old life. She puts on the nightgown. Mladen places his delicate hands on her stomach, and lowers his head, and I feel sorry for my sister, so sorry, but I keep on peering across the balcony of the hotel room right up to the moment when he tears the nightgown. I'll never understand the purpose of giving her that pointless gift, I never want to feel silk on my body, I abhor everything that's smooth and soft like that, and I abhor those loony, lovey-dovey clichés. These people do not, in fact, love each other, but who am I to say if those two monsters in my own house really do . . . I get down from the balcony and scrape my knee and step on the tail of a blind cat. The cat looks at me with the remnant of its deformed eye, for a long time, and then starts following me, like a stray dog, because I don't deserve anything better.

Harun isn't a Turk, I know. But they're all the same, all of them! Libya, Syria, Turkmenistan, Afghanistan, where does it end? They ogle my tits, my legs . . . They all have the same look on their faces. Dad raises hell with Mom because there isn't room in the summer kitchen for three more beds, to accommodate more illegals, who, although they're illegal since they haven't registered with the cops, have cash, and they'll pay more than legal ones. Ten euros a night times sixty days at minimum—and as you can see . . . We could even go to the seaside.

"What do you want with the beach? What the fuck will the beach do for you? What do you need the ocean for when you live in a spa town, you dumb cow?"

With great effort my mom opens her mouth, and in an even, monotone voice, as if she were giving the exact time of day, comes to my defense:

"Don't yell at the child what has she done wrong she hasn't done anything wrong!"

Mom always dispensed with punctuation, the same way she did with color, frequencies, and smells.

"Salt cures everything and so does sweat or tears or the sea because salt cures everything a spa does not cure rickets or sinuses from sinuses you can get terrible migraines from rickets your bones get bent Mila sweetie look at how big that bunion has grown does it hurt . . ."

For the umpteenth time I look down at my feet to confirm that all my ligaments were really present.

"Don't call me sweetie, and I don't have bunions."

Only Grandpa says nothing, because Grandpa is hard of hearing. But sometimes he reads lips. With great accuracy.

"You're still too young to be pushing daisies, daughter-in-law. Don't go asking for it."

While Dad counts the euros he's taken in for putting up immigrants, and jots down their names in a notebook (Rashid, Ahmadinedjad . . . Abbas . . .), Mom curses at him for taking Arabs into our courtyard.

"You're going to burn in hell, and the priest won't come to your name day . . ."

Grandpa, an old communist, swears at the mention of the priest and the fucking saints. He explains that the refugees are not just Arabs; there are also Iranians. I don't get the difference, but Grandpa worked in the Middle East and he knows.

"People are running from pogroms, from wars. But you, my boy, with what you earn from their trouble and poverty, well, that's why you can't sleep at night!"

I know that Dad doesn't sleep well anyway. I don't know if it's because of the money. I don't think so. I think it's because he was in a trench during the war in Kosovo. Dad pals around with Žare, who works for the city and leads the protests against the presence of the refugees. Žare drops by for a glass of *rakija* periodically, and is forever mixing it up with Grandpa over Tito's policy of friendship with third-world countries and calling the refugees *mujahideen* and Taliban until Dad calms him down and says the old fart's nerves are shot and it'd be better not to provoke him. Žare keeps on about the Arab Spring and what bullshit it was, and spouts plans to drive away all the refugees, open a new resort at the thermal spring, and bring back all those German and Swedish tourists. He reads Dad his new speech about our spa town, the touristic jewel of western Serbia. Dad takes in every word and nods his head, and orders Mom to iron his white shirt because state television will surely be there filming the demonstration and the shirt shouldn't look all wrinkled while he applauds in the front row as Žare talks about dignity and freedom of movement, as well as the right women have to wear skirts and dresses freely in their city. Dad will say straight into the camera—Let's expel all asylum-seekers from our city! Immediately! Out, out, out, out!— although in the yard of his home he is secretly harboring dozens of them for cash, and he knows no one's gonna throw them out, but he wants to go into business with Žare on this new hotel thing.

Everybody says that during the bombardment they fucked like crazy . . . Dad returned from Kosovo on a short leave and screwed Mom like a madman. I think I even felt it, and I doubt I was very far from coming out a boy, because the X and Y sperm mingled so much and came unglued and got smeared together because Dad had a very unhealthy case of blue balls. Mom thought he'd probably found somebody to fuck down there, but Dad said he'd never do that and would rather die first.

"Harun, have you ever fucked anybody? Is it true they cut you guys when you're little? It hurts less then, eh? I guarantee it! The smaller the dick, the smaller the pain. Let me see it!"

My hand shoots out toward Harun's zipper, even though I know I'd never actually touch it.

"*Na! Lotfan! Lotfan . . . lotfan . . .*" he pleaded in Farsi.

"Harun is saying words that Mila might misunderstand. Harun's not a good boy, no no, na na . . . He isn't, he isn't . . . Now Mila's going to undo Harun's zipper, gradually . . . sit down . . . easy now . . . Let me see it. Why are you so tense? Harun, stop it! Show me. I'm not going to tell anyone. Look, I'll show you mine, but it's nothing to write home about. The carpet doesn't match the drapes on blondes. They don't have black hair down there either. Instead it's sort of greenish. At any rate it's only hair. And I got my period today, just so you know, and it's a little gross, and sticky. Mom says women are martyrs from the day they're born and that just because I physically could become a mom now doesn't mean I'm cut out for it and I have to wait some more and if I wait I'll find somebody like my dad who will fuck my brains out, that's what Mom says. And I love my dad, you know, he sings beautiful songs when he's sad, beautiful songs. You can't imagine what his voice is like, he sings like a bird, except when he's screaming at Mom, but she deserves it, because she's gone senile, she can't get off her meds, weighs more than three hundred pounds, she's stopped dyeing her hair. Mom cracked up when she lost her job at the factory that makes synthetic fabrics in Loznica . . . Anyway, show me a little more of that cock, you moron! What, why are you looking at me that way?"

I knock Harun to the ground, and he says nothing, the imbecile. He doesn't resist. He just looks at me.

"Harun, why are you crying? Fuck it . . . And how do you think you're going to make it there in Holland or Germany or Sweden . . . or whatever the fuck dumb stupid places you're heading to . . . Well, how are you going to make it there? I mean, d'you think anybody's going to be waiting there for you . . . Are you thinking they're just up there waiting just for you? Well, they've got people like you coming out of their ass, you're going to wipe up their shit, d'you understand, and you'll be eating out of dumpsters, and you'll curse the day you set out from Iran with that father of yours. My dad tried it too, you know, twenty years back, but he as good as came back before he left . . . They deported him after two months."

Then I cry for a minute, to myself, so that Harun can't see, and I run over to the King Spa and hit Jelica up for some money but nooo . . . Mr. Jerk-off is there again and yet again they've locked themselves into the empty spa hotel. I can hear that she's nervous, and she asks him how long he's felt that way.

"We have three more hours . . . Do you want to waste those three hours on stupid questions? Come on, fill up the tub . . . Put in the aromatic salts . . . and the lavender . . . Lock the door . . . Just lie here beside me, OK?"

I don't know if this is pornography or romance, but I do know how pathetic it is, and Jelica knows too, but she yields.

"I'll turn out the light. So I can't see you lying. You know, it's obvious. Your eyes look to the side like that. A total lie is just a microsecond. It's just a small movement of the eye."

It doesn't last three hours but only a couple of minutes, and then

Jelica asks him about his wife. He says that it doesn't matter whether he told her about them or just said it to himself.

"Did you ever think that the only reality is what you project in your own head? And how no one can ever take that away from you? That that's the only free country. That's where I can do anything and that's when I do everything. Frustration doesn't exist there. There are no obstructions. Everything goes smoothly. High viscosity. And you know what the best part of it is? That I know that it really truly exists, somewhere, and at some time, and there always exists at least one world in which you and I are together. See what I mean?"

I don't understand what the words "viscosity" and "obstruction" refer to, but maybe Mr. Jerk-off is talking to her about matters of philosophy, because Jelica always needs to come across as intelligent.

"We still have two and a half hours . . . In that time . . . Hey, I know, I'll go off to another room and you can imagine me, like I'm really here, and I will, let's say, fuck somebody else, but it won't bother you, because really all that's real is what you project in your own head, which means here and now . . ."

Mladen lets the next few minutes pass in silence, and then he smiles and I understand why Jelica forgives all his nonsense; she forgives him because of his Brad Pitt smile . . .

"Come here, please. You have no talent for abstraction. Get on over here, and don't worry your pretty little head about multiple universes . . . Please. This stuff about the other room has made me hotter than I've ever been . . ."

It's such a drag to wait around so long; and it's such a drag that I looked up the definition of "multiple universes" on Wikipedia. I'm hungry, and I'm gonna show my tits to that guy Borko in the bakery for just a second when we're alone, and he'll give me whatever *burek* I want, and he'll tell me to be sure to come back tomorrow. Tomorrow, however, is lunch day with Mom; it's Sunday, and that is not something you want to miss.

Just a bit longer and it'll be summer break. Then I'm gonna buy the sickest bathing suit from that Chinese guy in the shop, one of the ones with three pieces. I'm counting the days till that. Every day is the same anyway, but maybe I'll miscount them and won't notice how many more there actually are . . .

Harun stands there in the park, intractable, like a shadow. He's waiting for me. He doesn't hang out with his fellow asylum seekers. He
doesn't sit in the café. He doesn't go to the betting shop. He's capable of
waiting around for me all day. I know it; I observe him in secret. When
I don't go to school, I stand behind a tree. Harun doesn't move; he sits
and draws. He only leaves in the afternoon to pray with his dad and
he promptly returns to the little wall. Then I jump him from behind.

"Salam, Mila!"

I unwrap one of my mom's cheese pitas from its paper bundle.

"Take this. Don't eat the crap from that bakery. Cheese and eggs.
What are you sniffing for? What the fuck, man! Eat it. I'm not a monster. Even I have a soul, sometimes . . . My mom still rolls out the filo
dough for the pitas on the table. Mom's from Bosnia. Across the Drina
there. Holy shit, just eat it . . . D'you have any dough? Cash—how
much you got? I know you have some, you piss-ant, and you have to
split someday anyway. Your permit is expiring . . ."

Harun pulls out a bundle of banknotes, all of them red . . .

"One, two . . . six, seven . . . around sixty euros, then . . . Will you
give them to me?"

Harun nods his head like an imbecile. I can't believe he's that much
of a dope, but it looks like he might actually be. He gives them to me
and keeps on laughing!

"Hold on—you've got cheese on your nose! Let me rub it off. There."

I wipe off Harun's nose with my thumb and lick the piece of cheese
off it.

*The crocodile leaps out, the crocodile leaps out, out of the deep river Nile,
river Nile, and caught the little Yuyu . . .*

That night, as I'm slowly sinking into sleep, I hear Dad yelling at Jelica
for staying out so late in town. Dad claims to be worried about her on
account of the asylum seekers, but Jelica knows that Dad is about to
renew his demand for refugees to be put up in the empty spa hotel, so
that we, as a family, make fat stacks of money and live super well, but
Jelica persistently refuses. Dad raises his voice more and more, for in
fact he's taken money in advance, and now he has to lodge the people
somewhere. But Jelica comes upstairs into our room while Dad keeps

jawing about this with Grandpa. All of a sudden Dad opens the door
and grabs Jelica by the hair, pulls her down the staircase, Jelica shrieks,
and then I hear our mother. I bolt down from the upper floor, and I see
that Dad has chucked Grandpa out into the courtyard and he's kicking
and kneeing Mother in the stomach. Mother drops and then he goes
on stomping on her. It's unbelievable how much force is in my puny
little father. I don't remember his ever laying a hand on Jelica, only
on Mom, but this is different. She's not his blood. Blood pours out of
Mom's eyebrow ridges, and Jelica can't see anything with her eye anymore; it must still be in there, that eye of hers, but the lid is all swollen
and a purple bruise is already appearing. Mom picks herself up off the
floor and takes a swing at Dad, but he dodges it. Grandpa puts his arm
around me and takes me into the house, but I do not cry. I just put on
water for Jelica's tea, made from thyme, and I pour out some *rakija* for
Mom, and Dad is nowhere in sight.

*Mama Kukunka cries, Kukunka cries, Daddy Taranta cries, Taranta cries,
give us back our Yuyu!*

Mom and Jelica lie there, wrapped in an embrace, and I wait till
Grandpa is asleep too, I finesse Mom's smokes, pack a few small things
in my backpack, and resolutely head for the refugee camp.

"I have to spend the night at your place tonight. It's a madhouse
at home. Understand? Why are you looking at me that way? I'm not
going to do anything to you. Don't be afraid."

Harun carefully takes off my backpack and lays it on the bed. Next
to the bed is a picture of a very pretty woman with incredibly black
eyes. So black you can't see her pupils, just like with Harun's. And
a vast mountain and sunset, and in that picture I also see the wind,
though there's not a single tree. I see it nonetheless. Harun takes off
my tennis shoes. And my socks. He looks at my feet and I'm ashamed
because I do not have attractive toes. Then he picks up a brush with a
number of teeth missing, unbraids my hair and brushes it out. I scowl.
What the fuck. I hate brushing my hair and I never do it! But Harun
persists, and then he tosses all my hair over one of my shoulders. It's
going to be a portrait, but I don't know what he's going to do about

my feet. He takes his charcoal and draws. I yawn because I'm really tired. Harun closes his sketchbook, turns out the light, and covers me with a blanket.

"*Duset daram*, Mila. *Duset daram.*"

I don't know Farsi, the language Iranians speak, but I know what that means. I drift off to sleep. Harun keeps on sitting there. He'll spend the whole night like that.

From the deep river Nile, river Nile, spoke up the crocodile, the crocodile, now bring me a roasted ox!

I know that Dad's yelling now at everyone in the house and threatening to kill them because his fucking cash has disappeared from the drawer, two grand in euros. He goes even more bananas when Mom tells him that I haven't been there for two days and he hasn't even noticed.

Mama Kukunka runs, Kukunka runs, and Daddy Taranta runs, Taranta runs, to get him that roasted ox.

Harun and I lie there naked, with our eyes on the stack of bills on the bed, but he couldn't care less about the money.

"Look, this is definitely enough for a month, maybe two, by the sea. I'll take Jelica's ID card so I can cross the border, and they won't figure out what I've done. And you'll cross it the same way you got here to us. Oh, you don't know—you've never been to the coast! And neither have I, actually. And you know, sometimes I catch this scent, seriously, in the summer when the weather's clear and calm in the morning and the wind blows up from the sea, and it comes along the Drina River till it hits me. I can smell the salt in the air, and now and then fat burst figs and black olives. People say this is impossible, that it all disperses in the atmosphere and disappears, but I know it isn't so. I can always tell when the wind is in from the sea . . ."

Harun smells my hair, and I feel certain that he also smells salt in the air here, and I know that no one is ever going to be as tender as he is. Then he gets up slowly, helps me into my dress, buttons up his trousers, makes a fussy little stack of all the money and puts it in my backpack. He puts his little drawing pad with his sketches in there too. And he removes his braided necklace and places it in the backpack. I start yelling.

"What the fuck, you cretin! We're going to the seaside, do you hear? We need to start now. We have to figure out which border crossing I'll wait for you at. And are we taking the ferry or going around the bay? It's longer that way, but the views are nicer. Actually, I'm afraid of that ferry, and that's why I say that. Listen, Harun! You can't give up now, now that we've planned it all out. I have to get to that sea, do you understand? Otherwise I'm going to die here. Know what I'm saying?"

Harun's unimaginably large eyes fill up with tears, and he hugs me so firmly that I can feel my ribs, and underneath them I can feel my soul, too. It's a slick little gray thing in the middle of my belly.

"You're a dick. How can you leave me now? No fair. Look, have it your way. We don't have to stay two months, exactly. Maybe ten days. No prob, right?"

Harun combs my hair out again and wipes away my tears, and I bite him so hard on the back of his hand that my teeth leave marks in his flesh. Harun doesn't yelp with pain at all. He's out of tears.

"Fine . . . Goodbye, then. I'm going now."

And I don't turn around once, although I was dying to turn around and kiss that bite mark and fall repentantly at his feet and say: Forgive me, you are going to the north, I'll be going south, and this is like birds who get their seasons mixed up. But I do not turn around.

So then, in the fall, Grandpa and Jelica head out for Grandpa's house in the mountains, with one suitcase between them. Jelica hugs me without a word and cries, Grandpa gives me a kiss on the cheek, and, as he did when I was little, gives me a Partisan salute, which I used to find so amusing back then. I'm happy that Jelica won't bug me anymore about combing my hair every morning and that I'll be able to read her forgotten diary in secret. And while they climb the mountain, Jelica's stomach is large, larger than the slope itself, but they're both quick, she and Grandpa, and they talk excitedly about the old walnut tree, mowing the weeds behind the house, and cleaning out the well. Jelica, perhaps, doesn't want to know how to milk the goats, but Grandpa's going to teach her. And the women from the village will teach her how to make goat cheese. She'll go down into the city only to have the baby, and then she'll come back up to the village.

Dad will be furious that she didn't tell him he has a grandson, but she has no desire to be in contact with anyone.

The crocodile speaks up, speaks up, out of the deep river Nile, the deep river Nile: You can have your Yuyu back.

On that day, Dad and I will be eating lunch in silence. Dad will prepare a pot of green beans with no meat, and I'll find it disgusting, but I won't be able to tell him. He worked hard on it, and that would break him. And he will cut flowers and put them in a vase. That day will be Mom's birthday, but she will still be in the hospital. Mom's not sick but she also isn't well, and they put her in the hospital because she can't try to off herself there. She didn't try it here, either, but Dad was tripping out. Dad will offer me a little sour cream, and stir it into what's on my plate, and he will mumble that some letter or other has arrived. I will swallow a big mouthful and ask whether the letter's from Mom.

"Hell no. Sweden."

I won't say anything for a few seconds.

"So maybe it's for . . . for Jelica?"

Dad will shake his head.

"I left it on the bed in your room."

I will jump out of my chair and run upstairs. Out of the letter will tumble an endless stream of mother-of-pearl dust, and the letter will be redolent of some other sea.

Because this sea is completely gray, but there is a breeze. Like on your sea. I chose the hardest shells, so they won't break before they get to you. The smell of oil from ships mingles with salt and mud. I think back to your hair. There's no hair anywhere that's that disheveled or has that color. Your bite is still there. I'm the only one who sees it, for here I constantly have on long sleeves and a jacket. You have a gap between your upper teeth, and that's the symbol of a lucky person. I sleep in a shack in the port. My father died. He suffocated in the false bottom of a tugboat. He didn't make it to Sweden. A little girl in yellow boots walked past me one day as I was drawing your portrait (I don't know if maybe you've cut your hair?), and stared, and smiled.

I gave her the drawing of a girl with green freckles, orange hair, and purple eyes. Her mother wanted to pay me for the drawing, but I turned her down. I hope you aren't mad that I gave you away.
  Harun

  PS: Is there some way to go up that Drina River in a ship made to go across the ocean? I'm leaving tomorrow. First stop Singapore. I don't know anything about boats except that you're afraid of them.
  Love, Harun
  (crossed out)
  I love you.

TRANSLATED FROM THE SERBIAN BY JOHN K. COX

KENAN GÖRGÜN

The Revolt of the Fish

I'M UP IN arms. The fact that I'm a fish in no way excuses the treatment I've had to endure. Ah . . . I can tell I'm about to get carried away.

Let me start over from the beginning.

I'm up in arms. The fact that I'm a fish in no way excuses . . .

In short: My present status as a fish (I say "present" because of my peculiar belief in reincarnation), my rare quality, then, of being reincarnated as a marine creature did not justify such harsh treatment. When I relive the bite of the hook in my flesh, I picture again, in all its cruelty, the time I was torn from the swells of the Marmara near the abutment of Galata Bridge in the glorious city of Istanbul.

I have a clear enough peripheral view of my situation for me to be able to carry out the resistance movement I plan to start, to end once and for all the abuse inflicted on us by those human beings who lord it over us with their *scornful arrogance*—I borrow that term from a valiant union organizer of bygone times (his race has since gone extinct, a little like some of ours) to describe the detestable attitude of a clique of business owners who were responsible for a restructuring that drove hundreds of thousands of employees out of work (all right, perhaps not as heavy a blow as extinction, but surely not far from it). Furthermore, among the pitiful men who are stalking my cohorts and me in pursuit of a bite of food on the cheap, I recognized some of those jobless men, those knights of sad countenance tilting against the windmills of destitution. For in this city poverty is a cunning beast, a mist that envelops the Golden Horn, impossible to neuter. It grabs your rotting organs like an infection that attacks the moment you lose your health insurance!

Sorry. My wriggling is becoming more frantic, I can clearly see. So, let me calm down a bit.

I sense that I'm on the verge of working out one of the knottiest complexities of this affair and I wouldn't want to get it wrong due to overexcitement. It makes me shiver to the tips of my scales. Agitation, together with a zeal for justice, sweeps over me in waves.

It was evening, a blustery evening that crenellated the Marmara, and the city shone with a thousand lights. The Galata Bridge connected the Old City—cradle of History, of mosques, churches converted into mosques, and palaces turned into museums—with modern Istanbul, which gathered to itself all that capitalism had invented in the way of garish signage. As always, the bridge was teeming with scores of fishermen, lining the guardrails on both signs of the roadway that led across the bridge, and all around the lights made the city sparkle like a trunk full of diamonds.

The fishermen's rods stuck out over the sides of the bridge, as if it were adorned with a sequined hat, and as if this effect were replying directly to the glittering points of light that radiated from the city.

I've never personally had that sweeping view from the Galata Bridge and its surroundings (although I've been dazzled more than my share by the panorama of Istanbul's several shorelines); it would not have been visible to me from my niche on the seabed, nor, surely, would I allow myself to ramble on about it solely to meet the aesthetic demands of the narrative. Rather, I'm recounting the description of our common living environment related to me recently by a gull, a creature that can survey it from the clouds.

My mention of gulls is apt, since those birds, which make up an integral part of the sky above Marmara, as we fish do its waters, are among the principal protagonists of the events I'm going to describe to you.

They were our predators at first, and later our allies.

At this point I must note that the need for nourishment prompts behavior that can't be gauged by morality alone. This is as true for the animals as it is for the twenty million souls who inhabit the metropolis. Gulls have been regarded as our natural enemy for a very long time. They're famous for diving beneath the surface of the water and plucking their dinner from our ranks before taking off again. I remember a first cousin who'd gotten snagged on a fishhook and, successfully freeing himself as he emerged from the water, had wound up in the beak of a laughing gull. It was all over for my cousin, like so many of my relatives before him. The men were decimating us from the land, and just above them loomed the gulls, implacable and endlessly vigilant.

Then that changed. But let's stick with the chronology.

It was on that gusty evening that I bit the hook.

There was nothing funny about it. It was a first for me, a baptism by fire, so to speak. Others have told me I'd already managed to slip off a hook in my early years, thrashing around so vigorously I'd caused the hook to detach from my throat without any damage to my organs. But I'd retained no memory of that, which in my system of values came down to practically not having experienced the episode, our memory being the definitive prism through which our life gains nuance and depth. To be sure, but on the other hand, what is it that assures you an event has occurred if the sole proof is the memory you retain of it? And although collective memories might possibly serve as such proof, I nonetheless doubt that much confidence can be placed in a single individual's memory. Memory and truth are not subjects taken lightly along the Galata, or beyond. If you consider it, the implications of this axiom are enormous. Imagine the possibility that History is strewn with Great Indisputable Official Facts, finding their basis in the declarations of one man or several, and yet we all know that if the flesh is weak, consciousness is equally so. In my case, if I set that anecdote from my youth alongside what I'm about to tell you, I deduce from it at best that what I'm about to tell you must have happened to me at one time or another (which isn't bad for a start).

Having swallowed the hook, cursing the bait that made it look so fetching and my weakness in succumbing to it, then explaining to myself that I'd been justifiably attracted by the prospect of keeping myself fed, I suddenly felt a powerful tug exerted on my body by the dynamic force at the other end of the line.

For a second or two, the fisherman and I had been perfect collaborators, closer than friends, relatives, or lovers. Connected by this fishing line that linked us together in a contest of strength whose outcome was relatively foreseeable—a line like a long, gleaming worm—we were each other's prisoner and guardian, locked in the ritual of a conflict we were eager to ignite. Then the power of my fisherman, perched on the bridge on the other side of the water, vibrated along the line and traveled to me via the hook, it was as if I'd been skewered by an electrical discharge of 100,000 volts. In the throes of an indescribable torment, I was snatched and yanked out of the water, in a rehearsal, I suppose, of my soul's imminent ascent to fishly paradise. That's what's called breaking the surface!

I already had plenty of practice lunging out of the water to impress finny females.

Surrounded by my schoolmates, I'd launch into an extravagantly showy routine. Intoxicated by my own agility, I'd do loads of stunts in the hope of getting it on with far-from-svelte lady tunas. But by the evening of my ordeal, those carefree times were eons away. At the end of the hook, I was doing a similar thing—albeit unwillingly—and the magnanimous tunas were watching with glimmers of anxiety as I spun out of control. I sensed that my life was, in every sense of the term, hanging only by a thread, and that I urgently needed to marshal my forces and wits in the service of immediate action. The sole order of the day: "Escape or die!"

Fate nonetheless seemed swifter than I, for it maintained the advantage and I found myself encircled by the flamboyance of the Istanbulian night, whirling ass over teakettle in tempo with the gyrations of the line. I sensed that the wind was blowing north-northwest and that the atmospheric pressure, as far as I was concerned, would soon skyrocket. I, too, was soaring upward and saw for the first time what my human predator looked like.

He was grindingly ordinary.

Scruffily dressed, his face lopsided and badly shaven, clinging to the handle of the rod with all the force of desperation, his eyes nearly overflowing with tears of gratitude; I had the dispassionate thought that I'd gladly have let myself be eaten by this poor wretch if my survival instinct hadn't been so insistent.

I would've preferred an adversary who inspired less pity and more rage.

But the line connected us and it was double or nothing.

The fact remains that my man wasn't a very skilled angler, and he manipulated his rod with such clumsiness that I soon passed over his head in a circular arc and landed on the sidewalk with a terrible thud! A shock that was no joke—I mention this to educate the people I heard laughing at the moment of impact, including a young European guy jabbering in a dubiously mongrelized mix of Turkish and English.

Pushed on by an unwavering idea, I was wriggling non-stop between the fisherman's fingers, the glistening lenses of my terror-stricken eyes taking in a number of details. Out of the water and its distorting undulations, I realized I was seeing closely for the first time those famous beings called humans. And though trickles of water continued to run down my eyeballs, they didn't prevent me from noticing a fine sample of Istanbul's population on the bridge.

I saw two old fellows who seemed to have just arrived from a far-away Anatolian village scarcely touched by modern civilization; I saw two young couples who'd come for a bit of fun and whom I had trouble distinguishing from the young European, they were so similar to him in their manner and apparel, as well as in some indefinable quality, which linked them profoundly to the West; I saw a man in his forties carrying two buckets full of fish and walking toward a wooden wagon mounted on caster wheels equipped with a hotplate, a tray of crudités and another of bread, and with the words GALATA FIŞBÜRGER painted in crude letters on the side of the vehicle; I saw a man with the sallow complexion of an office worker in a threadbare suit and a limp necktie, in the company of his son in a schoolboy uniform, buy from the vendor, for five lira each, two grilled fish sandwiches; I saw a veiled woman accompanied by a very young child, whom I think I would have resembled if I'd been human, and the woman, like the others, was trying to snare a few morsels to brown in a pan she'd purposely brought along. And, also, on Galata Bridge, surrounded by the twinkling city, were young tea vendors who carried, strapped to their shoulders, insulated dispensers with pressurized spigots for delivering hot drinks, one lira fifty a cup, sugar and stirrer included; vendors of a dish called *bulgur pilavi*, sold for the modest sum of three lira including a cup of yogurt to drink; a kid carrying on his head a platter of crown-shaped sesame bread and crying out, "*Si-miiiit!*" in a nasal voice; a bearded man, clothed in religious garb, pushing a dessert cart sheltered

under a glass canopy, who looked at me with a milder expression than
the one he'd shot at the young westernized Turks. All of them, otherwise so diverse, had something to sell, inexpensive little things, to drink
and eat, things that everyone could afford. For the most part, their carts
had a lantern for light, fastened to the top of a wooden pole. And yet,
surrounded by lights as dominating as those of the city's three waterside
districts, their lanterns—lightning bugs by comparison—struggled to
cast any visible illumination at all.

Finally free of the hook, I had only an instant's reprieve before the
hands of my fisherman, more adept by the second, picked me up from
the sidewalk and carried me toward a bucket with a hole drilled in its
lid, an ingenious and economical contrivance that would enable him to
slide me through it like a coin into a piggybank and also bar me from
attempting the journey in the opposite direction, since a well-behaved
coin never tries to leave its piggybank without permission. I thought I
was done for, I lamented the shortness of a life and, above all else, its
absurd, absurd fragility. Death hadn't the least bit of pompous cere-
mony. It arrived without elegance, without announcing itself, and the
very worst joke for a living creature was to discover in the final reckon-
ing the precariousness in which he'd been created and was destined to
remain until his last breath. There you are—that lesson was all I had the
luxury of taking away. Woefully meager, I told myself.

Then my silvery body passed through the pierced well of the sky-
blue plastic lid, and I was in the sky-blue bottom of the bucket, bathed
in an inch or two of water that had the sadistic purpose of keeping me
alive in a torpid state until the time came to toss me into the cooking
pot. I heard my undernourished fisherman accept a poke in the ribs and
the congratulations of a fellow angler. I glimpsed him again when he
leaned over to examine me quickly with a smile that was half victorious
and half regretful over the pain he'd inflicted on me for his own deliv-
erance. He had a very expressive face, with dense, bushy eyebrows, and
the structure of his nose was marked by a pronounced curvature, different from the more delicate or more bulbous noses I'd seen on the faces
of other humans with lighter complexions. He admitted to his neighbor that the few fish he'd managed to catch had made up his entire food
intake in the two weeks since his release. He then spoke of his arrest

for political reasons I didn't grasp very well. He'd had quite a good job before being thrown in the slammer. That said, it was only thanks to the remarks of his neighbor that I understood they were talking about prison, for the person concerned, my fisherman, preferred to say he'd been "retained as a guest for a long stretch," a cryptic formula I found full of dignity. An endearing man, truth be told.

Alas, in our nascent yet all-but-ended relationship, the shiny fishing rod and our zero-sum combat had set his hardship and mine at odds, and prevented me from dwelling on his woes. So, I started wriggling again. No, in fact, I did much more than that, I spasmed, I contorted myself, I leaped repeatedly, and boosting myself up with all my strength, I succeeded in bashing the lid again and again, until I'd jarred it loose, escaped from the bucket, and ended up a short distance away, thrashing on the sidewalk, while the lid, a counterfeit sky blue, was rolling on its edge beneath the actual sky, black and moonlit.

Catching sight of the water through the guardrail bars, I felt life stir again in my gills, just as a redemptive wind inflates the sails of a doomed ship to save it unexpectedly. The only thing I felt was the purely physical will to get to the water. The one time the fisherman's hands closed around me, I thanked the fish gods that I'd chanced upon a novice, and it wasn't very hard to extract myself from his fingers. Still, I felt a terrible pang when I heard him moan, and then I was through the bars, and the immensity of the Marmara's shimmering waters called me with the dulcet song of its welcoming depths.

As I was poised to jump, I caught sight of a gull flying over me with unmistakable intentions. Recalling the life-saving escape I'd first managed as a child and had just now repeated, I sensed suddenly above me the mythological shadow of my destiny—more dominating than the gull's presence—exhorting me to take heart. The gull was diving with his beak already gaping when I shot him a steely look that left no doubt he ought to spare my life. And, to my surprise, I saw my wish granted. I even detected a touch of perplexed admiration in his eyes. As he passed me, he shrieked that he would share the message with his flock and that I could thereafter rely on their commanding view of the territory whenever it was a question of protecting us from intruders and pointing us toward the nearest underwater channels where we could find refuge, all in exchange for permission to feed on us in reasonable quantities, or, in lieu of that, on nutritive sediments we would churn up from the sea floor for the gulls' consumption . . . I was astonished by the effect my daring had had on this bird, who was proposing to me in no uncertain terms to organize a concerted resistance against the oppressors. I owe to that radical gull—at least as much as to my own aspirations—the seeds of the revolt presently rumbling in the depths of the seas. That being so, the proposed give-and-take seemed to me to be in deep harmony with ecological values (although it implies the sacrifice of some of our kind in submission to slanted criteria, as is so often the case when necessity shapes the rules).

In my fall toward the water, amid the rush of air streaming through my exhilarated scales, I noticed enormous fishing trawlers crossing the waters beyond the industrial port. These ships are designed to sweep clean a broad swath of the seabed. I recognized, attached to the sides of the vessels, systems of sophisticated nets, as well as the steel claws I had already encountered in the world down there, the scene of some of the worst tragedies to have befallen my race. I'd seen firsthand that those claws were responsible for the destruction of so many of our spawning grounds, stealing the lives of millions of my cohorts and causing our species losses incomparably more severe than any that could ever be inflicted by the fishermen of Galata Bridge. I was sure that if I swam up to the claws, I'd see the pulverized residue of those millions of eggs encrusting their surfaces like an indelible stain of guilt, one that a doomed future would hurl at the shameless face of a grossly selfish and rapacious present.

In my fall, I understood that despite the terrifying aspects of the situation I had just experienced, I had confronted my destiny, and that refusing to recognize it would be a fatal error. In the world on the other side of the waters, human sharks, comparable to the ones we fear at the bottom of the ocean, were imposing their law on timid shoals of tiny fish. In the final moments of my existential fall, while the water wrapped me in its tangy scent, angelic voices were raised atop the minarets that dotted the city's unforgettable landscape, and I realized I'd come to understand the need of a great many human beings, when things go badly on terra firma, to believe that mythical and benevolent spirits are gliding above their heads and looking after them. In those moments—amid the ambient chorus of calls to prayer—everything seemed calmer to me.

Space, spirits, and sea—a calm that preceded the storm.

A storm that's called change.

TRANSLATED FROM THE FRENCH BY PAUL CURTIS DAW

IRAKLI QOLBAIA

Penurious Words of the Parsimonious

It's never night when I die.

Intense! naked! A human fire fierce glowing, as the wedge
Of iron heated in the furnace. His terrible limbs were fire . . .

IN THE MORNING once more you ascended from the underworld—a gray day, the kind you'd love, if you still loved anything—and searched through the pockets of your coat, a painful procedure that revealed you had three euros and three cigarettes left, which means that beginning tomorrow you'll have nothing left to smoke and—because money appears only out of nowhere—you'll be unable to pay the rent; you don't notice now the people around you (why do you never notice people around you when you're feeling bad, when that is the only time there's any point in noticing people), on the corner of the street a strong smell seized you: *the smell of glue and paint,* when you die, too, they will glue you up against the wall and paint you the color of the wall—so that's where everybody's gone, this phantom city, the sharp cylindrical pencil-top of the Catholic cathedral is floating in the saturnine blue, since you gave up using your glasses, since you decided why should there be such a thing as *seeing correctly,* every kind of seeing must have an equal right to existence, and if Cézanne could, and if El Greco could, if Brakhage could, and, in general, there's no need whatsoever anymore for you to see anything, anything at all, anything whatsoever anymore—except maybe two steps ahead, if you prefer to be a little more pragmatic, you try to cut all the unnecessary words out of your vocabulary, such as hello, thank you,

same to you, could you please, and could you possibly, please, and so
on, but this has proven a task much harder than taking off your spectacles and throwing them into one of two rivers, which is much too
easy (and then the democracy of words, for instance, how long since
you last said the word *cone*), at one time you knew beauty (each night
I see you in my dreams, so each night before sleep I rehearse in front
of the mirror), how does the lunar Pierrot move, and how can you
touch what the magic lantern reflects, today you observed your reflection in the metro window, its sad eyes looked back at you, that it had
sad eyes would have once been a very joyous piece of news, you built
this malkuth of your solitude with hellish geometry, only to find out
later that you're ashamed of your own solitude, this morning your
head hurt you, which means that birds have already made a nest out
of the hair they stole from you, the hair you dropped while you were
smoking, perched on the windowsill, never let the magician have
your hair (*you know, you look a little like Mondrian, and you know, you
look a little like shit*), you went through your pockets and once it
turned out they had nothing in them but holes you jumped for joy,
you clapped your twin soles and lit out on the road (but of course this
is no silly Kerouac story), two curves vertically mirrored, one horizontal curve set upon them, one arrow-straight horizontal running in
the higher part of the figure and from its center a straight vertical line
hung head down, a tiny triangle gazing downward positioned in the
extreme low point of the vertical, and two black dots sitting in paral-
lels in respect to the vertical $(0; -2,5)$; $(0; 2,5)$—this is what you saw
reflected in the dirty window, and do you still wonder why you're
alone, you saw how a fat man was torturing a small cat the color of
rubbish, the Japanese seem to have believed that when somebody
offends you the shame is yours and *you* should go kill yourself, you
believe that when you witness the violence the fault lies in your eyes
and it's your eyes you should pluck out, but *eyes see more than the
heart feels*, but they see less than they should, but you can punch in
the code number on the entrance door to your building without looking, as you shall do right now, for you are standing in front of it and
now either get inside or go to hell, for example, in the middle—down
straight—upper left—right pole, the door opened and you entered
the building, the second floor of which contains an apartment where

you live, and this is interesting: you got used to the fact that your apartment was on the second floor even though you always thought it a third floor, but then you were told that in truth your apartment is on the first floor, for what you thought was the first floor turns out in fact to be a sort of basement, a non-floor anyway, and the semi-floor between the basement and your floor is in fact no floor at all (even if there is a lonely crooked door hanging from it), so now begin your ascent of the floor and a half to get to the first floor, for on your own you're unable to grasp anything, when they ask you what you think about the schools and universities of Europe (this is a synthesis of about a thousand different questions, but has one sole answer) you answer that you think the same as Blake did, but—and here's where the trouble comes in—when they ask what was it that Blake thought about the Schools and Universities of Europe you can't answer any-more, for you can paraphrase the first part of it (I fix my gaze on the schools and universities of Europe) but the rest of the phrase is quite unsayable, at least for you, sometimes you cheat: you skip this part and go straight to: the wheel without the wheel, not like (and here once again you skip a few more words: Garden of Eden, for if you'd say "not like the ones in the Garden of Eden" surely no one will listen any further, something you can try one day, if you decide to be Blake-like yourself), wheel within the wheel and so on, on the stairs that follow on the entrance to this building—mostly in the areas of the basement (with a womb-like space for mailboxes carved into it) and the half floor, which turns out is no floor at all—three times you saw a blond girl aged about six who'd always hide in the strangest of places and, sadly, at that moment you thought of Dostoevsky, yes (admit here that the pretty phrases in your writings are all stolen), *and if your thought-dreams could be seen they'd probably put your head in a guillotine* (but no one can ask originality of you for if the point is for your writing to be completely unlike any other writing you'll have to come up with new arrangements for letters, and if they themselves will ever try to sneak into the verbal part of their own minds, like you're trying to do right now, for instance, they'll hardly be able to find many original lines there, only ones they remember, you think, that should they label you with a label that begins with, for example, the letter *p*, you'll visit them in their dreams and cut them to little pieces), you've

reduced the objects in your room to the least possible number: one
table, one chair, and one mattress on the floor, and somebody's piano
that you can do nothing about, once this room was hemmed in with
the color reproductions and pictures of world masterpieces, of which
you left only two (down with the photos, down with Miró, down
with Klimt, down with the rest): one Klee and one Kandinsky, and,
of the numerous books, only two: one Joyce and one Flaubert (but
the Flaubert too will be thrown away in a couple of days, and there
will be just one book left, that you can read ad infinitum), in your
head there are two holes through which you see the world, and every
room you've ever been in was perfect, a place where every object is
close enough to be clearly seen, with the same logic that God created
woman, yesterday a woman asked you for a lighter and then disappeared into the mist, what were you to do, you could, for instance,
pull the whip out of your socks and cry, be not ashamed, love is not
sin, or else you could talk to her, but even so the conversation wouldn't
end up being set down here, and besides, as the family idiot put it,
nothing's harder to write than a trivial conversation, but then again
he does it anyway, and this act fills him with the—equally—trivial
pleasure of the *enfant gâté*, the pleasure of laughing at people when
you have no wish whatsoever to do so (and after all, had you been a
cynic, you'd be perfectly happy in the country whose most beloved
national [*voire mondial*] novelist is Flaubert and whose most beloved
national [*voire mondial*] poet is Baudelaire), and by the way, you
found something curious reading it this time around: in the book
there are (at least) three characters whom the author gives the same
name as he gives the book, and of these three not one is (in contradis-
tinction to what is generally believed) less important than the other
two, all three have a colossal impact on the life of the character whom
you've always considered the protagonist of the book, but this point
of view, too, had to be altered reading it this time around: the protagonist of the book makes his appearance only on the first (two) page(s)
of the book (and thereafter haunts it like a ghost) and he addresses
himself—as does every other character in the book—in the first person, a point that, apparently, most everyone missed, so he himself had
to explain (he who was so meticulous about how his work would be
received by society), Madame Bovary is me (a statement that was

understood by still fewer of its readers), all three and all the other
Madame Bovarys, and, it goes without saying, this would have been
so even if the protagonist hadn't manifested himself on the first (two)
page(s) of the book, and he knew this, that is he knew what a discovery he'd revealed in this novel, and that's why he could say, later, that
it's a novel about nothing, one evening you took a walk and were able
to see how the evening phantoms mingled, a few of them recognized
you, saluted you, and told you they were visiting friends, whereas you
were going nowhere, and then you got lost and hardly found your
way back home, and arrived home in five minutes after having left it,
as did Odysseus who had erred for twenty years, but meanwhile had
got inside a thousand houses, and would get out of each one of them
for five minutes or sometimes more, *Cars are dignified, men despair,*
the lower right-hand side of one of the two reproductions informs
you, today you saw an announcement in the street that read "*le jour
je suis un étudiant, la nuit je vends mon cul—Jonathan, 22 ans (s'in-
staller à Lyon!)*" There is Zeno's Trieste, there is Clarissa's London, and
there is your Lyon, which looks like this:

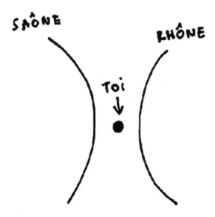

and here's to Heinrich, Robert, Scott, and all the others who wished
to disappear, even though no one ever said the dot vanishes more
quickly than the cities, on the contrary, the first to go are always

cities, planets, worlds, each human is a world, and so is each public toilet, recently a professor (who resembled a cat but whose surname was horse) said, *Artaud—a great French poet*, in the past you'd have thought that this four-worded phrase contained three mistakes, or rather that the given conjunction of the four words in this phrase results in a false whole, which would have made Artaud himself, as they say, roll over in his grave, this is what you'd have thought in the past, but now you see the matter more dimly and the ideas behind it more clearly, and so you thought, sadly, about how culture digests everything, even Artaud, who said the only thing that interested him was what lay outside the culture, and who wrote a totally cryptic letter to Hitler (who is, by the way, quite probably, the only painter, writer, and public figure that the culture will never quite digest), who fought for the same thing as all the universities in the world: white man's culture, white man's civilization, the way, in the first years of school, you often ate chalk (*chalk*—another word it seems you haven't said for a century), teachers would say this meant you lacked calcium, which sounded good and you believed to be true, but, later, you understood what you lacked was not calcium, what you lacked was whiteness, and then the cigarette replaced the chalk, which is also white on the outside and has exactly the same shape as the chalk in your school, generally, white things were always of great importance for you, for example the eternal white noise in your ear, for example such foods as rice, milk, Moby Dick, and the natural, awkward association that you have forces you to change the subject of contemplation, why did cinema die at the end of the sixties, because it was invented as an academic subject, Genet (a wholly cultured writer) and Bolaño (not quite cultured yet, though he's been dead for ten years) both stole books (an act which already makes one an honorary member of culture), you could never have stolen a book alone (it takes guts), but together with a comrade of yours you did, in a certain bookshop in Tbilisi: you stole a book by Orhan Pamuk, called apparently *My Name Is Red* (red was your favorite color up to the third grade, and you were ashamed of it, for at school they said that the devil was red and, therefore, red was the devil's color), which ended up among your belongings and which you never read, but hopefully, one day, the roofs of all the literary cafés and bookshops of Tbilisi will collapse and crush all the books and people under them, and then no one will be able to steal anything, and Tbilisi will become a just and law-abiding city, on the other hand, if the bookshops and literary cafés do come down, there may also be less culture left in Tbilisi, and less coffee and cakes—this is how far you've come from the natural and awkward association, but if you're to go back to what is white you might remember that a German girl suggested you go to the cinema but you couldn't come up with a way to accept, in your world there are few whites, but lots of blues and grays, which makes you realize, as a quite minor student of the history of art, what a zero your world is, in German universities it's said they love foreign students very much, in French universities (empiric knowledge) they truly love the invalids: T.E.E., in older times it was something else that the Europeans loved, Proust wanted to write (but didn't) an essay in defense of pederasty, which was later carried out by Gide, who wouldn't publish Proust because of his faulty command of French grammar, you write a teleological history of mankind vanishing from wheel to internet, or about the increasing hegemony of intellectual fascism in the upper crust of your country ever since this body got to you, the reason why you're thinking about all this is probably that a couple of minutes ago you arrived at your table, one evening, when together with your flat mate you were coming back from the intersection and you passed the window of an art gallery, which usually shows the work of exponents of contemporary art, though that evening your eyes met no canvases in there, only three little parallel zigzag lines, four identical such things, one on each wall, and you remarked out loud that apparently the exposition had changed, at which your sociologist walking-companion laughed and explained that the blue zigzags were not a part of the exposition, but just a decoration on the wall that could be seen for the simple reason that nothing was on display in the transparent room at the moment, which was further revealed (this too was indicated to you by your companion) by the writing on the glass door, and, as he said this, he added, you aren't such an exemplary student of art, which is all too true, as illustrated by what had just transpired, but even you know that art has but one criterion, that if you put down three little parallel zigzag lines in your notebook it will not be art, but if you paint three little parallel zigzag lines and call them art, it will be so, and if Picasso paints a masterpiece and burns it right away, this masterpiece will never be art

ceci n'est pas de l'art

you dreamed your life would become a nightmare, like *Eraserhead,* but it's come to resemble a wet dream, but a wet dream so dull that the dreamer doesn't even get a hard-on, you wanted your life to be blue poetry and music, like "Dress Rehearsal Rag" or "Famous Blue Raincoat," but it's come to sound like the beeping that the street-sweeper trucks make at six in the morning, or else a MIDI from some low-quality Polish computer game, computer games opened a huge abyss in our childhoods, you saw the blind who asked for help, the legless who asked for mercy and bread, bearded women who asked for caresses, snails squashed on the pavement who asked for the return of their third dimension, but you never once saw a woman who asked for the body of her unborn child, it would be good if you could create a text so complete unto itself that if just a single word was taken out, the rest would lose all meaning, and you would bring it to the publisher, who is in the habit of putting an excerpt from the book on the back of it, but since in your text there would be no isolate passage that had any meaning of its own, he would have to put the entire book on the back cover, and so the reader would first read a transcription on the back cover, and then he would buy the book and reread it, but you don't care for literature except for what you can explore through it (as Mondrian said of his painting), and what's more, literature for you is the only thing that allows you to explore without leaving the room, also it would be nice to have a cigarette that would never end and would fill the room with ashes and smoke, also sun would be nice, a beautiful sun, the one you find only in winter,

and at that moment you stood up and approached the piano to smoke
one of the three cigarettes that remained in the pack, you often think
the best music is the music made by glockenspiels, as the best theater
is the theater of marionettes, and now tell me, if you remember, when
did the darkness come in, when you woke up, when you came out of
the metro, when you came back to your room, no, all three options
are wrong, the darkness came suddenly, directly, in a moment, in the
interim between the second and third puffs on the cigarette, and by the
fifth puff you were already so overwhelmed by it, before the sixth, the
cigarette fell out of your hand, and what was the darkness: indescribable pain in the left ear, and as you have plenty of time and are in no
hurry whatsoever, I'll wait for you, and we can pass a couple of minutes in complete silence, for there's no such thing as a transcription
of screaming, and that exactly was the only thing that occupied your
mouth, body, and mind for these few minutes, when you fell down on
the ground and folded in two, later, because the left side of your head
did not explode, you slowly got used to the pain and could resume
your train of thought: because pain causes the human boundless suffering, the human wishes to avenge, which is obvious in the complete
discrediting of pain, pain is bad, it tortures and makes one suffer, but
now (for you've already got back your ability to think) it seems to you
rather that pain itself is not to be blamed, and you sense that pain is
not the same as its cause, but that it's between you and the cause and
mostly acts as a middleman, and most likely it suffers just as much as
you do, if not more, pain is a desperate creature, a creature that has the
right to exist only when everything is worse than bad, its only function
is to serve as a physical equivalent of ennui, and when you track back
the last couple of minutes, when you found yourself down on the floor,
you notice that at a certain point pain and screaming became one, and
after all both are simple (and unhappy) messengers to another world

and in this whole scheme pain is the only one that's on your side and (almost) pities you, so you must come to love the pain, and pity it in return, and by the way it's only now that you stand up off the floor and find that the cigarette has left a thick black spot and fizzled out, and right then, when you thoughtlessly fixed your gaze on the piano, there amid the piles of incomprehensible documents and envelopes and letters you caught sight of a book, the existence of which had completely slipped your mind, in fact not a book really, but almost a chapbook (and why *almost?*), a book of thirty pages big enough to cover only two-thirds of your palm, and even though it was only by accident it survived the great expulsion, now the very thought it might also have easily made its way on to the blacklist terrifies you, for now you're certain that this is the only piece of writing you might still want to read till the end of your days, "On the Marionette Theater," by Heinrich von Kleist, and you sat on the piano bench and drowned yourself in this amazing creation with all your might, true though it may be that you're only reading a French translation, all the same you have the firm belief that Kleist himself is talking to you, he lays your head on his knees and tells you of this curious incident with his gentle, sweet voice, and you feel a second body that also caresses you, Henriette of course, and if you remember correctly, the space-time between this book and the last act of mankind is but six months, only six months and this is the way he wrote, with the kindest voice in all of literature, patron saints of all the vanished, and so, on their knees, you fell asleep, and those minutes were an oasis in the hellish desert of your existence, until the second increase of pain, out of which you could not pull yourself, plunged you back into the space of your room

you go back to the table, you could have written the story of your life like a tragic song of love, a sort of unromantic *Tristan and Isolde*, the title characters of which are totally unsympathetic, if you were to tell that story it would cover more than half your life, or rather a whole two-thirds of it, which is a lot, and what's more the subject wholly exhausts everything meaningful that's ever happened in your life, or else you could write a teleological version of your life, of how your final act will redeem the error of your mother, who didn't have an abortion, or else you could write your parallel life, in which Sophia would be born instead of you, your nonexistent sister (yes, admit now that you searched for her inside you and didn't find her), you also wanted to write a book of forty-four volumes each volume of which would reveal one of Ante Sumisu's incarnations, and the book would be called *Forty-Four Lives of Ante Sumisu*, after all his English emanation was the single most important figure in your own current life, and that's when you looked through the window and your gaze was captivated by a scene that was totally opaque to you, a scene in which one moving body was acting upon another unmoving body and when you approached the window you discovered that it was a young woman hanging out laundry, the simple beauty of the scene captivated you, as if you were seeing the movement of the human body for the first time, and you sat on the windowsill, then remembered that you had two more cigarettes left and stood up again to get one, after which you'd get straight back to your vantage point, the pack was lying on the piano, you pulled one out, you put it between your lips exactly in front of the upper right front tooth and then picked up the lighter that doesn't light, won't light, for a while you searched for some other source of fire, all the while afraid that the woman wouldn't be where you left her, but you find nothing, and suddenly you remember what somebody once told you (in a winter skiing camp), that a lighter can be brought back to life by being thrown on the ground, and so that's what you did, but an instant before it left the palm of your hand you remembered that someone else had told you something else again, that if too strongly thrown against the floor, a lighter might explode, which, indeed, is what happened, a second later, and right away the fire consumed the clothes which had somehow been transported from the room across the street directly to the floor of your own, apparently while you were looking for the matches, and this made you think of irreversibility, or something like that, but the thought didn't get to take a firm shape, for you rushed to get past the fire before it blocked your path to the other side of the room, and you lay down on the mattress and pulled the blanket over your head, up over your nose, which still left you your eyes, which you could still see through, but then everything grew slowly dim and distorted and you thought that probably your eyes were melting, and gradually everything became the way it was in the picture on the wall, which you thought about, in the final instant. That's how you're going to disappear.

TRANSLATED FROM THE GEORGIAN BY THE AUTHOR

ALOIS HOTSCHNIG

The Major Meals

At SEVEN, at *eleven*, at *three*, and at *seven*, not at *six*, at *ten*, at *two*, and at *six*. An hour before meals, Father. At *seven*, at *eleven*, at *three*, and at *seven*.

You don't need to tell me that. It's her you need to tell. She says at *six*, at *ten*, at *two*, and at *six*. The doctor told her at *six*, at *ten*, at *two*, and at *six*.

He told me at *seven*, at *eleven*, at *three*, and at *seven*. And that's what he told you, too, Father. He told us both. You eat an hour later. You can eat at *eight*, at *twelve*, at *four*, and at *eight*, he said.

That's what I said, at *seven*, at *eleven*, at *three*, and at *seven*. At *eight*, at *twelve*, at *four*, and at *eight*. That's what I've been saying the whole time. But then I sit at the table and I want to eat, and *she* shakes her head and says at *six*, at *ten*, at *two*, and at *six*.

Hans? Is it Hans? It is Hans, isn't it? How long is he going to stay, ask him how long he can stay.

Tell me, how are your parents? You do see them every now and again, you say.

Whenever possible. I can't go more often than that, you know.

And they can manage all right on their own?

More or less. At least I think so, Father.

That's good then.

I'll come tomorrow, Mother. As usual, at two.

An hour before meals, that is. An hour later you can eat. I know that.

It's just that, how will I know, an hour beforehand, whether or not I'll be hungry an hour later. How am I supposed to know at *seven*, at *eleven*, at *three*, and at *seven*, if I'll want to eat at *eight*, at *twelve*, at *four*, and at *eight*? What if I don't feel like it, an hour later?

You didn't come yesterday. He's hungry, you know.

How do you think I'm doing today? And what about her?
    You could be doing well, Father. And Mother, too. The both of you might be fine, now. I don't know. You could be hungry. You could be cold. You are cold, am I right?
    Yes, cold. No, I'm not cold. Did she say that?

I'm asking you, Paul, what should we tell Hans when he asks about Father? Best to say he's not at home.

She wants to know when you're coming. It's seven.
    You don't want to take your pills, you say? Whyever not?
    Because I'm hungry. Because I want to eat. Now. I've been looking forward to it all day. To finally feel full, for once.
    But you've already eaten today? Breakfast. It's seven o'clock at night, Father.
    Well then, isn't it time to take the thing? At *seven*, at *eleven*, at *three*, and at *seven*, that's what you keep saying. Or I'll eat breakfast *now* and take it at eight. Although if I take it at *eight*, then I won't be able to eat again until *nine*. She says that if I had swallowed it at *six*, then I'd be able to eat something now, at *seven*.

I know, Paul, it's early.
    It's two in the morning, Mother. Is he cold?
    Cold, yes. It's not seven yet, he says.

At *three*, that is, Father, at *three*, and then again at *seven*. It's now *four*. You can eat.
    I can't eat now, you know that. One hour after.
    An hour after *three* is *four*. Just enjoy it. She's fixing you something, isn't she?

I have to take it at *two*, she says. At *two* and at *six*.

You didn't take it at *three*?

She says the doctor told her at *six*, at *ten*, at *two*, and at *six*. Not at *three*. That was the mistake, that was the mistake the entire time, she says. Besides, it's *four* now. I'm hungry. I didn't know at *three*.

He's often so warm in the daytime. During the day he just glows and glows.

She'll tell you herself. Why don't you tell him?

Who is it, then, is it Hans?

Not Hans, Mother, it's me, Paul. At *seven*, at *eleven*, at *three*, and at *seven*. It's just not that hard. The note is on your night table. At *seven*, at *eleven*, at *three*, and at *seven*.

But that's not right, Hans. It always makes him so warm. I don't want it to be my fault, you know.

He's coming on Monday, he said. Today is Monday. And he's always come when he said he would.

And if it's not Monday today? For him, I mean. It's happened before. What then?

That's what it says, an hour before, that is what it says. It's just that we don't eat an hour after. *Before what* then, an hour *before*? If there's nothing to eat an hour *after*, then there's nothing to take an hour *before*. She says it's all wrong, the way it is.

I see that you're here. And I'm still asking you when you're coming. I'm asking when you'll be coming again.

But I just got here, Mother. I'm here.

And you'll be leaving soon. You only come so that you can leave again. Today is Tuesday, you're telling me. But you don't come on Tuesdays, ever. Don't tell me it's Tuesday today, Paul.

We get up, it's daytime, and I ask myself, did the cat eat? The cat isn't eating, she says.

Father?

Who, me?

Yes, Father. The two of you aren't doing so badly, you know.

He came after all. Can you hear me? Are you awake?

I told you, he has always come before.

But on a Tuesday, Franz. What on earth next?

He's so cold at night now. When he sleeps and can't sleep, as he says. He lies there and is cold.

Then she wakes me up. She grabs my head and my throat and my hands. After that, I'm awake.

Then I wake him to make sure he's still here.

I'm here, we're awake, and I wait till she falls back asleep and will let me sleep through till morning, till seven.

During the day he's too warm. That's from the pills. After an hour, he gets warm. And then hot. At night he cools down and is cold.

She keeps touching me, my hands, my head, always the same, and then I wake up.

He's so still at night. As if he were gone. He lies next to me and is still. So I wake him up.

It's too early, I tell her. But she doesn't hear. Her hands stroke my head and my throat. I try to sleep, I hope she won't notice, and to breathe loud so that she'll hear. But she doesn't hear.

He's not breathing, I think. So I reach for him and bring him back.

She stands next to me and strokes my head and my throat. And I think, it's late. It's already seven. But it isn't. It never is seven. Where are you, she asks. I'm here, I say. What's going to happen, she says. What do you think will happen, I say. It's night and then it will be day. That's what will happen. It will be seven.

He stands in the rose bed. He stands in the roses, just stands.

Say, Paul, since I'm feeling all right, can I just skip it this time? Once a day I should be able to do without it, since I'm not doing badly, what do you think?

If he doesn't take it at *three,* by *four thirty* he can barely walk. Then he shuffles his feet but doesn't move. He says he feels better. But when he feels better, he also won't take it at *seven*. Then all he can do is stand there, just stand.

That Frau Wagner is no longer alive, I just can't believe. You must have misheard. I'm sure you misheard.

Look on the back. You have to turn the picture over, then you'll see who's still alive and who's not.

If it's true, with the crosses. Who knows how many people think we're already dead. Anyway, I just ran into her shopping.

You haven't been shopping for ages, think about it. We talked about her. That she had died, you said. And who would be next, you asked.

You always ask that, not me. What will happen, you wonder. Nothing will happen, not a thing.

But him, in the third row, the second from left, next to Georg, you do know him. That's you.

I'm the one next to who? Do we have any children? How many kids would that be? The one next to who, are you telling me?

Now he bends down to the roses. He's going to get pricked. He grabs and then bleeds. What now?

Yesterday I told her you'd be coming tomorrow. Now you say that you're not coming until tomorrow. She says there's nothing to be done for the cat.

Before, I was often glad when he was away. But now. He just stands there and stands.

If I just skipped one, what do you think, it would all be the same, an hour before or one hour after, it's the same, if I swallow or not, don't you think? It's just, what happens with the one hour *after* if there was no hour *before*?

I talk and I hear myself talk and I think, does he hear me or not? Is it my voice from back then that he hears or is it me now?

———

And whether Frau Wagner still shops. For five hungry people, she shops. In any case, that's what it looks like. The trouble she goes to, as if she were bearing a cross that we had painted on her back. But she won't let anyone help her, you see. She goes shopping and carries it all back herself. Why don't we wave her in, even if only to show her that we're still here, too.

There's nothing we can do for the cat. It eats outside the house.

TRANSLATED FROM THE GERMAN BY TESS LEWIS

STEFAN BOŠKOVIĆ

Transparent Animals

THE TRAFFIC LIGHTS were green but Mr. Slick didn't cross. I stood several yards further back and filmed him. He didn't even notice me. The street was deserted. I pressed Stop, put the camera back in my pocket, lit a cigarette, and waited. He watched the spot from which the street emerged. Identical stone houses stretched along its entire length. From time to time a salty night gust would lash us. I stared at the lampposts. They lit up and went out again like fireflies. The reflection in the sea extended to the horizon. I surveyed the broad intersection. He had vanished. I chucked away my cigarette and ran across the street. I looked around, applied what logic I had, and dashed for the nearest alleyway. My heaving lungs made my windpipe constrict. The houses squeezed together, stone crumbled, and the intense pressure robbed me of the air I needed. I lost my balance. I expected to feel the cold on my back. The concrete was warm.

I lay in bed, exhausted. It was almost the end of my sick leave and I had to go back to work in a few days. I had found out almost nothing about him—not one piece of information more than I had at the beginning. I opened the camera and changed the card. I'd go through the material later. Before I put my weight on both legs, I lifted the glass vessel from the stool. The insides of the dead, transparent fish were shot through with red and blue specks. Mr. Slick stood in front of a huge glass window in the mall. Trapped birds flitted above people's heads. I carefully lowered the vessel back onto the stool. The body of the fish glided elegantly to the bottom.

I found a good position. I zoomed in by twenty-five percent and rested the camera on a cold samovar. He was sitting at the same table in the corner, gazing at the floor. He blew smoke at his reflection on the table. She couldn't stand the smell of tobacco. He ordered an omelet with truffles. I gave the waiter a sign to bring me the same. I wasn't hungry but I loved the smell of pan-tossed fungi. He chewed some more ice. The battery was running flat and I was far from the nearest socket. I followed him to the beach. He stood on the pier and scurried back whenever a big wave came. I decided to give him a push. I tip-toed up. Young guys in short diving suits were jumping into the sea like frightened pelicans. He asked for a lighter. His fingers were yellow. I didn't reply.

Eighteen days earlier, the phone had rung. The clock showed ten twenty. There'd been a bad traffic accident on a highway some-where in Europe, four people were killed. Among them my wife. The policeman expressed his sincerest condolences. I didn't ask a single question. I kept holding the phone for a few moments longer. Then I collapsed.

Thousands of red bursts illuminated the beach. A countdown and fireworks. The end of carnival is celebrated by frolicking in the sea. Men and women go wild on the sand. Froth spouts from a metal cannon. It covers people's heads. I watched that Mediterranean circus from the promenade. Mr. Slick was drunk and leaning against the rail-ing. He could hardly keep his head up. I went and offered him another drink. He asked me to switch off the camera. I zoomed in on his eyes. Pink capillaries glimmered beneath the fireworks. He turned away and tried to go. He staggered, people pushed him. He ran up to the rail-ing and vomited on the dancing, foam-covered bodies. A thread of saliva dangled from his mouth halfway down to them, and he sucked it back up.

Our childless marriage ended in a collision with a semi-trailer doing ninety-five miles an hour. I waited three days for them to deliver the body. The messages on my cell phone made things easier for me. She was bringing home a dead fish in a jar from an exhibition in Japan. The dead tissue soaked in chemicals became transparent after a time, she explained, and the bones and cartilage took on a red-and-blue hue.

I often rewound the videos and watched things over and over again. He was sitting on the wet sand, the waves lapping at his legs. He didn't change position until nightfall. I filmed a cruise ship enter-ing the bay. It blocked the sun. When it had passed, the red had already sunk below the horizon. Crabs came up on shore and leaping mullet thrashed behind the boats. He took off his trousers and walked back to the house.

When her black, deformed suitcase arrived, I leaned it up against the wardrobe and stared at it for several days. It unsettled me while I slept, too: in my dreams it was open, or it turned into a big black dog. I moved it to the smaller bathroom. I sat on the bed and rubbed my hands. I hauled it up and opened it. Little pieces of glass spilled over the parquet floor. I don't remember when I lost consciousness.

I was lying on the floor. I pulled the sharp pieces out of my hands and washed the others off in the shower. Timidly, I turned over her clothes, smelled the little boxes of makeup, and piled the soft things carefully on her side of the bed. Her cell phone was still on. I browsed through the messages. I found the video. We were running along the beach, I drew a heart in the sand. I cut my finger on a piece of rusty iron. The next was a hello from the Imperial Palace in Tokyo. She spoke in profile. She was puffy. She brandished the vessel of glycerin. "Translucent specimens have created a new world. First the scales are removed, then the body is preserved in formaldehyde. The animals are soaked in solvent and take on the color of cartilage. Once the muscles and protein break down, the process is stopped as soon as the fish becomes transparent. The bones turn red. And the brilliant beast floats." She waved once more and sent a kiss.

Then I came across the photos. The two of them looked tired and happy.

It wasn't hard to find out what he did and where he lived. He ran from the darkness. He played tennis at dawn, spent the mornings at the mall, and sat on the beach at dusk. Once he forgot a book at the bar. I wanted to take it, but my movements were clumsy, and the waitress was faster.

My physical state went downhill. I didn't eat for days. A rash appeared on my shoulders and neck, my mouth went dry, and my knees swelled. I gathered the necessary strength, went up to him, and told him who I was. He was finishing his morning training. He wrung out his sweatband on the orange sand. Lightning struck somewhere nearby, a summer shower rustled. We stopped beneath the porch of a building. He looked at his own reflection in the shop window. The plastic models smiled vacantly. He took a swing and smashed the glass. A dazzle of shavings rained on his hair and shoulders. He pulled his arm out gingerly. He said he knew who I was. It had been her choice. A mob soon gathered. The alarm howled.

TRANSLATED FROM THE MONTENEGRIN BY WILL FIRTH

MIKI LIUKKONEN

A Cookbook for Neurotics

I TURN MY head and look at Alle, who sits on my right side smashing steaming pulpy potatoes with a fork and then adding pats of butter, which melt juicily among the chunks. We're sitting in the kitchen
around the square table, which is also set with oily feta salad, sun-dried
tomatoes, mustard, and salmon in square porcelain serving dishes. In
my parents' house everything is pointedly non-round. In this house
Alle and I spent our childhood. Everything is still more or less the way
it was back then. Only the garage has been torn down, the asphalt
ripped up, and a vegetable garden hoed into its place; in it our mother
grows carrots, peas, parsnip, chervil, and rhubarb. The stone walls are
painted a bright white, with great rainbows sculpted into the plaster.
In the wall across from the kitchen sink is a small apse, which works
perfectly as a spice shelf, the spice jars in a neat row on the narrow
stone slab. The furniture is dark, either nut hardwood or stainless steel.
One wall, perpendicular to the one with the apse, has been jammed
full of photos of our childhood, vacation trips, Christmas celebrations,
official class photos from our school days, grainy and orange-tinged
photos of our grandparents, but also the odd watercolor by Alle and
me from fifteen years ago (our parents taller than our house, gigan-
tic V-shaped birds in the background, and a smudgy blue-violet sun),
and one enlarged photo of good old Bruce pecking happily at a leg of
the sofa, the same sofa still there in the living room, its honey-colored
left rear leg still showing the indentations from those pecks, which you
wouldn't notice if you didn't know to look.

The living room walls are white-painted stone with plaster designs
too, with vinyl black furniture, leather, glass, rust-brown rhomboids
in curtains the color of a summer evening, a black TV table made of a

slab of honeycomb, standing on adjustable legs and holding a 32" LCD
TV, on either side of which stand enlarged photos of Alle and me at
some pre-school age slipped behind shiny glass rectangles and framed
with narrow metal frames, a three-legged birch stool holding a large
Guinean-style red clay pot, hanging on the wall above it a black man-
dolin that my father inherited from his father, with only the two bottom strings still strung on it. The lights burn bright in every room, low
and round the clock. Wall recesses, ferns, and two impressively large
angel's trumpets; in the hall a winter-rosy clerestory and a decorative
brass handle from which hangs a black velvet tassel. In the back yard
stands a trampoline that's seen better days, lilting miserably to one side
year-round as if some heavy creature had died on it. I don't remember
that Alle and I ever jumped on it much. In front of the trampoline, for
my mother's mental health, is a fence hiding it from view.

Alle, who has rolled his dirty sleeves up loosely over his bony
elbows, stares straight ahead with his small watery eyes, not saying anything. His fork grinds up the potatoes into a white-and-yellow mush. I
glance over at him surreptitiously, reading the signals, but can't make
anything out. Money worries again, probably. Or else some woman.
Alle's hair is dark brown, cut short and combed to one side. Around
his neck he has a thin silver chain from an ex-girlfriend, the chain
peeking out from behind a missing button and Father asking what it
is. I can hardly get my fork into my mouth, though I'm famished. I
haven't eaten a bite since breakfast. Mother's in such a good mood she
doesn't notice anything, just jerkily cuts the salmon with a long knife
and babbles on. At his feet Father has a paper bag he's brought in from
the living room, some surprise apparently, and he keeps asking Alle
all kinds of questions, but Alle stays on his own wavelength, answers
when asked, but doesn't look up from his plate. I'm thinking. I hav-
en't told them about the thing at Physicum. Should I? Everyone will
be talking about it in horror tomorrow anyway, probably even today.
Mother spoons feta salad onto Father's plate, though Father hasn't said
he wants any. Alle and I are here for tradition's sake. Every Wednesday
at six, unless I have swim practice. Workout times vary, but the days
usually don't. These family dinners, despite Mother's cheerful chatter, are vaguely melancholic meetings in high-backed chairs, brightly
lit by a long fluorescent bulb hanging from two wires almost down to

the table. When Mother falls silent, the conversation turns random, with long silences, puffing out and then blowing away like a stutterer's smoke signals. My stomach is still upset from what happened this morning. The kitchen is too bright and white, which I never noticed as a kid. Was it this bright back then? After a moment's silence Father contentedly rubs his greasy palms together under the table and then hauls up a book, which he hands Alle with a wordless smile. Alle takes the book in embarrassment, almost reluctantly.

"What's this?"

"Mother and I thought you might like it," Father says, nodding.

"Why? I mean, thanks . . ." Alle flips through the book quickly. "Uh, a cookbook?"

I raise my eyebrows: "Written by who, Meila Enkroos? Right? That's the book Mikael mentioned once."

"Do you know Meila?" Mother asks with her knife and fork in a greasy X in front of her chest.

"She was Mikael's teacher in middle school."

"A cookbook for neurotics," Father says and nods again.

"But why did you think . . . for me . . ." Alle stares at the book as if it were a pair of ice skates bought in the summer.

"You don't cook," Father says.

"What, me? No, not really . . ."

"Maybe you could make something out of that."

"But—for neurotics? Do you mean I'm . . ."

"No, no. It's a bestseller, apparently. The saleslady recommended it."

"It would suit you better," Alle says, handing the book to me with a smirk.

Father leans forward and points a flat index finger at me with a serious look: "But Jerome cooks. Don't you?"

"Let me have a look."

I take the book from Alle and start paging through it. I remember Mikael mentioning the book to me last year on Yrjönkatu Relaxation Day.

For a moment Frank Sinatra's cover of "The Girl from Ipanema" plays in my head, I have no idea why. Meila's author photo on the back flap: long black hair, a black gaze, a red blouse, in front of a sepia background: *Meila Enkroos (b. 1962, Als) is a Danish-Finnish writer. She moved to Helsinki in the early 1980s and taught religion in various middle schools until becoming a full-time writer in 2010.* A Cookbook for Neurotics *is her debut work.*

"A religion teacher, what shit," I mutter, and open the book to a random page.

Meila Enkroos
A COOKBOOK FOR NEUROTICS
Recipes: Poultry

Chicken Fricassee

An inexpensive and tasty dish for lunch or dinner.
Preparation time: Depending on the degree of your neurosis, 90 min—2 days.

Ingredients:
1 oven broiler, unseasoned

Sauce
3½ cups water
1 cube chicken bouillon
1 tsp curry powder
2 tbsp lemon juice
½ cup wheat flour
½ cup whipping or single cream + ½ cup water

N.B. Check to make sure you add *exactly* the amounts listed in the ingredients. "A little," "a pinch," "according to taste," and other such approximations are not to be tolerated *under any circumstances.* Possible consequences of careless measurements include anxiety, despair, hyperventilation, night terrors, panic attacks, contamination phobias, somatic obsessions, dysphoria, blurred sense of reality (depersonalization/derealization), amnesia, conversion disturbances, flashbacks, sweating,

arrhythmias, migraines, aggressive venting, frustration, faint-
ing, compulsive praying, hypochondria, tics, mental paralysis,
uncontrollable sobbing, physical paralysis, narcolepsy, mic-
ropsia/macropsia, epileptic fits, acute stress reasons, alcohol-
ism, terror of social situations (even if cooking alone), coffee
cup neuroses, incontinence, vestibular neuronitis, compulsive
whistling.

Instructions
Take the oven broiler out to thaw one hour before cooking.
Check the time. Check the time. If you're not sure whether
you will be hungry at 4 p.m., or 5 p.m., or 3:30 p.m., or what
the time even will be an hour from now, put the broiler back
in the refrigerator. What time is it? If you think you'll be hungry in an hour, put the broiler on a clean table after all. But
don't put the broiler on the table until you're sure it's clean.
There may be tiny crumbs or grease on the table. Disinfect the
table and dry it with a rag. Throw the used rag in the trash.
Wash the table with water and dry it with a new rag. Throw it
in the trash as well. Now you can put the broiler on the table.
Maybe. You can. Can you? What if . . . But OK, put it on the
table. In the middle of the table. Not on one side. *In the middle.* Estimate the exact center of the table with a measuring
tape if need be. If you don't own one, buy one. Write it down:
buy a measuring tape. Write it on clean paper and put the note
somewhere where you can't help but bump into it. Tape it to
the bathroom mirror. Now that you're in the bathroom, wash
your hands. Wash them again, and maybe a third time. Fixate
on one specific number of washings. Obsessives tend to love
the number three, while the chronically anxious tend to vac-
illate between the numbers seven and eleven, OCPDers rebel
against the notion that they need some specific agreed-upon
number of repetitions to remain calm and balanced but can't
help thinking obsessively about the fact that they don't have an
obsession about a certain number.

Exit the bathroom. The broiler is on the table, right? Is it
in the center of the table? Check, but avoid touching it. Check

the time. Leave the kitchen quickly and try not to think about the broiler for a moment. Look out the window. Imagine that the window is LARGE and BREATHING, clean, fresh. Imagine yourself floating through it, but don't sink too deeply into the thought if you have a tendency to let your sense of reality fade. Check the time. If forty-five minutes have passed, you can walk back into the kitchen, but if not, sit down. Put your hands on your knees, or read. Breathe. Don't start doubting the eventual tastiness of the spiced chicken. Don't think about other dishes. HITLER. There. I managed to distract your attenSEXCOCK-PUSSY. Check the time. If forty-five minutes have passed, or if you use an egg timer (which of course is the best option), walk into the kitchen. If more than forty-five minutes have passed, stay calm, all is not yet lost. Use the egg timer next time. Don't worry. No one will be angry with you. Everything is soft, but not too soft. Remove the broiler from its package with rubber gloves and wipe it with paper towel (from an *unopened package*), and when you're finished with the piece of towel, throw the remainder of the roll in the trash. Put the broiler on a baking tray lined with baking paper or in a glass casserole. Don't panic. Bake the broiler at 175 (Celsius) in the exact center of the oven for exactly 1½ hours. Throw the rubber gloves in the trash. Ovens are different, but it doesn't matter, so long as the broiler is in the oven exactly 1½ hours. Set the timer. Check that you set it. Breathe. Check the timer.

Try to pass the 1½ hours without collapsing. The world is beautiful. The leaves on the trees. Fluffy clouds. Fluff. Think: what is fluff? *I'm singin' in the rain, I'm singin' in the rain.* You can of course take a tranquilizer if the wait seems impossible. Of course. Fontex or Sepram: of course. Seromex: go ahead. Doxalin, Prozac®, Celex, Lexapron: toss them in too. Fevarin: why not. Just be careful not to fall asleep. Remember that you've got a chicken in the oven. Check the time. Do you even like chicken?

The timer rings. Now quickly. Stick to the schedule that *you yourself set.* Don't be ashamed. I understand you. Remove the broiler from the oven, using rubber gloves again. You have a drawer full of them. That's why you're alone. Even in company you're alone, because you control your world so that others will not be able to reach you, they have no way to enter your world. If there are others in your house, make sure they don't touch you. They are dirty and impulsive. They are *Them*.

Peel the skin off the chicken. *Rip it.* You may even enjoy it. Imagine you're tearing to shreds the skin of whatever Jere or Tiina it was that used to torment you in primary school. Ah. Those sowers of the seeds of your trauma. Tear the broiler into strips that please *YOU*. Freedom. Do you feel it? Isn't it wonderful? Tear slowly or in a huge hurry. Don't worry about me. Tear any damn way you want: don't let me bruise *YOUR* routines. Imagine that I am a harmless cactus in the shadows of your room. Next boil water in a kettle, to wash it. You might want to listen to jazz. When the water has boiled and you have poured it off, measure the correct amount of water and pour it into the kettle. Check the amount. It was 3½ cups, but what if the amount has changed? What if you read it wrong and your whole family dies? Or your dog? Worst of all: what if you *don't need any water at all?* But you do. 3½ cups. Three and a half cups. Add a chicken bouillon cube to the water. Think: a cube. Hopefully it's a perfect cube: no flaked or worn corners. Keep your fingers crossed. If you can't stand the uncertainty, throw the chicken bouillon cube in quickly. It can't see you. If you accidentally throw the paper in with it, don't worry: *It. Can't. See. You.*

Add the lemon juice. Mix the wheat flour with the cream and water mixture. I know, I know: I should have warned you in advance. Why does everything have to be so fucking difficult? It's not. Jesus Christ, concentrate. You're free. You can quit any time you want. The worst is over. Chicken is tasty even without all this other crap. But please do continue, I beg you. Make the mixture. Add it to the water. Let the mixture boil for exactly ten minutes. Use the egg timer. Quick. There. Nothing else matters, only your nerves. You don't have to taste the food at any point during its preparation. You'd only burn your tongue and your whole day would be ruined. If that happened you might as well just go to bed and hope that some day . . .

So. Don't taste it. Add in the pieces of *the reason for all your traumas*, your victim, Jere/Tiina. Ah. It's suffering. Ah. Or else *no*: if you start feeling bad about this and don't want to hurt anyone, even if your somatic thoughts are trapped inside the most horrific imagery of violence/rape, don't listen to me. I'm a cactus, remember.

The food must be about ready by now. It is. It's definitely good. *You* did it. You succeeded. And what could feel better than that? You don't even have to eat this garbage if you don't want to. There are other recipes in here.*

Hopefully you feel better. Check to make sure the coffee-maker isn't on.*

---

* Try, for example, the pudding for psychosis patients and/or kleptomaniacs on p. 12. Other recipes in the book include:
- Boiling water for sufferers of dementia
- Sushi for hysterics (separate instructions for male and female hysterics, p. 43 & 44)
- Palak paneer for sufferers from conversion disturbance
- Kimchi for dysthymics
- Hammering hamburger for rage syndrome sufferers
- Garlic clove soup for onychophagics
- Cleaning coconuts for trichotillomaniacs
- Powerful detox smoothies for sufferers from Rapunzel syndrome (/trichophagics)
- Eggplant for sufferers from koro/shuk yang (genital retraction syndrome)
- Carrot salad for tanorexics
- Several colorless snacks for sufferers from Stendhal syndrome
- Flamed duck for pyromaniacs
- Bone marrow soup for lycanthropes
- For misophonics: how to enjoy food just by sniffing it
- "The many forms of whipped cream, relief for dance-maniacs"
- "Dietary advice for sufferers from Klüver-Bucy syndrome"

And:
- "Simple thyme lard for voyeurs with vascular cognitive impairment"

———

"Mm, I see," I say and hand the book back. "Interesting."

"Does it look good?" Alle asks.

Father nudges Mother with his elbow: "I told you."

Mother smiles: "It's good you're going to learn how to cook. You're so thin."

Alle says, "Thank you," and closes the book.

TRANSLATED FROM THE
FINNISH BY DOUGLAS ROBINSON

ÁDÁM BODOR

From *The Birds of Verhovina*

Anatol Korkodus

Two WEEKS BEFORE he was arrested my stepfather, Brigadier Anatol Korkodus, bought me a brand-new Stihl petrol chainsaw. He said he'd ordered it from Czernowitz; the parcel was already here and I should collect it from Edmund Porchiles at the Sign of the Two Queens. I could pick up the present in the morning on my way back from the station.

It seems that, even if he suspected something, he dissembled because, as if there were nothing brewing, another of his protégés from the reformatory at Monor Gledin was due, and he asked if I'd meet his train at daybreak, and take him to the office.

He was intending to keep to his bed that day, so I was to make sure the youngster was fed, talk to him, and generally keep him entertained until the afternoon, when he had time to speak to him himself.

Normally it was Balwinder, the office dogsbody, that he dispatched to the station when the facility had a visitor, or indeed a new arrival such as this, but on this occasion for some reason best known to himself he wouldn't hear of it.

As the timetable here had recently been canceled and all you could know for certain was that this first train, which comprised chiefly freight cars and just a single decrepit third-class carriage, would arrive before clocking on time at the timber yard, I decided to trot out to the railway station well before daybreak and waited patiently near the exit, huddled on a bench covered in hoar frost. I set down next to me, in a clearly visible spot, the piece of cardboard on which the gaffer had written the newcomer's name with a thick felt-tipped pen, in big letters and bold strokes, so that even in the meager lighting of the station it was easy to read.

He was called Daniel Vandyeluk, like some seedy sexton reeking of old age, though he was clearly just a delinquent street kid. He had been sent over from the reformatory at Monor Gledin for re-education, to stay at the outpost until he found his feet and learned to behave.

Anatol Korkodus readily took in young misfits, boys who'd gone off the rails, so that far away from the temptations of the city, amid rolling mists, sulfurous hot springs, and abandoned bunkers and sla-gheaps, they might revel in untrammeled freedom and find them-selves, as well as a path to a better future. But he never got very far with them. Nor did he delude himself that he did. He called them his birds, knowing that it always ended, one fine day, in their fly-ing away. Some would leave for parts unknown within days of their arrival, disappearing without trace. Many, once their probationary period was over, were sent by Anatol Korkodus back to the refor-matory. And there had not so far been a single one who had sought his final resting place in the area, with the intention, when the time came, of being buried here, on the slopes of the Paltin.

I had by then spent quite a few years in Verhovina. Many years ear-lier I, too, had been brought one frosty morning from the same place, by the same rundown local train.

On nights when there is little wind, especially when the valley is cov-ered by a dome of thick cloud, the train can be heard an hour or two before it gets in, as it begins its climb along the Jablonka and clanks its way over the hundred-year-old iron bridges. To the experienced ear, just the occasional sound from the far distance is enough to work out exactly where the train might be at any particular time. But today the hollows of the groves, the ditches lined with bushes along both sides of the embankment, were hugged by a blanket of dismal fog that muf-fled even the barking of the dogs nearby. An indication that somewhere beyond the recesses of the valley the train was indeed getting close came only from the little groans of the sleepers, an occasional squeak or rus-tling that shivered along the rails like an electric current.

Apart from me the only person waiting for the train was Stationmaster Stehtz; it would seem that these days people are no longer inclined to travel by train. A recent rumor had it that the station was about to be axed and perhaps even the rails taken up and sold together with the iron bridges, because the Jablonka Valley line, from the ford at Tuverkan Pasha and all the way up to the loading bay of the timber yard, was said to have been measured up by persons unknown; some even claimed to know that the valley and all its extensive iron equipment had been bought by a rich foreigner called Bazil Haraklán, allegedly from a faraway, rich plain beyond the mountains, Coltwildgarden, Holtwildgarden, or some such mythical-sounding place. Allegedly even the letters sacking the railwaymen were ready to be sent out; no wonder, then, that the stations were becoming so deserted.

So it was that when the first train of the day pulled in, hissing, puffing, and wreathed in clouds of steam, from the window of the third-class carriage only a single head, wearing a black and yellow striped cap, poked out to survey the empty platform. Nor did its owner seem in any hurry to make a move, and it was only when he saw the uncoupled engine, exhaustedly trundling off by itself in virtual silence toward the engine shed, that he realized this was the end of the line, and finally got off, making hesitantly for the exit.

It was immediately apparent that he was not, in fact, wearing a cap on his head; rather, his closely cropped hair had some design painted on it. Amid his original dark locks shone streaks of a golden yellow, prominent in the grayish mist. He wore a jacket of cheap denim that he had long outgrown, had no luggage, and when he came close enough to be illuminated by the light of the lamps, it could be seen that he wasn't even wearing shoes. He walked the length of the platform barefoot, cracking the edges of the frozen puddles as he did so. He had no choice but to pass in front of me, so that when, as he came closer, he saw the piece of cardboard on the bench and slowly deciphered his own name, he came uncertainly to a stop.

Hell's teeth! Not waiting for me, are you? I was supposed to be coming tomorrow.

Anatol Korkodus had a sense that you'd be coming today.

And there I was thinking I could take it easy for a while in the station bar, spend my savings, suss out the lie of the land, and then turn up tomorrow. You've ruined my day.

He spoke in a thin, reedy voice; none of his teeth could be seen. He had icy, bluish-gray eyes, like Edmund Porchiles's husky at the hostelry. The yellow stripes glaring in his hair gave his head a fluffy bloom.

I looked him up and down: Then come to your senses. Can you see a bar anywhere around here?

The station here consisted of just two buildings: in one, the station-master and the traffic controller, a girl, working in shifts, dealt with the freight and other traffic, and issued tickets through a small hatch open to the elements, while at the back, in a more spacious room behind a swing door, lived Stationmaster Stehtz with his family. In the old days, what was now a ramshackle and dust-laden hut, with a sticky-topped metal table and a couple of broken-backed tubular chairs, had served as a bar, but that had been shut down long ago.

As there was no bar to be seen, Daniel Vandyeluk turned round and round in his disappointment. Then he stopped in his tracks and took several huge gulps of air.

It stinks here. What the hell is that smell?

I have no idea what you're talking about. You need to have your nose examined.

What he must have picked up was the choking smell from the thermal springs in the Paltinsky meadows, which clings even at break of day to the bottom of the valley, until dispersed by welcome winds.

Crossing the square in front of the fuel depot and the timber store, we trudged along Jablonska Poljana's deserted high street, carefully skirting the frozen clods of earth. Only the soles of my boots could be heard tapping on the ground, the barefooted Daniel Vandyeluk lagged a good half step behind me, negotiating the frozen puddles noiselessly.

What, if I may ask, happened to your shoes?

Threw them away.

You're joking. Keep a civil tongue in your head when you speak to me.

You heard. I threw them away, like I said.

He halted on the Pissky bridge and stared down into the Jablonka, black and silent as it wound its way between the blanket of ice that overlaid its banks. I stood behind him, wondering what he would do. But in the end he just spat into it.

At this I assumed my most withering tone: Don't let me see you doing that again. Spit where you like but not into the water. Best of all, just swallow it.

From Nyegrutz's bakery the yellow light spilled out into the fog, and before its open entrance swirled the smell of roasting chestnuts and burning oil. I grasped Daniel Vandyeluk lightly by one elbow and steered him over to the doorway. He had a scrawny little arm, like a child's.

I looked about. The street was deserted.

You will now wait here nicely and talk to no one. If anyone stares at you wondering who or what you are, you take no notice. Pretend you're not here. Understood? Act as if they'd seen an apparition.

And why would they stare?

I looked him up and down again, from the top of his head, aglow with its yellow streaks, down to his bare feet.

They might.

There was no one yet in the bakery. Behind the counter sat Irina Nyegrutz, preparing the dough for the fried flatbreads in a blue dish covered by a checkered cloth. In a roasting pan on the gas stove lay hot chestnuts, smoking, their shells burst open. I ordered half a kilo of chestnuts and two flatbreads with curd-cheese topping. While Irina Nyegrutz rolled out the dough, added the curd cheese, and pushed and patted the bread around in the sizzling oil, I walked up and down the empty room, taking a look out of the open door and the steamed-up windows from time to time. It was exactly six o'clock; behind the looming curtains of fog, the saw mill's siren boomed out dully. The veins of condensation dribbling down the purple glass of the window made the image of my unshaven face quiver, as if I were weeping.

Daniel Vandyeluk stood obediently on the threshold, like a dog tied up by its owner in front of a shop, plumes of steam rising from his nostrils, his hands in his pockets, one bare foot rested on top of the other.

Irina Nyegrutz slipped the flatbreads into a paper bag, putting the roast chestnuts into another. She peered out of the door.

Who's the other one for?

As you can see, no one.

New kid. I can see he's not up to much. He won't stay long.

We live in hope.

Daniel Vandyeluk and I went on. After just a couple of steps, he piped up, a touch testily.

Tell me, why did you leave me outside?

Next time you can come in, if you like.

But for some reason this time you left me outside.

I didn't want your smell to bother Irina Nyegrutz.

I've been on the road since yesterday. I'm sure I must smell of the train a bit.

I said nothing about smelling of the train. Go on, tell me why you threw away your shoes?

They'd been shat in.

Are you serious? That shouldn't have stopped you putting them on. In case you didn't know, it's lucky. Someone likes you a lot.

Little Zsanett did. Poor thing was angry they let me out.

You may meet again. Be sure you repay her affection in kind.

At the entrance to the Man-Gold courtyard, I once again brought him to a stop by grasping one of his elbows. The sun was coming up, the sky had a congealed yet translucent look, but in the courtyard, entered through a wide, high archway and enclosed by four single-story buildings, there still lingered the hemmed-in murk of the departing night, and on the steps of the scone bakery it was possible to make out only the bottles of goat's milk, laid out ready in four rows. I picked up a couple of the bottles, and when we went on, barely two houses later, but by now on the far side, I knocked on one of the windows of the Augustins' house. Or rather on the plank covering the window.

The Augustins' window, which looked out onto the street, was nailed up with planks, up and down as well as diagonally, leaving just a small gap in the crudely knocked-up trelliswork for a hand to poke out and take in the odd item, say a bottle of milk. The Augustins were a couple we'd been holding under house arrest for years. As the jail in Jablonska Poljana had burned down long ago, there was no choice but to keep them locked up in their home.

I put one of the bottles on the windowsill and waited for the window to open. From behind the planks came the voice of Mrs. Augustin:

Is it true that Madame Subprefect Vaneliza has run away? And that things are also looking black for Anatol Korkodus? My husband

and I had the same dream, for the second time. Because if it's true, we're being kept here under false pretenses. Would you kindly have a word with Constable Hamilcar Nikonuk and have him set us free this very day.

Dream on, you two. Events could take one of several turns. But for the moment you are both keenly awaited by the examining magistrate in Gledin. You'll have a leash around your waists when you're taken before him.

I gripped Daniel Vandyeluk by the arm again, and gave him a meaningful look: They think, in there, behind the planks, that I've nothing better to do than pass the time of day chatting with them.

They done something, or d'you sometimes just lock people up?

It depends. I don't know if you'll appreciate what I'm about to say. These folk hooked up school kids to an electric current. One was seven years old, another eight, the rest eleven. Actual electric current, 220 volts.

An experiment, or what?

I waved my hand dismissively. Does it matter?

At the Sign of the Two Queens I brought Daniel Vandyeluk to a halt again. The petrol chainsaw, still in its original Stihl packaging, a colorful cardboard box secured by metal bands, lay on a bench in Edmund Pochoriles's kitchen. They were just having breakfast; there was my niece Danczura, a waitress in the hostelry, and also hovering about was Lutheran pastor Lorenz Fabritius. They knew where I'd been and could also see Vandyeluk by the door, which was slightly ajar. He stood there with his head hanging down, air curling out of his nostrils, as from a horse, in two different directions. He doesn't look too promising, remarked Edmund Pochoriles.

No, he doesn't, I nodded. I don't know what the gaffer will make of him.

Fabritius jabbed a finger at the box as I put it under my arm.

Expensive piece of stuff. What d'you need it for?

Well, what d'you think. I can take it to the Silent Forest, or I can use it now to chop firewood in the yard. But if need be, I can dismember my enemies with it.

As I was leaving, Pochoriles remarked: It's not as simple as that, you know. It's not so much the bones, but the blood, the flesh, and the innards that clog up the bearings. That makes the motor stall and you have to clean it all out. You're better off with a good ax, or a sharp cleaver.

I had a nice ginger cat, Tatjana. At one time I called her Charlotte but when she began to run to fat and a bulging collar of fur formed around her neck, I gave her a new name. She was just short of eight kilos in weight, with stripes and a thick tail, her ears with tufts like a lynx; if a dog met her in the street, it would hurry over to the other side. Now she was crouched, waiting, on the transom of the gate, but as we approached she jumped off, and though she was not inclined to be friendly by nature, she first fixed Daniel Vandyeluk with a stare, holding her head up high, then, moving behind him so that she could brush his trousers with her tail, slipped slowly between his legs. She sat down facing him again and stared him in the face, into those icy eyes. When we got going, she trailed in our wake, a couple of steps behind, slowly and ruminatively, her head held low.

Yours?

Whose did you think it was?

Why's it wearing a cat collar?

It's not a cat collar, it's her own collar of fur. She does have a cat collar as well, when needed. Should I happen to be afraid on the night shift, say, I take her along on a leash.

Start kissing her goodbye, because I want her. Name your price.

He may have been serious, but inwardly I just laughed.

In the office I asked him to empty his pockets completely and lay everything out in an orderly fashion on Anatol Korkodus's writing desk. Apart from his release slip he had only thirty-two coupons. He could have used these to get at least a pair of slippers or shoes of some sort for the trip and still had enough left over for a change of underwear and a pair of socks. But he had nothing else on him. When, after thoroughly patting him down, I had satisfied myself that this was indeed the case, I led him around the waterworks brigade's courtyard, at the far end of which I lived, with the gaffer, in the former Czervensky mansion. This was a barren courtyard, overgrown with weeds and with bare tracks traced in the frozen mud. In the open-topped granary lay a rusty snowplow, an ancient sand buggy covered in dust, and beside them the clapped-out old Willys Jeep belonging to Hon. District Commissioner Hamilcar Nikonuk, with its flat tires. Where we walked in the courtyard Daniel Vandyeluk left footprints glistening darkly on the frozen ground. He stopped at the entrance to the outhouse and asked for permission to relieve himself.

As I waited for him I caught sight of our brown Balwinder, the office dogsbody, by the open gate. I had no idea how he came to be there, as earlier there was not a living soul to be seen. Without so much as a "good morning," or even a nod in my direction, he was just standing there motionless, squinting into the yard. The yard where there could not have been anything for him to see but us. I walked over.

Anything wrong? What on earth are you doing hanging around here?

Why should anything be wrong? I'm just looking around. Isn't that allowed?

Well now! It seems to me you're doing this on purpose. There's not much point, that much I can tell you.

Perhaps there is.

Phooey! I spat out in my fury.

Meanwhile Daniel Vandyeluk had come out of the outhouse.

Is this where I'm staying too?

Where you're staying tonight is in quarantine. For a full three weeks. That's how we do things here, as you know. Because of the germs.

You could see he didn't quite understand what I said. Perhaps he didn't even know what quarantine was or what germs were, but since he didn't ask, I didn't explain. I sat him down in the kitchen, laid a piece of carpet before him, and told him that if he was cold he could cover his bare feet with that. Though it wasn't especially warm indoors either, his features relaxed and his nose began to run; he wiped it on the sleeve of his jacket. He was a pale, thin-skinned, scrawny kid, his frozen, bluish-gray dog eyes swiveled to and fro among the walls. On the back of one hand he sported a crude, inked-in tattoo, mysterious relics of a mysterious, criminal past: dots, lines, crosses.

Anatol Korkodus had told me to be friendly toward him and talk with him, and when lunch was brought from the canteen, to get him to eat, and to send him in to see him on his sickbed once he had been properly fed. But that morning I was in no mood to make polite conversation. Various points flashed through my mind, and I was about to take a deep breath, but whenever I looked at him and my eyes met his, I got cold feet. Rather, what occurred to me was: how much better it would be if it were not Daniel Vandyeluk sitting there but someone else.

Whenever there's a lengthy silence, one that seems to go on and on, it eventually, all of a sudden, finds a voice. It begins by sighing gently, like a distant waterfall, then it starts to crackle, and then, when it's going full blast, raging unbearably, all of a sudden, as if it spurted right at you, the whole world comes dripping icily through your ears. Now, for the moment, only the whistling of the hearth's chimney was audible, then the ticking of the alarm clock, as if somehow borne on the wind from far-off meadows, now fading away, now becoming more intense.

TRANSLATED FROM THE
HUNGARIAN BY PETER SHERWOOD

LARS PETTER SVEEN

The Stranger

HE STOOD IN the kitchen, but didn't see her. Ingebjørg, he said. Where are you. He walked over to the stove, looked at the pots and pans that still hadn't been washed up. The bread was on the bench. Ingebjørg, he said. By now it had grown dark outside. He opened the door. Ingebjørg. Everything was quiet. He put on the boots that were standing there and closed the door behind him.

He walked towards the barn, but stopped outside. There was no lamp burning in there. A gust of wind shook the aspen trees and the leaves crackled in the dark. He turned and walked down to the small courtyard. From there he could see the field, or what was visible as an outline, against the night sky. He stood there and screwed up his eyes, and when the wind calmed and the aspen leaves stopped rustling, the sound of voices swept across the courtyard. He opened his mouth, then closed it again. Looked up at the house and the light from the kitchen window. It seemed as if there was someone sitting in there, but there wasn't. No, there isn't, he whispered, and started to walk across the field.

The voices came from the birch over at the far end of the field. He stopped about thirty meters from the tree. He bent his head, stood like that for a little while. Then he walked closer. Ingebjørg, he said, and the voices stopped. Ingebjørg, he said once more, and almost ran the last few meters. And his wife emerged from the dark into his field of vision. Without any overcoat, her apron still tied around her waist. Ingebjørg, he said. I'm here, she said. He grabbed her shoulders. Who else is here, he said. No one, she said. He let her go and looked around. There was no one else there, just the two of them. Who else is here, he said again. There's just the two of us, she said. He turned to her. There was a fresh

gust of wind, and the sound of the aspen trees came fluttering across
the field toward them.

He had kept the farm going for the whole length of the war. The
Germans didn't try to prevent things like that. But he didn't have much
of a patch of land, and the supply of stocks from the outside had dried
up. So, each summer, he traveled around to some of the bigger farms in
the district to help with the hay-drying. Sometimes he'd be away for as
long as two or three days. He slept outside when the weather allowed.
Those light, starless nights. It's as if there's nothing up there, he said
to her one night when he was at home. It's as if everything has been
packed away, he said. And she looked out the window in the kitchen
before patting his hair where he sat in front of the fireplace. Other
times he slept in some outbuilding or other, when the rain hung over
Fræna and even the summer evenings weren't light enough. Then he'd
wake in the middle of the night, sit up, and mumble her name.

When the war was over, she became pregnant. When summer
arrived, he decided to take jobs only at the farms nearest by. He left
early in the morning and came home late. She said she didn't mind if
he stayed away longer. You're only here at night anyway, she said. But
he kept coming home. I can't be away from you now, he said.

It was on one of those nights that he found her out in the field.

He wrapped her in a woolen blanket when they got back to the
kitchen. What are you doing out so late, he asked. But she didn't
answer, just stood up to put more wood on the fire. You want me to
make you something to eat, she asked. He walked over to the window
and looked out at the field. It was impossible to see anything but shadows in the world out there.

The next morning before he left he walked down to the field. There
were no footprints around the birch except those he and his wife had
made. He stroked the bark with his hand and looked up at the house.
Then he walked back up to the farmyard, and down to the road, out
through the gate.

He came home late that night and found her sleeping in bed. The
kitchen was still warm and he walked down and sat there without
lighting the oil lamp. After a while he got up and walked over to the

window. The colors had faded from the sky, the mold of the night had descended. He stood there and looked out on the realm that had risen from the soil, the realm that lay hidden all day but now revealed itself in shadows and murky shapes. He rubbed his eyes and put his head in this hands.

Sitting there, he heard a sound from the living room. He stayed totally quiet. The sound was still there. He lifted his hand, took down a wooden ladle hanging on the wall. And then, wearing a woolen sweater over her nightgown, his wife stepped into the kitchen. She walked straight to the door, opened it, and disappeared outside. He stood there at the window, wrapped in the dark, without saying a word. She had walked right past him. He opened his mouth, but nothing came out. The door was closed, not a lamp was lit. Ingebjørg, he said in a low voice. Ingebjørg. He walked into the living room, turned, and came back to the kitchen at a run. He threw the ladle away, tore open the door, and stood there in the opening. His wife was on her way across the field, the leaves of the aspens were flapping. He put on his boots and closed the door behind him.

He walked out to the yard and turned right along an overgrown path leading to the forest. When he arrived among the trees he made a sudden turn to the left and followed the edge of the forest by the field. He approached the birch, and stopped. His breath was like a thin flame stretching toward the sky above him. The trees were quiet. His wife's voice came flowing toward him from the field. He took a few steps. Stopped, and looked back to the farm. Between the trunks and the foliage, the houses were like two dark spots. He turned, and walked slowly toward the sound. He stopped when he stood right at the forest's edge, as close to the birch as possible. And now he could hear not only his wife's voice. A male voice came drifting to him, almost whispering. There was something stilted about it, as if the words didn't belong to the mouth of the one who spoke them. Then his wife interrupted. She spoke slowly, with long pauses between the words. He stared in the direction of the tree, but could only see her. It was impossible to get even a glimpse of another person.

They stopped talking and she started to walk across the field up toward the house. He stayed lying on the ground. His wife disappeared from view and he heard the door opening and closing. After a few

minutes he stood up, quickly, and almost ran toward the tree. Come
out, he said when he was standing in front of the birch. Come out, he
said, but nothing happened. He walked around the tree. There was
no one there. Where are you, he asked. Come out. The summer night
around him was darker than usual, as if the clouds had clogged the sky.
He put his hand on the tree and looked down at the ground. Then he
walked up to the house. He walked into the kitchen, through the living room, and up the stairs to the bedroom. He stood at the end of the
bed and said, Ingebjørg. But she didn't move. Ingebjørg, he said, and
she answered with a mumble. He undressed, and lay down next to her.

The following day he went to the Skjelbrei brothers' farm to help with
the last of the hay-drying. The Skjelbrei brothers had arrived from
County Trøndelag in the spring and had bought up fields enough to
cover two farms. But no one wanted to work for them, so they were
grateful when he turned up. He had been there several times this summer, and had always been gratefully received.

   They had been out in the sun for several hours before they moved
into the shade to rest. The brothers sat down leaning against a rock
just inside the fence posts. The youngest pointed to the fence and said
he couldn't understand why they'd left the rock lying there. It's just a
few meters, he said. The oldest shook his head and looked down at the
ground. We'll have to move it next spring, he said. They drank from
a bucket of water standing there. He sat down with the brothers, and
asked if they liked it here. They nodded. Perhaps it's stuck farther down
into the ground than we think, the youngest said, and stood up and
tried to shift the rock. Won't be budged, dammit, he said. The youngest brother sat down again, and they didn't say anything for a while.

   He stared down at his shoes, at the ground and the grass beneath
them. Have you seen any strangers around here, he asked the brothers. They looked at him, at each other. No, the oldest answered. But
then we're strangers ourselves. Well, yes, he answered. Why do you ask,
the youngest asked. The brothers looked at him and he covered his face
with his hands. There's been someone over at our place at night, he
said. I don't know who it is, but it's a man. Have you seen him, asked
the youngest. No, I don't know what he looks like. But he talks funny.
The oldest one stood up, wiped his pants. You'd better tell us if he steals

something or causes trouble, he said. The youngest stood up too, and they both began to walk toward the heaps of grass lying in front of them. He got on his feet, followed the brothers.

On his way home he dropped by two of the neighboring farms and asked about the stranger. No one had seen or heard anything. They asked about his wife and he said she was fine. Not long now, they said, and he nodded and said yes, not long now. He was told about a whore who used to run with the Germans, who'd been run out of Molde Town a few days ago. The farmer who told him shook his head. None of it's right, the farmer said.

Both places offered him supper and he said thanks but no. The light of day was fading, and he was walking through twilight. He pulled his jacket from his backpack and put it on. The heat of summer would soon disappear from the evenings.

When he came to the gate, he stopped and stood watching the house. The light from the kitchen window fell onto the front yard. The evening had gone, night had returned, filling everything. He stood at the gate and looked at his own house, walked over to the gate and followed it a few meters along. When he came to the third or fourth gate post, he stopped. He tugged at it, and tore it up from the ground. He loosened the steel wire from one tip and from the middle. Then he went back to the road and up toward his house. Outside the kitchen he put the pole down next to the doorway. Then he went into the barn, found a can of oil, a bit of rag, and a box of matches. He put the matches in his pocket and stuffed the rag in the can. Then he placed the can next to the pole.

She fell asleep with one hand on his shoulder. He was awake, and looked over at her. Her face was divided into two halves; one half was hidden in the pillow, while the other was only barely visible in the dark room. He lifted her hand away from his shoulder. Then he closed his eyes for a few seconds. He opened them again, and looked over at her. She was still lying next to him. He closed his eyes again. A twitch went through him, and the room became silent. Outside, a wind came down from the mountains, into the forest, and across the fields. All at once his eyelids flew open, and he was lying on his back looking up into the ceiling. A small flare appeared on the black surface, and he smiled and

got out of bed. Come here, he said, and stretched out his hands. And
then he held his child in his hands, its soft skin against his fingers. He
held the child to his chest, and closed his eyes, and when he opened
them, he looked up into the black ceiling. He rubbed his face, and
glanced over at his wife, but she wasn't there.

He got out of bed and got dressed. No lamp was lit, either in the living room or in the kitchen. He put on his jacket and his boots and stood
in the doorway looking across the field. Everything was outside his field
of vision now. He bent down and picked up the post lying down by the
doorstep. He took the rag out of the can and wrapped it around one
end of the post. Then he walked down into the yard and over to the
forest where he had been the evening before. He crouched between the
trees and crept over to where the forest bordered the birch. He squatted and held both hands around the post. His wife's voice floated over
to him. He stood up and said, Ingebjørg. There was only silence. He
saw the birch ahead of him, a black root that grew up toward the sky.
His wife was standing next to it. She had her face to him and he said,
Ingebjørg. She didn't answer, and he walked toward them. Who are
you, he said. He lifted the post now. Who are you with. The birch
grew larger the closer he came. His wife said something, but it was only
a whisper. And out from the tree stepped a tall, imposing man he had
never seen before. Who are you, he asked the stranger. But there was no
answer. What are you doing here, he asked. But the stranger still didn't
say anything. He took the matchbox from his pocket and lit the end
of the post. The flame blazed blue before it caught fire and lit up. He
stared at the stranger standing in front of him. The man was dressed
in a dirty uniform spotted with black. His hair was combed back, but
his skin was pale. Who are you, he asked, but the stranger stayed silent.
Who is this, Ingebjørg. She stared at him, and then she put her hands
on the stranger's shoulders, and whispered into his ear. They stood like
that in front of him, her hands around the shoulders of a strange soldier, her mouth close to his ear. The stranger didn't move. Run, she said
to him then, and suddenly the stranger tore himself loose, and ran away
along the field. They stood there and looked at the dirty uniform disappearing out of the light of the flaming torch.

Who is he, he asked. But she didn't answer. He went to her, took her
arms, shook her. Who is he, he asked. She fell to her knees. My God,

Ingebjørg, who is he. You're only wearing your nightgown. Who is he, he repeated, and looked toward where the stranger had disappeared. You'll freeze to death, he said, and lifted her up. She looked down at the ground. Who is he, he asked. Ingebjørg, answer me, who is he. He held the torch in front of her face, but she didn't lift her head. Look at me, Ingebjørg, he said. For Christ's sake, look at me. She twisted around, and he let her go. She stumbled a few steps away from him and turned toward the dark field. Suddenly a wind came tumbling over them and the fire went out. For a brief moment her shadow changed shape and she said: It has nothing to do with you. He dropped the burning post. The birch swayed, and from the yard they could hear the sound of the aspen leaves. Why has he stayed behind, he asked, why didn't he leave with the others. She turned to him. He came back, she said. He came back for us, she said, and put her hands on her stomach.

He pulled her after him up to the house. She sank down on the floor in the kitchen. He took her under her arms and dragged her into the living room. There he put her in a chair, found a blanket, and wrapped her in it. You mustn't get cold, he said, and went back to the kitchen. There he lit an oil lamp and took it into the living room. Ingebjørg, he said. You mustn't tell anyone about this. She looked at the lamp. Ingebjørg, he said, listen to me. This must be between us. He took her hands between his. Go back to bed now, he said. She was shivering under the blanket. He's here for us, she said. He let go of her hands, and stood up. Go back to bed, he said.

He put the lamp on the stove and walked over to the window. The house was quiet. Madness, he said, and his voice hung for a few seconds in the kitchen air. The night outside was darker than ever, and now he could hear the sound of rain against the tin roof. The wind took hold of the house and blew it out into a bottomless ocean. He turned away from the window. Then he saw the stranger. He sat at the kitchen table with his gray eyes, as if the water had filled them.

The stranger put his hands on the table, and said *mein Sohn*. Who are you, he asked the stranger. But the creature just beat his hand on the table again, and said *mein Sohn*. He stood still. The stranger grew quiet and turned his head toward the lamp. Then he stretched his hand up at the flame in the glass. His fingers were pale, and as he held them up against the light, they almost disappeared. The stranger pulled his hand away and hid it in one of his armpits. *Licht*, he mumbled, and crouched down. Then he straightened up. *Mein Sohn*, the creature said, and pointed to where he was standing. What are you saying, he asked. *Mein Sohn*, the creature whispered, and his hand disappeared in the light. The stranger bent his head. *Licht*.

Then he tore himself loose, took a step toward the stove, lifted the lamp, and stared at the uniform, at the skin wrapped like a shawl over his knuckles. The night rattled the house, whipped up the world outside. He lifted the lamp to his mouth. And as he was blowing out the light, as darkness was closing around them, he heard the voice: *dein Sohn*.

He stood in the darkness in the kitchen without saying a word. He took the matchbox from his pocket and he lit the lamp again. The creature had disappeared. He walked over and stroked the tabletop with his hand. Then he held the lamp above his head and looked around the kitchen. There was no one there. He walked into the living room, and did the same. He found no one. He walked up the stairs to the loft and the bedroom. There he doused the lamp and undressed on the floor in front of the bed. Then he lay down next to his wife. Ingebjørg, he said, but she was asleep, and didn't answer. He put his hand on her stomach. Come here, he said.

TRANSLATED FROM THE
NORWEGIAN BY MAY-BRIT AKERHOLT

AUTHOR BIOGRAPHIES

Sheila Armstrong is a writer and editor. She grew up in the west of Ireland and currently lives in Dublin. In 2015, she was nominated for a Hennessy Award in the First Fiction category and was featured in New Island's *Young Irelanders*. In 2016, she was first runner-up in the Moth Short Story Prize. She is currently working on her first collection of fiction.

Ádám Bodor, born in Kolozsvár (today Cluj, Romania) in 1936, was convicted of being a political criminal at age sixteen, and spent the years 1952–54 in prison. From 1955 to 1960, he was a student at a Protestant theological college and worked for a while at the Diocesan Library of the Transylvanian Protestant Church. His first book (*The Witness*) was published in 1969 in Romania, while in Hungary his debut was a collection of short stories entitled *A High Mountain Pass* (1980). He has been living in Hungary since the early 1980s; for a time, he was editor at Magvető Publishing. In the 1990s, he became familiar to the wider reading public after the publication of his novels *The Sinistra Zone* (1992) and *The Archbishop's Visit* (1999), the most comprehensive collection of his short stories to date, *Back to the Long-Eared Owl* (1997), and a confessional, autobiographical work, which takes the form of an interview, *The Smell of Prison* (2000). Bodor's books have been published in more than twenty languages, including Paul Olchváry's admirable English translation of *The Sinistra Zone*, published by New Directions.

Stefan Bošković was born in 1983 in Podgorica, Montenegro. In 2010, he graduated in Drama from the Faculty of Dramatic Arts at the University of Montenegro in Cetinje. Bošković has written scripts for a feature-length film, several short films, a sitcom serial, and a large number of documentaries. Several of his short plays have been staged. He has published a novel, *Šamaranje* (Slap in the Face), and a book of short stories, *Transparentne životinje* (Transparent Animals), whose title story is in this edition of *Best European Fiction*.

Deyan Enev was born in Sofia, Bulgaria. He graduated from Sofia University, where he studied Bulgarian language and literature. Among his various occupations are house-painter, hospital attendant, teacher, and copywriter. As a writer, Enev has published twelve short story collections to date. One of them—*Everybody Standing on the Bow*—has been published in Austria (Deuticke) and in the UK (Portobello) under the title *Circus Bulgaria*. The English edition of this collection, translated by Kapka Kassabova, was long-listed for the Frank O'Connor Prize.

Teolinda Gersão was born in Coimbra, Portugal, and has lived in Germany, São Paulo, and Mozambique. She is the author of seventeen books. Among her literary awards are the PEN Club Prize for the Novel in 1981 and 1989, and the 2001 Short Story Prize of the Portuguese Writers' Association. She was writer-in-residence at the University of California, Berkeley, in 2004. Her novel *The Word Tree* was published in Brazil by Planeta and in the UK by Dedalus Books; *City of Ulysses* was published by Dalkey Archive Press in 2017. Her most recent book is the short story collection *Prantos, amores e outros desvarios* (Tears, Love, and Other Madness, 2016).

Kenan Görgün (b. 1977), a Belgian of Turkish heritage, left school at seventeen to devote himself to writing . . . meanwhile his great dream was to be a trucker and he hadn't read a single book in his life. Stories, novels, screenplays, songs for rock bands, gonzo journalism backstage at Cannes, his truant's education made him a scrappy pamphleteer, never ceasing to seek out new challenges. With *Détecteur de mes songes*—the collection from which "The Revolt of the Fish" is taken—Görgün returns to the short form, ten years after the publication of his first book of short stories with Quadrature Editions, *L'Enfer est à nous*.

Georges Hausemer (b. 1957, Differdange, Luxembourg) lives as a writer, translator, and publisher in Luxembourg, in a small village in the North Eifel, and in San Sebastián, in the Basque Country. Recent publications include *Der Schüttler von Isfahan: Karawansereien* (2016) and *Fuchs im Aufzug: Erzählungen* (The Fox in the Elevator: Stories, 2017). In 2017, he was awarded the Batty Weber Prize in recognition of his literary work.

Andrej Hočevar (b. 1980) is a writer and an editor. He has published six books of poetry (most recently *Seznam* [A List], 2017) and one book of short stories (*Dvojna Napaka* [Double Fault], 2016). For over ten years, he has been an editor at LUD Literatura, first as a review and essay editor for the literary magazine *Literatura*, then as the editor of the Prišleki imprint. In 2013, he founded an online magazine [www.ludliteratura.si] and he has been its editor-in-chief since then. Hočevar has organized various literary projects, plays the bass guitar, and writes music for his band.

Alois Hotschnig is the author of two novels and several collections of stories. He has been awarded the Gert Jonke Prize, the Italo Svevo Prize, and the Erich Fried Prize. Two of his books, *Maybe This Time* (Peirene Press, 2011) and *Ludwig's Room* (Seagull Books, 2014), have been translated into English by Tess Lewis.

Christos Ikonomou (b. 1970, Athens) has published three collections of short stories, *The Woman on the Rails* (2003), *Something Will Happen, You'll See* (2010, winner of the Best Short Story Collection State Award), and *All Good Things Will Come from the Sea* (2014). The latter two are published by Archipelago Books in English translations by Karen Emmerich.

Helena Janeczek, born and raised in Munich in a Polish-Jewish family, since adulthood has lived in northern Italy and writes mostly in Italian. A novelist, poet, and critic, her books include the non-fiction book *Cibo*, the non-fiction novel *Lezioni di tenebra,* about a daughter confronting her mother's time in Auschwitz, and the multiple-award-winning novel *The Swallows of Monte Cassino* (translated by Frederika Randall), on the soldiers from around the globe who fought that World

War II battle. *The Girl with the Leica* is a novel about the photographer Gerda Taro, a partner of Robert Capa, who died at the front during the Spanish Civil War, aged twenty-seven.

Gary Kaufmann (b. 1994, Vaduz) is a young Liechtensteinian writer. He studies German philology and media at the University of Innsbruck in Tyrol, Austria. His book *Drei Verräter, ein Täter* (Three Snitches, One Culprit) challenges the image of a peaceful, devotional principality. It was published by van Eck Verlag in 2015. Other stories have appeared in various German anthologies. He is also the chief editor of the national scouting magazine *Knota*.

Josefine Klougart (b. 1985) is the author of five novels, including, most recently, *New Forest* in 2016. Twice nominated for the prestigious Nordic Council Literature Prize, she received the Danish Crown Prince Couple's Stardust Prize in 2011, the committee calling her "one of the most important writers, not just of her generation, but of her time."

Olivera Ḱorveziroska (b. 1965, Kumanovo) is a prose writer, poet, essayist, and literary critic. She has published two poetry collections, *Third Floor* (1982) and *Tall Whites* (1999); and five short story collections, *Sorrows of the Young Proofreader* (2000), *(Inter)woven Stories* (2003), for which she won the Stale Popov Award, *Two Pillows* (2010), from which "Events Agency" is taken, *Short Stories without Sugar* (2016), and *Sewn Stories* (2017). She is the author of two novels and a picture book for children. In 2005, she published her first novel for adults, *The Locked Body of Lou*, which was short-listed for Novel of the Year by the daily newspaper *Utrinski Vesnik*. Her stories have been translated into numerous languages.

Haro Kraak (b. 1986) is an author and journalist living in Amsterdam. His novel *Lekhoofd*, about a young boy who can taste sounds and who sees letters and numbers in colors, was well received and nominated for the Bronzen Uil (Bronze Owl), the prize for the best Dutch and Flemish fiction debut of the year. As a reporter, interviewer, and critic, he writes about music, literature, pop culture, and media for the Dutch newspaper *De Volkskrant*. Currently he is working on his second novel.

Hélène Lenoir is a French author of numerous novels, including *Elle va partir* (She's Leaving) and *Son nom d'avant* (Her Maiden Name), and two volumes of short stories, including *La Brisure* (The Break). Since 1980 she has lived in Germany, where she is a professor of French. Her short story, "L'Entracte," appeared in English in *Narrative Magazine* in 2015, translated by Elly Thompson.

Caryl Lewis's latest novel is *Y Bwthyn* (2015) and her latest story collection, *Y Gwreiddyn*, in which this story appears in its original version, was published in November 2016 by Y Lolfa and won the Welsh-language fiction category in Wales Book of the Year 2017. Lewis has twice been the overall winner of the Wales Book of the Year (Welsh-language categories), for *Martha, Jack a Sianco* (2004) and *Y Bwthyn*. This translation, by Gwen Davies, first appeared in the *New Welsh Reader* 116 (Winter 2017).

After publishing two acclaimed collections of poetry, **Miki Liukkonen** (b. 1989) made his novelistic debut with *Children under the Sun* (2013). The book was short-listed for the 2014 Runeberg Prize. The second novel from Liukkonen, *O* (2017), painted on an outrageously large canvas, is a megalomaniacal and encyclopedic narrative of ordinary people and extraordinary events, neuroses, stubbornly fixed ideas, and the irrational things we fear. The novel has been short-listed for the 2017 Finlandia Fiction Award.

Xabier López López was born in Bergondo, Galicia, in 1974. He is the author of several novels, short stories, and young adult and children's literature. He has won many awards for both his adult and children's writing, including the Xerais Prize in 2011 for *Chains* and the Spanish Critics' Prize in 2003 for *The Life That Kills Us*. The majority of his work has been translated into Spanish, along with various translations into Portuguese, Arabic, Chinese, and English.

Colm Ó Ceallacháin was born in 1966 in Cork, Ireland. His Irish-language fiction has appeared in numerous literary journals and in English translation on the website www.otherworldsliterature.eu, the result of a writing residency in Donostia / San Sebastián in 2017. An essay based on the talk he gave at the first Irish-language literature conference to be held at Charles University, Prague, will be included in the anthology arising out of that conference, which is scheduled to be published in 2019. His first collection of short stories, *I dtír mhilis na mbeo* (In the Sweet Land of the Living, 2017) was awarded joint first prize for a work of prose at the Oireachtas literary awards.

Alberto Olmos (b. 1975, Segovia, Spain) has been chosen by *Granta* as one of the best young Spanish-language novelists and as a finalist for the 1998 Herralde Prize for his first novel, *A bordo del naufragio*, which was published by Anagrama. It was followed by the novel *Trenes hacia Tokio* (winner of the Community of Madrid Novel Award, 2006), *El talento de los demás* (2007), *Tatami* (2008), and *El estatus* (Ojo Crítico RNE Prize, 2009). Literatura Random House published his most recent works, *Ejército enemigo* (2011) and *Alabanza* (2014), as well as *Guardar las formas* (2016), the collection of short stories from which "Every Last One, Place and Date" is taken.

Patrik Ouředník (b. 1957, Prague) is a Czech writer living in France. The author of more than a dozen novels, he is also a translator who has brought Henri Michaux, Claude Simon, and Samuel Beckett into Czech. His novels *Europeana*, *A Brief History of the Twentieth Century*, *The Opportune Moment, 1855*, and *Case Closed* are published in English by Dalkey Archive Press. *The End of the World Would Not Have Taken Place* will be published by Dalkey in 2019.

Vesna Perić, a fiction writer, dramatist, and film scholar, is an editor in the drama division of Radio Belgrade. She has published stories in a variety of Serbian literary magazines and in three recent anthologies. Her work has also appeared in German and English translations.

Irakli Qolbaia (b. 1995, Tbilisi, Georgia) is a writer, a translator, and a student of French literature. After completing his studies, he moved to France, where he studied art history and the history of cinema. His translations include poetry by Rimbaud, Apollinaire, Reverdy, and Alejandra Pizarnik, among others.

Olena Stiazhkina is a writer, journalist, and historian from Donetsk, eastern Ukraine. She has been nominated for, and won, several literary prizes in Ukraine and Russia, including the prestigious Russian Prize, for Russian-language writers working outside of Russia. When she collected her award in Moscow, in April 2014, after the annexation of Crimea and in the early stages of the war in the Donbas, she gave a powerful speech against the conflict, stating that: "The Russian language does not need military defenses. The Russian language does not need blood. It needs knowledge, critics, publishers, writers, teachers, and children." Later that year, she was forced to leave her hometown because of the war. Stiazhkina is the author of several novels and collections of short prose.

Paweł Sołtys (b. 1978) is a Polish musician, singer, and songwriter. Under the name Pablopavo, he has recorded over a dozen albums and played over a thousand concerts. He studied Russian language and literature. His short stories have appeared in various magazines in Poland, including *Lampa*, *Rita Baum*, and *Studium*. His debut short story collection, *Mikrotyki*, was published by Wydawnictwo Czarne in 2017. It has been nominated for the prestigious Polityka Passport Awards 2018 in the Literature category (in 2014 Sołtys, as Pablopavo, received the award in the Popular Music category).

Lars Petter Sveen (b. 1981) made his debut with the short story collection *Driving from Fræna* (2008), from which "The Stranger" is taken. His breakthrough came in 2014 with his third novel, *Children of God*, for which he was awarded the prestigious P.O. Enquist Prize in 2016. The book is forthcoming in Danish, Swedish, French, and English.

Gábor Vida (b. 1968, Kisjeno, Romania) is one of the most critically acclaimed prose writers of his generation and the winner of several prestigious literary awards. A graduate of Babes-Bolyai University, Cluj/ Kolozsvar, Romania, where he read Hungarian and French, he has so far published three collections of short stories and two novels. *History of a Stutter* is his most recent book, a hybrid of novel and memoir. At once a merciless family history, an anatomy of the Ceaușescu regime, and a diagnosis of Hungarian nationalism in Transylvania before and after the regime change, the book is written in a prose that is both raw and sensuous, analytical and empathetic. Vida lives in Tg. Mures / Marosvásárhely, Romania.

Lina Wolff (b. 1973) has lived and worked in Italy and Spain. During her years in Valencia and Madrid, she wrote her short story collection *Många människor dör som du* (*Many People Die like You*). *Bret Easton Ellis and the Other Dogs*, her debut novel, was awarded the prestigious Vi Magazine Literature Prize and was shortlisted for the 2013 Swedish Radio Award for Best Novel of the Year. Her second novel, *The Polyglot Lovers*, was published by Albert Bonniers Förlag in 2016 and was awarded the August Prize for Novel of the Year in 2016. It was also awarded an English PEN award for the translation featured in this volume. Lina now lives in southern Sweden.

Christopher Woodall grew up on the edge of London in the 1950s and '60s and spent much of his early adulthood in Germany, France, and Italy. His debut novel, *November*, re-imagines and sometimes celebrates the experience of migrant workers in late 1970s France. He is currently working on a sequel. His first collection of short stories, *Sweets and Toxins*, from which "Lying to Be Cruel" is taken, is forthcoming from Dalkey Archive Press.

Ulf Erdmann Ziegler (b. 1959) is a fiction writer and an art critic living in Frankfurt am Main, Germany. He has published five literary books, three of them novels, one labeled an "auto-geography," and a collection titled *Schottland und andere Erzählungen* (*Scotland and other tales*, 2018) from which "Detroit" is taken. Ziegler was a newspaper editor and an art-academy teacher before he began writing his first novel, inspired by his stay in St. Louis, MO, in January 2002. His books are published by Suhrkamp Verlag, Berlin.

After completing her undergraduate degree at the University of Fribourg, **Céline Zufferey** obtained a master's in contemporary art at the Bern University of the Arts, where she wrote her first novel, *Sauver* *les meubles* (Gallimard, 2017). A two-time winner of the Prix du jeune écrivain francophone (in 2014 and 2015), she is also the author of *New York K.O.* (Paulette Éditrice, 2016).

TRANSLATOR BIOGRAPHIES

Martin Aitken is a freelance translator of Scandinavian literature. His work, mainly from Danish, includes Josefine Klougart's novels *One of Us Is Sleeping* and *Of Darkness*. His co-translation (with Don Bartlett) of the sixth and final volume of Karl Ove Knausgaard's *My Struggle* was recently published by Harvill Secker and Archipelago Books.

May-Brit Akerholt, born and raised in Norway, now lives in Australia, where she is the recipient of a fellowship from the Theatre Board of Australia Council. She has lectured on theater at the National Institute of Dramatic Art, worked as a dramaturge and literary manager at the Sydney Theatre Company, and has translated numerous plays, poems, and novels, including works by Edy Poppy and Jon Fosse for Dalkey Archive Press.

Uilleam Blacker is a lecturer in comparative East European culture at the School of Slavonic and East European Studies, University College London. His translations of contemporary Ukrainian authors have appeared in Dalkey Archive's *Best European Fiction 2015*, *Words Without Borders*, *Modern Poetry in Translation*, *Ukrainian Literature in Translation* and *Words for War: New Poems from Ukraine* (2018). He has also published prose in the *Edinburgh Review*, *New Writing Scotland*, and *Stand*, and is a member of the Ukrainian-British theater group Molodyi Teatr London.

Jason Blake is employed in the English Department at the University of Ljubljana. He is the author of the (pre-Melania) guidebook *Culture Smart! Slovenia* and a series of writing guides aimed at Slovenian students of English. His translation of Jasmin B. Frelih's *IN/HALF* was published in 2018 by Oneworld.

Jeffrey D. Castle is a literary translator and PhD candidate at the University of Illinois at Urbana-Champaign.

John K. Cox is a professor of East European history at North Dakota State University in Fargo. He is currently translating novels by Biljana Jovanović and Erzsébet Galgóczi.

Gwen Davies is a literary translator whose titles include *Martha, Jac & Shanco* by Caryl Lewis (Parthian, 2007) and, as co-translator, *White Star* by Robin Llywelyn (Parthian, 2003). She has also previously published in *Best European Fiction 2011* and is editor of the *New Welsh Review*.

Paul Curtis Daw is a former lawyer repurposed as a translator. The University of Virginia Press published his translation of Evelyne Trouillot's novel *Memory at Bay*. His translations of stories and other texts from France, Haiti, Belgium, Quebec, and Réunion appear in *Words Without Borders*, *Subtropics*, *Asymptote*, *Indiana Review*, *Cimarron Review*, *carte blanche*, and *K1N*, among other publications, and in the 2016–2018 editions of *Best European Fiction*. He has served as an officer and director of the American Literary Translators Association.

Karen Emmerich is an Associate Professor of Comparative Literature at Princeton University, and a translator of modern Greek poetry and prose. She has translated two books of stories by Christos Ikonomou, *Something Will Happen, You'll See* (Archipelago, 2013) and *Good Will Come from the Sea* (Archipelago, 2018), as well as several other volumes.

Paul Filev is a Melbourne-based literary translator and editor. He translates from Macedonian and Spanish. His translations from the Macedonian include Vera Bužarovska's *The Last Summer in the Old Bazaar* (Saguaro Books, 2015), Sasho Dimoski's *Alma Mahler* (Dalkey Archive Press, 2018), and the anthology *Contemporary Macedonian*

Fiction (Dalkey Archive Press, 2018). From the Spanish, he has translated Eduardo Sánchez Rugeles's *Blue Label* (Turtle Point Press, 2018).

Will Firth was born in 1965 in Newcastle, Australia. He studied German and Slavic languages in Canberra, Zagreb, and Moscow. Since 1991 he has been living in Berlin, Germany, where he works as a translator of literature and the humanities (from Russian, Macedonian, and all variants of Serbo-Croatian). His best-received translations of recent years have been Robert Perišić's *Our Man in Iraq*, Andrej Nikolaidis's *Till Kingdom Come*, and Faruk Šehić's *Quiet Flows the Una*. See www.willfirth.de.

Alexander Hertich is an Associate Professor of French and Chair of World Languages and Cultures at Bradley University. His translation of René Belletto's *Dying*, which was a finalist for the French-American Foundation Annual Translation Prize, was published by Dalkey Archive Press in 2010. His translations of Nicolas Bouyssi and Christian Gailly have appeared in previous editions of *Best European Fiction*. In addition to translation, he is an active literary scholar and has published in French and English on Patrick Modiano, Jean-Philippe Toussaint, Marie NDiaye, and Raymond Queneau, as well as other modern French writers.

Eric Kurtzke is a literary translator and assistant editor at Dalkey Archive Press. His translation of Carlos Maleno's *The Irish Sea* (winner of the Premio Argaria) was published by Dalkey Archive in 2017. He has translated Maleno's second novel, *The Endless Rose*, and is currently working on Daniel Guebel's novel *Collapse*, both of which will appear in 2019.

Tess Lewis is a writer whose essays and reviews have appeared in *Bookforum*, the *Hudson Review*, and *Partisan Review*. Her translations from French and German include works by Peter Handke, Kalus Merz, Pascal Bruckner, and Jean-Luc Benoziglio. She is the recipient of a John Simon Guggenheim fellowship and was awarded the 2017 PEN Translation Prize for her translation of the novel *Angel of Oblivion* by Maja Haderlap.

Dustin Lovett is a freelance translator and PhD student of Comparative Literature at the University of California, Santa Barbara. Translations of his have also appeared in previous *Best European Fiction* anthologies in 2010, 2011, 2012, and 2015.

Elizabeth Lowe is founding director of the Center for Translation Studies at the University of Illinois and professor of Translation Studies at New York University. She translates Brazilian and Lusophone writers, most recently a novel by Mozambican writer Abel Coelho, titled *Elephants Never Forget* (Tagus, 2017). Her translation of J. P. Cuenca's *The Only Happy Ending for a Love Story Is an Accident* (Tagus Press, 2013) was on the long list for the 2015 IMPAC award.

Eliza Marciniak is a literary translator and an editor. Her translations include *Swallowing Mercury* by Wioletta Greg (published by Portobello Books in the UK and Transit Books in the USA), which was long-listed for the Man Booker International Prize 2017 and short-listed for the inaugural TA First Translation Prize, as well a series of classic Polish children's books by Marian Orłoń (published by Pushkin Press): *Detective Nosegoode and the Music Box Mystery*, *Detective Nosegoode and the Kidnappers*, and *Detective Nosegoode and the Museum Robbery*. She lives in London.

Erika Mihálycsa is a lecturer of twentieth-century British and Irish fiction at Babes-Bolyai University Cluj, who has published mostly on Joyce's and Beckett's language poetics. Her translations from English to Hungarian include works by Samuel Beckett, Flann O'Brien, William Carlos Williams, Anne Carson, Paul Durcan, Julian Barnes, Patrick McCabe, Jeanette Winterson. Her translations of contemporary Hungarian prose and poetry have come out to date in *World Literature Today*, *Trafika Europe*, *Two Lines*, *Envoi*, *The Collagist*, *Numéro Cinq*, *B O D Y*, *The Missing Slate*, *Music and Literature*, *Asymptote/The Guardian*, as well as being selected in Best European Fiction 2017. She has published short prose and essays in both Hungarian and English. Together with Rainer J. Hanshe she edits the literary and arts journal *Hyperion: On the Future of Aesthetics*, issued by Contra Mundum Press.

Kalina Momcheva is a young translator from Sofia, Bulgaria. In 2016, she graduated from Sofia University with a degree in English and American studies, then continued her education in the university's Translation and Editing MA program. Her translation of Deyan Enev's short story "The Underpass" was done for a Translation from Bulgarian into English course taught by the American literary translator Angela Rodel.

Frederika Randall, a cultural journalist and literary translator, was born in Pittsburgh and lives in Rome. Her translations include Ippolito Nievo's *Confessions of an Italian*, Guido Morselli's *The Communist*, Luigi Meneghello's *Deliver Us*, Ottavio Cappellani's *Sicilian Tragedee*, as well as the historian Sergio Luzzatto's *The Body of Il Duce, Padre Pio: Miracles and Politics in a Secular Age* (author and translator awarded the 2011 Cundill Prize), and *Primo Levi's Resistance*.

Douglas Robinson has been translating from Finnish since 1975, and has previously translated Finnish texts for *Best European Fiction* 2010, 2015, and 2016. His translation of Aleksis Kivi's *The Brothers Seven*, Finland's greatest novel, appeared in 2017. He is Chair Professor of English at Hong Kong Baptist University and author of a dozen books on translation.

Jacob Rogers is a translator of Galician poetry and prose living in Spain. Previous translations have appeared in *Asymptote*, *Your Impossible Voice*, *PRISM International*, *Nashville Review*, *The Brooklyn Rail In Translation*, and *The Portico of Galician Literature*, along with his translation of Carlos Casares's novel, *His Excellency* (Small Stations Press).

Peter Sherwood, a widely published translator, studied Hungarian and linguistics in the University of London before being appointed, in 1972, to a lectureship in Hungarian at the School of Slavonic and East European Studies (now part of University College London). He taught there until 2007. From 2008 until his retirement in 2014 he was László Birinyi, Sr., Distinguished Professor of Hungarian Language and Culture in the University of North Carolina at Chapel Hill.

Jan Steyn is a translator and critic of literary works in Afrikaans, Dutch, English, and French.

Elly Thompson was born in Oregon. She has an MA in French literary translation from New York University. She has lived in France and the UK and now lives in New York City. Her translations include *I Don't (Really) Need You* by Marie Vareille.

Saskia Vogel, a Los Angeles native, is a writer and Swedish-to-English translator. Her debut novel is forthcoming in 2019 from Coach House Books (North America), Dialogue Books/Little, Brown (UK), Mondial (Sweden) and the "Héroes Modernos" collection at Alpha Decay (Spain). She has written for publications such as *Granta*, *Literary Hub*, and the *Paris Review Daily*. In 2017 her story "Sluts" received an Honorable Mention from the Pushcart Prize. Her other translations include works by Karolina Ramqvist, Katrine Marçal, and Lena Andersson.

RIGHTS AND PERMISSIONS